Final Friends

VOLUME ONE

Also by Hodder Children's Books

Christopher Pike

THE LAST VAMPIRE

Volume 1 (books 1 & 2): The Last Vampire/Black Blood
Volume 2 (books 3 & 4): Red Dice/Phantom
Volume 3 (books 5 & 6): Evil Thirst/Creatures of Forever
Book 7: The Eternal Dawn

REMEMBER ME

Volume 1: Remember Me/The Return part 1
Volume 2: The Return part 2/The Last Story

L. J. Smith

NIGHT WORLD

Volume 1: Secret Vampire/Daughters of Darkness/
Enchantress
Volume 2: Dark Angel/The Chosen/Soulmate
Volume 3: Huntress/Black Dawn/Witchlight

THE VAMPIRE DIARIES

Volume 1 (books 1 & 2): The Struggle/The Awakening
Volume 2 (books 3 & 4): The Fury/The Reunion
Book 5: The Return – Nightfall
Book 6: The Return – Shadow Souls
Book 7: The Return – Midnight

Jackson Pearce

Sisters Red
Coming soon:
Sweetly

Final Friends

VOLUME ONE

The Party

The Dance

PART I

CHRISTOPHER PIKE

Hodder
Children's
Books

A division of Hachette Children's Books

For Ashley

THE
PARTY

CHAPTER 1

I should never have gone on vacation in Europe, Jessica Hart thought. *After climbing the Matterhorn, starting high school again feels ridiculous.*

The day was Friday, the last day of the first week of school, but Jessica's first glimpse of Tabb High. Less than twenty hours earlier she had been enjoying the crisp, cool air of Switzerland's Alps. Now she had Southern California's worst to breathe; the morning was as smoggy as it was hot. Plus she had a terrible case of jet lag. She probably should have skipped what was left of the school week and rested up over Saturday and Sunday, but she had been anxious to see her friends and to check out the place where she was doomed to spend her one and only senior year. So far it had not impressed her.

'I want to have a party,' Alice McCoy was saying to her as they wove through the crowds in the outdoor hallway

1

towards Jessica's locker room. 'We could get, say, thirty kids from Mesa, with thirty kids from Tabb.'

Mesa High had been their alma mater until midsummer, when those in power had decided that the district could not afford two partially full high schools. Tabb had absorbed perhaps three-quarters of Mesa's students. Although Tabb was older than Mesa, it was far bigger. The other twenty-five per cent had ended up at Sanders High, five miles further inland. Fortunately for Jessica, the majority of her friends had moved with her to Tabb, not the least of whom was Alice McCoy. Two years younger, she was – in Jessica's unbiased opinion – the sweetest girl in the whole world.

'You mean as a get-to-know-each-other sort of thing?' Jessica asked.

'Yeah. I think it would help break the ice between us.'

'I wouldn't worry about any ice today,' Jessica said, brushing her dark hair off her sweaty forehead. On hot days like this she wished she had Alice's bright blonde curls; they seemed to reflect most of the sun's rays. 'Does this joint have air conditioning?' Jessica asked.

'In some of the rooms.'

'Some?'

'The teachers' lounge is really cool. I was in there yesterday. They want me to paint a mural on the wall.'

Alice laughed. 'They want a mountain glacier.'

'It figures. I hope you're charging them?'

'I'm not.'

'Fool. Back to this party business. How would you know which thirty Tabb kids to invite?'

Alice nodded. 'That's a problem. But maybe in the next week we'll meet some nice people. Have you run into anyone that you like yet?'

Jessica shook her head. 'No, and I've been here all of thirty minutes. But maybe by lunch I'll get some guy to fall in love with me.'

The words came out easily, but were accompanied by a slight feeling of uneasiness. She had gone on few dates while at Mesa High. Guys just didn't ask her out much. Her best friend, Sara Cantrell, said it was because they were intimidated by her beauty.

'You're right, Sara, that must be it. All those guys watching me from across campus and thinking to themselves that there's a babe beyond their reach. Really, they have a lot of nerve even looking at me.'

Actually, Jessica knew she was pretty. Enough people had told her so for enough years, and they couldn't all be wrong. Besides, she had only to look in the mirror. Her face was a perfect oval, with a firm chin and a wide, full mouth that she had trained to smile even when she didn't feel much like smiling. Her hair and eyes matched beautifully. The former was dark brown, long and wavy, with a sheen that had stayed with her from infancy; the latter, an even darker brown, large and round, giving her either a playful or nasty look, depending on her mood. And with a carefully controlled diet and daily jogs around the park, she kept her figure slim and supple. She'd even picked up a tan this summer.

I sound practically perfect!

But, no, she wasn't perfect. She believed, like most teenage girls who don't date much, that there was something wrong with her, something missing. Yet she didn't know what it could be. She didn't understand how Alice – a nice enough looking girl, but certainly no fairy princess – drew girls and guys alike to her in droves. Some people were charismatic, she supposed, and others weren't, and that was that.

Just then Jessica caught sight of a girl in a cheerleader's uniform standing beside a tree and chatting with a group of what appeared to be football players. A stab of envy touched her. The past spring she had successfully tried out for the cheerleading squad. And all summer she had been looking forward to entering the mainstream of her school's social life. But then *her* school had disappeared, and those who decided such things – who were those jerks, anyway? – had felt that Tabb High should be allowed to maintain its pep squads without integrating those from Mesa High.

God, now there's a girl that looks out of reach.

Jessica stopped Alice, gestured in the direction of the cheerleader. Her blonde hair teased and highlighted, the girl appeared hip, arrogant in a flirty way. Even from a distance, Jessica could see the eyes of the guys gathered around her flickering down her long tanned legs. 'Who is that?' she said.

'Clair Hilrey,' Alice replied. 'Funny you should ask. She was one person I had already decided should come to my party.'

'Why?'

'She knows everybody. She's probably the most popular girl on campus. She's gorgeous, isn't she?'

Jessica had already taken a dislike to her. It had been a dream of Jessica's, since her freshman year, that she might be nominated homecoming queen. Back at Mesa, she would have had an excellent chance. Here it already looked as if the odds were stacked against her. She shrugged, started up the hallway again. 'She's all right.'

Jessica had been at her locker half an hour earlier to deposit her notebook before checking in with her senior counsellor. The man had seemed nice enough, but sort of slow and boring, and she couldn't remember his name any more than she could now remember her locker combination. Stopping in front of the locker, she searched her pockets for the slip of paper with the three magic numbers.

'Whoever you put on your list,' she said, finding the paper and twisting the steel dial, 'be sure to invite that new guy you're seeing. What's his name, Kent?'

Alice looked doubtful. 'Clark. I don't know if he'd come. He doesn't like to be around a lot of people.'

The dial felt as if it had gum stuck under it. This school was gross. 'Where does he take you when you two go out, the desert?'

Alice smiled briefly. 'We don't really go out. He just comes over.' She added quickly, almost nervously, 'He's an incredible artist. He's helped me so much with my painting.'

Jessica paused, studied her. The topic of Clark disturbed Alice, and Jessica wondered why. More than that, she was concerned. She had always felt the urge to take care of Alice. Perhaps because Alice had lost both her parents when she was only ten.

'I'll have to meet him some day,' she said finally, brushing a curl of hair from Alice's face. The younger girl nodded, kissed Jessica quickly on the cheek, and began to back away.

'I'm glad you had a happy vacation. I'm even more glad you're home! Catch you later, OK?'

'At lunch. Where should we meet?'

Alice had already begun to slip into the crowd. 'I'll find you!' she called.

After waving a quick farewell, Jessica turned and opened her locker and discovered that the light blue cashmere sweater her mother had bought for her in Switzerland for two hundred francs was being spotted with *somebody's* grape juice. The juice was leaking from a soggy brown-paper lunch bag perched on top of a thick notebook that didn't belong to her and which she felt by all rights did not belong in her locker.

'Damn,' she whispered, hastily pulling the bag and the notebook out of the locker and dumping them on the ground. Her face fell as she unfolded her prize gift and held it up. She had known it was to be in the high nineties today; she'd only brought the sweater to show off to her friends. Now it had a big stain over the heart area. It was dark enough to be a bloodstain. Suddenly she wished she had never got on that plane in Zurich.

'Excuse me, I think these are mine,' somebody said from below her. There was a guy crouched down at her feet, picking up the notebook and lunch bag. When he had his things in hand, he glanced up, clearing his throat. 'Are we sharing the same locker?'

Jessica put her sweater down and sighed. 'You mean you don't even get your own locker in this school? What kind of place is this? I had my own locker in kindergarten.'

The guy stood, frowning as he noticed the juice dripping from his bag. 'I guess it does take some getting used to. But I don't think I'll be getting in your way much. I only keep my books in my locker.'

'And your lunch.'

The fellow noticed her sweater and did a quick double take, from it to his bag. 'Oh, no, did my grape juice leak on your sweater?'

'Somebody's grape juice did.'

He grimaced. 'I'm sorry, I really am. Do you think the stain will come out?'

'I'll probably have to cut it out.'

'That's terrible.' He reached a hand into the bag. 'It's all my fault. Boy, can I make it up to you? Could I buy you a new one?'

'Not around here.'

'Well, how much did it cost? I could pay you for it at least.'

'Two hundred Swiss francs.'

'How much is that?'

'I don't know.' Jessica leaned an elbow on the wall of lockers, rested her head in her hand, blood pounding behind her temples. What a lousy way to start the day, the whole school year for that matter. 'I can't remember.'

The guy stood staring at her for a moment. 'I really am sorry,' he repeated.

Jessica closed her eyes briefly, taking a deep breath, getting a hold of herself. She was making a mountain out of a molehill. Fatigue often made her overreact. Chances were the dry cleaners could get the stain out. And if they didn't, they didn't. Her bedroom closet was overflowing with clothes. When she thought about it, she realised she had little right to blame this guy. After all, she was invading his territory. He had probably had this locker since he was a freshman.

She straightened up, letting the sweater dangle by her side, out of the way. 'Don't worry about it,' she said. 'I have another one at home just like it.' She offered him her hand, lightening her tone. 'My name's Jessica Hart. I'm a Mesa High refugee.'

The guy shook her hand. 'I'm Michael Olson.'

'Pleased to meet you, Michael.' She wondered if this were their first meeting. She could have sworn she had seen him before. 'Are you a senior?'

'Yeah.'

'So am I.'

'I thought so. Did you just get here? I didn't see you earlier this week.'

'Yeah, my family's vacation ran a few days too long.'

Michael nodded, looking her straight in the face, and as he did, Jessica realised that, besides seeming familiar, he was rather attractive. He had thick black hair and eyebrows, pleasant friendly features. Yet it was his eyes that sparked her interest. There was an extraordinary alertness and intelligence in them, a sharpness she had never seen before in anyone her age. But perhaps she was imagining it. For all she knew, he could be the local druggie, high on something.

But he seems nice enough.

'I bet you were in Switzerland,' he said.

She laughed. 'How did you guess?'

'Your accent.' He glanced about. 'I suppose this place looks old to you after Mesa.'

She nodded. 'And crowded. And hot. We had air conditioning.'

'Some of our rooms are cooled. The gym is. We take our basketball very seriously here at Tabb.'

Jessica brightened. 'Oh, now I know who you are! You're on the basketball team. I saw you playing last year.

You killed us, didn't you?'

Michael shrugged. 'It was close most of the way.'

'Yeah, right, all through warm-up.'

'Well, you guys were never very nice to our football team. What did we lose to you, the last nine in a row?'

'The last ten. And you know what's worse? Practically our whole varsity was transferred to Sanders High.'

'I guess we couldn't expect to get beauty and brawn both.'

Did he just compliment me? It sounded like a compliment.

Jessica didn't take compliments well. To simply accept them, she felt, was to acknowledge that her looks were important to her, and she always thought that was the same as saying to the world that she was superficial. On the other hand, she did love to be complimented. She was nuts, she knew it.

She laughed again. 'Before the football season's over, I know you're going to think Tabb got the raw end of the deal.'

'I hope not,' he muttered, lowering his head, pulling a tissue from his pocket, and wiping up the few remaining drops of juice from the locker. 'I'm going to pay you for that sweater no matter what you say. What's a Swiss franc in U.S. money these days?'

'One and a half pennies. Forget about it, really. I have

parents who can't spend enough on their darling daughter.'

'It must be nice. Did you enjoy Switzerland?'

'Yeah. And the Greek islands. It was neat floating on a raft in the Mediterranean. The Vatican was amazing too.'

He nodded, repeated himself. 'It must be nice.' Then he began to back up. 'Well, I have to go. I hope you like Tabb. I'm sure you will. If you need help finding your way around, just let me know.'

'Thanks, Michael. See you later.'

'Sure.'

Michael was gone no more than ten seconds when Sara Cantrell appeared. It had been Sara who had been kind enough to pick Jessica and her parents up at the airport at three that morning. Sara had grumbled about it, naturally, but that was to be expected, and wasn't to be taken seriously. The two of them went back to the beginnings of time; they had taught each other to talk. Or rather, Jessica had learned to talk, and Sara had learned to make astute observations. Sara had a biting wit and was usually hungry for potential victims. Tabb High did not yet know what it had inherited. It would know soon, though.

'Hello, Jessie, can't believe you dragged yourself in today. God, you look wasted. You should go home and put your face back under a pillow.'

Jessica yawned. 'I didn't even go to bed. I was too busy unpacking. What are you doing here? When you dropped us off at home, you said you were taking the day off.'

'I was until I remembered my mom wasn't working today. She would just drive me nuts. Hey, do you know who that guy you were talking to is?'

'Michael Olson.'

'Yeah. I hear he's the smartest guy in the school. Better get on good terms with him. You're taking chemistry, and I hear our young Olson wrote the lab manual they use here.'

'Are you serious? I thought he looked clever.' Then she winced. 'Did you really sign me up for chemistry?'

'You told me to.'

'My *dad* told you to. What do I need chemistry for?'

'So you can get into Stanford and find a smart young man to marry who'll give you smart little kids to play with in a big stupid house.'

Jessica groaned. 'I didn't know that's why I was taking chemistry.'

Sara pointed to her sweater. 'Did your ears explode while going up in the plane or what? That looks like a bloodstain.'

'I didn't get it on the trip. It's something old. I got it at Penney's.'

Sara grabbed the tag. 'Is Penney's charging us in francs these days?'

Jessica pulled the sweater away and shut it in the locker. 'Don't hassle me, all right? I'm still getting acclimatised.' She wiped at the grape juice on her hands. 'Last night you said we share first period. What class is it? I've lost my schedule already.'

Sara wrinkled her nose. She could do a lot with her nose. She had the same control over it that most people had over their mouths. This did not mean, however, that it was an unusually large nose. Sara was cute. By her own estimation – and Sara could be as ruthless with herself as she was with everybody else – she rated an eight on a scale of one to fourteen. In other words, she was slightly above average. She had rust coloured hair, cut straight above her shoulders, hazel eyes and a slightly orange tan that somehow got deeper in the winter. Because she frequently wore orange tops to complement her colouring, Jessica told her she looked like Halloween.

'Political science,' Sara said. 'And we've got this really liberal ex-vet for a teacher. He was in Vietnam and slaughtered little babies, and now he wants us selling the communists hydrogen bombs so he can have a clear conscience.'

'He sounds interesting.' Jessica didn't believe a word of

it. 'Come on, let's get there before the bell rings. I'm already four days late.'

The teacher's name was Mr Bark, and Sara hadn't been totally off base in her analysis. The first thing the man did when they were all seated was dim the lights and put on a videotape of a nuclear attack. The footage was from the big TV movie *The Day After*. They watched a solid ten minutes of bombs exploding, forests burning and people vapourising. When the lights were turned back on, Jessica discovered she had a headache. World War III always depressed her. Plus she wasn't wearing her glasses as she was supposed to; watching the show had strained her eyes. Sitting to her right, Sara had put her head down and nodded off. Jessica poked her lightly, without effect. Sara continued to snore softly.

'I hope my purpose in showing this tape is clear,' Mr Bark began, leaning his butt on the edge of his desk. 'We can *talk* on and on about how incredibly destructive nuclear weapons are, but I think what we have just seen creates an image of horror that will stay with us a long time, and will remind us that above all else we can't allow the political tensions of the world to reach the point where pushing the button becomes a viable alternative.'

If Sara hadn't been lying about his being a vet, then Mr

Bark hid it well. He didn't look like someone who had seen battle. In fact, he looked remarkably like a plump, balding middle-aged man who had taught high school political science all his life. He had frumpy grey slacks, black-rimmed glasses and an itch on his inner left thigh that he obviously couldn't wait to scratch.

Jessica poked her friend again. Sara turned her head in the other direction and made a low snorting sound.

'One Trident submarine,' Mr Bark continued, raising one finger in the air for emphasis, striding down the centre of the class, 'has the capacity to destroy two hundred Soviet cities. Think about it. And think what would happen if the captain of a Trident sub should go off half-cocked and decide to make a place in history for himself, or to put an end to all history. Now I know most of you believe that the fail-safe device the president has near him at all times controls—'

We should have had someone else pick us up at the airport.

Mr Bark paused in midstride, suddenly realising he didn't have Sara's full attention. Impatience creased his wide fleshy forehead. He moved to where he stood above her.

'She had a late night,' Jessica said.

Mr Bark frowned. 'You're the new girl? Jessica Hart?'

'Yes, sir.'

16

'And you're a friend of Sara's?'

'Yes, sir.'

'Would you wake her, please?'

'I'll try.' Jessica leaned close to Sara's head, hearing scattered giggles from the rest of the class. Putting her hand on the back of Sara's neck, she whispered in her ear, 'You are making fools of both of us. If you don't wake up this second, I am going to pinch you.'

Sara wasn't listening. Jessica pinched her. Sara sat up with a bolt. 'Holy Moses,' she gasped. Then she saw the stares, the smirks. Unfazed, she calmly leaned back in her chair and picked up her pen as if to take notes, saying, 'Could you please repeat the question, Mr Bark?'

'I didn't ask a question, Sara.'

Sara stifled a yawn. 'Good.'

'But I'll ask one now. Were you awake through any of the videotape?'

'I got the highlights.'

'I'm glad. Tell me, what was your gut reaction while watching the bombs explode?'

Sara smiled slowly. 'I thought it was neat.'

Mr Bark shook his head. 'You might think you are being funny, but I can assure you that you are—'

'No, no,' Sara interrupted. 'I'm telling you exactly how

I felt. The whole time I was watching it, before I nodded off, I was thinking, 'Wow.'

Mr Bark grinned in spite of himself. 'Granted, Sara, the visual effects were outstanding. But didn't the wholesale destruction of our civilisation upset you?'

'No.'

'Come on, be serious. I had girls crying when I showed this tape in fifth period yesterday.'

'Mr Bark,' Sara replied with a straight face, 'when I was watching that part where the bomb exploded outside that university, I honestly thought to myself, "Why, those lucky kids. They won't have to go to school any more."'

The class burst out laughing. Mr Bark finally gave up. He tried to dig up more heartfelt testimonials from the less bizarre minded, and while he did so, Jessica noticed a handsome blond fellow sitting in the corner. She had to fight not to stare. What kind of place was this Tabb? First there was Clair Hilrey, who belonged in *Playboy*, and now there was this hunk. It was a wonder that they couldn't put together a halfway decent football team with all these great genes floating around. She poked Sara again.

'Who's that in the corner?' she whispered.

'The football quarterback,' Sara whispered back.

'What's his name?'

'He hasn't got one. But his jersey number is sixteen.'

'Tell me, dammit.'

'William Skater, but I call him Bill. Pretty pretty, huh?'

'Amazing. Do you know if he has a girlfriend?'

'I've seen him hanging out with this cheerleader named Clair.'

'God, I hate this school.'

'Miss Hart?' Mr Bark called.

'Yes, sir?'

He wanted to know about her feelings on radiation, and of course, she told him she thought it was just awful stuff. When the class was over, Jessica did her best to catch Bill's eye, but he wasn't looking.

I've been here less than two hours. I can't be getting a crush on someone already.

She ditched Sara and tailed Bill halfway across campus. He had a great ass.

The following period was the dread chemistry, and the teacher's lecture on molecular reactions proved far harder to absorb than Mr Bark's on atomic explosions. This was definitely one class she wouldn't be able to BS her way through.

Towards the middle of the period, they started on the first lab of the year. Jessica ended up with a quiet Hispanic girl named Maria Gonzales for a partner. They hardly had a chance to talk, but she struck Jessica as the serious type. Jessica just hoped she was smart and took excellent notes. She wondered if Michael Olson really was a wizard at science. It would be asking too much, she supposed, to hope William Skater was.

Maybe Bill will be in another one of my classes.

Break came next. Before leaving for school that morning, Jessica had spoken to another friend of hers, Polly McCoy — Alice's older sister — filling her in on everything that had happened on her vacation. She had known Polly almost as long as she had Sara, although she was not nearly so close to Polly. A lot of their friendship was founded on simple geography; since they were kids they had lived only a few hundred yards apart; it was hard not to be friends with someone your own age who lived so close.

Polly had what at best could be described as a nervous disposition. It showed particularly when she was around Sara, who enjoyed picking on Polly. Keeping the two girls apart was difficult, however, because none of them really had any other close friends, and they usually ended up going to movies, the beach or wherever together. Three bored girls each looking for one exciting guy.

When Polly and Alice's parents had died, they left the

girls a large construction company. It was at present managed by a board of directors, but both girls were potential bosses and millionaires. They lived in a big house with a partially senile aunt who was their legal guardian. They lived as they wanted. Only the McCoy sisters could think of throwing a party to introduce two schools to each other.

But it turned out that Alice had not told Polly about the party.

'She's going to do what?' Polly asked as they waited in line at the soda machines. Polly had already got hold of a candy bar. She ate a lot of sweets these days, and it showed, especially in her face. It was a pity. When thin, Polly was a doll.

'She's going to invite thirty of our own people and team them up with thirty of Tabb's people,' Jessica said, casting an eye towards the front of the line. Apparently the machines here took kicks as well as quarters. The guy up front was busting a toe for a Coke.

'She never told me.'

'Maybe she just thought it up.'

'I don't care. We're not having it. They'd rip up the house.'

'No, they wouldn't.' The guy kicked the machine one final time and then stalked off. He was from Mesa. 'But

21

let's not invite that guy. Hey, is there another place we can get something to drink?'

'There's the mall. It's less than five minutes away in the car. But I don't want to go there now. And I don't want a party at my house.'

Jessica decided she'd let Sara and Alice argue with Polly. She had already made up her mind that they had to have the party if only to invite Mr Football Quarterback. 'All right, all right, we'll have it in my bedroom. What did you do while I was gone?'

'Nothing.' Polly took a bite of her candy, her bright green eyes spanning the jammed courtyard. Then she grinned. 'I take that back. I did do something funny. They were running a contest on the radio to see who could send in the best album cover for a new heavy-metal band. I can't even remember the group – it was Hell and Steel something. Anyway, I sent in one of Alice's paintings. She won!'

'What did she win?'

'A free trip to one of their New York shows and a backstage pass. The DJ said the group is seriously considering using her artwork.'

'Is Alice going to go?'

'No. You know she hates loud music.'

'Wait a second. One of Alice's paintings on the album

cover of a heavy-metal band? Since when does she paint anything that doesn't have flowers and clouds in it?'

Polly shrugged. 'It's none of my business.'

'What's none of your business?'

'What Clark has her drawing.'

'Her boyfriend has her drawing whips and demons?' Boy, I hope he hasn't seduced her.'

Polly did not appreciate the remark. She was fanatically protective of her younger sister. 'He's not her boyfriend. He's just someone who comes over and eats our food.'

'What's he look like?'

'Not bad, pretty good.'

'You wouldn't want to give me too many details, would you?'

Polly smiled. Unlike her sister, her hair was dark, almost black, with red highlights. Indeed, in almost every respect, their looks differed. Alice was a waif. Polly was a peasant. She had big breasts and a bigger butt. 'He's got great hands,' she said.

'How do you know?'

'I'm not saying anything.'

'For someone who doesn't like to pry into Alice's business, you've said a lot.' The subject was beginning to bore Jessica. She noticed a booth near the centre of campus, pointed it out. 'What can we sign up for over there?'

Now Polly was bored. 'Student office. They've lengthened lunch today so all those who want to play politics can tell us why we should vote for them. You're not thinking of running for anything, are you?'

Jessica had a brilliant idea. 'No, but Sara is.'

'Sara? She doesn't like to get involved in choosing what to wear in the morning.'

'You say the candidates are supposed to speak at lunch today?'

'In the gym, yeah. It's the only cool building on campus.'

'Let's sign her up.'

'We can't. You have to sign up in person.'

'Then you be Sara for a few minutes.'

'We'll never get her out on the floor to speak.'

'We'll worry about that later.'

'She'll be furious.' Polly paused, thought about that for a moment. 'All right, I'll be Sara. What should we have her run for?'

'What else? Student body president.'

CHAPTER 2

Michael Olson had not heard Jessica Hart's comment to Alice McCoy about finding a guy to fall in love with by lunch, but had he been listening, he might have believed her to be a beautiful witch capable of casting potent spells. Michael had thought of Jessica, and nothing else, all morning. He had a terrible feeling he was going to spend a substantial portion of the remainder of the year thinking about her.

And I'm going to have to see her every day, several times a day, until June.

Whereas most guys would have been delighted with a set up that would bring them repeatedly in contact with a girl they found attractive, Michael didn't for the simple reason that he knew he'd never be able to get past the hello-how-are-you? stage. It was true that he had said much more to her than that during their first meeting, but that had been before he'd had a chance to fantasise about her. Now just the memory of her made him uneasy. He didn't know what it had been about her that had hit him so hard. He wondered if her effect on him hadn't been largely because of his own state of mind. His summer had been particularly lonely. He had worked and read a lot, and gone out seldom; and never with anyone of the opposite sex. Since school started he'd been looking over the new girls from Mesa. There was no doubt he was ripe for a crush.

Or a heartache.

'Remember that scene in *War Games* when Matthew Broderick changes the girl's grade with his computer?' Bubba asked as he and Michael strolled across the deserted campus. Fourth period had just begun, but neither Bubba nor Michael was cutting. Because of extremely high scores on IQ tests taken when they were in junior high, both guys were in the MGM (Mentally Gifted Minors) Programme. They had a free period each day to pursue individual projects that their superior intelligence qualified them to pursue. In actuality, they probably were cutting. So far this year, they had used fourth period primarily to get an early start on lunch.

'I remember the scene,' Michael said. 'You couldn't do that here, though, could you?'

Bubba was a wizard with computers, and at life itself. He was five feet four, and because he enjoyed food and denied himself nothing, he was also rather round. But stature and weight were no obstacle to Bubba. He went out with practically any girl he wanted and enjoyed the reputation as the coolest person in Tabb High.

'Not without the codes that give access to the school district's data files.'

'I didn't think the scene was very realistic,' Michael said. 'Hey, why are we going to the administration building?'

'To get the codes.'

'What?'

Bubba smiled faintly. He endeavoured to maintain a serene countenance, like the holy Buddha, from whom his nickname had been derived. Michael couldn't remember who had thought up the nickname. Perhaps it had been Bubba himself. His real name was John Free.

'Mr Bark wants me to write a program that will automatically read and count the votes on the cards that will be used in the voting for student body officers,' Bubba explained.

'But you don't need the district data files to do that.'

'Does Miss Fenway know that?'

Miss Fenway was a secretary in the administration

27

building. 'What does Miss Fenway have to do with any of this?'

'She has the codes written on a little piece of white paper taped to a board that slides out from her desk above her top left drawer. I saw them there yesterday.'

'Did you memorise them?'

'No, I didn't have a chance. But I will today.'

'But what does this have to do with the program you're writing for Mr Bark?'

'Absolutely nothing.'

Once inside the administration building, they went straight to Miss Fenway's office. She was busy sorting files at a corner cabinet when they entered. Michael had always liked Miss Fenway. She enjoyed playing mother to every kid in school, and she took special pride in him because he got straight As. But she was no dummy, and he doubted Bubba would trick her into giving out confidential information. She had a computer terminal on her desk.

'May I help you boys?' she asked, putting down her papers and stepping towards them. A thin woman with a warm, wrinkled face, she had never married nor had any kids.

'Yes,' Bubba said. 'Mr Bark has put me in charge of

tabulating the votes for student body officers this afternoon. I need the codes that will allow me to connect the old card reader in this building with the new PC in the computer science class.'

Miss Fenway was puzzled. 'I hadn't been informed about this.'

'Mr Bark is free this period. You'll find him in the teachers' lounge, I believe. He'll explain what I mean.' Bubba took a seat, making it clear he was going to wait in her office until she did what he wanted. Miss Fenway looked at Michael.

'Do you know what this is all about?'

'Not me.'

The instant Miss Fenway left, Bubba sprang to his feet – he was remarkably agile given his physique – and closed the door. He had the desk board with the page of codes pulled out in two seconds. Swiftly, but carefully, he began to copy them down.

'I didn't see you do this,' Michael said.

'See me do what?'

Miss Fenway returned a minute later with Mr Bark. The latter explained to Bubba that all he had to do was write a program that broke the count down into fresh-men, sophomores, etc. He would do the rest. Bubba nodded and apologised for not understanding the first time. As they were leaving, Mr Bark told them about a video he wanted them to see.

'From the TV movie *The Day After?*' Bubba asked.

'Yes.'

'I've seen it,' Bubba said.

'What did you think?'

'It was neat.'

Mr Bark sighed. 'I have this new student you should meet.'

The computer room was empty fourth period. They had the place to themselves. Using the stolen codes, Bubba called up the files containing the transcripts of every kid in the school district. Michael wondered at his motivation. Although as intelligent as himself, Bubba never worried much about his grades. He had no intention of attending college. He wanted to go straight into business. In fact, he already invested in commodities and stock options. He also bet the horses through his uncle, who was a bookie with mob connections. Financially speaking, Bubba's family occupied the same position as Michael's, lower middle class. And yet Bubba drove an old but well-kept Jaguar and wore only the finest clothes. And he didn't even have a job. Since Michael had to slave six days a week at a local 7-Eleven to help his divorced mother make ends meet, he knew if he were to criticise Bubba's *businesses*, he would only be doing so out of jealousy.

'Here you are,' Bubba said, pointing to the screen. Michael leaned closer. Semester after semester – rows of As, except for one C his junior year. He'd got it last year in calculus. A pal of his had desperately whispered for help in the middle of a test. Being such a swell guy, Michael had slipped him a piece of paper with a few answers that, through bad timing and bad luck, had ended up in the hands of the teacher. Regrettably, the test had been the final exam and the teacher had given them both automatic Fs. It had slashed his overall semester grade in half. His hopes of being valedictorian had gone out the window then and there.

'You can't change it,' Michael said. 'Everyone on the faculty knows I got that C.'

Bubba's fingers danced over the keyboard. Then he frowned. 'We can't change it, anyway. The file's protected. I should have known. Once transferred to the district offices, the grades are carved in stone.' He thought for a moment, then jumped out of the file and into another that was the same except for the absence of recorded grades.

'What's that?' Michael asked.

'This semester's records.' Bubba moved the cursor beside Michael Olson's MGM fourth period, put in an A. 'This file hasn't been transferred yet. We can manipulate it up until the day it is.' He erased the A. 'You know, Mike, I think this is going to be a pretty laid-back year for the two of us. Would you like me to pull Dale Jensen's record?'

Dale Jensen had the only gradepoint average higher than Michael's. It was a perfect 4.00. But Dale hadn't taken a difficult class in all the time he had gone to Tabb. He specialised in subjects where he could get up and indulge in longwinded monologues about how screwed up all the screw-ups in the world were. He was really a despicable character. If anyone stopped to tell him something, he always interrupted with the sarcastic line, 'I'm impressed.'

'No, leave him alone.'

'Are you sure? Who wants to listen to him on graduation day?'

'We're not going to sneak a phoney grade on to his transcript for this year without him knowing it.'

'I suppose you're right,' Bubba replied without much conviction, sitting back from the screen and stretching.

'I wanted to tell you about this girl I met,' Michael began.

'Ask her out.'

'No, let me tell you about her first.'

'What for? I'm sure she's the greatest discovery since sliced bread. Just ask her out. What's her name?'

'You probably haven't seen her. She just got here this morning. Jessica Hart.'

Bubba nodded approvingly. 'I know her, she's hot. A friend of hers is having a party for the whole school.'

'Where did you hear that?'

Bubba shrugged. He seldom revealed the sources of his information. He was seldom wrong about anything. 'I don't think you should wait until the party to go after her. She won't last, not around here. Someone will nab her. It may as well be you.'

Michael chuckled at the crude manner in which Bubba referred to Jessica. He knew that Bubba had a strong admiration for the female species, or at least a powerful appreciation of them, which was almost the same thing. Girls who went out with Bubba once wanted to go out with Bubba twice. He knew how to satisfy them.

'Why don't you ask her on a date?' Michael asked.

'I can't. I've got to save myself for Clair Hilrey.'

'I thought Clair was going with our esteemed quarterback, Bill Skater?'

'They've dated a few times. They went to the Baked

Potato Restaurant last Saturday night. But it's nothing serious.'

'Does Clair know this?'

'Give me a couple of weeks, and I'll make it clear to her.'

Michael scratched his head. 'Didn't Clair tell you last spring that she thought you were the most disgusting human being in the whole school?'

'It makes no difference. Over the summer your average teenage girl forgets nine-tenths of what happened the previous school year. I'll ask her out at tonight's game, during half-time. She'll say yes.'

Michael shook his head in amazement. 'I'm going to enjoy watching this.'

Bubba sat up, speaking seriously. 'I'll let you in on a profound secret. Only the very elect of males in our society know this. And once you know it and ponder its significance for any length of time, your whole perspective will change.'

'The earth is really flat?'

'No.' Bubba leaned closer. 'Girls want to have sex exactly as much as boys want to.'

Michael laughed. 'Bubba, I just met Jessie. I don't even know her. I don't want to sleep with her. I'm afraid to talk to her.'

'It's much easier to have sex than to talk. When you talk, you have to think. You think too much, Mike. That's your problem. And you're lying to yourself. Of course you want to sleep with Jessie. You don't have to be ashamed. Chances are she probably wouldn't mind sleeping with you if she thought she could do it and not have to pay for it later in some way. That's why girls love me so much. I let them know that with me everything is OK.'

'But you kiss and tell. With what you just said, that makes you a hypocrite. Take how you carried on about Cindy Fosmeyer.'

'Who do I tell except you? And I know you would never damage a girl's reputation.' He smiled. 'And since we're talking about Cindy, did I ever tell you she has the hots for you?'

Cindy Fosmeyer had huge breasts. They were so huge they fairly blotted out any personality she might have had. 'You never did because it's not true.'

'Believe what you want, buddy.' Bubba stood. 'But I give you my word on this – if you don't ask Jessica out by Monday, I will.'

Michael was not amused. He had known Bubba a long time. They'd had a lot of good times together. But there was a lot about him he didn't know, that he didn't want to know. 'Is that a threat?'

'Think of it as an incentive.'

'What about saving yourself for Clair?'

Bubba patted his bulging gut. 'There's enough of me to go around.' He turned towards the door. 'I'll be back in a minute.'

Bubba was gone much longer than a minute. While waiting, Michael entertained himself scanning Jessica Hart's transcript. He felt mild guilt at prying, but couldn't resist. He was mildly surprised to discover she was taking chemistry. She must be smart, but then, he had observed that talking to her. Perhaps she would need a tutor. He knew the subject so well that a rumour had gone round last year that he had written the lab manual. It was incredible the things people would believe.

When the door opened behind him, he assumed it was Bubba. The cool, soft hug from behind caught him by surprise.

'Hi, Mikey!'

'Alice, what are you doing here?'

Michael had met Alice McCoy the previous winter, a couple of weeks before Christmas. Wearing what he was later to discover to be her typical sunny expression, she had popped into his 7-Eleven and asked if she could paint Santa Claus and Frosty the Snowman on his windows. He had been immediately taken by her enthusiasm. She told him he could pay her what he thought it was worth, and if he didn't like it when she was done, he wouldn't have to pay her at all. It sounded like a good deal, but the owners of the store were Muslims from Lebanon, and he didn't know if they'd appreciate Christmas decorations all over their place of business. A quick call dispelled his fears; the two brothers were eager to have their store look as American as possible.

The next day was a Saturday. Alice showed up at nine o'clock in the morning. He expected her to chalk out a few reindeer and spray in a couple of featureless snowmen and call it done. Her supplies threw him for his first loop. She had a huge, flat black case of paints and brushes. She spent a half hour cleaning and polishing the windows before starting, and when she finally did begin, she worked steadily for seven hours, slowly, patiently, meticulously unfolding a rich colourful tapestry of sparkling elves, joyous children and racing sleighs. When she finished, she sprayed on a sealer that she promised would protect the paintings. When he finally did wash away her work, near Easter, it had been with a heavy heart. But by then he'd had something greater than her pictures to enjoy. He had Alice herself, as both a regular visitor and a good friend. She was a true gift of holiday magic. She had charm and grace, kindness and wit.

She was everything he had imagined his little sister would have been.

Michael's mother was only seventeen and in high school when she had given birth to him. Old man Jerry Olson split for parts unknown five years after that – Michael still had a few clear memories of his dad – and since then his mother had dated a seemingly endless succession of men. Two years ago one of them had got her pregnant. The guy had had no wish to marry her – he, too, would eventually disappear and his mother had vacillated about having an abortion. Finally, over Michael's bitter protests, she had decided on the operation – sort of late. He did not understand why the doctor had told his mom it had been a girl, or why she had told him.

By a strange quirk of fate, he'd always thought of his unborn sister as *Alice*. After the incident, he often dreamed of what she would have been like. His little Alice. He still loved his mother more than anyone, but he doubted he'd ever totally forgive her for what she had done.

But now, with Alice McCoy here to see him, it was easy to pretend what had gone before had been only a bad dream.

'What am I doing? I'm cutting, just like you,' she said, releasing him and walking around the room, lightly tapping the keyboards on Tabb's brand new PCs, touching a printout page. Like a perpetually curious child, Alice was fascinated with everything around her.

'You have an art class now, right?'

'Yeah, I'm supposed to be at the park across the street studying tree branches. But they've just sprayed there with an awful-smelling insecticide.' She giggled. 'I did start on this one sketch of a giant mosquito sucking the sap out of a tree. It was really gross.'

'Can I see it?'

'No.'

'Did you throw it away?' She shook her head. 'But I'm going to, right after I show it to Clark. It really is weird. I can't believe I drew it.'

'Clark's your new boyfriend, isn't he?'

'He's not that new. I see him a lot.'

'I'd like to meet him. What's he like?'

Alice shrugged, tossing her bright head of hair. 'I don't want to talk about him. I want to tell you about a friend of mine I want you to meet. She's from Mesa, like me. She's really wonderful.'

'What's her name?'

'I'm not going to tell you. I want to be the one to introduce you so that when you both fall in love, and get married later on, you'll be able to look back and say it was me who made it all possible. Are you going to the game tonight?'

'I'm going to try. I have to work, but I should be able to catch the second half.'

'Could you get there at half-time? I could introduce you to her then.'

Michael chuckled. He wasn't really interested in Alice's friend, not after meeting Jessica Hart, but he saw no harm in saying hello to the girl. 'What's wrong with today at lunch?'

'I won't be here. I have a doctor's appointment.'

He paused. 'What for? I mean, are you sick?'

Alice brushed aside the question. 'It's nothing, I just have to stop in.'

'How are you going to get there? I could give you a ride.' For some reason, the thought of Alice going all alone to the doctor disturbed him. He knew she had no parents, and that her guardian aunt didn't get out often.

'I'm taking a taxi.'

'They're expensive.'

'I have money. Don't worry about it. Just be there tonight at half-time. I'll get her to come.'

'I'll do my best,' he promised.

She smiled. 'Thanks, this means a lot to me. Oh, what's

that you have on your screen? It looks like a report card.'

Michael explained how through the use of special codes – he didn't say where they had obtained them – he and his friend were able to tap into the school's files. Alice was fascinated, but before she could ask any questions, Bubba returned. And when Bubba realised that Alice had been made privy to what he obviously considered inside information, he quickly tried to present a more innocent picture of their doings.

'What's on this screen is only a photocopy of existing records,' he said. 'It's not the records themselves. We're just looking at them, that's all. It's no big deal.'

Alice grinned slyly. 'Sure, you're getting ready to turn the school upside down, and it's nothing? I'm not that dumb. Come on, where did you steal these codes?'

'What codes?' Bubba asked, glancing at Michael. 'These photocopies aren't confidential. You don't need codes to access them.'

She laughed gaily, much to Bubba's displeasure. 'I don't believe you!'

Bubba feigned nonchalance, quickly manoeuvring out of the file, leaving the screen blank. 'Suit yourself,' he said.

'In fact, I think you could get into lots of trouble if certain people knew about this,' Alice said playfully.

Bubba stopped, stared at her a moment. 'No one's going to get into trouble. No one's going to talk about this. OK?'

She didn't understand what he was really saying.

'He's right,' Michael said. 'This isn't something that should get around. Do me a favour, Alice, and forget what I showed you here.'

'All right,' she said cheerfully. 'But I know it was all your idea, Bubba. Michael wouldn't fool with people's grades.'

'Nor would I,' Bubba said curtly.

Alice laughed again, oblivious to the tension in the room. Giving Michael a quick kiss on the cheek, she reminded him to be sure to get to the stadium by half-time. The instant she was gone, Bubba turned off the screen and shook his head.

'Mike, you're not improving your chances of being valedictorian by trying to get us both expelled.'

'Alice won't talk. She's my friend.'

'Alice is a fifteen-year-old girl who is not my friend. I don't trust her.'

'Don't worry about it. She was only kidding.'

Bubba thought for a moment. 'All right, Mike, whatever you say.'

* * *

Michael and Bubba went to the mall for lunch shortly after that. It was crowded. Michael remembered when the mall had been nothing but a piddling collection of failing stores. Put a roof over something and people swarmed in.

Michael ordered a turkey sandwich from Ed's Sandwich Selection. His mother was usually too tired after working all day as a secretary in a downtown high-rise to cook; he had grown up eating most of his food wedged between two slices of bread.

He was practically finished with his sandwich before Bubba had even decided what to order. Bubba finally opted for Indian food, which took time to prepare (to his specifications). By then many of Tabb's students had already come and gone so they could be back for the special assembly of candidate speeches. Michael also had a mild interest in hearing the talks. Plus he hoped to run into Jessica Hart again. He had begun to take Bubba's threat seriously. At Michael's prodding, Bubba got his dishes to go.

The assembly was well under way when they entered the gym. The bleachers were jammed. They stood near the ticket booth beside the entrance, Bubba holding his aromatic spiced dahl and rice in a white cardboard container, surveying the audience for a seat. In a high, cracking voice, a girl at the microphone was talking about school spirit and how great she was.

'Do you see her?' Bubba asked.

'I'm not looking for her.'

'I believe you. I see her.'

'Where? Don't point.'

'Sixth row on the far right, two rows behind Fosmeyer's body.'

Michael saw her. It was amazing how her beauty had magnified since morning. The shine of her long brown hair seemed to jump right out from the crowd. 'All right, let's leave,' Michael said.

'But you dragged me back here. No, we're going to sit behind her.'

Michael didn't like that idea. 'There's no room.'

Bubba ignored him. 'Come on.'

They didn't actually get the seats directly behind Jessica, but a couple of rows back. Bubba obtained the space by gesturing to a couple of sophomores to move to the rear. Bubba did not have a reputation for being violent; nevertheless, the kids jumped when he pointed. Climbing the steps, Michael had kept his head turned away from Jessica. He didn't know if she'd noticed him.

Sitting in the row between Michael and Jessica were a couple of Tabb's football players. They cheered loudly as the next speaker was announced: Bill Skater. Bubba began to lay out his Indian delicacies, opening a bottle of Perrier and spreading a cloth napkin across his lap. Michael saw Jessica lean forward as Bill strode towards the microphone. She had a pudgy girl with dark hair on her left and an orange-haired girl on her right. These two girls turned and spoke to Jessica when Bill appeared. Michael leaned forward, trying to block out Bill's opening statements, straining to hear what the girls were saying.

'He walks like a stiff board,' the one on the left said.

'I hear he's the worst quarterback in Tabb's long history of terrible quarterbacks,' the one on the right said.

'Shut up, both of you,' Jessica said.

'Oh, but I think he's cute,' the one on the left said.

'He should take his shirt off and give his speech,' the one on the right agreed.

'Shh. I want to hear what he has to say,' Jessica said.

'What for, we've heard it all before,' the one on the left said.

'Yeah, I wish I could get down there and tell them what this school really needs,' the one with orange hair said.

This last comment caused Jessica and her pal on the left to break into laughter. Michael didn't know what was so funny. He wondered if Jessica was interested in Bill Skater.

Michael listened to Bill's speech with an open and unprejudiced mind, but never did figure out what he was running for, much less why anyone should vote for him. Bubba continued to savour his meal. When Clair Hilrey's name was announced next, however, Bubba looked up.

'Isn't she something?' he muttered as Clair swaggered to the microphone in her cute blue-and-gold cheerleader uniform.

'She's an empty phoney devoid of an iota of intelligence.'

Bubba nodded. 'True. But if you look past those superficial qualities, you'll see her true value.'

'Which is?'

'It's hard to express in words. Just imagine her naked.'

Clair's speech had a content similar to Bill's, which is to say it had no content at all. But she giggled a lot, whereas Bill had been as stiff as the board Jessica's friend had compared him to, and she did have an alluring way of propping her hands on her hips at the top of her undeniably gorgeous legs. Clair made it clear she wanted to be school president.

The name Sara Cantrell was called next.

'What the hell?' the girl on Jessica's right said.

'Go ahead, tell them what this school really needs,' Jessica said.

'No way. I'd have to start by telling them it doesn't need me.'

'Coward,' the girl to Jessica's left said.

'Don't call me a coward, you spineless fish.'

'Sara Cantrell, please?' the announcer repeated.

'It took you three years to alienate everyone at Mesa,' Jessica said. 'Just think of the power you'll have behind that microphone. You can do it all in one afternoon here.'

The logic appealed to the strange girl named Sara. Michael watched as she stood and made her way down the bleacher steps and on to the gymnasium floor.

'Hi, I'm Sara,' she began, completely at ease. 'I'm not really running for anything. My friends Jessica Hart and Polly McCoy signed me up because they thought it would be funny to get me down here.' Sara pointed towards her friends. 'They're sitting right over there. Let's give them a big laugh to show them that at least we think *they're* funny.'

The audience cheered loudly. Jessica and Polly turned beet red and buried their faces in their knees. Michael burst out laughing.

'But since I am here,' Sara continued, 'I do have a few things I'd like to say. First, I don't think you should vote for anybody who's spoken this afternoon. They all struck me as a bunch of insecure idiots, looking to get their egos stroked. Second, I don't believe we need student officers at all. What do they do? I'll tell you. Nothing! And finally, I don't know who out there stole the chewing gum from my locker, but I hope you choke on it. Thank you.'

Sara received a standing ovation and thunderous applause. She walked back to her place as though she were just another spectator taking her seat. But she grinned when she reached her friends.

'How did I do?' she asked.

'You'll probably be expelled,' Polly said.

'Or elected,' Jessica said.

'I think your girlfriend's right,' Bubba whispered in Michael's ear.

CHAPTER 3

Nick Grutler did not go to the mall for lunch nor did he attend the afternoon assembly. He didn't own a car to drive anywhere, and no one had told him about the election. Indeed, although Nick had been in school every day since Monday, no one at Tabb had even spoken to him outside of class, and that included his teachers. Nick Grutler was six feet four, wiry as a hungry animal and as black as midnight. No one had spoken to him for the simple reason that they were afraid of him.

Tabb High had several black students – four to be exact, two girls and two boys – but none of them was a recent transfer from East L.A. where youth gangs ruled. None of them had the pent-up emotion that came from having to master the use of a switchblade by age twelve just to survive. Nick had not killed anybody – no one he had been forced to stab, at least, had died in his presence

– but he had seen more violence than most war vets. And he had always hated it, and worse – in his own mind, for someone of his size and strength – had been afraid of it. None of the teachers that had yet to speak to him had noticed that the new boy from the other side of the city who sat so still during class actually had tremors beneath his skin. Nick had a lot he wished he could forget.

But it was his intention to forget, or if that was not possible, at least to put the past behind him. He considered the new job his divorced father had landed in a nearby aerospace firm as a gift from above. Another summer in East L.A. like the past one, Nick knew, probably would have seen him killed. On the other hand, Tabb High was no paradise either, so far.

He was enrolled as a senior, but he had to admit to himself that he hardly qualified as a freshman in this part of town. He was going to have to read the text books they had given him. He was going to have to *learn* to read.

He had absolutely no one to talk to. The white kids at school were all caught up in things that he had always imagined were just for TV characters. They went to the beach and parties and worried about what they were going to wear to the next dance. In a way they were like children to him. They had never stared down the barrel of a sawn-off shotgun and been ordered to kiss cold metal. They had lived incredibly sheltered lives. And yet, they were light-years beyond him. They knew all kinds of stuff. They could get up in front of a whole class and speak what was on their minds. They had nice clothes, nice cars and lots of money. They could laugh at the drop of a hat. He had spent Monday through Thursday feeling superior to them. But now that it was Friday, he realised he was jealous – and all alone.

His counsellor had put him in sixth period P.E., where all the athletes were. The only connection Nick had had with any sport was basketball. He used to play in a lot of pick-up games in the inner city. Of course, basketball season was months away. The coach who oversaw the P.E. class hadn't known what to do with him. Finally he'd asked if Nick would like to lift weights. Sure, Nick had said.

Nick was working up a sweat with over two hundred pounds on the bench press that Friday afternoon when the big, fat-legged dude with the thin-lipped mouth began to hassle him.

'A little heavy for you?' the dude asked, taking up a position near Nick's knees. Lying on his back, Nick could see that the weight room was fairly crowded, about twenty guys pumping iron. He suspected they were all on the football team, and that not a single one of them would rally to his side if this guy started to get rough. He knew instantly the guy was looking for a fight. He had an instinct for such things.

'It's not bad,' he muttered, letting go of the bars and sitting up. Perhaps if he went on to another machine, he thought, there was a chance the guy would leave him alone. Unfortunately, the guy was blocking his way.

'What did you say, boy?' the big white kid asked.

'Nothing.'

'Yeah, you did. I heard you say something. What was it?'

Nick scooted back to where he was able to swing his leg around the bench press table without touching the guy. 'I said, it was not bad. The weight wasn't.'

The guy smiled. A couple of his buddies behind him stopped lifting to watch. 'You must be pretty strong, boy. How many pounds were you lifting there?'

'I don't know.'

'You don't know? How come you don't know?'

Nick stood up. 'I wasn't keeping track.'

The guy followed him to the next machine, which exercised the hamstrings. To use it, Nick would have to lie face down, which was not something he wanted to do at the moment. He stood undecided as all around him more guys stopped working out to stare.

'What are you waiting for?' the dude asked, moving closer. Nick estimated the guy had forty pounds on him, but knew that his gut was soft, a swift fist in the diaphragm and the white kid would go down. Nick also estimated that about twenty guys would jump in the moment the guy hit the floor.

'Nothing.' Nick had never mastered the art of talking his way out of a fight.

'Aren't our machines good enough for you?'

Nick lowered his head. 'They're all right.'

'Just all right? You sure spend enough time on them, time that someone else on the team could be using. Are you getting my meaning, boy?'

Nick got it very well. But suddenly he didn't feel that he should. This is how it had always been with him. He would try to avoid a confrontation up to a point – and then he just wouldn't bend any more. He would explode. He hated being called boy.

'No.'

The guy lost his smile. 'No what?'

Nick looked him straight in the eye. He hadn't really looked anyone in the eye all week. 'I have as much right to use this equipment as you do. If you think I don't, that's your problem.'

'Really? Well, I think it just became your problem.' And with that, the guy shoved him hard in the chest.

Nick had been expecting the move, and it was still his intention to floor the guy without seriously injuring him. But what followed proved unexpected. Absorbing the blow without losing his balance, Nick moved slightly to the right and forward. He planned to grab the guy by the left arm, spin him around and put him in a choke hold. He figured that would be the best way to keep his teammates at bay. He couldn't believe it when the overweight tub anticipated *his* move and caught his right hand, whipping him into the nearby wall with incredible force. On the wall hung a mirror the guys used to admire themselves. It splintered on impact beneath Nick's skull, cutting into his scalp. Then he was on the floor, trying to stand. Blood trickled down the side of his face. The guy's feet were approaching.

'You goddamn piece of—' the dude swore as he let fly a kick towards Nick's forehead. Nick was through treating him carefully. He ducked the fat foot and crouched, coiling the power of his legs. The momentum of the misplaced kick left the white dude twisted at an awkward angle. Nick launched himself upward, grabbing the guy's hair with both hands and snapping his right knee into his groin. The bastard couldn't even scream out. Doubling up, making a strangled gasping sound, he fell to the floor, turning a sick pasty colour.

'Who's next?' Nick barked, glaring at the remainder of the room. He doubted that he'd scare off the whole gang, and he was right. You couldn't bluff people out of a twenty-to-one advantage. A few of the stockier fellows began to close in. Instinctively, Nick knelt and grabbed hold of a large jagged slice of mirror. The players paused warily, glancing at one another. It was then that the head of the football team, Coach Campbell, barged in.

Nick had seen the man before. Approximately forty years old, he had tanned leathery skin and a wide blunt face Nick thought particularly ugly. Although below average in height, he was built like a tree trunk and had one of those thick raspy voices that was usually the result of years of shouting.

'What's going on here?' he demanded. He saw his player rolled up on the floor and then saw Nick bleeding, with the glass knife in his hand. A look of pure disgust filled his already disgusting face. 'Put that down!'

Nick set the piece of mirror on the floor. He had been gripping it so hard, it had cut into his fingers and they were bleeding as well. Coach Campbell moved so close to Nick that Nick could feel his hot breath on his bare chest. 'What did you do to Gordon?' he asked.

'He attacked m-me,' Nick stuttered.

'He attacked *you*? Why would he attack someone carrying a knife?' The coach backed off a step, scowled down at Gordon. 'Skater, Fields, help The Rock to the infirmary.'

The Rock, Nick thought.

The players did as they were told and soon the guy was cleared away. From the outside, Nick knew he was standing perfectly still, but inside he was shaking. He half expected the coach to belt him in the face. Worse, he had no doubt at all that he was to be expelled, and that his father would kick him out of the house when he heard.

'What's your name, son?' Coach Campbell asked.

'Nick Grutler.'

'Where you from? What are you doing here?'

'This is where I go to school.'

'Who gave you permission to use the facilities in this room?'

'The other coach.'

'Who?'

'I don't remember his name.'

Coach Campbell folded his arms across his chest, nodding to himself. 'I know who you are. You're that transfer from Pontiac High downtown. I was warned about you. I see I should have listened.'

Nick swallowed. 'He started it.'

Coach Campbell looked around the room. 'Is this true?' He waited for an answer. No one spoke up. The coach sighed, shook his head. 'Grutler, either you're a liar or else no one here gives a damn about your hide. I don't know which is worse. But I can tell you one thing, you're on your way out, out of this room and off this campus.' He began to walk away. 'See someone at the infirmary about your cuts. Then come to my office.'

A heavy weight descended on Nick, and for the first time an outsider might have noticed a crack in his reserve. He was stooped over slightly; he couldn't quite catch his breath. He really had wanted to fit in.

Then the unexpected happened for the second time in a few minutes. One of the guys in the corner began to laugh. The sound caused Coach Campbell to stop in the doorway and glance over his shoulder. The guy in the corner kept right on laughing, louder and louder. The coach turned towards him glaring.

'What are you giggling about, Desmond?' Coach Campbell demanded.

The guy got up slowly, shaking his head. 'It's just that you remind me, Coach, of a sheriff in a movie I saw last night on TV. The sheriff tried to put a black fella behind bars just 'cause he didn't like his looks. Sitting here, I was thinking you talked just like him. You see that movie, Coach? You would have liked it. The sheriff ended up going to jail.'

'What's your point?'

The guy yawned. 'Seems to me if The Rock wants to pick on people that can kick his ass, I don't see why it's anybody's business except his and the guy he's hassling.'

'Are you saying The Rock started this? Why didn't you speak up earlier?'

'Couldn't be bothered, I guess.'

Coach Campbell glanced at Nick, then back at the guy. Nick could see Desmond was no slouch, either. About six feet with a head of thick brown hair, he had a powerfully developed physique. More important to Nick, though, when he had begun to laugh, the other guys in the room had backed off slightly, as though even his humour intimidated them. Coach Campbell seemed to take him seriously enough.

'What are you doing in here, anyway, Desmond?' the coach asked. 'Don't you have a cross-country race to run this afternoon?'

'I do, yeah. So what?'

'You shouldn't be tiring yourself out beforehand lifting weights.' Then his tone took on a bitter edge. 'You shouldn't be running at all. Why don't you suit up for tonight's game? We need some help at full back.'

'I'll tell you why, Coach. 'Cause I don't feel like it.'

'You're wasting God given talents. You could go to college on a scholarship. You have the potential to go to Notre Dame!'

Desmond looked bored, sat down. 'No way, I ain't even Catholic.'

Coach Campbell let out an exasperated breath, turned to Nick. 'All right, Grutler, we'll let it pass this time. But in the future, try to stay out of trouble.'

Nick had not expected an apology. 'Yeah, sure.'

When the coach had left, everyone went back to pumping iron, except for Desmond, who pulled on a torn cross-country jersey and strolled outside. Nick caught up with him on the hot asphalt between the weight room and the gym.

'Hey, I just wanted to thank you,' Nick said.

The guy didn't even slow down. 'No problem. I got a real kick out of seeing you knee The Rock between the legs. I bet that pig can't stand up straight for a week.'

'Well, I won't forget it. I owe you one.'

'You don't owe me nothing. But if you want to buy me a case of beer someday, I'll drink it.'

And with that, Desmond walked away.

*　*　*

Nick did not go to the infirmary. He didn't know where it was, and he didn't want to run into The Rock and his pals if he *was* able to find it. He took a shower instead and afterwards held a wad of toilet paper to the cut on his scalp. Eventually the bleeding began to subside. The resulting scar would be hidden under his hair, but because he had hit the mirror with the side of his head, and not the back, the flesh between his left temple and left eye had also begun to swell. He worried what his father would say when he saw it. His father had a violent temper.

Besides having given him walking orders to stay out of trouble, his father had also told him not to come home that afternoon without a job. Nick had figured his best bet would be the nearby mall. He knew roughly where it was and thought he might be able to walk there in less than a hour. He'd worked before, in his old neighbourhood, loading freight at the docks. He wondered if the stores in the mall would want him to fill out all kinds of papers before letting him show what he could do. He hoped not.

Before he set out for the mall, he stopped at the soda machines in the courtyard. He was disappointed to discover he didn't have enough money to buy a Coke. He was standing there, fishing through his pockets for a possible hidden dime, when a small Hispanic girl came up at his side.

'May I?' she asked. He was blocking her way. He stepped aside hastily.

'I don't have the right change,' he mumbled. He'd seen the girl before, at lunch, sitting by herself beneath a tree hugging her knees. She had long black hair tied back in a ponytail that reached to her waist.

'Oh.' She put in her change, made her selection. A can of orange soda popped out below. 'What do you need?'

'Nothing, I wasn't that thirsty.' He was dying for a drink. 'Thanks, anyway.'

'No,' she said, glancing up at him with big, lustrous eyes, a serious, perhaps sad, expression. 'I have change.'

Nick shrugged. 'I need a quarter.'

She reached into her tiny purse. 'I have three dimes.'

He took out his dime and three nickels. This was all the money he had in the world. He'd gone without lunch. This was another reason he needed a job in a hurry. He had to buy almost all his own food. He took her dimes and bought his Coke, giving her back the spare nickel. 'Thanks,' he said, opening the can, shifting nervously on his feet. She was staring at him.

'Do you know you're bleeding?' she asked finally.

He touched the side of his head. It had started again. 'It's nothing. I cut it.'

'Does it hurt?'

'No. A little. It will stop in a minute.'

She went to touch the area. He recoiled automatically, and she withdrew her hand. 'I'm sorry,' she said.

'It's really nothing,' he said quickly.

'You were in a fight, weren't you?'

He began to shake his head, stopped. 'Yes, I was.'

Her next question caught him off guard. 'Did you win?'

'I don't think he'll want to fight me again.'

She offered her hand. 'I'm Maria Gonzales. You're Nick, aren't you?'

He shook her hand briefly. Her skin was cool, very soft. 'How did you know?'

'I've watched you this week. You walk from one place to another. You never talk to anyone. I did that when I first got here.'

She had a strong Spanish accent. He wondered if she had only recently come into the United States. He'd had experience with a variety of ethnic groups in his old neighbourhood. He suspected she wasn't from Mexico, but from farther south, from El Salvador or Nicaragua. 'I don't know many people here,' he said.

'Do you know anybody?'

'I know the name of the guy who threw me into the mirror.'

She smiled faintly. She had deep red, heart-shaped lips, smooth high cheeks untouched by make-up. Her pink dress hung loose and cool but he could tell she had a fine figure. She had a freshness about her he had seldom seen in his old neighbourhood. She had probably led a clean life.

'And I bet he knows your name,' she said.

Nick smiled, too, pleased with himself for having made a mildly funny remark, and happy to be talking to someone who was kind. Yet at the same time he felt the sudden urge to curtail the conversation. Perhaps he wanted to quit while he was ahead. Maybe he didn't think he was good enough to be talking to someone like Maria.

'Nice meeting you,' he mumbled, backing up a step. 'I better be going.'

'Do you take the bus home?'

'No.'

'Oh, you have a car?'

He stopped. The truth sounded so poor. 'Not really.'

'Where do you live?'

In a shack.

'Near Houston and Second.'

'I live over that way. You don't walk home every day, do you?'

'Sometimes I hitch a ride.' No one had picked him up so far.

'You should take the bus. There's one coming in about ten minutes. You shouldn't be walking home after getting hit like that on the head.'

The urge to get away intensified. He felt exposed, as though any second this girl was going to see something repulsive in him. He took another step back. 'I'll be all right. I've got to go. Thanks again for the Coke.'

'Take care of yourself, Nick.'

He hurried off the campus, walking in the direction of the mall. He didn't understand it. She had sounded concerned about him.

CHAPTER 4

Sara Cantrell approached the soda machines seconds after Maria Gonzales and Nick Grutler finished talking. Sara was feeling pretty good. She was glad she had spoken her mind about the candidates in the assembly that afternoon. The whole country was in love with phonies, she felt. The bimbos on sitcoms, the rock dopers on MTV, the rich liars in D.C. It made her sick just going into the supermarket and having to look at all those fakes on the covers of *People* magazine. One day she'd like to start a magazine of her own where she could interview people like herself, people who knew it was all a big joke.

Sara had a bad thirst. But when she put her quarters in the soda machine and punched the 7-Up button, nothing happened. She tried the other buttons, then the coin return, and still nothing happened. Her good mood went right out the window. Those were the only two quarters she had! What did this stupid machine expect her to do, drink water? She pounded it with her fists, kicked it with her feet. Her quarters must be stuck.

The administration's probably behind this. Trying to weasel extra money out of us kids to buy themselves magazines for their goddamn lounge.

She remembered a move a guy had done on one of the soda machines at lunch. He had grabbed hold of it with both hands and tilted it slightly on edge, coughing up not only his money but a couple of free cans as well. Setting down her books, she stretched out her arms, trying to get a grip on it. She was not a big girl, nor was she particularly strong. Nevertheless, when she tilted the machine to the right, she was surprised to see it rock right out of her hands. It hit the asphalt with an incredible bang, causing her to jump. Taking a quick look around to make sure no one had seen her, she collected her books and hurried towards the front of the campus. At Mesa High she'd never once had a soda machine fall over on her. This was a stupid school.

Sara was supposed to meet Polly and Jessica in the parking lot directly across from campus. They had been forced to put their cars there; Tabb's lot was filled. Sara was temporarily without wheels. Her dad had taken them away when she had received her third ticket in a month for running a red light. It was a real drag – and totally unfair. She had only gone through the lights after stopping and looking both ways. Why, she thought, should she have to sit and wait on a mechanism that didn't care if she crossed the road or not?

Her dad didn't know she had picked up Jessica and her folks at three in the morning. She'd run half a dozen red lights driving to the airport.

A row of bushes separated the school from the pavement that ran along its west side. They were tall, thick shrubs, and putting one foot on to the pavement, Sara couldn't see more than a few yards in either direction. She didn't even hear Russ Desmond coming.

When he hit her, she hardly felt a thing. One second she was walking, the next, flying. She must have closed her eyes. When she opened them, she was sitting in the bushes with a branch running up her trouser leg and a flower stuck in her ear.

'Oh, wow,' she breathed. A guy with the greatest set of legs she had ever seen was standing over her breathing hard.

'You all right?' he asked.

'What happened?'

'You got in my way.'

'Really?' Did this guy throw every girl that got in his way into the bushes? She sat up with effort, a muscle in her lower back protesting. The guy grabbed her arm and pulled her on to the pavement as if she were light as a feather. The second he let go of her, she reeled backwards. The pavement wobbled under her feet.

'Thanks a whole bunch,' she muttered, blinking. 'Who the hell are you?'

'Russ Desmond.' He wiped his sweaty face on his arm, still panting like a dog. 'You've got leaves in your hair.'

'I didn't grow them, believe me.' She tried to brush them away and poked herself in the ear. Her hands were trembling. Maybe she had a concussion or something. The guy looked pretty wild, like a biker in a track uniform. 'I'm Sara Cantrell. You must have seen me at lunch.'

'Huh?'

Just then a multicoloured herd of various-shaped teenage boys came storming down the pavement. They had appeared from around a corner, and there was only a second to get out of their way. Russ Desmond watched them pass without a great deal of interest.

'Do the guys migrate at Tabb or what?' she asked, getting back down from the steps where she had run for safety.

'We're just having a little race, that's all. What did you mean, I must have seen you at lunch? What happened at lunch?'

It hit Sara then what was going on. 'Wait a sec, you're in the middle of a race?'

'That's what I just said.'

'No, I mean, *you're* in the race?'

'Yeah.'

'But you were winning!' She looked down the pavement in the direction of the rapidly vanishing group of cross-country runners. 'Get going. Go after them. Hurry!'

'I will,' he said, sounding vaguely annoyed. 'In a minute. I just want to make sure you're all right.'

'I'm all right. Get out of here.'

'First tell me what happened at lunch?'

'I gave a speech. Didn't you hear my speech? It doesn't matter. I'm sure someone taped it. You can listen to it after your race. Now get out of here. Go. Scoot. Goodbye.'

He nodded, gave a quick smile. 'You've wrecked my time, Sara.'

Watching him run off, pulling leaves from her hair, she muttered, 'Well, you wrecked my make-up, Russ.'

Russ Desmond.

Polly and Jessica showed up a few minutes later. They were talking about Alice's party, or rather, arguing about it. Sara loved arguments. She hated to simply discuss things.

'Food doesn't have to be a big deal,' Jessica was saying. 'We don't have to feed everyone dinner for God's sake. All we need are a few sweet and salty dishes, and plenty to drink. Isn't that right, Sara?'

'That is true.'

'But people are going to be showing up with beer,' Polly said. 'You remember what happened at Alice's last party? Claudia Philips got drunk and threw up all over Kirk Holden.'

'So we won't invite Claudia,' Jessica said.

'Or Kirk,' Sara added.

'And we can put on the invitations that no alcohol will be allowed,' Jessica said.

Polly grimaced. 'We have to print up invitations?'

'Of course,' Sara said. 'We have to show these barbarians we have class.'

'Who's going to pay for all this?' Polly asked. 'Me?'

'No, of course not,' Sara said. 'Alice will.'

'Alice has the same account as I do,' Polly complained. Then she paused, staring at Sara. 'What happened to you? You have leaves in your hair, Sara.'

'Well, you have a fat ass, Polly. And this evening I'll wash my hair and look just wonderful, and you'll still have a fat ass.'

'You wouldn't look wonderful if a car full of plastic surgeons ran over you on the freeway,' Polly retorted.

Sara wrinkled her nose. 'Huh?'

'Stop it, you two,' Jessica said. They had reached Jessica's and Polly's cars. Jessica had a Toyota; Polly, a Mercedes. Both cars were brand new. Sara had had a nice car once, before she had run into a stupid telephone pole. Jessica continued, 'We have to decide whether we want to make it a swimming party or not. What do you think, Sara?'

'Definitely. We can go skinny-dipping.'

'We're not going skinny-dipping,' Polly said. 'It's against the law.'

'Only when you've got a fat—' Sara stopped, looking around. 'Where's Alice?'

Jessica and Polly glanced at each other. 'She went home early,' Jessica said.

'What's the matter?' Sara asked. 'Does she have cramps?'

Polly hesitated. 'Yeah.'

'That's a shame,' Sara said. She liked having Alice around. That girl could take an insult better than anybody; she always just laughed.

71

Jessica yawned. 'Let's talk about this later, at the game. I've got to take a nap now or I'm going to turn into a pumpkin.' She opened her car door. 'You want Polly or me to take you home, Sara?'

'I'll go with you.'

'I can drive us to the game,' Polly said eagerly.

'Whatever,' Jessica nodded, still yawning. 'Get in, Sara.'

When they were cruising down the road, the air conditioner on full and Polly following on their tail, Sara asked, 'Why are you going to the game? You should stay home and rest.'

Jessica rubbed her tired eyes beneath her glasses. She had only put on the glasses at Sara's insistence. Lately Jessica's sight had got so bad that Sara hated to get in the car when she was driving. That morning in political science, before she fell asleep, Sara had noticed Jessica straining to see the screen. The girl had a history of allergies; her eyes were too sensitive for contacts, even for soft lenses. Yet she resisted wearing her glasses, even when there was no one else around; simple vanity, there was no question about it.

'I would, but I told my journalism teacher I'd take some pictures for the paper,' Jessica said.

'You volunteered?'

'Not exactly. The teacher saw the pictures I'd taken last

72

year for Mesa's annual. She likes my work. I think she's been waiting for me and my camera to show up. I don't mind. I've got to do something now that I'm not a cheerleader any more. And I promised Alice I'd come. She has this guy she wants me to meet.'

'What's his name?'

'I don't know.'

'Bill Skater?'

Jessica smiled. 'I wish. It'll be fun watching him play tonight.'

'It might be *funny*. I wasn't kidding in the assembly when I said I'd heard he was awful.'

Jessica shrugged. 'I could care less what he can do with a football.'

Sara sneered. 'What makes you think you're ever going to find out what he can do with you?'

Jessica grinned. 'It's only September. I've got till June. I'm going to invite him to the party.'

'I know.'

Jessica lost her grin. 'You don't think we're pressuring Polly into something she doesn't want to do, do you?'

'Polly's just being Polly. If we didn't give her a shove every now and then, she'd be mummified in her bedroom closet. Besides, the party was Alice's idea.' Sara rubbed her aching arm. A purple bruise was beginning to appear below her elbow. 'I have someone I'm going to invite, too.'

'Who?'

'This guy I ran into.'

CHAPTER 5

Michael Olson was doing inventory at the 7-Eleven when Nick Grutler walked in. Michael had seen Nick at school – it was hard not to see that tall, black body – and wondered if he played basketball. He had thought of asking him. It was not fear of Nick that had kept Michael quiet. Once Bubba had accused Michael of being especially kind to minorities because he felt guilty about not fully trusting them. It was Bubba's contention that everyone was prejudiced to a degree, and the best anyone could do was to try not to let it interfere with how he treated other races. But Michael was genuinely colour blind. People were people to him.

Michael had not approached Nick because Nick did not look as if he wanted to be approached. It was as simple as that. The Rock probably wished he'd had as keen instincts. Michael had heard what happened in the weight room. But unlike Russ Desmond, he did not take pleasure in The Rock's downfall. Michael disliked violence in any form.

But now that Nick had come into his store, Michael felt no qualms about introducing himself. He nodded as Nick approached the counter. 'Hi, how are you doing? Don't we go to school together?'

A flicker of surprise crossed Nick's eyes. 'I go to Tabb,' he mumbled.

'So do I.' Michael offered his hand. 'I'm Michael Olson. Nick Grutler, right?'

Nick shook his hand. He had a mean grip. 'How did you know?'

'You can expect most people at school to know your name after you floored The Rock.'

A note of wariness entered his voice. 'Was he a friend of yours?'

'The Rock doesn't have many friends.' Michael had only brought up the weight room incident because he wanted to answer Nick's question honestly. He wanted to get off the subject. 'You look like you've been out in the sun all afternoon. Can I get you something to drink? You know we sell soft drinks in glasses here as well as bottles and cans.' Michael picked up the king-size cup behind him. 'These are only fifty-five cents.'

Nick looked vaguely uncomfortable. He pulled a couple of silver dollars out of his pocket and laid them on the counter. 'These are good, aren't they?'

Michael picked one up. 'Yeah, sure. Though you don't see many of them around. Did you get them at the bank?'

'No. At the Italian market.'

'In the mall? Man, I love the smell in that place.'

'Their warehouse in the back don't smell so good.'

'What were you doing back there?'

'They needed some boxes moved.'

Michael knew the owner of the market. He had probably worked Nick to death for a couple of hours and then given him the two silver dollars, probably thinking Nick would imagine they were worth more or something.

Michael was looking for a new employee. The owners had told him to hire whomever he wanted. They trusted his judgment.

'Was it a temporary job?' he asked, knowing it was. Who would hire a black guy with bloody hair?

'Yeah. I'll have one of those big Cokes for fifty-five cents.'

'Sure.' Michael reached over, scooped some ice into the paper cup. 'Have you done enough work for one day?'

Nick seemed interested. 'I could do more.'

'I'm rearranging our storeroom. But because I have to keep coming back up front to handle the register, it's taking me for ever. It's back-breaking work – all you're doing is lifting – but someone like you could probably finish most of it in a few hours. I could give you thirty bucks under the table, no tax taken out?'

Nick accepted his Coke, took a deep swallow. 'Show me where to start.'

Michael led Nick to the rear of the store and gave him an overview of how disorganised things were. Nick grasped immediately what had to be done. After a couple minutes of discussion, Michael left Nick alone. He needed help with the storeroom, true, but Michael was also using the chore as a test. If Nick did good work, he would offer him a permanent part-time job. It would be handy having someone around who could reach the top shelves without a ladder.

Two hours later, as it began to get dark outside and the faint sounds of Tabb High's band drifted through the open door from the direction the school stadium, Nick reappeared and announced he had finished. One look in the back and Michael was astounded. Not only was everything neatly arranged, Nick had obviously used his own initiative – and used it wisely – in setting up certain sections. This meant a lot to Michael. He'd previously had a couple of employees who had been fine workers except that they had required constant supervision. Obviously Nick had common sense as well as powerful biceps.

Getting three tens out of the cash register, Michael made his offer. He could guarantee him at least twenty hours a week, although some weeks he'd need Nick close to thirty. He gave him a brief summary of what his responsibilities would be, and what he would start at. Nick listened patiently, and from his stoic expression, it was impossible to tell what was going on in his head. He asked only two questions.

'Will I be working with you all the time?'

'Most of the time,' Michael said.

Nick thought for a moment. 'Why are you doing this for me?'

'I'm offering you the job because you've proven to me you know how to work. I'm not *doing* anything for you.'

Nick nodded. 'I appreciate it, anyway. The only one who would even talk to me at the mall was that Italian guy, and I know he just ripped me off.' He put his thirty dollars in his pocket. 'Can I just keep working now?'

Michael smiled. 'You'll take it then?'

Nick smiled, too, finally letting his pleasure show.

'Yeah. But I'll have to call my dad to tell him I've got a job.'

Michael pulled the phone from beneath the counter. 'Sure, then take a break. There's a lot to do here, but you don't have to kill yourself.'

A half-hour later Michael wondered if he'd lied to Nick about not killing himself. They got held up by a guy with a gun.

Nick was in the cooler, putting the beverages in from behind, and Michael had returned to the inventory report and the register when the masked man entered. He wore a dark nylon stocking over his head on top of a blue knitted cap and a pair of silver sunglasses. He had his gun drawn as he entered.

'Get your hands up!' he snapped, waving his revolver nervously. Michael carefully set down his note board and pen. His first reaction was not one of fear, but of pure amazement. It was only eight-thirty. Who would be stupid enough to try to pull off a hold-up now, when anybody could walk in at any second? The 7-Eleven was open twenty-four hours a day, for God's sake. But Michael didn't consider suggesting to the guy he come back later.

'What can I do for you?' he asked calmly, slowly raising his hands. There was a button located beneath the counter that would sound an alarm at the local police station. Unfortunately, it was so situated that Michael would have to ask permission of any thief to use it. The clink of bottles continued to sound from behind the cooler. Nick must not know they had uninvited company.

'What's that?' the fellow demanded. He wasn't very good at this. Outside of his obvious anxiety, he had a rather squeaky voice. Shifting the gun from one hand to the other, he scratched under his nylon stocking.

'What was what?' Michael asked.

'Do you have someone back there?' He peered towards the cooler. It must have been hard to see through the disguise. 'Hey, you back there! Get out here before I blow your buddy away!'

'Yeah, come out here, Nick. We've got a guest.'

Nick appeared a moment later, his arms hanging by his sides. 'Mike?'

'It's nothing to worry about,' Michael said, trying to relax everybody concerned. 'We're all cool here, aren't we?'

'Yeah, it's cool,' the guy spat out, cocking his revolver. 'Give me your goddamn money. No funny business.' He gestured towards Nick. 'And you, get your hands up and come over here.'

Michael did not want to give him the money. In no

way did he plan on risking his or Nick's life to save it, but he did feel a responsibility to the owners of the store to get to the alarm button if at all possible. Opening the register, he rapidly began to toss all the change on the counter, like he was scared and didn't know what he was doing. The masked man shook his gun angrily.

'Just the bills, man! Just the bills!'

'Yes, sir, the bills,' Michael answered breathlessly, pulling the drawer out still farther, past the point of no return. The drawer slipped from the register, the money pouring loudly on to the floor. Michael feigned shock. 'Wow, I'm sorry.' He bent over. 'Here I'll pick it up.'

'Man you're a peach.' The masked man chuckled, falling for Michael's chicken act, leaning forward to watch him better. But it was already too late. Michael had hit the button the instant he crouched down. At this very second, several patrol cars would be changing direction and moving towards them.

Michael didn't know when he had hired Nick that Nick had never depended on a cop for anything in his life. He didn't know about Nick's incredible reflexes.

As Michael began to collect the money behind the counter, Nick lashed out with his foot at the gun, sending it ricocheting off the ceiling and into the cereal row. Startled, the masked man twisted around to retrieve it.

Before he could get halfway there, Nick grabbed hold of his arm and whipped him into a stack of beer bottles. The guy slid towards the freezer in a wave of broken glass, foam and noise.

'Oh, God,' Michael whispered. Moving quickly, Nick collected the gun and turned on the fallen thief. Seeing him coming, the guy frantically began to rip at the nylon over his face.

'Mike, don't let him kill me!' he cried. 'It's me! It's Kats!'

'Kats,' Michael said, disgusted. 'I should have known.'

Carl Barber, better known as Kats, was a nineteen-year-old loser. He had gone to Tabb High for five years, taken advance pottery and Shop I, II and III, and still hadn't graduated. He'd had a lifelong dream of joining the marines, but without the diploma, they wouldn't take him. He worked at the gas station up the street from Tabb High. He had oil under his fingernails a surgeon couldn't have removed. Whenever kids from the school drove into the station – dozens of students cruised by every morning and afternoon – Kats got into a fight with them. Admittedly, Kats usually didn't start the fights. He was one of those rare people that *no one* respected. Guys would pull into the full-service area and tell him to dust their tyres. According to Bubba – who took Kats about as seriously as everyone else but who nevertheless spent a fair amount of time in his company – Kats had been genetically cloned from Rodney Dangerfield. Nothing ever went his way, that was for sure.

'Stop, Nick,' Michael said. 'I know this guy.'

Nick looked bewildered. He shook the weapon in his hand. 'This is real, Mike. He was pointing it right at us.'

Michael came from behind the counter, furious. 'So you hold us up with a real gun! What the hell do you think you're doing?'

Kats grinned, his ugly teeth protruding from beneath his thin black moustache. It was not true, like some said, that he greased his hair and moustache with oil from the gas station, at least not intentionally. But it was a fact he was always running his hands through his hair even when he was labouring beneath filthy dripping heaps.

'I was just trying to give you boys a little scare.' Kats giggled. 'I did, too. I saw the way you fumbled that cash register!'

Michael turned to Nick. 'All right, go ahead and waste him.'

'Mike!' Kats cried, squirming in a pond of Miller Lite.

Michael took a step closer. 'I fumbled the drawer on purpose! I hit a button to call the police. It also trips an alarm in the homes of the owners. They're all going to be here in minutes. What am I supposed to tell them?'

Kats tried to get up without cutting himself, brushing off scraps of glass knitted together with torn beer labels. 'Christ, Mike, what's the big deal? The gun wasn't loaded. It was just a prank.' He grinned again. Michael really wished he would stop. 'How'd you like my disguise? I knew you wouldn't recognise me with that voice I was using. Got it off an old gangster movie I watched last night. What do you think of my piece, huh? Picked it up at the swop meet last Saturday. It fires a twenty-two—'

'Shut up,' Michael said wearily. 'Just take your piece and get out of here before the police arrive. I don't know what I'm going to tell them.' He tried to count the broken bottles. 'But I do know one thing, you're paying for this mess.'

Kats tried to snap the revolver from Nick's hands, failed. Nick did not appear to trust Kats any more now than when Kats had been holding them at gunpoint. Nick gave the weapon to Michael, instead, who accepted it reluctantly. Michael had never understood why anyone made handguns. They were no good for hunting. They were only good for killing people. Had Kats been stowing it in his refrigerator, he wondered. The steel felt unreasonably cold in his hand. He was anxious to be rid of it.

'Why should I?' Kats said angrily. 'It was this big lug here who tripped me. I ain't paying for it, no way.'

'If you don't,' Michael said flatly, 'I'll give the police your address.'

Kats saw he was serious, nodded. 'OK, lighten up. I'll pay for the beer. And I'll leave now.' He started towards the door.

'Go out the back,' Michael said. 'I don't want some cop taking a shot at you.' He held out the gun. 'Take this with you.'

Kats smiled as he accepted the revolver, slipping it into his belt beneath his shirt. He had a fetish for guns. It was probably part of the reason he wanted to join the marines. His crummy single-room apartment was packed with rifles, shotguns, all kinds of ammunition. 'Good thinking. Hey, you're not really mad at me, are you, Mike? You know I would never try to rob you. You and me, we go way back. Coming to the game later?'

'Yeah, maybe.' Michael chuckled in spite of himself. This was turning out to be a weird day. 'Go ahead, get out of here. Go home and take a shower. You stink.'

'Thanks, Mike. See you later.'

When he was gone, Michael called the police. Turned out they had received no alarm. He called one of his bosses, told him he had accidentally bumped the button.

The boss gave him the same story as the police; no alarm had gone off. Hanging up the phone, Michael pulled on the wiring attached to the button. It was burned out, shorted.

'At least now we've got your feet to protect us,' he told Nick. 'That is, if you haven't changed your mind and want to quit?'

'I'm not quitting, Mike. I'm just beginning to feel at home.'

Between the two of them, they cleaned up the mess. The equivalent of three cases had been destroyed. Michael decided to juggle the numbers on the store inventory until Kats came up with the money, if he ever did. Michael figured he'd probably end up paying for the damage out of his own pocket.

Michael's replacement, the twenty-year-old son of one of the bosses, came in at nine o'clock. Amir went full-time to the local junior college and spent most nights at the store. As a result, he was chronically exhausted, and did little during the wee hours of the morning except run the cash register and study. He simply nodded when Michael introduced Nick as their new employee. Michael hoped Amir's father had the same reaction.

Michael and Nick were walking out the front doors of the 7-Eleven when the phone rang. An hour had passed since the phoney hold-up. It was Bubba. Michael took the call in the small office in the back.

'Did you invite Nick Grutler to come to the game with us?' Bubba asked.

'Yeah.' The invitation had surprised Nick, but he had accepted without hesitation. He seemed to be looking forward to it. 'Where are you? You said you'd pick me up at nine.'

'Kats is here,' Bubba said, lowering his voice. 'He tells me Grutler tried to kill him.'

'Did Kats also tell you that he pulled a gun on us?'

'Yeah, but that was a joke, Mike. What's wrong with this guy? I hear he practically cut The Rock's throat this afternoon.'

'Get off it, Bubba. You know as well as I do, The Rock started it. Nick's cool. Are you going to pick us up or not?'

'If it was just up to me, I'd be there already. But Kats wants to go to the game, and he says if Nick comes with us, things might get ugly. He's full of it, I know, but why don't you and Nick go on alone?'

'Since when does Kats tell you what to do?'

'It's no big deal. Let's not fight about it. I'll meet you there. Come on, it's getting late, and I want to talk to Clair before half-time ends.'

Michael was disappointed in his friend. 'Whatever you say, Bubba.'

Michael owned his own car, an off-white Toyota that had had over a hundred thousand miles on it when he bought it. The interior was clean, and although the engine drank a quart of oil every month, it ran smoothly. Yet as he opened the passenger door and adjusted the seat for Nick's long legs, Michael thought how plain it would look to a girl like Jessica Hart who had just returned from sunbathing in the Aegean Sea. He was hoping to see her at the game, maybe say hello.

The parking lot was packed; they had to park a block away in a residential area. Walking towards the stadium, Michael caught a glimpse of the scoreboard: Tabb High 0; Vistiors 6. The marching bands and drill teams had taken the field. The snack bar was beset with thick lines. They had definitely made it for half-time.

'Have you ever played any sports?' Michael asked Nick as they hurried up the steps that led to the entrance.

'Nope.'

'How about some pickup basketball games?'

'Oh, yeah, we used to play those.' Nick chuckled. 'But we never followed many rules. You had to knock a guy unconscious for a foul to be called.'

'Have you ever thought of going out for the team here?'

Nick looked uncomfortable. 'I don't think I'd fit in on a team.' He reached for his back pocket. 'How much is it to get in?'

'When you're this late, it's free.'

Once inside the gate, they both caught a whiff of the hot dogs and decided they were starving. Nick insisted it would be his treat and went to wait in line while Michael made a quick stop at the rest room. He was heading back to the snack bar when he ran into Alice McCoy. She had a guy with her, a thin redhead who was literally dragging her towards the exit.

'Mikey!' she called, disengaging herself from her date and running to give him a quick hug. 'Where have you been? I've been looking for you all night. Remember, I wanted you to meet my friend?'

'Well, I'm here now,' he said cheerfully.

She glanced back over her shoulder. Her date had turned away, staring into the brick wall behind the snack bar. Alice smiled quickly, nervously. 'Did you have to work late?'

'No later than usual. Do you have to leave now?'

'Yeah. We – we have to go somewhere.'

'That's too bad. I can always meet your friend another time.'

'No, I want to be there when you meet her.' Again, she glanced at her date, obviously trying to come to some sort of decision. Michael nodded towards the guy.

'Is that your new boyfriend?'

She didn't seem to hear him.

'Could you stay here a sec?'

'Sure.'

Alice walked back to the guy, spoke softly to him. First he shook his head. But as Alice persisted, he shrugged, pulling out a comb and running it through his long, thin red hair. Touching him gratefully on the arm, Alice returned to Michael.

'I'll go get her,' she said. 'Stay here, right here. OK?'

'All right.' Watching her disappear into the crowd, Michael wondered why Alice had not introduced him to her date. Ordinarily she was extremely polite. Something about the way the guy stood, his hands ploughed into his pockets, completely ignoring everyone around him, disturbed Michael. He decided he'd introduce himself.

'Hi, I'm Michael Olson,' he said, walking up and offering his hand. 'I'm a friend of Alice's. You're Clark, right?'

The guy had the brightest green eyes Michael had ever seen. They practically glowed in the dark. His gaze lingered on Michael's outstretched hand for a moment before he lazily shook it.

'I suppose,' he said. He had a deep southern accent, a disconcerting stare. His black leather biker jacket hung loose over his shoulders; Michael suspected there was nothing but skin and bone beneath it. The guy needed to see a doctor. His palm was warm and clammy.

'Alice tells me you're also an artist?'

Clark found the comparison amusing. 'She loves pretty colours. I like sharp lines, black and white.'

'Huh. What's that mean?'

'That I'm unique.'

What does she see in him?

The question made Michael pause and consider how well he knew Alice. From day one, he'd neatly classified her as a carefree darling. He should know better by now that no one was that neat, or that unique.

'She told me you've had a big influence on her work,' he said.

'She's talked about me?'

'On occasion.'

'Alice doesn't work. Alice's got too much money to work. Alice's got too many dresses.' He grinned suddenly. 'Do you like the dress she's wearing tonight? I like when her sister wears it. It looks a lot different on Polly.'

Michael had met Polly once. Alice had brought her by

his store last spring. He assumed Clark was making a lewd reference to her large breasts. His dislike for the guy deepened. 'Where are you from?' he asked.

Clark lost his grin. 'Why?'

'I was just wondering, that's all. Do you go to school around here?'

'No.'

'Where do you go?'

'The other side of town.' Clark's gaze wandered towards the playing field. 'Our team's as lousy as yours. But in our stadium, you can always lean your head back and look at the trees in the sky.'

Michael frowned. 'I don't mean to be rude, but are you stoned?' He was worried about Alice driving home in the car with him.

'I'm here man, right here.' Clark yawned, turning again to face the wall behind the snack bar. 'Alice had better get back soon. I've got to get out of here.'

'Why?'

Bubba and Kats appeared. Since Clark had not bothered to answer his last question, Michael felt under no obligation to introduce him to them. Bubba had on a black suede jacket, a red handkerchief tucked in the pocket, a white silk shirt underneath. Kats was no longer dripping but still stunk of beer. Bubba had probably thrown Kats's clothes in the dryer without washing them. Clark continued to stare at the wall. It didn't even have graffiti on it. Michael allowed Bubba to pull him aside.

'Have you seen Clair?' he asked.

'No, I haven't been here long,' Michael said. 'But I think the cheerleaders are finished with their half-time routine.'

'Good.' Bubba gestured in the direction of Clark. 'Who's that?'

'A friend of Alice's.'

'Wonderful. He looks dead.' Bubba turned to Kats, pulling out his wallet. 'Get me a large buttered popcorn and a medium size Dr Pepper without ice.' He handed Kats a ten. 'Treat yourself to whatever you want. Bring it to the fifty-yard line. But if I'm talking to Clair, keep your distance.'

Kats accepted the money. The side of his face had begun to colour from his bout with Nick. 'Going to bag her, Bubba?'

'I'm going to wrap her up in aluminium foil and toast her. Go get in line. Tell them to watch the salt on the popcorn.' When Kats was gone, Bubba said, 'Let's do it, Mike.'

'I'm waiting for Alice and Nick. I should stay here.'

Bubba waved his hand. 'Don't worry, they'll find you. Come on.'

Michael really did want to see Bubba in action, especially going after Clair. He figured he'd be able to catch Alice on her way back to Clark. And locating Nick would be no problem. He followed Bubba out on to the bleachers. The mood of the crowd appeared upbeat; Tabb High hadn't been down at half-time by only six points in years. The cheerleaders were gathered beneath the stands on the track, near centre field. Standing nearest to the microphone, Clair was giving her voice a rest, sucking on a soft drink while waiting for the team to return to the field. With her shiny blonde hair tied up in twin gold-ribboned ponytails, her legs deeply tanned beneath her short blue skirt, Michael had to admit she looked awfully sexy.

'Are you sure you want me with you?' Michael asked.

'I consider this a necessary part of your education. Just stay close, like we're hanging out together. But let me do all the talking.'

A chest-high chain-link fence separated the audience from the track. Leaning casually into it, Bubba waved to Clair, calling, 'Hey, come here. I want to talk to you.'

Clair did not quite know what to make of the order. Holding on to her drink, she approached slowly. 'Yeah, what?' she said, looking up at him.

Bubba smiled. 'How are you doing, Clair? Good? You look good.'

Clair took her straw out of her mouth. 'I'm all right. What can I do for you, Bubba?'

Bubba rested an elbow on the top of the fence, dropped his smile for an unhappy expression. 'I don't know, maybe you can do something. I'm having a bad day, a really bad time.'

'What's wrong?' Clair asked.

'Well, like I was telling Mike here – you know Mike, sure you do – it's no wonder they speak of the stock market like it was a woman. You never know what she's going to do. The same day you think you've got her figured out, she turns around and stabs you in the back.'

Clair showed interest. 'Oh, yeah, someone told me you fooled around with stocks. What happened, did you lose some money?'

'It was all on paper, you understand. I was investing dollars I'd made on earlier trades. But it still pisses me off to be outguessed. I probably shouldn't talk about it. But the market, she's one nasty lady. How are things with you? I love your hair up like that. You should wear it like that all the time, even when you're taking a shower.'

Clair played with one of her ponytails. 'If I did that, I'd get my ribbons wet.'

Michael recognised Bubba's strategy. It was Bubba's opinion that money and sex were inseparable in the female mind; thinking about credit cards and spending power, in his opinion, got them more excited than browsing through a *Playgirl* magazine.

'Then you could blow them dry,' he said. 'Hey, can I ask you something? This has really been a miserable day.'

'What?'

'Let's go out together sometime. I'm always working, I've got to have more fun in life. Let's go out next weekend, next Saturday night.'

Clair nodded. 'Sure, we could – wait a second. I don't know. I don't think so. I'd like to, but I'm seeing Bill Skater. I don't think he'd like it if I went out with someone else.'

Bubba waved his hand. Sometimes Michael thought Bubba could convince the Pope to break his vows with a wave of that hand. 'Bill won't, I know the guy. He doesn't want to totally monopolise your life. Don't worry about it, we'll have fun.' He smiled. 'I just got new leather upholstery in my Jaguar.'

'That's right, you've got a Jag.'

'I sure do. Hey, you like music, Clair? You like U2?'

Bubba must have researched Clair's taste in music. She

lit up. 'They're one of my favourite bands!'

'They're going to be in town next week. We'll go see them.'

'But I heard they were sold out.'

'I've already got tickets. Third row, dead centre. We can eat first and then head on over to the forum. Give me your phone number.'

Clair glanced around uneasily. Bubba had come a long way in less than a minute, but Clair was obviously hesitant about handing out her number to a short, overweight guy in front of the entire community. 'You really have third-row tickets?'

'They could be second row.'

She paused, sizing him up. She wasn't a total airhead. 'You're not just throwing me a line, are you? I've heard about you.'

Bubba was sly. 'What have you heard?'

Clair blushed. 'Stories.'

'Well, they're all true.' Bubba leaned over the fence, spoke seriously. 'If you don't want to go, Clair, just say so. A lot of guys don't mind wasting their time. But I do.'

Michael had followed Bubba's moves perfectly up until this point. But when Clair suddenly blurted out her number, he realised he was completely lost.

'Five-five-five-four-three-two-six,' she said. 'I don't have anything to write on. Will you remember it?'

Bubba nodded, moved back from the fence, straightening his jacket. 'I'll call you tomorrow.'

Clair returned to the microphone, her fellow cheerleaders quickly gathering around. Bubba led Michael back in the direction of the snack bar. 'No sweat,' he said.

Michael nodded. 'All right, you were smooth. But if you hadn't brought up the concert, she would never have given you her number. Do you really have tickets in the third row?'

'Nope, I don't have any tickets. And I'm not going to pay scalper prices to get them.'

'You're kidding? She'll freak when you pick her up.'

'No, she won't. Ten minutes alone with me and she won't even remember how to spell U2.'

Michael laughed. 'I'd like to see that.'

'I'm hoping you will. You noticed I made the date for next Saturday, and not tomorrow? I wanted to give you time to talk to Jessica Hart. We can make it a double date.'

'I don't think I can move that fast.'

'Then stop where you are and let her come to you.' Bubba stopped, gestured towards mid-aisle. 'She's coming down the steps now. See her? She's got that Sara chick with her.'

Michael would not have believed his heart could start pounding so hard so quickly. Jessica had changed into white trousers, a bright green T-shirt. A 35mm camera with a telephoto lens hung around her neck. Her long brown hair bounced with each step she took down the bleachers. He turned away.

'Let's get out of here,' he said.

'Leave if you want. I've been looking forward to a private conversation with Jessie about her tastes in music.'

'I'll stay,' Michael grumbled. He hoped – and feared – that Jessica and Sara would pass them by without noticing them. Perhaps they would have. But Bubba stepped right into their path.

'Ladies,' he said. 'My name is Bubba. You may have heard of me. This is my friend, Michael. You may have heard of him, too. We are both fairly popular.' He extended his hand. 'We would like to welcome you to Tabb High.'

Giggling, Jessica shook his hand, introducing herself. Sara was more reserved. 'I *have* heard about you,' she said. 'This girl in my P.E. said I should watch out for you.'

'Did she tell you why?' Bubba asked innocently.

'No.'

'Then she must have a guilty conscience, and you shouldn't listen to her.' Bubba pulled his gold pocket watch from his jacket. 'I have a few minutes, Sara. Come with me. I want to discuss your political future.'

'I'm not running for anything.'

'But you like hot dogs, don't you?' Bubba asked.

Sara threw Jessica a quick glance. 'I love hot dogs,' she said slowly.

Bubba reached over and took Sara by the arm. 'Then you should have one, with *everything* on it. Nice meeting you, Jessie. See you later, Mike.'

When they were gone, Jessica continued to giggle. 'Is he really your friend?' she asked.

'I think he considers me more of an apprentice.' He cleared his throat. 'I hope he doesn't overwhelm your friend.'

'Sara can take care of herself.'

'That's right, I almost forgot. I was there at lunch.'

'I saw you when you sat down.'

'Really?'

'Yeah.'

The conversation ran into a hitch right there. Michael couldn't think of anything to say. Jessica started to fiddle with the focus on her camera. It was a Nikon. The previous year, Michael had constructed an eight-inch reflector telescope. He had a dream of taking time-lapse photos of the sky through it from out in the desert. Jessica's camera would have been ideally suited for the job. Except it cost close to five hundred bucks.

'It's jammed again,' she muttered, getting frustrated. A roar went up from the crowd. Wiping her hair out of her eyes, Jessica looked up. The team was coming back on the field. 'Damn, the teacher wanted me to get a shot of the players running out of the tunnel.'

'May I see it?' Michael asked.

'It does this all the time,' she said, holding it out without removing the strap from her neck. He gently twisted the lens, trying not to brush up against her breasts; they weren't all that far away. She added, 'I think I was sold an incompatible attachment.'

It was indeed jammed. 'Did you just take the telephoto lens out of its case and screw it in a moment ago?'

'Yeah, how did you know?'

'The camera's warm. You must have been holding it in your hands most of the night. But the lens is cool. Let them both sit out for a moment. When the temperatures average out, the jamming will stop.'

She nodded. 'That makes sense. You know a lot about cameras?'

He shrugged. 'I've played around with a few.'

'You should be the one taking these pictures, not me.'

'Are you doing this for the paper or the yearbook?'

'Both, I guess.' Jessica's attention wandered to the football players. She had a striking profile. He hadn't realised she had such thick lashes, such big eyes. He wondered what it would be like to touch her face.

'Who are you looking for?' he asked.

'A girlfriend.'

'Is she on the football team?'

'She plays quarterback.' Jessica turned his way again. 'Hey, do you know a guy named Russ Desmond?'

Michael felt a pang of jealousy. 'Yeah. But he's not on the football team this year.'

'He runs cross-country, right?'

'Yeah.'

'Do you know him well?'

'Not really.'

Jessica smiled. 'I suppose I can trust you. Sara's been searching for him all night.'

Michael felt better. 'She's searching in the wrong place. Russ would never come to a football game.'

'Why not?'

'He hates the coach. And the coach hates him. It's a long story.'

Jessica nodded, her lovely brown eyes drifting up into the stands this time. 'Where is she?' she whispered.

'Sara?'

'No the girlfriend I mentioned. You wouldn't know her. She's from Mesa. She's only a sophomore, an old friend.' Jessica chuckled. 'All day she's been telling me about this fantastic guy I've got to meet.'

'What's her name?'

'Alice McCoy.'

Michael leaned into the fence. He was lucky he didn't flip over and land on the track. 'Oh, my,' he said.

'Pardon?'

'Nothing.'

Jessica suddenly turned her head towards the field. Tall, blond and handsome number sixteen was walking towards the sidelines. Jessica quickly raised her camera, trying to focus her jammed telephoto lens. 'Damn,' she muttered.

Had Jessica not tried so eagerly to take Bill Skater's picture at that precise moment, Michael probably would have admitted he was the fantastic guy Alice wanted Jessica to meet. Later, he was to wonder if he *had* told Jessica, if the tragedy that was to follow Alice's party would have been avoided. It would be a possibility that would haunt him the entire year. It would be a possibility based solely on a young girl's strange dream.

'You might want to give it a few more minutes,' he said softly.

Jessica did not appear to hear him. She had lowered the camera, and her eyes. Bill had stopped at the microphone to talk to Clair.

'I'd better go,' Michael said.

Jessica raised her head. 'Huh? No, don't go, please. I'm sorry. What were you saying?'

'Nothing.' He edged away. 'I really have to go.'

'That's too bad. Thanks!'

'For what?'

She forced a smile. 'For everything, what else?'

Michael did not head in the direction of the snack bar, but away from it. Alice would have to forgive him for ditching her. He couldn't bear the thought of witnessing Jessica's probable – if she went for the likes of Bill Skater, it was virtually certain – disappointment when she learned Michael Olson was Mr Fantastic.

He only remembered that Nick had gone for their dinner when Nick came up to him with a box full of goodies.

'I hope you like junk food,' Nick said. 'I live on it.'

Michael accepted a hot dog, a tub of popcorn and a large orange. Nick again refused Michael's offer to help pay for the stuff. They continued to walk in the direction of the scoreboard. 'I bet you've had to search all over for me,' Michael said. 'Sorry I took off.'

'I knew where you were,' Nick said. 'I was watching you talk to that girl.'

'Jessica? You should have come over. I could have introduced you.'

'No, I couldn't do that.'

'Why not?'

'I don't know. I would have got in your way.'

'Don't say that.'

Nick glanced over at him. For an instant, something glimmered deep within Nick's black eyes. But all he said was 'OK, Mike.'

They sat at the end of the bleachers away from the crowd. Nick began to dig into his food. Michael realised he'd lost his appetite. He sipped his drink, stared at the clock on the scoreboard. He didn't even know what he was doing at the game. She had smiled at him, thanked him, all the while thinking about the quarterback. Bubba would steal Clair away from Bill. Bill would find solace in Jessica's arms.

It's like the earth going around the sun – a vicious cycle.

'This is going to be a long second half,' he muttered, referring to the rest of his life.

'Want to leave?'

'Do you?'

'Whatever you want, Mike.'

'Whatever I want,' he repeated quietly. He chuckled sadly, shook his head. 'No, not today. Maybe tomorrow.' He slapped Nick on the back. At least he'd made a new friend. 'Tell me about yourself, Nick?'

'What do you want to hear?'

'Everything.' He thought of Jessica's line. 'What else?'

It took them a while until they returned to the topic of girls. Finally, however, Michael heard of Maria and spoke of Jessica. They both agreed that something had to change.

CHAPTER 6

Polly McCoy noticed that her arm was bleeding. A drop of red trailed from beneath the bandage inside her left elbow all the way to her wrist. She had given blood that afternoon; it was a habit of hers to give blood every two months, as frequently as she could. Once Jessica had joked that she must have been a vampire in a past life, that she was working off karma. Polly didn't know about that. She had all this money and she had never done anything to earn it. She felt as if she had to help people, give something back. And she didn't believe in reincarnation, anyway, or even life after death. When you died, you were dead. It was pretty simple. On the other hand, she occasionally did wonder about vampires, about demons in general. So many terrible things happened to so many nice people. There had to be something evil behind it all.

Taking out a Kleenex and wiping away the blood, Polly saw Alice making her way up the stadium steps. Polly was sitting in the very top row. She liked the view. She could see what everyone was up to. Of course, when half-time finished, she would rejoin Sara and Jessica closer to the field. They had all come together. But for now she didn't mind being alone. Actually, she preferred it. She was not in the best of moods. She was mad at her sister. Sara and Jessica had been looking for him, but only she had seen Clark. She'd watched him and Alice carrying on the whole night.

And it was me who saw him first.

Polly had met Clark three months ago, during the last week of school at Mesa High. The day had been beautiful. She and Alice had decided to go for a hike in the woods. They had driven up into the nearby mountains and set out along a trail adjacent to a stream. They quickly ran into trouble.

Approximately two miles from the car, Polly stepped on a loose stone and twisted her ankle. The sprain was nasty. They both decided she should stay where she was while Alice went for help. While waiting for her sister's return, Clark appeared.

Polly's initial reaction to him had been one of fear. He talked weird. He looked weirder. But he had a certain *touch*. When he took her swollen ankle in his delicate hands – over her shy protests – and began to massage points on either side of the bone, the pain vanished. Polly had read about acupressure and stuff like that. What he did went beyond that. The swelling even stopped.

And the more she listened to his voice, the less strange it sounded. He had lots of interesting ideas. He told her how the mountain they were on had once been used by the Indians as a sacred spot for the channelling of the spirits of long-dead medicine men. What made his point of view so unique was that he neither believed nor disbelieved what he said. He was just being 'open'. He told her she had to open up. He had a pad and pencil with him. He wanted her to take off her top and let him sketch her. When she refused, he began to draw her as if she were completely nude. He finished the sketch minutes before Alice returned with the ranger. He gave it to her as a present. She didn't remember having given him her number. But he called her the next day.

Over the next two months, they never went out once. They spent most of their time together necking in her bedroom with the door locked. She finally did take her top off for him, and her pants, but they never had sex. He would push her right to the limit and then back off. She knew it was probably for the best – what with all the talk of herpes and AIDS going around – nevertheless, it still frustrated her. She wondered if he truly found her attractive. She wondered that a lot when he started chasing Alice.

It happened just like that. Overnight. Hello, how are you, Polly? Let me speak to Alice. And from then on Alice and Clark were always together. The only thing that kept Polly from freaking out altogether was that their relationship appeared to be a brother-sister sort of thing. Alice said it was, and of course being the considerate sister that she was, she had still asked Polly a thousand times if it was OK. Polly told her not to worry. She wanted what was best for Alice. And there was no denying Clark was 'opening' her up to all kinds of artistic inspirations. Alice had paintings in progress in her studio that the special-effects people in Hollywood couldn't have dreamed of.

Yet Polly was finally beginning to wonder if she hadn't got a raw deal. Tonight, for the first time, she had seen Clark put his arm around Alice. If you would do that in public, there were a lot of other things you might do in private. Clark had such hypnotic green eyes, like a cat. And those long fingers. She couldn't stand the thought of them all over her baby sister.

'Hi. Have you see Jessie?' Alice asked, panting from her hop up the steps.

'Last time I saw her, she was down by the cheerleaders. But she's not there now.'

Alice searched the stands, sighing. 'I've got to find her right away. Clark wants to leave.'

'I could give her a message for you.'

'No, it's not that. I want her to meet somebody.'

'Why are you leaving with Clark now?'

'I told you, he wants to leave.'

'Why does he want to leave?'

'He didn't tell me.' Alice stopped. 'What's wrong?'

'With my arm? It's bleeding, can't you see? I gave blood today. You should, too, sometime. There're a lot of sick people out there who need it.'

'No, I mean, you sound mad?'

'Why would I be mad?'

'I don't know.'

'I'm not mad.'

Alice smiled. Polly could remember the first time Alice had ever smiled. Polly had only been two years old at the time, and Alice two months, but Polly remembered everything. 'Are you having fun?' Alice asked.

'Sure. How about you?'

Alice beamed at the whole stadium. 'I'm having a great

time. I love this school. I love the people here.' Suddenly she leaned over and embraced her sister. 'And I love you most of all!'

Polly returned the hug. 'I know you do,' she said softly, feeling the bones of Alice's ribcage under her fingers. When they had both been kids, Alice had tended towards chubbiness. Now, Polly could barely get her to eat one full meal a day. 'Would you like a candy bar?' she asked, reaching for her purse.

Alice straightened herself. 'No, chocolate gives me acne.'

'It doesn't do that to me,' Polly replied, getting the candy out for herself. The nurse at the hospital this afternoon had told her to go home and have a big meal. She had to make up for what she had lost. She didn't appreciate Alice suddenly staring at her as if she were a pig. 'I gave blood today,' she repeated.

'What about your diet?'

'Leave me alone, all right?'

Alice knelt back down beside her, holding her hands. 'Are you upset 'cause Clark's here?'

Polly swallowed on the lump in her throat. 'No. I see Clark all the time at the house. What difference should it make seeing him here? Anyway, why have you been hiding him away all night? Jessie and Sara want to meet him.'

Alice leaned back on her heels. 'I don't want them to see him.'

'Then why did you bring him here tonight?'

A note of anger entered her voice. 'I didn't. He insisted he come. Now he wants to leave early.' She looked away, her expression strangely flat. 'I've got to get away from him,' she whispered.

Polly felt a thrill. She softened her voice. 'Why?'

'He's not very nice.'

'What?'

'He talks about mom and dad.'

Polly closed her eyes, the thrill gone. 'What does he say?'

'Nothing.'

'Tell me!'

'No, it has nothing to do with you.'

Polly opened her eyes, took a bite of her candy, smiled slowly. 'All right, let's drop it. Let's talk about the party.'

Alice brightened. 'Can we have it?'

Polly nodded. The bad moment had come, and the bad moment had gone. All of a sudden she felt greatly relieved. 'Yes, I think it would be all right. But we'll have to take Aunty over to Uncle Tom's for the night. The noise might upset her.'

Alice nodded, leaned over, and kissed her cheek.

'Thanks! I owe you a million.'

Polly smiled at her. 'You only owe me a penny. Don't invite Clark to the party.'

Alice didn't hesitate. 'I won't even tell him we're having one.'

Alice left to search for Jessica. Polly remembered a textbook she had forgotten to take home that afternoon. She debated about waiting until after the game to get it from her locker. She finally decided that Sara would get mad if she did. Sara had been getting mad at her a lot lately; it was really beginning to bother her.

Polly accidentally ran into Sara at the bottom of the steps.

'Do you know where Jessie is?' Sara demanded.

'No. Alice doesn't either.'

'What are you talking about? Where is Alice?'

'I don't know.'

Sara grabbed her stomach, groaned. 'I just ate three hot dogs.'

'Why three?'

'My political adviser insisted. Where are you going?'

'To my locker.'

'Is the locker hallway open now?'

'The door lock is busted. It's always open.'

'What did you forget?'

'Nothing. Don't say anything mean.'

Sara laughed loudly. 'Don't get mugged. I could see the school from the snack bar. They don't waste electricity here. There isn't a light on.'

No greater truth had ever passed Sara's lips. After leaving the stadium and heading around the silent gymnasium, Polly found herself in a disquieting land of darkness. Tabb High had a lot of trees. The branches blocked much of the sky, as did the overhanging roofs. She wished she had a flashlight. She had never cared much for the dark. It had been on a dark and lonely road her parents had died. She remembered it well. She remembered everything.

What did that bastard say about them?

Her steps echoed softly as she strode down the empty open hallway. She was uneasy, yes, but she also enjoyed the emptiness. Sometimes during the day she wished she could be this alone, strolling the campus free and easy, meeting only those people she chose to meet, hearing only those voices she wanted to hear, touching only those who wanted to touch her . . .

What did Clark say about me?

Polly was crossing the courtyard, passing beneath what she had heard referred to as the varsity tree, when the can landed on top of her head. It startled her something awful; she practically had a heart attack right there on the spot. She jumped away from the tree and cried in a trembling voice, 'Who's there?'

A vague figure shifted above her in the branches. She leaned slightly forward – all the while telling herself to run the other way – straining to see better. 'Hello?' she croaked.

The figure croaked back. No, it was more of a belch. She reached down, picked up the can that had struck her on the head, smelled the beer. Her fear disappeared as quickly as it had come. Somebody was just getting drunk in private. Laughing, she walked towards the tree trunk.

'Hey, if I was you, I wouldn't be drinking up there. You could slip and hurt—'

A flash of metal and wood whipped by, inches from her face. Polly leaped back a step. Embedded in the ground in the grass at her feet was a huge axe.

Polly screamed bloody murder.

The guy fell out of the tree. Polly kept screaming. He rolled over and looked up at her. 'What time is it?' he mumbled.

Polly bit her lip. 'Past nine-thirty.'

The guy sat up, rubbed his head. 'Where are the birds?'

'What birds?'

'I heard birds.' He burped again, deep and loud, and reached for his axe.

'That was me. Excuse me, what are you doing with that?'

He was using it, Polly realised a moment later, to climb to his feet. She relaxed a notch. There were empty beer cans littering the ground. This guy wouldn't be chasing her anywhere.

'Do you need some help?' she asked tentatively. He briefly gained an upright position, clinging to the axe handle, before swaying forward and smacking his skull directly into the tree trunk. 'Oh, no!' she cried, jumping to his side. 'You'll kill yourself.'

'What time is it?' he breathed in her face. With the lack of light, she couldn't see what he looked like. She could, however, smell him. He must have poured half the beer over his shirt.

'I told you, past nine-thirty. Why do you keep asking me that?'

He tried to get up again. 'Got to chop this down before morning, before the birds get here.'

'You can't do that.' She tried to pull the axe from his hands. 'No.'

He wouldn't let go of the handle. 'Why not?'

'Because it's a pretty tree. Leave it alone.'

The guy turned, stared at the trunk, and then spat on it. 'Those faggot foots – footballs. They all stand here.' He leaned into the axe, pushed himself up. 'It's got to go.'

Polly moved back a step. He'd raised the axe over his head. It looked capable of flying in a dozen different directions. 'Stop!' she pleaded.

He let go with a wild swing. The tip of the axe sliced into the bark. Leaning back, he tried to pull it free. His hands ended up slipping from the handle, and he was back on his ass. Before he could get up, Polly knelt by his side, putting both her palms on his chest. Even through his soggy shirt, she could feel the curves of his well-developed pectoral muscles. 'Look, you've got to stop. If you kill this tree, you'll be killing all the birds who live in it.'

'I can't hurt the birds,' he said, trying repeatedly to get up, not realising it was she that was holding him down.

'That's right. So why don't we take your nice axe and put it in my car and I'll drive you home.' She wasn't exactly sure why she had made the offer. It could have been because of some distant streetlight. A sliver of white had fallen across his face, revealing a rugged – rough would probably have been closer to the truth – handsomeness.

He belched again, his jaw dropping open.

'Is it you?' he asked, amazed.

'Who? What?'

'You! I stopped the race for you. The foots – Coach made them kick me off the team. All because of you.'

'No, it wasn't me.'

He wiped the back of his arm across his nose. 'You're pretty, Sara.'

'Thank you. Let me take you home.'

'Your place or mine?' he slurred as she helped him up.

'Your place. What's your name?'

'Rusty – Russ.'

'I'm Polly.'

'Sara Polly?'

'I'm whoever you want me to be.'

It took time getting the axe out of the tree. It took longer getting Russ and the axe into her car. Fortunately, he remembered where he lived. She assumed it was the right house. She deposited him in the front yard without knocking on the front door and then headed back for the stadium. She decided to keep the axe for now. In his intoxicated condition, there was no telling what he might do with it.

She liked him. And she didn't care that he was the guy

Sara had been searching for all night. She'd seen Clark first and look where that had got her. Nowhere.

When it came to love, you were a fool to be nice.

CHAPTER 7

Mr Bark stopped Sara the following Monday morning as she was leaving his political science class. Jessica was with her.

'What is it?' Sara asked defensively. 'I stayed awake the whole period.'

'It's not that. I have some news for you.' He paused, and there was no denying from his expression that he thought it was bad news. 'You know I am the faculty adviser to the student government?'

'It doesn't surprise me,' Sara said cautiously. 'What's up?'

'You've been elected student body president.'

Sara laughed. 'What the hell? No, you're kidding. What are you talking about?'

'You were elected by a landslide.'

Sara swallowed. 'But I wasn't running. Jessie, tell him it was all a joke.'

'You didn't want to be president?' Jessica asked in surprise.

'Your name was on the ballot,' Mr Bark said.

'Now hold on a second,' Sara said. 'I explained this to the whole school last Friday. Jessie put my name down.'

Jessica smiled. This was great. 'No, I didn't.'

'Polly did then. It makes no difference. I can't be president. I hate politics. I hate politicians. No, absolutely not.'

'I don't want you as president, either,' Mr Bark said. 'I think you have a bad attitude. But the student body doesn't think so. Your nearest competitor didn't get a quarter of your votes. You have a responsibility to your peers. There's a lot of business that has to be taken care of immediately. We don't have time for another election.'

'Who's the new vice-president?' Sara asked.

'Clair Hilrey.'

'I thought she was running for president,' Jessica said.

Mr Bark frowned. 'I thought she was, too. Maybe she put herself down for both offices. She shouldn't have done that.'

'Make her president,' Sara said quickly.

'I can't do that,' Mr Bark said.

'Then I'll do it,' Sara said.

'No, you can't do that, either. It's against the rules.'

'The President of the country never follows the rules, why should I? No, wait. If you won't accept my resignation this instant, I'll intentionally break every rule in the book. Then you'll have to impeach me.'

Mr Bark was getting angry. 'You don't impeach student body presidents.'

'Why not? This is a free and vicious society.'

'Why are you being so difficult? There are kids in this school who would give almost anything to have the honour that's been bestowed on you.'

Sara started to speak, stopped, silently shook her head.

'It might be fun,' Jessica said. 'It might make you popular.'

Sara glared at her. 'No,' she said firmly.

Mr Bark had run out of patience. 'I can't stand here all day arguing with you. We're having our first student council meeting tomorrow at lunch in Room H-Sixteen. If you should change your mind and want to accept the office, see me sometime this afternoon. There're notes on the student body's financial status you should go through before the meeting. If not, then I guess we'll have to carry on without you.'

Jessica had chemistry next. She had to go. Once outside

Mr Bark's class, Sara refused to speak to her, anyway. She went off in a huff. Jessica couldn't help laughing.

The laughter did not stay with her. She'd had a miserable weekend. She was still sleepy and tired from her travels. She'd had to take long naps Saturday and Sunday afternoons just to be awake at dinnertime. Also, she'd been lamenting Bill Skater's obvious interest in Clair Hilrey. The disappointment was silly, she knew. She had only started at the school. She couldn't realistically expect the resident fox not to have some sort of girlfriend. Nevertheless, she had spent hours since the football game wondering how she could get his attention. In Mr Bark's class just now, Bill hadn't looked at her once. And she'd worn her shortest skirt.

Her gloom deepened when her chemistry teacher announced a surprise quiz in the middle of lab. She practically fell off her stool. 'He didn't say anything about a quiz on Friday,' she complained to her lab partner, Maria.

'Last Monday he warned us to be ready for a quiz at any time,' Maria said, pushing aside their rows of test tubes, getting out a fresh sheet of paper. 'You weren't here. But I wouldn't worry, it shouldn't count for much.'

Jessica worried anyway. To get accepted at Stanford, she had to keep her GPA close to a perfect four. She hadn't even glanced at the textbook over the weekend.

The teacher let them stay at their lab desks. He wrote several molecular formulas on the board and asked for their valence values. It appeared no big deal for the bulk of the class; they went right to it. Jessica sat staring at the board. She'd left her glasses at home again. She could hardly read the formulas.

What's a valence value?

When Jessica finally looked down, she saw that Maria had slipped her a piece of paper with two rows of positive and negative values. Sitting across the grey-topped table, Maria nodded.

'I can't,' Jessica whispered.

'Just this once,' Maria whispered back.

The teacher wasn't watching. Jessica scribbled the numbers on to her paper. The teacher collected them a few minutes later. Then he wrote the answers on the board. Maria knew her stuff; they each got a hundred. Jessica thanked her as they returned to the lab.

'I've never cheated before,' she said, embarrassed.

'But you didn't know there could be a quiz,' Maria said, adding softly, 'Sometimes it's hard not to lie.'

'Well, if I can ever make it up to you, let me know.'

Maria nodded – she didn't talk a lot – and they continued with their acid-base reactions, which made no more sense than they had before the quiz. Jessica swore to herself that she would study chemistry for at least two hours every night until she caught up. She even entertained the idea of asking Michael Olson for a couple of tutorial lessons. She wasn't getting much out of the teacher; he talked too fast, and seemingly in a foreign language. Michael obviously had a sharp mind. She'd felt rather silly when she'd needed his help at the game with the camera. He had been right about the jamming disappearing when the temperatures evened out. Although she found his intelligence somewhat intimidating, he was easy to talk to. Yet she worried what he thought of her. He would start out friendly enough, and then after a couple of minutes talking to her, he'd be in a hurry to get away.

He probably thinks I'm an airhead.

Sara had cooled off by lunch. When Jessica met her near the snack bar, she even laughed about how her election had proved beyond doubt the substandard intelligence of the majority of Tabb's students. She had not changed her mind about the job.

Polly joined them midway through break. She had not heard of the election results, and neither Jessica nor Sara brought it up. She had, however, already printed up the party invitations – elegantly lettered orange cards in flowery orange envelopes. Jessica and Sara both agreed the printers had done a fine job. Polly gave them six each.

'But don't invite anyone weird,' she warned.

'You'll have to give one to Russ,' Jessica told Sara.

She fingered the envelopes uneasily. 'I'll think about it.'

'Are you talking about Russ Desmond?' Polly asked suddenly.

'Yes,' Sara said warily.

Polly giggled. 'You can't invite him. You're the one who got him kicked off the cross-country team. He hates you.'

Sara didn't respond immediately, which surprised Jessica. 'What are you talking about?' Jessica asked.

'Russ had to stop in the middle of his race last Friday to help Sara up. She had jumped right in his way, and he accidentally knocked her down. He ended up losing the race, and the football coach got furious and kicked him off the team.'

'How does the football coach have the authority to kick someone off the cross-country team?' Jessica asked. Sara had told her about the race incident, but from a slightly different perspective.

'He's also the athletic director,' Polly said.

An odd look had crossed Sara's face. She was angry,

128

certainly, but also – was it possible? – upset. 'You lie,' she said.

'I'm not,' Polly said indignantly. 'The whole school knows about it.'

'If that's true, then why did the whole school just nominate me president?'

Polly sneered. 'Since when are you president?'

'I am president. Ain't I president, Jessie?'

'Unquestionably. But why does Russ hate Sara? He can't blame her for what happened.'

Polly shrugged. 'He does.'

'How do *you* know?' Sara demanded.

'He told me so when I took him home Friday night.'

Sara snorted. 'You took him home? Where did you take him home from?'

'It's none of your business,' Polly said.

Sara held up her finger. 'Polly, if you're lying to me, or even if you're telling me the truth, you're going to have a party at your house you're never going to forget 'cause I'm going to drown you in your goddamn swimming pool.'

And with that, Sara whirled around and stalked off.

'What's got into her?' Polly asked.

'I don't know,' Jessica said. 'Maybe it's love.'

Polly departed to eat large quantities of sugar. Jessica

was left holding her six invitations and wondering who to give them to. It took her all of a fraction of a second to realise she had to get one to Bill Skater. It didn't take her much longer to spot him. He was alone, walking towards the parking lot. She had never seen him alone before; he usually had a bunch of guys around him. This could be a rare opportunity. Quickly she strode towards the other exit. She should be able to circle around part of the lot and run into him coming the other way.

Her plan worked better than she expected. She ended up coming up the aisle where he'd parked his car. He stopped when he saw her, nodded.

'Hi.'

She looked up, smiled. 'Hi! You look familiar. Do we share a class?'

He put the key to his red Corvette in the door, his eyes on her. They were as blue as the Bill in her fantasies. 'I don't think so,' he said. 'What's your name?'

'Mr Bark. I mean, we're in Mr Bark's class together. My name's Jessie. What's yours, Bill? Is your name Bill?'

He nodded. He did not appear to notice she was suffering from momentary brain damage. She was so nervous. 'I remember you,' he said. 'You sit next to the girl who snores.'

What notoriety. 'That's me,' she gushed.

'Right.' He opened his car door. 'See you around, Joan.'

'Jessie. Wait!'

He sat inside on the black leather upholstery. 'Yes?'

'Ah – you were great last Friday, you know, in the game. I thought you were.' Tabb had lost sixteen to three. Bill had thrown only one interception and an equal number of completions.

'Thanks. Bye.'

'Bye. Would you like to go to a party?'

He shut his car door, rolled down his window. 'What did you say?'

'My friend's having a party. She gave me all these to pass out.' Jessica waved her half-dozen invitations as if they might multiply into hundreds any second. 'Would you like to come? It's not this Saturday, but next Saturday. In the evening.'

He took one of the envelopes, opened it, nodding as he read the contents. 'Are you going to be there?' he asked.

'Sure, yeah. The whole time.'

He nodded again, tossing the card on to the passenger seat. 'I'll see you then.'

He drove away. Her approach had set women's lib back twenty years, she realised. But she didn't care! He had asked if she'd be there! He was only coming to see her!

Right, and your name's Joan.

Jessica decided to dwell on the positive. It didn't require much willpower. She floated back up the steps and into the courtyard. She bought a milk and sat by herself in the shade beneath a tree. Polly had specified on the cards that everyone was to bring a bathing suit. Jessica had a new bikini she could wear – blue with white polka dots. It left little to the imagination. Maybe he would bump up against her in the water . . .

If she went in the water. She'd almost drowned as a child in a backyard pool. She didn't know how to swim.

Jessica looked up. Michael Olson was coming over to say hi. How sweet.

They were in the computer room. Nick was listening. Bubba was talking. Michael wanted to get it over with. They had finally decided to do it, Nick and himself. They were going to ask the girls out.

'It's important you do everything in its proper order,' Bubba was saying. 'Get her alone. Start a conversation. Bring up a movie. A movie doesn't sound as heavy as dinner. Of course, once you're on the date, you can always go to dinner. But it's easy to work a movie into the conversation. Do each of you know what's playing?'

'Yes,' Michael said.

'No,' Nick said, hanging on to Bubba's every word. He had looked more relaxed during Kat's hold-up. Then again, Michael wasn't exactly enjoying a period of low blood pressure. It struck him as ironic that the fear of one little word could have such an effect on two grown boys. Would you like to get together this weekend?

No.

A big little word.

'It doesn't matter,' Bubba continued. 'She'll know what's playing. Then ask if she's busy this weekend. This is a better question than asking outright if she'd like to go out. It eliminates a possible objection before she can raise it.'

'But you asked Clair outright?' Michael said.

'Yes, but neither of you is Bubba. Now, after she has said no—'

'What if she is busy?' Nick interrupted.

'Then ask about another time. Don't be discouraged if this weekend is not good. Even teenage girls have other commitments. But if she puts you off twice, then back off. Keep your dignity.'

'Go on,' Nick said.

'Arrange the date. Set a definite time and get her phone number and address. Be sure to paint a picture that the whole thing is casual. That way she'll know how to dress without asking. Also, you don't want her to think she's overly important to you.'

'Get off it,' Michael said.

Bubba spoke seriously. 'That may offend your romantic ideals, Mike, but it's a fact the human animal only desires what it can't have. True, you have to make her feel wanted, but never *loved*. If she knows you can't live without her, then she'll also know she can see you whenever she wants. You want to operate from a position of strength. Always keep her in the dark, unsure of where she stands.'

'Go on,' Nick said again.

'That's it, for now. When the date's set, come back here and I'll give you the next lesson: how to get her clothes off.'

'We have a problem,' Michael said. 'Nick doesn't have a car.'

'Let him borrow yours,' Bubba said.

'Then what is Mike supposed to use?' Nick asked.

'He can borrow my car. And I'll get Clair to pick me up.'

'You'll make her drive, and you don't even have the concert tickets?' Michael asked.

Bubba smiled. 'Mike, you worry about the most unimportant things.' He stood and slapped them both on the back. 'Make me proud of you, boys.'

Michael and Nick left Bubba to his computer. Lunch was more than half over. They had to locate the girls quickly. They hurried towards the courtyard.

'Why are we doing this?' Michael muttered.

'We don't have to,' Nick said with more than a note of hope in his voice.

'Let's not start that again.' They had talked about this moment all weekend at work. Without this mutual encouragement, Michael realised, neither of them would have got this far. Yet Michael had another reason for having decided to ask Jessica out. He'd had a dream.

It had been beautiful. He had been on a roped bridge stretching between two lands, one a desolate desert, the other a lush green forest. There had been a churning river running beneath his feet, and above – in contrast to the brightly lit lands – a black sky adorned with countless stars. He had been standing in the middle of the bridge facing the desert, hesitating, when a female voice had spoken at his back.

'I will follow you,' she said. And when he started to turn around, she added quickly, 'No, don't. You can't see me.'

'Why not?'

'Because of the veil. I'm still wearing it. But you're

young. Go forward, I will follow you.'

The desert beyond looked most unappealing, particularly compared to the green wood that he could glimpse out of the corner of his eye. 'Who are you?' he asked.

'You have forgotten.' There was no censure in her voice, only mild amusement and a rich, enduring love. Michael could almost, but not quite, figure out who it was. 'It happens sometimes. It doesn't matter. Just remember that I am behind you. That you can't fall. No, don't look down, either. Go forward.'

'Then can I see you?'

'Yes, but not today. Later, another time. I will see you first, and then we will meet again, like we always do. Go now, and don't be afraid. You are my love, Michael Olson . . .'

And then he had woken up, and the stars outside were fading with the approaching dawn. He hadn't gone back to sleep. He had just lain there feeling content. That had been Saturday morning.

The dream had left him with a measure of courage. Enough to risk the big No. Walking beside Nick, he continued to wonder who the girl had been.

They split up when they reached the centre of campus. Nick had spotted Maria. She was by herself, next to the low adobe wall that surrounded Tabb. Michael wished him luck. He had to chuckle when Nick crossed himself.

Michael sighted Jessica minutes later. She was sitting alone beneath a tree, drinking a milk. And he had thought Nick superstitious; he would have recited a Hail Mary on the spot had he been able to remember the opening line. Jessica waved to him. He was trapped.

'How are you doing?' she asked as he approached. She looked positively radiant. Could she be this happy to see him?

'Fine. How about you?'

'Fantastic.' She patted the grass beside her. 'Have a seat. I was just thinking about you today, in chemistry class.'

He sat down. The ground felt solid, better than his feet. 'Really? I thought they only studied guys like me in psychology.'

She laughed, and he secretly congratulated himself on his witty remark. 'No, I was remembering how you wrote the lab manual they use.'

Michael almost gagged. 'Who told you that?'

She paused. 'It's not true?'

'No. All I did last year was discover a couple of procedural errors in the manual. I didn't write it.' He smiled. 'I am still in high school, after all.'

She laughed. 'With your reputation, it's hard to remember that.'

Michael had never thought of himself as having a reputation. 'Are you having trouble in the class?' he asked.

She set down her milk, folded her hands between her bare legs. He couldn't help noticing how much of her legs there was to notice. Nice skirt. Nice legs. 'Yes,' she admitted quietly. 'I think missing the first week has thrown me off. We had a quiz today, and I didn't even know what the question meant.'

'Did you flunk it?'

She giggled. 'No, I got an A.' She continued in a serious voice, 'No, I really am confused. And I was wondering if maybe you could possibly tutor me a tiny bit? I could pay you for your time and all.' She looked at him with her big brown eyes. 'I really need the grade, Michael. My parents are on top of me all the time about my GPA.'

He couldn't believe his luck. It almost seemed unnatural. A corner of his mind wondered if Bubba had not somehow set it up. 'Sure, I could help you. But you wouldn't have to pay me. I think you'll catch on quickly, once you get used to the chemical language. Physics, calculus, chemistry – they all have a jargon that can be frightening at first. I sometimes think scientists keep it that way to make themselves look smart. Honestly, chemistry is as easy as basic maths.'

'I have a lot of trouble with that, too.'

'When do you want to start?'

'I want to do something for you first.' She brightened. 'I know what! I'll take you to a movie. Yeah, that would be fair. I pay for the movie and you teach me about valence values. How does that sound?'

Michael had to take a breath. Very unnatural, this whole conversation. 'I have some free time this Saturday. Can you get by in class until then?'

'Yeah, we won't have another quiz that soon.' She pulled a pen from her bag, began to write on one of the funny orange envelopes by her side. 'I'll give you my number and address, and you give me yours. If you want, I can drive.'

'No, that's OK, I have a car.' He would have a Jaguar Saturday night. He began to feel rather happy about the whole dating business. All these lonely years he had suffered in silence. There was nothing to it. All you had to do was decide to ask them out and then they asked you. Sure.

This won't happen again in another three hundred years.

They exchanged the vital information. He noticed she

lived in Lemon Grove. Big bucks. Maybe he wouldn't tell her he had borrowed the Jag. He nodded to the orange envelope in his hand. 'What is this?'

'Oh, an invitation to a party my friend's having. Alice McCoy – I told you about her at the game? You're welcome to come.'

His heart skipped as it had last Friday when she had mentioned Alice's name. But this time the reasons were different. This time there was no reason at all, only the voice in the dream. '*I will follow you.*' Why would Alice have been standing behind him, covered in a veil? Even his subconscious should have a purpose in putting her there.

'Thanks.' He began to get up. He didn't think he would go to the party. He would have to be Mr Fantastic again. For now, he was doing all right as Michael Olson. He hadn't seen Alice at school today. He hoped she wasn't sick. 'I've got to go,' he said.

Jessica looked up, surprised, got slowly to her feet, brushing off her bottom. 'I didn't mean to keep you.'

'You haven't. I'm not that busy. I'll give you a call.'

She smiled. 'Or leave me a note in our locker. I seem to keep missing you between classes.'

He had missed her on purpose today. 'We'll talk,' he said, turning away. 'Take it easy.'

'Bye!'

He wanted to be happy. He had been looking forward to this moment – he had better be happy. He was going out with Jessica Hart, he told himself. She was sweet, beautiful, charming. He had her number. She needed him. Bubba would be proud of him . . .

Do you want her to need you? Or to care about you?

He decided, as long as he got to see her, *he* didn't care.

He hoped Nick was all right.

'Hello, Nick,' Maria said. 'How's your head?'

'My head? It's OK.'

She put down her sack. It appeared packed with oranges, nothing else. He felt as if he had an orange stuck between his ears. He couldn't remember what Bubba had told him to say first. 'The swelling looks like it's gone down?'

'Yeah.'

She nodded. 'Would you like an orange?'

Nick accepted the fruit. 'You have a lot of them.'

'My dad brings them home.'

Her dad probably worked the orchards. The possibility reinforced his suspicion she had not been in the country more than a year, two at the outside, that her father was working for slave wages picking the fruit. Bubba had told him to bring up the movies. 'You can't get oranges like these at the movies.'

Maria blinked. 'They don't sell them there.'

'Yeah, that's what I mean.' He put his hand on the nearby wall for support. Unfortunately, he used the hand that held the orange, and crushed it. A squirt of juice hit Maria right in the eyes. 'Damnit, I'm sorry!' he cried, dropping the offending fruit. She calmly reached for a handkerchief in her bag.

'You got a ripe one,' she said.

'I'm really sorry.'

'It's nothing.'

'It must hurt.'

She looked up at him, her face serious. 'If I ever did get hurt, I don't think I could take it like you did last Friday.'

'That was nothing.'

'Someone told me this morning that you got thrown into a mirror.'

Nick scratched his head. 'Well, yeah, I didn't walk into it.' She liked that. She smiled. She was the kind of girl who needed to smile more often. So solemn.

'Would you like another orange?' she asked.

He waved it away, feeling a sudden surge of confidence.

She admired how he had fought! She wasn't afraid of him. 'Would you like to go to the movies Saturday night?'

She nodded. 'Could you pick me up at the library? I'll be there studying.'

'I could, yeah.' He would have to ask Michael where the library was. 'What time would be good?'

'Six. That's when the library closes.'

That Bubba was a genius. 'I'll see you then.'

CHAPTER 8

Sara had decided to attend the student council meeting Tuesday at lunch after all. When she arrived with Mr Bark's papers on the financial status of the council tucked under her arm, the other officers were already gathered around the large table in Room H-16. She recognised only three: Clair Hilrey, Bill Skater and that football player everyone called The Rock. She knew of the latter because of the stories that had been circulating about his fight with the tall black guy. The Rock sat slightly hunched over in his chair. He had not played in Friday's game. Sara heard the new guy had almost killed him.

Two adults were also present: Mr Bark and Tabb's principal, Mr Smith, both sitting unobtrusively in one corner. They were there to oversee, she had heard, not to interfere. The promise of the principal's presence was one of the reasons she had decided to come. She hoped to speak to him about allowing Russ Desmond back on the cross-country team. That lying Polly had been feeding her a line – there was no doubt about that – but she did feel somewhat guilty about having stepped in his way. She certainly didn't want him hating her.

Another factor had brought her to the meeting. The biggest problem she had with school, and life in general, was that it bored her. After thinking about it a while, she had come to the conclusion that being president couldn't make the situation any worse. Of course, if the job ever got to be more of a hassle than it was worth, she could always walk away from it – and to hell with any responsibility she owed to her peers.

'Have you been waiting for me?' Sara asked, sitting at the head of the table, all eyes on her.

'Yes,' Mr Bark said.

'That's a shame.' She cleared her throat, glancing around. 'What are we supposed to do first?'

'I'm the sergeant at arms,' The Rock said. 'I have to call the meeting to order.'

'Do it,' Sara said.

The Rock stood and smashed his gavel on a wooden block and mumbled a few lines about the date and the time. Sara thought it a pathetic comment on student councils across the land that the sergeant at arms was an elected position. The Rock sat back down.

'Can I begin?' Sara asked. No one moved to stop her. 'All right, I want this meeting to be short. I haven't eaten yet. I want all our meetings to be short, no longer than ten minutes.'

'Sara,' Mr Bark said, interrupting. 'That is ridiculous. A lot has to be accomplished during these meetings. Ten minutes is not enough time. But we don't want to keep you from eating. We offer a class here at Tabb called leadership. All the students in this room, except you, are in that class. Of course, we understand you did not expect to be nominated. For that reason, the faculty would be happy to rearrange your schedule so that you may join the class. That way we can take care of business during leadership and you can have the majority of your lunches free.'

'Does leadership replace political science as a requirement?' Sara asked.

'No, it doesn't,' Mr Bark said.

'Then I don't want my schedule rearranged.'

'Be serious—' Mr Bark began.

'Rocky,' Sara interrupted.

'I'm called The Rock.'

'Whatever. Don't I have to recognise someone before they can speak?'

The Rock nodded. 'It's in the by-laws.'

'Mr Bark,' Sara said. 'I don't recognise you. I'll tell you when I do.' She glanced at her notes on the financial papers Mr Bark had given her to review. 'Let's get going. First, we're broke. We have a sum total of nineteen hundred and sixty-two dollars and thirteen cents in our activities account. With this we're supposed to put on both the Sadie Hawkins and the homecoming dances in the fall quarter. Now the senior class controls homecoming – and I'll get to that in a second – but the juniors are supposed to take care of Sadie Hawkins. Who's junior class president?'

A thin Japanese girl on her near right raised her hand. 'I am.'

'If I give you half of what we've got,' Sara said, 'can you book a band, print up tickets, buy a truck-load full of hay, and do whatever else you need to get this thing going?'

The girl hesitated. 'I don't know everything involved.'

'It's a question of cash flow. Figure out approximately how many people will attend, how much you'll have to spend to keep them happy. Then decide on a ticket price. The grand or so I'll give you will be to get you started until you can start collecting money. Do you understand?'

'Yes.'

'Can you do it? I don't want to have to think about it.'

The girl nodded. 'The junior officers will take care of it.'

'Good. We're making progress. Let's discuss homecoming. I think we should cancel it this year.'

Now they were really staring at her. Clair – sitting to her left and looking sickeningly gorgeous – protested. 'Are you out of your mind? It's the biggest event of the year.'

'I have to recognise you,' The Rock said. 'Can I?'

'Yeah, she's recognised,' Sara said, leaning towards Clair. 'What do you mean it's the biggest event of the year? For you maybe, and four other *princesses* in the school. But for the rest of us slobs it's just another occasion to have dirt rubbed in our faces. So we're not as pretty as you? Whoever said good looks make a good person? Look at history. It's full of ugly kings and queens. Look at all the suffering that's gone on – wait a second. Never mind. If the kings and queens had all been good-looking, it probably would have been worse. Let's get back to the issue. How many dances do we really need? Last year at Mesa, I never went to a single one. We already have Sadie Hawkins. I say that's enough. The alumni won't be coming back, anyway. I went to the game last

Friday. I felt like leaving after the first quarter. What a bunch of clods.'

Bill Skater raised his hand. 'Can I speak?'

Sara sat back. 'Rocky, recognise our quarterback.'

The Rock did so. Bill stood, and Sara had to admit he had an imposing physique. She could see Jessica's reasons for wanting to get him alone in a dark and secluded spot. She wondered if perhaps she should have skipped the clods part.

'I don't think you have any right to knock our football team,' he said. 'One game doesn't mean nothing. Last year, the Super Bowl champs lost their first four games. And they ended up with the gold ring.'

'Yeah,' The Rock said.

'But that's not what I want to talk about,' Bill went on. 'I'm the treasurer. I've looked at our books, too, and I think we can afford homecoming. How much money do we need, anyway? It doesn't have to be that fancy. Homecoming is a tradition. Traditions are important. They're what makes this country great.' He sat down.

'Yeah,' Clair said. 'Just because no one's going to vote you on to the homecoming court doesn't mean you've got to spoil it for the rest of us.'

'What officer are you?' Sara asked.

'I'm vice-president,' Clair said proudly.

'You were running for president. How did you get nominated for vice-president?'

Clair frowned. 'I don't know.'

Sara sighed. 'I should have you all shot.' The whole gang went to protest. Sara raised her hand. 'All right, we'll keep homecoming. But we can't have it in the next few weeks, and I don't care what our treasurer says. We simply don't have the money. We're going to have to raise it somehow, and to do that, we need time. Let's have it during basketball season.'

'That's absurd,' Clair exploded. 'Homecoming is always during football season. You can't change that.'

'Why not?'

'Because you can't, that's why.'

Sara strummed her fingers on top of the table. 'I will give you another reason why it must be postponed. If the elections are held in the next couple of weeks, the girls from Mesa won't stand a chance of being nominated to the court. Transfers from Mesa like myself make up only a quarter of the student body. Hardly anyone who was originally from Tabb knows us. It wouldn't be fair.'

Clair grinned. 'Does Mesa have anyone we would vote for if we knew them ten years?'

The group giggled. Sara leaned towards Clair again. 'Jessica Hart – remember that name. When the final count comes in, pimple brain, you won't be smiling.'

Uncertain, Clair turned to Bill. 'Who?' she whispered.

Bill nodded. 'I've met her. She's pretty.'

'How pretty?'

Bill shrugged.

'Rocky?' Sara said.

He pounded his gavel. 'Order in the council.'

Mr Smith, the principal, raised his hand. 'May I speak?'

'I recognise you myself,' Sara said.

He stood. An older man close to retirement, he always wore – no matter what the weather – tailored three-piece suits. He had a faint English accent and was known for his exquisite manners.

'What you people decide is, of course, strictly up to you,' he began. 'But I would like to say that, in my opinion, Sara has made a persuasive argument for a postponement. This is, however, not the reason for my interruption. I was curious, Sara, how you plan on raising funds for homecoming outside of ticket sales and the like?'

'I don't know, maybe we can have a raffle.'

Clair scowled. 'This isn't a church. What are we going to raffle? A new TV set?'

Sara smiled faintly. 'Maybe your body.'

There followed cries of outrage and protest, plus plenty

of good laughter. In the midst of it all – especially when Clair called for a presidential impeachment – Sara realised she was having fun. The remainder of the meeting – she let it run twenty minutes – passed quickly. It was decided homecoming could wait until winter. Naturally, she didn't recognise the vote of anyone who thought different.

Sara caught up with the principal in the hallway afterwards. 'Excuse me, Mr Smith?'

He turned. 'Ah, Sara, you're a strong-willed young lady. You've put a spark back into the council that's been missing for a number of years. But a word of advice from an old gentleman. In the future, please watch the personality attacks. I realise you say all those things in the spirit of jest, but as you must know, not everyone shares your sense of humour.'

'I'll remember that, sir. Could I ask a favour of you?'

'Certainly.'

She told him about Russ Desmond's expulsion from the cross-country team and the reason behind it. When she had finished, he said, 'Russ is one of our finest athletes. It sounds like a misunderstanding that can easily be patched up. I'll have a word with Coach Campbell.'

'Thanks a lot. I appreciate it.'

'I do have a piece of bad news for you. It doesn't have

to be taken care of immediately by the student council, but we have a soft drinks machine that needs to be replaced. The accountants at the school district refuse to cover the cost. Apparently, one or more students had the bad sense to tip the machine over. It can't even be repaired.'

Sara shook her head. 'The barbarians.'

CHAPTER 9

Stepping on to the track near the runners, Jessica had to shield her eyes from the sun. Heat radiated in rippling waves off the ground over her bare legs. She couldn't imagine how anyone could run three miles on a day like this.

'They should postpone their race till evening,' Alice said, wiping the sweat from her brow. 'They'll get heatstroke in this.'

'Maybe it'll rain,' Sara said. There wasn't a cloud in the sky. She pointed towards the shadow cast by the scoreboard. 'Let's go over there.'

'Where's Polly?' Jessica asked.

'She said she was stopping for a drink,' Alice said.

'Not a bad idea,' Jessica said, turning to Sara. 'See Russ?'

'No.'

'You haven't even looked for him,' Jessica said. 'You've got to tell him you're here.'

'I'm under no contractual obligation to do so,' Sara said.

'Why wouldn't you?'

'He's here to run a race. Why should I bug him?'

'You're just afraid he won't remember you,' Jessica said.

'You're right, I should have him knock me down again in case he's forgotten,' Sara snapped. 'Get off my case, Jessie. If he wants to talk to me, he can come over and talk to me.'

'Sorry,' Jessica muttered, surprised at her tone. Sara was usually about as sensitive to personal remarks as a brick wall.

They reached the shade and sat down. The grass tickled Jessica's legs. Alice continued to wipe at her head, the sweat literally pouring off her. 'Are you all right?' Jessie asked.

Alice smiled quickly. 'I'm fine, just glad I'm not running.'

'But you were sick, weren't you? You didn't come in Monday or Tuesday.'

Alice found a tiny yellow flower, plucked it. 'I was painting.'

'What?' Jessica said.

Alice threw her flower into the air, watched it fall directly to the ground. No breeze. 'The blue wind.'

'Really? Sounds interesting,' Jessica said. 'You'll have to show me. Hey, what are you doing this weekend? Want to go to the beach?'

'I'm painting.'

'Couldn't you set it aside for a few hours.'

'I've got to finish it.'

'That's too bad,' Jessica paused. 'I'm going to the movies Saturday night. You won't believe it, I asked the guy. His name's Michael Olson.'

Alice nodded slowly, leaning back, looking up into the clear sky. 'Polly told me. That's neat that you found – someone you like.'

'We're just friends. He's going to help me with chemistry. That reminds me, where's that fantastic guy you were going to introduce me to?'

Alice lay down, closed her eyes. 'Ask me after your date.' She yawned. 'I could go to sleep here and never wake up.'

Jessica patted her arm. 'You go ahead and rest.'

Polly reappeared a few minutes later. Seconds before she reached them, however, Sara nodded in the direction of the stadium ramp. 'That's him over there with the shaggy brown hair, the muscles,' she said.

Jessica cupped her hand over her eyes again. 'He looks tough.'

'You don't like him?'

'I didn't say that. He's very attractive.' He belonged in a black leather jacket on the back of a motorcycle. 'He's the one who stopped that black guy from killing that football player?'

'Yeah,' Sara said. 'So what do you think?'

'I just told you,' Jessica said. 'He's attractive.'

'Attractive. Phonies on TV are attractive. Do you like him?'

'Yes, I *really* like him. He's a total dreamboat,' Jessica laughed.

'Shut up. I was only asking.'

Polly waved. 'What are you guys doing over here? They start and finish by the bleachers. Come on, let's move. What's Alice doing?'

'Dreaming,' Alice whispered, her eyes still closed.

'She's taking a nap,' Jessica said. 'Sara wants to stay here in the shade.'

Polly plopped down beside them, her face flushed with blood. 'You won't believe who I was just talking to. Russ Desmond. He—'

'Shut up,' Sara said.

Polly looked to Jessica. 'What did I say?'

'It's the heat,' Jessica said.

They stood – except for Alice, who appeared to have caught an early train to sleepyland – for the start of the race. The bang of the gun echoed off the mostly deserted stands. In a colourful jumbled herd – Russ lost in the centre – the runners circled the track and vanished out the gate. 'That's exciting,' Jessica remarked. 'What happens now?'

'We wait till they come back,' Polly said.

Jessica preferred races where she got to see the runners running. She contemplated joining Alice in sleep on the grass.

Fifteen minutes later Russ reappeared, coming up the ramp. He had company, a short Japanese fellow clad in green dogging his heels. A cheer went up from the people gathered near the finish. Jessica leaped to her feet, her interest level taking a sharp upward climb. It was going to be close.

'Come on, Russ!' she yelled.

Russ accelerated sharply as he hit the track, opening up a ten-yard lead. He added another five yards as he went into the curve of the track, momentarily heading away from the finish but quickly approaching their vantage spot. Jessica poked Sara in the ribs.

'Cheer.'

'Shh,' Sara said, intent on the race.

'Shout his name,' Jessica said.

'Shh.'

'Go!' Jessica yelled with Polly.

'Damn,' Sara muttered. With a surge of his own, the Japanese guy had cut his lead in half. 'Russ!!' Sara cried.

At the sound of her voice, he twisted his head towards them. He even raised his hand, shielding his eyes to see better. Then his left foot stepped on to the slightly upraised narrow cement strip that circled the inside of the track. The rhythm of his stride faltered; he practically tripped. When he had recovered, the Japanese guy was ten yards in front. Russ went after him.

'Go!' they screamed.

He lost by inches. Maybe he would have lost, anyway, without the stumble. His competitor obviously had a powerful kick. Jessica told Sara as much. Sara would have none of it.

'I should have kept my mouth shut,' she said. 'Two races, two screw-ups.'

'But it sure was exciting,' Alice remarked, still on the ground, fresh from her snooze.

'What makes you think he was looking for you?' Polly asked Sara. 'He could have been looking for me.'

Jessica expected Sara to explode. Sara, however, ignored Polly completely. 'Let's get out of here,' she said.

'No, you should congratulate him on his effort,' Jessica said. 'I'll go with you.'

Sara surprised her again. His loss seemed to have depressed her. 'All right.'

'I'm coming, too,' Polly said.

'No,' Jessica said. 'Stay here. Stay with Alice.'

'Why should I?'

'Because I'm asking you to. Please?'

Polly gave in reluctantly. Jessica and Sara approached the gang at the finish slowly, watching as the winner embraced Russ, hanging back for a few minutes while the coach and several of the other runners spoke to him about the race. Finally he separated himself from them and grabbed a can from the ice chest, heading for the shade behind the bleachers.

'You want to talk to him alone?' Jessica asked as they followed after him.

'No.'

He must have been totally exhausted. Sitting with his back to a wooden plank, he didn't notice them coming. He had a beer in his hand, Jessica realised. Quite an ice chest they had here. Or else he filled it with his own private stock.

'Hi,' Sara said.

He glanced up briefly. 'Hi.'

'This is my friend, Jessie.'

Russ grunted. Sara looked at Jessica, uncertain. 'That was a great race you ran,' Jessica said quickly. His rough edges were more apparent up close, and yet, he also seemed somehow younger, more of a boy than she had thought from a distance.

'I've run better.' He took a slug of beer, his eyes wandering to the baseball field.

'It's a shame you lost,' Jessica said.

'You win some, you lose some.'

'I didn't mean to distract you,' Sara said.

Russ belched. 'Hey, you got my axe?'

Sara paused. 'What?'

'My axe. You took it the other night.'

'No, I didn't.'

'I need it back. It belongs to the store where I work.'

'I don't have your axe.'

'What did you do with it?'

'Nothing. I don't have it.'

'What are you talking about?'

'What are *you* talking about?'

Russ looked vaguely annoyed. 'You know, you're a weird girl.'

Sara sucked in a sharp breath. 'I'm weird? I'm weird? I'm not the one who's worried about some goddamn axe that he thinks he's lost.'

He sharpened his tone. 'I didn't lose it. You took it.'

'Why would I take it?'

'You didn't want me to chop down the tree.'

'What tree?'

Russ rubbed his head, growing tired of the whole discussion. 'What are you doing here?' he muttered.

Sara chuckled. 'I came over so *you* could thank *me* for getting you reinstated on the cross-country team.'

'Huh?'

'In case you didn't know, I'm the school president. It was me who talked to the school principal. It was me who made it possible for you to run today.'

She'd caught his attention. 'No kidding?'

Sara nodded. 'You better believe it.'

He had a short attention span. He finished his can, crumpled it up in one hand, and threw it aside. 'You shouldn't have bothered.'

She stared at him for a long moment, and Jessica was just thankful Sara didn't have the missing axe in her hands. She probably wouldn't have killed him, but she might have taken a foot off. As it was, she turned and stalked off. Russ observed her departure with mild surprise. 'Is it that time of month or what?' he asked.

'I think you might have hurt her feelings,' Jessica said diplomatically.

'Oh, really?' he said innocently. 'Well, I didn't mean to. Tell her I'm sorry.'

Jessica knelt by his side. 'This is probably none of my business, but do you like Sara?'

'Huh?'

'When she shouted for you in the race, I couldn't help noticing how you looked over. I was wondering if you liked her?'

'Yeah, she's all right. She's got a temper, though. God.'

'Would you want to go out with her?'

'Where?'

'Anywhere, you know, like on a date?'

'I don't know. I guess.'

She supposed that would have to do in place of yes. 'Are you busy tomorrow night?'

'No.'

Jessica took a pen and paper from her bag. It would be hopeless to give him Sara's number. He would only lose it. 'I'll tell you what. Come over to my house tomorrow at six. Sara will be there. You can pick her up and the two of you can go out to dinner. How's that sound?'

'I don't know where you live.'

'I'll draw you a map. Will you come?'

He shrugged. 'All right. As long as she gives me back my axe.'

CHAPTER 10

Michael was no expert when it came to dressing for a date. Part of the reason, he supposed, was he had never gone on a date before. The other problem was his lack of nice clothes. He finally settled on a pair of grey jeans and a white shirt. He figured he was playing it safe. Bubba said he looked like an altar boy.

The three of them – Michael, Bubba and Nick – were spending the last minutes before the *Big Night* in Michael's house. Bubba only lived around the block, and of course Nick had had to come over for the car. Michael's mom had already left for the weekend. Her current boyfriend, Daniel Stevens, owned a condo by the beach. Michael liked the man. Mr Stevens taught music at UC-Irvine. He had an easy-going manner and treated his mother like gold. Michael suspected his mom liked him, too. Maybe this one would work out. She deserved someone nice.

'Did any of you go to the game last night?' Michael asked, sitting on his bed, sipping a lemonade. Nick – he couldn't seem to relax – had glued himself to the far wall. And Bubba was at the desk in front of the mirror, trying on a bag full of garish forties ties his gangster uncle had left him in a will.

'I didn't,' Nick said.

'We got stomped: thirty-seven to fourteen,' Bubba said. 'There's a rumour circulating that Bill Skater's quarterback days are over.'

'Did you start the rumour?' Michael asked.

'I did, but it's gathering momentum. I've also started a Draft Russ Desmond campaign, whether he wants to play or not.' He turned away from the mirror. 'What do you think of this one?'

Not only was it a depressing brandy-red colour, it had a dime-size hole in the centre. 'It's awful,' Michael said.

'That looks like a bullet hole,' Nick said.

Bubba nodded. 'My uncle was wearing it when he got wasted.' He tightened the collar. 'Clair will love it.'

'What did Clair say when you told her she had to drive?' Michael asked.

'We'll see,' Bubba said, reaching for the phone. He dialled the number from memory. She answered on the second ring. 'Clair? This is Bubba. How are you doing? . . . Hey, that's great. I can hardly wait myself. But I've got a small problem. You know Michael Olson? . . . Yeah, he sure is smart. He's going out with Jessica Hart tonight . . . What? No, she's cool. Never mind what you've heard. Anyway, he has to borrow my car. Could you pick me up? . . . What a sweetheart! Let me give you my address.'

He chit-chatted a minute longer before signing off. 'She loves me,' he said as he put down the phone.

'Do you swear you don't have those tickets?' Michael asked.

'U2 played their final L.A. show last night. How could I have tickets?'

'What did she say about Jessie?'

'She called her a stuck-up bitch. Don't take it personally. It's only because Jessie's pretty. Pretty girls always hate other pretty girls. It's biological.'

Nick ventured away from the wall. 'I better get going.' He had a long face.

'Hey, loosen up, Nick,' Bubba said. 'You're just going out with her. You don't have to kill her afterwards.'

Michael stood, setting down his lemonade. 'Are you worried because she's having you pick her up at the library?'

Nick looked at the floor. 'I don't know, when I think

about it, maybe she's ashamed of me.'

'She's probably just worried her dad will blow your head off when he sees how dark you are,' Bubba said sympathetically.

Nick smiled faintly. 'Yeah, that must be it.'

Michael escorted Nick to the front door. 'I filled the car with petrol this afternoon,' he said. 'The air conditioner works, but the window's usually a better bet. And forget about the radio. It only gets AM.'

'Thanks, Mike.'

'The car's ten years old. It's no big favour.'

Nick went to touch his shoulder, hesitated. 'I mean, thanks for everything. You're a real friend. Where I come from, you learn to appreciate your friends. Any time you need a favour, no matter what it is, I'll be there for you.'

Michael was touched by the sentiment. 'You just have yourself a good time.'

Nick promised him he would. Michael watched him drive off, and was heading back to his room when Kats pulled up. Kats drove an old Mustang that never needed an oil change; it leaked a quart a week. 'Don't park that thing in the driveway!' Michael called.

'You let that black dude take your car?' Kats asked a minute later, after having stowed his heap out of sight around the corner. He had obviously just come from work. He needed a bath. 'You must be out of your mind, Mike.'

Michael ignored the comment – people did that all the time with Kats – fetched him a glass of lemonade, and told him not to sit on anything. Bubba came out of the bedroom with a box of condoms in his hands.

'You sure you don't want at least one of these?' he asked.

'That's all right, you might need the whole box,' Michael said.

Bubba nodded. 'I did use a whole box once. Lost three pounds that night. Gained it right back, though. It was mostly water.'

Michael groaned. 'If you're going to talk like that, we better go in the bathroom.'

'Don't be a prude. They advertise condoms on national television. Safe sex, all that stuff.' Bubba pulled one from the box, offered it to him. 'Come on, she'll thank you for it afterwards.'

'Give it to Kats.'

Kats was excited. 'How many of those have you got to wear?'

Bubba glanced at Kats's filthy fingernails. 'You? Eleven.'

Michael pointed to the orange envelope with Jessica's

address on it. 'Kats, hand me that paper on the oven, would you?'

Kats picked the invitation up, stopped to read it. He was nosy on top of everything else. His grin widened. 'Polly and Alice McCoy! They come into the station all the time. Always pay with a gold credit card. You know them, Mike? Are they having a party? I'd like to go to that. Wooh, that Alice sure is a tasty number.'

Michael took a step forward, snapped the invitation from Kats's hand. 'Shut up. You have to be invited. You can't come.'

'Hey, Mike,' Bubba said. 'Cool down.'

Michael realised he was overreacting. 'Sorry.'

Kats stared at him a moment, his black eyes strangely flat. Then he grinned again. 'I bet you were just afraid I'd break in carrying my gun, hey, Mike?'

Michael folded the invitation, put it in his back pocket, out of sight. He remembered that gun all too well. 'Yeah, I guess, something like that.'

He had asked Jessica yesterday if she'd like to get a bite to eat before the movie. She had said sure. He was supposed to pick her up at six-thirty. He would be early if he left now, but suddenly he wanted to get out of the house, get away from the others. He told them he had to hit the road. Bubba left with Kats in the dripping Mustang.

Michael was familiar with Jessica's neighbourhood. And although he had never been to the McCoy residence, he knew Alice lived around the block from Jessica; he had both addresses on the invitation. Cruising down the road in Bubba's Jaguar, he decided to swing by and say hello to his favourite artist.

He had expected a huge house. He wasn't disappointed. You could use up a lot of petrol, he thought, going up a driveway like this every day; it was as long as a football field. He parked beside a silver grey Mercedes, climbed out.

An elderly lady answered the door. He assumed she was the guardian aunt Alice talked about. Her posture was terrible; in better years, she must have been half a foot taller. She was one of those old ladies it was hard to imagine had ever been young. She had a sweet smile, however, which reminded him of Alice's. Parents and relatives always smiled when they saw him. As Bubba had observed, he had that altar boy aura.

'Is Alice here?'

'She's around the back. Are you a friend from school?'

'Yeah, I'm Michael Olson.' He offered his hand. She shook it feebly.

'Alice has told me about you. Please come in.'

They had cream-coloured carpet, deep and soft. The

171

living room cathedral ceiling went way up; twin tinted skylights spread a faint rainbow of colour over the elegant contemporary furniture and towering fireplace. The place was spotless. *They'd better lay down protective sheets for the party*, he thought. The aunt pointed towards a sliding glass door. 'You'll find her near the rose bushes.'

'Thank you. Is Polly here?'

'She's at a friend's.'

The pool was large even for a house as big as this one. It was not, however, exotically shaped, simply rectangular. Mr or Mrs McCoy had probably enjoyed swimming laps.

Alice had set up her easel in the corner of the yard, between the wall of the house and the beginnings of an exotic garden of flowers, bushes and trees that stretched perhaps fifty yards to a tall adobe brick wall. The McCoys could do all the shouting they liked and their neighbours wouldn't even know about it.

An overhang from the second-storey roof cast a shadow over her spot. She had compensated by erecting a silver-dished lamp behind her right shoulder. He thought the arrangement unusual since she could have painted practically anywhere else in the yard and enjoyed direct sunlight. Perhaps the strange mixture of artificial and natural lighting was what suited her mood best. Although he could scarcely see the painting, her work in progress appeared – from the colours – to have a distinct surreal quality.

He thought how content she seemed with a brush in her left hand, a song on her lips. Maybe she was in the middle of a creative high. He decided not to interrupt her, after all. He circled around to the other side of the house and climbed back in the Jaguar. The aunt would probably wonder what had become of him.

It hit him then, hard as a rock, that he was going to pick up Jessica. *Jessie!* The nervousness came quick, but also, an exhilarating joy. This could be the start of something. She could fall in love with him. It was theoretically possible.

He drove around the block, parked in the street in front of her house. Ringing the doorbell and waiting for her to answer, he aged five years.

When the doorbell rang, Jessica was upstairs in her bedroom with Sara and Polly, trying on earrings. She sent Polly down to answer it. 'If it's Michael, tell him I'll be down in a minute. Offer him a Coke.'

'What if it's Russ?' Polly asked.

Jessica glanced at Sara. 'Give him a beer,' she said.

When Polly had left, Sara went to the bedroom door

and peeped out. 'It's Mike,' she said a moment later, disappointed.

'He'll be here, Sara. He's only a few minutes late.'

'Thirty-two minutes is not a few.'

'Guys have a different sense of time than girls.'

'Are you absolutely positively sure it was his idea to go out?'

'Yes.'

'You're lying. You talked him into it.'

'He likes you. He told me so.'

'Did he say that? What were his exact words?'

'He said you were an all-right girl.' She decided against any earrings at all. They were just going out for fun, after all. She turned to Sara. 'Look, why don't you call him? He may have got lost.'

'Already did! – no signal.'

'Oh. Maybe you could talk to his mom. I'm sure their number is listed. She could tell you when he left.'

Sara folded her arms across her chest. She'd broken from tradition and put on a beautiful white dress. 'I'm not talking to his mom.'

Jessica squeezed Sara's arm. 'Be patient. He'll be here. Now, I've got to go. Wish me a good time.'

'Have a good time,' Sara grumbled.

'Don't you want to come down and say hi to Michael?'

Sara plopped on the bed. 'No. I hate men. All of them.'

Michael was sitting on the couch with Polly when Jessica entered the living room. He stood up quickly when he saw her and smiled. His grey jeans and white shirt looked a bit plain next to her bright yellow trousers and silky green top, but who gave a damn? The degree of her pleasure at seeing him again surprised her. He had such lovely black eyes.

'You look nice,' he said casually, stepping towards her. On impulse, she gave him a quick hug.

'Thanks, so do you.' His arms felt strong beneath his shirt. She took a step back. 'Did you have any trouble finding the place?'

'No.'

'Where are my manners? Have you met Polly?'

'I met Mike last year,' Polly said. 'He's a good friend of Alice's.'

Jessica stopped, frowned. 'You are? Alice didn't tell me that.'

Michael was watching her. 'She's a nice girl.'

'Alice? She's a doll.' Jessica picked her bag off the TV. 'I'd introduce you to my parents, but they went out for dinner. Which reminds me, where do you want to eat? Remember, I'm paying.'

He mentioned a local restaurant – one of her favourites

– but insisted it would be his treat. She told him they could argue about it when the bill came.

As she was leaving, she remembered that Maria would be coming over later to spend the night. All this last week, since Maria had helped her on the quiz, they had begun to talk more, outside of class as well as during chemistry lab. Maria was a different sort of friend for Jessica. She was serious, someone who weighed every word before speaking it. She appeared totally uninterested in local gossip, and yet she was fun to be around. She had a quiet dignity that Jessica found inspiring.

On Thursday Maria had admitted she had a problem. Nick Grutler, the tall black guy, had asked her out. She wanted to go; she had, in fact, told him she would. But her parents would kill her if they found out. They weren't prejudiced, she said, just *extremely* conservative. She had told Nick to pick her up at the library, but she knew that when he dropped her off at home, her parents would be awake and waiting. She didn't know what to do.

To Jessica, the solution was obvious. Spend the night at her house. The offer had delighted Maria. To further ensure that Maria's parents did not learn of the date, Jessica had called Friday afternoon after the cross-country race and had casually spoken to Mrs Gonzales about Maria's coming over. The lady had sounded pleased her daughter had made such an upstanding friend. You just had to know how to handle parents.

'Are you going to hang around for a while?' she asked Polly. 'I forgot to tell my mom and dad about Maria spending the night.'

'I might stay for a while.'

'Until Russ shows up, right?' Polly started to get mad. 'Don't say it. If you do leave before they get back, could you leave them a note for me?'

'Sure, Jessie. I hope you two have fun.'

Michael was probably going to think she was a jerk. The second they left the house, she told him she needed to make a quick personal call and asked him if he wouldn't mind pulling over.

'Your house phones aren't working?'

'Yeah.'

They stopped just down the road. Excusing herself, she rang Information. There were three Desmonds. The first one didn't have a Russ. The second – it sounded like his dad – said he'd go get him. Russ didn't seem all that wide-awake when he came on the line.

'Hello?'

'Hi, Russ, this is Jessica Hart. Remember me?'

'Yeah.'

Jessica gestured to Michael that she would be off in a

moment. 'Russ, where are you? Don't you remember you were supposed to go out with Sara tonight?'

He yawned. 'It was tonight?'

Jessica wondered if she should stop where she was. Chances were, Sara would eventually kill a guy like this. 'Yeah, how could you forget?'

'I don't know. Can I come tomorrow? I'm watching *Star Trek*.'

'No, you can't come tomorrow. Sara's waiting for you at my house this minute. She's all dressed up. You get over there right away.'

'Right now? I'm hungry.'

'You made a date, Russ. You should keep it. Do you still have that map I drew you?'

'I think so.'

'Good. Now whatever you do, don't tell her I called. All right?'

'All right.'

Nick's worst nightmare was coming true. They were in the car together, driving down the road, and they had absolutely nothing to say to each other. He didn't even know where he was taking her. He had assumed she would suggest a place she wanted to eat, the movie she wanted to see. Now he suspected she was waiting

178

for him to make the decision. Unfortunately, he hardly knew the area. He didn't want to risk taking her to the local doghouse. The silence between them dragged on and on.

'How was the library?' he asked finally.

'Fine.'

'Did you get a lot of homework done?'

'I should have done more. What did you do today?'

'I worked at the store in the morning. Then I just hung out.'

'Oh.'

They'd had a couple of other mini-conversations like this. They had also ended with 'oh'. The word could be used in practically any situation. Nick worried that they would keep coming back to it all night. He felt he had to say something different, something to break them out of their rut. Actually, he wanted to tell her how happy he was that she had agreed to go out with him, but since he was feeling rather miserable at the moment, he was afraid it would come out sounding insincere. He decided on a different tack.

'How do you feel?' he asked.

'Good.'

'That's good.'

'How do you feel?'

'Good. I mean I'm OK.'

'Is something wrong?' she asked.

'No. Why do you ask?'

'No reason. I was just asking.'

'Oh.'

See – now he had said it. He was seriously debating whether he should give up right then and there and take her home when he noticed her staring at him.

'What is it?' he asked.

'You're mad at me, aren't you?'

'Why would I be mad? I'm not mad.'

'I didn't invite you to my house.'

'That's all right. You were working at the library.'

'That didn't fool you, Nick.'

Her saying his name – on top of her confession – seemed to loosen something in the air. At home, he seldom heard his name. He didn't think his dad had said it in the last five years. 'Is it your parents?' he asked.

She nodded. 'They don't know I'm out with you.'

'They don't let you date?'

She hesitated. 'Not exactly.'

'Oh.' The light turned red. Stopping, he rolled down the window. The outside air had cooled significantly. They must be getting close to the beach. Naturally, what she said did not surprise him. That was the thing about

being one of the few black guys in the neighbourhood –
you got used to everything. 'Do you feel guilty?'

'No. I'm not doing anything wrong.'

'But I could be getting you into trouble?'

'You won't. I'm spending the night at a friend's.'

It stung to hear how she'd had to set everything up
beforehand. Maybe he was mad at her, a little. 'Does this
friend have parents?' he asked. 'You know, they might see
me accidentally.'

She turned towards him. 'I'm sorry.'

The regret came swift. 'No, Maria, I shouldn't have
said that.'

'My parents are good people. They just feel they have
to be cautious. They haven't had easy lives.'

He waited till the light turned green, then drove across
the street and parked near the curve. Behind Maria,
through a patch in the bushes along the pavement, he
saw a blue slice of ocean, the warm brown of sand. He
turned off the engine. 'And you feel you have to be
cautious, too, right?'

She nodded, watching him.

'Why?'

'I just have to be.'

'Then what are you doing with me?'

She didn't answer, but continued to stare. She seemed

scared, not of him, but of what he might say. He said it anyway. 'You and your parents are illegal immigrants, aren't you?'

She trembled, ever so slightly. 'Yes,' she whispered.

'There were lots in my old neighbourhood.'

She nodded. 'I knew.'

'What?'

'You would know. When I met you at the soda machines, you looked like someone – who knew, who didn't belong.'

He chuckled. 'I suppose a bloody head might give someone that idea.' Then he got serious. 'What's the big crime? They've loosened the laws. Stay here a few years and they'll make you a citizen.'

'That's not how it works. We got here after the amnesty deadline. In Washington there's talk about changing the requirements, but until then we could be sent home any time.'

'How did you get registered at school?'

'My dad paid this man some money. He made me a phoney birth certificate.'

'How long have you been in the country?'

'Almost two years. We're from El Salvador.'

'How is it there?'

She tensed. 'Not good. I like it better here.' She gently

touched his knee. He could not remember when he had last been touched by a female. Probably by his mom, before she had split eight years ago. 'I'd rather not talk about it, if you don't mind? I worry too much about it as it is.'

'What would you like to do?'

She brightened. 'Eat. I'm starving. You don't know where you're going, do you?'

He smiled. 'No.'

She told him about a Mexican restaurant next to the pier. Nick restarted the car. She hadn't asked him to keep her secret. She'd automatically trusted him to do so. He was glad.

Russ had half a roast beef sandwich in his hand when Sara answered the door, the other half in his mouth. 'Sorry I'm late,' he mumbled, chewing.

He had on blue jeans, a torn red T-shirt and sandals. Sara silently cursed Jessica for talking her into dressing up. He hadn't even combed his hair. 'Did you have trouble finding the place?' she asked diplomatically.

'No.'

Polly popped her head out the side of the door. 'Hi, Russ! How are you doing?'

He grinned. 'Hanging in there, babe. How are you?'

Sara pushed Polly out of the way. 'We've got to go. Remember to feed the cat.' She stepped outside, shutting the door in Polly's face. That girl only liked a guy when he belonged to someone else. 'Where's your car?'

'I don't have a car. I've got a truck. It's right there.'

Sara grimaced. It looked like he used it for hauling. She pointed to the mound of grass piled in the back. 'Do you keep a cow, or what?'

He didn't think that was funny. 'My old man's a gardener. What's yours do?'

'He shuffles papers.' He was a bank president.

'Does he use a truck to deliver them?'

Jessica had warned her to watch her mouth. Jessica said guys didn't appreciate being made fools of. 'Ah, yeah.'

'What do you want to do?' he asked as they walked towards his truck.

'I'm hungry.'

He took another bite of his sandwich. 'You haven't had dinner?'

'No. I thought we were going to eat together?'

'That's cool. Let's go to the McDonald's in the mall.'

'The McDonald's?'

He opened the passenger door, and as he did so, she caught a whiff of his breath. The empty beer cans littering his front seat only confirmed her fears. 'You've been drinking,' she said.

'Is there a law against it? If you want, we can go to the Burger King instead.'

'How many beers have you had?' Judging by his empties, he'd put away several six-packs, but that seemed unlikely.

'Why? I can drive.'

'How many?'

'I can't remember.'

'I'm driving.' She held out her hand. He stared at it a moment before giving her the keys.

'Do you know how to drive a stick?'

'I learned on a stick,' she said, reaching into the passenger side and removing what was left of a six-pack. 'I'm putting these in the back, under the grass. I don't want some cop stopping and arresting us.' As it was, her licence was still in suspension.

'They'll get warm,' he protested. 'One of them's half-full.'

'I don't care.'

The driver's seat was encrusted not only with dirt, sweat and more dead grass, but also had a dozen or so of those little thorny balls that get stuck on clothes at picnics. She looked down at her white dress, running her fingers over the clean smooth fabric. She'd bought it in Hollywood at a designer shop for big bucks. Then she looked over at Russ: food in his mouth, hair in his face, not much going on behind his eyes.

What the hell am I doing with this guy?

But it was right then that he showed the first trace of decency he had since their collision when he stopped during the race to see if she'd been hurt. Without her even asking, he pulled off his shirt and draped it over her seat. And sitting there naked from the waist up, his powerfully developed chest warm and brown in the evening sunlight, he seemed to her, if not perfect, at least worthy of consideration. She got in.

'You've got to watch the brakes,' he said as she fiddled with the clutch. King Kong could hardly have pressed the thing in.

'What's wrong with them?'

'They don't always work.'

She stopped. 'You can't be serious?'

He shrugged. 'If you don't like it, let's take your car. That'll give me a chance to look in your boot.'

She didn't have her car; Jessica had picked her up. 'What's in my boot?'

'I think that's where you put my axe.'

Sara leaned her head on the steering wheel, totally

reversing her opinion of a moment ago. 'Jesus,' she whispered.

Dinner had been fabulous. Probably because the restaurant overlooked the ocean, they'd both been in the mood for seafood; she'd had a shrimp salad, and Michael, swordfish. Although she was already stuffed the pastry tray the waitress had brought by a moment ago was too much of a temptation. Fortunately, Michael promised to eat half the chocolate cake she had ordered. She was going to have to jog a few miles this weekend to make up for tonight. She didn't care. She was having a great time.

Initially, while thinking about the date that afternoon, she had worried she would come off seeming stupid, shallow. She had always done well in school, but since third grade, she had felt she was faking it. She got good grades, she thought, because she studied twice as much as anybody else. She saw herself as an overachiever and feared that one day, some day, she would be found out. Everyone would know she didn't really belong in the accelerated maths class, or chemistry for that matter.

Yet rather than trying to hide her insecurity from the smartest guy around, she found herself confiding in him about it. She wasn't even sure why, other than that

Michael was an excellent listener.

'I keep reading about the average GPAs of the kids who get into Stanford,' she said. 'And their SAT scores. They're so high! I'm not taking the test until December, and I've already bought a couple of those study guide books. I took a trial test a couple of nights ago. I won't tell you what I scored. Let's just say if I do as well on the real test, I'm going to save my dad a lot of money on tuition fees. I swear to God, sometimes I think I'm going to end up at the local junior college.'

'What do you want to major in at Stanford?' he asked. He had taken a fancy to the candle on their table and was playfully running his fingers above the flame. She didn't doubt she had his full attention, however; he wasn't staring, but his eyes seldom wandered far from her face. Once again, she wondered how he saw her.

'My parents eventually want me to get into broadcasting. They tell me I've got the voice, the personality. They think a major in journalism, with a minor in communications, would give me a solid background. I know some of those girls on the news make a lot of money. What do you think?'

'I think I asked the wrong question.'

She smiled. 'What do you mean?'

He momentarily took his hand away from the

candle, caught her eye. 'You keep telling me what your parents want.'

She started to answer, stopped. He'd hit pretty close to home with that one. 'They are paying the bills,' she muttered.

He backed off. 'I didn't mean they were giving you bad advice. They obviously care a great deal about you.'

'No, you're right. I need to hear this. I should major in what *I* want. It is my life, after all. But that's the problem. I don't know what I want. Being an anchorperson on TV looks glamorous. Everyone knows who you are. You're where the action is. But that's looking at it from the outside in. For all I know, I might hate it.'

He nodded. 'That's true. But if you really are interested, you could probably get a summer job at a TV station. You might only change lights, but at least you'd get a feel for the environment.'

'That's an idea.' She made a mental note to check on that.

'What about Stanford?'

'What about it? Don't you think it's a good school?'

'It's one of the best. Is that why you've chosen it?'

He'd caught her again. 'My dad went to Stanford,' she admitted. 'I grew up browsing through his college yearbooks. I know all the sororities on campus, even the

189

Stanford school song. I don't know, it's so hard to get into, I've always felt that if you graduated from Stanford, you would be one of the elite.' She leaned forward. She really wanted his approval. 'Does that sound like too snobbish a reason?'

He chuckled. 'I'm the last person to ask.'

'Why?'

''Cause I'm jealous. *I* won't be going to Stanford.'

'Why not? You've got the grades. You'll probably get super-high SAT scores.'

He looked down. 'I can't afford it.'

She had to remember that not everybody's dad made six figures a year. He must have borrowed the Jaguar for their date. 'Couldn't you get a scholarship?'

He shrugged. She may have been embarrassing him. 'It's a possibility, but I'd hate to be that far away from my mom. She sort of likes having me around.'

He'd said nothing about his family. 'Is your mom divorced?'

'Yeah.'

'You don't have any brothers or sisters, do you?'

'No.'

'Neither do I. I wish I did. I sort of envy Polly sometimes. She's got Alice.' He glanced up suddenly. 'What is it?'

'Nothing,' he said.

'It really surprised me that you knew her. She never told me. When did you meet?'

'Last Christmas.'

'Really? Where?'

'At the store where I work. The 7-Eleven on Western.'

'I've been in there a couple of times. I never saw you. Is it a part-time job?'

'Fifty hours a week.'

'Wow.' He lived in a different world, she realised. He made money, carried his own weight. She charged everything, ran up the phone bill. And from what he said, he watched out for his mom, when all she did was fight with her parents about nothing. She lived such a superficial life.

But what can I do? I'm already spoiled.

She decided she couldn't possibly accept his help with chemistry. He undoubtedly had little time to himself.

She leaned over, blew out the candle beneath his hand. 'Come on, Michael. We don't need the cake. I'm taking you to that movie I promised.'

They called for the bill. She put up a fight, but he insisted on paying. Out in the car, they checked a paper he'd brought. They couldn't make up their minds what to see and decided to head back to the mall near campus where they would have six shows to choose from.

Driving along Pacific Coast Highway, the salty air pouring in through the open windows, the sun setting over the water, they slipped into a quiet spell. Relaxing into the seat, she glanced over, studying his profile. For a moment she wished that it had been him who had asked her out, that this was a *real* date. He didn't have Bill Skater's startling blue eyes, his strong jaw. But his face was appealing, particularly now, with his dark eyes intent on the road, his thoughts seemingly far away. And he had something else she liked. He was kind.

Twenty minutes later, while reviewing the movie posters outside the mall's theatres, they heard their names called.

'Maria!' she cried, turning.

'Hi, Nick,' Michael said. 'It's a small city.'

They made an interesting couple. Maria couldn't have been five feet tall, and Nick had to be pushing six and a half. They were not holding hands, but Jessica noticed how close they stood, how their arms and sides brushed as they approached. She had been curious to meet Nick. She'd heard such contrasting stories: that he was a bloodthirsty maniac; that he had risked his life to protect Russ Desmond from a huge toppling mirror; that he had the strength of ten guys. Watching him now shaking Michael's hand, shyly saying hello

192

to her, she marvelled at his politeness.

They decided to team up. But if it was difficult for two to choose a movie, it was impossible for four. Not that they were each insisting their own personal taste be the deciding factor. On the contrary, Michael, Nick and Maria refused to volunteer any preference, and Jessica didn't know what she wanted to see. They had time. They decided to have an ice cream first.

They ran into Bubba and Clair inside the 31 Flavours.

Meeting him at the game, Jessica had thought Bubba a wonderful character, not someone she would like to get too close to, but a guy it would be nice to run into from time to time when she needed a taste of the extraordinary. He obviously had Sara's highly developed sense of self-confidence, as well as her wit. Yet he seemed somehow both more fun loving and more devious. She had been surprised to learn he had been a friend of Michael's for many years.

Bubba took charge of the introductions. When it was time for Jessica to meet Clair formally, Jessica found herself becoming defensive. She'd heard what Clair had said in the student council meeting about how all the female transfers from Mesa were dogs.

'Clair, this is someone you have to know,' Bubba said, excited. 'Miss Jessica Hart. She used to be a cheerleader at

Mesa. The best they had, I've been told. Jessie, meet my pal, Clair Hilrey.' He chuckled. 'Clair *is* the best.'

Clair blushed at Bubba's remark, remaining seated beside a half-consumed banana split. She had an overall flushed look, as if she had just been out in the sun, or exercising. A thin gold necklace glittered at her throat. Crossing her exquisite long legs, she offered her hand. 'I've heard about you,' she said sweetly. 'I've been wanting to meet you.'

Jessica shook her hand. She wondered what Clair was doing with short, fat Bubba, whether this meant Bill and she weren't a couple any more. She forced a smile. 'I've seen you at the games.'

'Yeah?'

'Cheering, you know.' Who did this girl's hair? Jessica wondered. That person should be doing her own.

Clair glanced at Bubba, giggled. 'That's what we cheerleaders do here at Tabb.'

'Yeah,' Bubba said. 'They're full of spirit. They never get tired. Hey, why don't you guys join us? We're going to go to the movies in a few minutes.'

Michael and Nick didn't react to the suggestion one way or the other, although Maria did not seem particularly enthusiastic. The three of them appeared to be waiting for her decision. Clair smiled at her again, the fine lines of arrogance beautifully arranged around her wide, sensual mouth. Jessie almost felt as if Clair were challenging her to stay. *Come on, girl, see who all the boys start fawning over.* Jessica met her eyes. 'That sounds like fun,' she said.

They ate ice cream, lots of it, until they were all sick and groaning. Then they headed back to the theatres. They didn't have to worry about selecting a movie. Bubba did it for them. He'd read the reviews and heard the inside Hollywood buzz, he said, and they would be crazy to see anything else. It was something about a female vampire from outer space who didn't wear any clothes.

Michael had been right. It *was* a small city. They bumped into Sara and Russ next, standing in line for the same movie. Russ must have picked it; Jessica knew how much Sara hated anything sci-fi. Indeed, Sara didn't appear to be having a thrilling night. She pulled Jessica aside the first chance she got.

'I'm going nuts,' she hissed, while the others talked together in line. 'Do you know where he took me for dinner?'

'Where?'

'I'll let you guess. The menu was fabulous. We had a choice of hamburgers: Big Mac, Quarter Pounder, Double

Cheeseburger. Then we had our choice of shakes: vanilla, strawberry, chocolate. Of course, if you ordered the full dinner, you got complimentary french fries.'

'That sounds like McDonald's?'

'Very good. But dinner was the fun part. Before that, he let me take him for a scenic drive in his garbage truck. And guess what? Two local civil servants stopped us to point out the twenty bushels of dead grass we had flying out the back.'

'You were driving? Did they ask for your licence?'

'That they did. Fortunately, my less than sober male companion ingeniously told them I had accidentally left it in the back before we had piled in the grass. The cops didn't mind. They told me to dig it out. They even helped me. And guess what they found?'

'More dead grass?'

'No. Beer. Alcohol. That stuff they sell to people after they are twenty-one years of age. They found three cans, and one of them was open. That's against the law, in case you didn't know.'

'Did you get a ticket?' Sara's licence was already in suspension; another ticket and they would probably tear it up.

'No, I got arrested!'

'No!'

'I had to take a breath test. I had to walk in a straight line and breathe in a bag. And get this, all the while Russ – drunk out of his gord – got to sit there and watch!'

'Did you get a ticket?' she repeated. Sara had not been arrested.

'No, I got humiliated! Then I had to eat a greasy hamburger, which gave me indigestion. And now I've got to watch some goddamn flick about a blood-sucking pin-up.'

She glared in the direction of her date, fuming. 'I wish the cops had given me a urine test. Then I could have thrown it in his face.'

'But do you like him? Are you having fun?'

'Shut up. What are you guys going to see?'

'The same thing you are.' Jessica noticed Clair fixing Michael's collar, her polished nails brushing the back of his neck. Bubba noticed, too, and didn't seem to care. Jessica couldn't say the same for herself.

Am I jealous? I can't be jealous. He's just a friend.

'Let's get back in line,' she said.

Clair backed away from Michael the moment they returned. For the first time that night, Jessica took Michael's hand. Clair whispered something in Bubba's ear, causing him to laugh.

'What's up?' Michael asked innocently. Jessica pulled him close, squeezed the top of his arm, smiled.

'I am.' Maybe just maybe, he would be more than a friend.

The fireworks between Sara and Russ were not over. When Russ reached the ticket window, he discovered he didn't have enough money for two admissions. He asked Sara if she could spring for a few dollars. Sara stared at him for a long time before responding. Jessica silently hoped Sara was using the time to calm herself. She might just as well have been hoping for a gallon of petrol to put out a fire.

'What?' Sara asked softly. 'You want money from *me*? You want *me* to pay for *your* movie? Is that what *you* want?'

Poor Russ, he was looking right into the face of a volcano and he couldn't feel the heat. The girl behind the ticket window waited with an expression of infinite boredom. 'Yeah,' he said.

Sara took out her purse, opened it for all to see. She must have had forty bucks, in tens and fives, and plenty of change. She smiled when she saw the money, and Jessica shivered. It was a crooked smile Sara saved for special occasions, immediately before she exploded into a frenzy.

'Hey, why don't we make this my treat,' Jessica said quickly, stepping up to the window, pulling out a twenty. 'Why don't I—'

'She's got plenty of cash,' Russ interrupted. He stretched his hand over to pluck a bill from Sara's purse. Sara held it out of reach. He frowned. 'Hey, come on, we're holding up the line.'

'No,' Sara said.

'What do you mean, no?' Russ demanded.

'You didn't say please.'

'Please what? Please give me a couple of bucks? Man, you're – All right, all right, please give me a couple of bucks.'

Sara stopped smiling. 'No.'

'What do ya want to see?' the girl in the window finally asked. The people behind them began to stir.

Michael took out his wallet. 'Russ, I could lend you a ten if you need—'

'No,' Sara interrupted, her eyes fixed on Russ. 'No one's loaning this buffoon a red penny.'

Russ shook his head, disgusted. 'You know what your problem is, girl? You're spoiled. You get everything handed to you on a platter. You've got no class.'

Sara started to laugh, loud and high, like a hyena. She did this for maybe three seconds, then suddenly cut it off and poked a sharp finger into Russ's chest. 'I have no class!' she screamed. 'You're an hour late! Your truck smells like a cow stall! You practically get me thrown in jail, and now you're pinching money out of my purse!'

'That's telling him,' Bubba said, enjoying the exchange. The others held back. It was too late, Jessica knew, to go back.

'My truck doesn't stink,' Russ said indignantly. 'And I'm not pinching your money. I'm just short is all. I didn't know I was going to have to pay for all this tonight.'

Sara went to snap at him, stopped. Jessica began to feel faint. 'What do you mean?' Sara asked quietly.

'I didn't know we were going out until your friend called me. If I'd known, I would have gone—'

'Stop,' Sara said. She glanced at her, spoke to Russ. 'Jessie called you? When did Jessie call you?'

Russ lowered his head, realising his mistake. 'I don't know.'

Sara nodded. 'Jessie set this all up, didn't she? Yeah, that makes sense. You're being a jerk 'cause you don't want to be here. Well, I can understand that.' She took a breath. 'I'm sorry.'

'What do ya want to see?' the girl asked again. She had the line down pat. Sara reached into her purse, threw all her money under the window.

'The vamp flick,' she told her, glancing at the rest of them. 'It's on me.'

Then she left, in a hurry, and Jessica was not able to catch up with her until they were halfway across the mall, near the central fountain. Fortunately, none of the others followed. Sara was crying. Jessica would not have thought it possible.

'I didn't know this would happen,' Jessica said. 'I didn't know.'

Sara didn't tell her to go away, didn't blame her. Removing a handkerchief from her bag, she slowly wiped away her tears, blew her nose. Jessica watched with a mixture of guilt and amazement. Who was this fragile creature? It couldn't be her best friend. That girl *never* cried, not in the twelve years she had known her. Sara looked at her with red eyes.

'I would call a cab, but I spent all my money,' she said.

'I'll go get Michael. We'll give you a ride home. You stay here until I get back.' She put her arm around her. 'I really am sorry.'

Sara smiled faintly, embarrassed. 'This is stupid.'

Jessica hugged her. 'No, this just means you like him.'

Michael met her midway between the theatres and the fountain. She explained how Sara would rather not have to see the others any more tonight. He understood immediately; he went for the car.

They drove to Jessica's house; Sara had planned to spend the night, anyway, and Jessica wanted to talk to her. Sara didn't say a word, except to thank Michael when she got out of the car. Jessica watched her hurry to the front door, disappear inside. She turned to Michael.

'I guess I still owe you a movie,' she said.

'That's OK.'

'You know, you're being awfully cool about all this. I think I would feel better if you were a little put out or something.'

He played with the keys in the ignition. Now he wouldn't look at her, and for a moment she wondered if he was nervous. But he hadn't asked her out. He couldn't be thinking of kissing her goodnight.

What if I kissed him?

'Sara seemed pretty upset,' he said, rolling down his window and placing his left elbow halfway outside. In the confines of the front seat, he had placed himself as far away from her as possible. She decided to take the hint. He didn't want her kisses. He probably just wanted to get back to see the movie. She couldn't blame him.

'Yeah, she is. I better go see her.'

'OK.' He glanced up the street. 'I have some free

202

time tomorrow evening, if you still need help with chemistry?'

He probably had to work all day, and would be exhausted when he got home. She would be stealing his own study time. 'Oh, that, never mind. I've been reading the textbook like mad the last few days. I think I've caught up on my own.'

'Are you sure? It's no bother.'

'I'm sure.' She reached over, touched his arm. 'Thanks.'

Now he turned his keen dark eyes on her. 'For everything?'

He remembered! She smiled. 'What else?'

A sweet note to finish the evening. Nevertheless, walking towards her front door, alone, the sound of his car disappearing around the corner, she felt a little sad. She would have to remember to make sure Michael came to Alice's party next Saturday.

CHAPTER 11

A week later, riding to the party in the Jaguar with Bubba and Nick, Michael was still thinking of Jessica's goodnight, and feeling bad. A couple of hours alone with him and she decides she doesn't even want his help with her homework. Hell of an impression he must have made. Yet for a few happy minutes here and there, over dinner and standing in line for the tickets before the Sara-Russ blow-up, he had actually believed she liked him. He'd caught her staring at him a couple of times, watching him, thinking, he had imagined, how great he just might be.

She had probably been wondering when the night would be over.

Since then he had spoken to Jessica only in passing. He had taken to timing his trips to their locker so he would avoid her. He did so not because he was angry with her, but because he didn't want to bother her. She was so sweet; she might feel obligated to be nice to him even if she didn't feel like it. And he had another reason. She'd been spending a lot of time with Bill Skater the past week, at lunch and during break.

Beyond their mutual great looks, Michael couldn't imagine what those two had in common. Of course, from their point of view, that was probably more than enough.

'You're awfully quiet back there, Mike,' Bubba said, driving. Nick sat to his right in the passenger seat. After dropping Sara and Jessica off last Saturday, Michael had gone straight home. He had, however, seen Nick the next day at work and heard how well things had gone with Maria. But he had not spoken to Bubba about the *Big Night*, about Clair or Jessica. After all these years, Bubba usually knew when to leave him alone. Then again, it was Bubba who was dragging him to this party. If it hadn't been for him, and a fear of offending Alice, he would be at home now reading a book.

'That happens to me when I don't talk. You make a left here, in case you didn't know.'

Bubba took one look down the road and drove past it without turning. Michael quickly saw his reason. The street was jammed, with cars everywhere. Though a quarter of a mile away from Polly and Alice's house, he could clearly hear the rhythm of the music, the sound of people laughing and carrying on.

'Your babe's going to be here, isn't she?' Bubba asked Nick.

'Yeah, Jessie invited her. And me, I guess.'

'It doesn't look like they're turning away anyone,' Michael said. Bubba couldn't find a spot anywhere.

'Is Clair coming?' Nick asked Bubba.

'Yeah. Wait till you see her in this new bikini I bought her. For all the material they used, it could have been cut from a red handkerchief.'

'How did you keep her from exploding when she found out you weren't going to the concert?' Nick asked.

Bubba looked over at him. 'Do you consider yourself a gentleman?'

'I suppose.'

Bubba pointed to the glove compartment. 'Open that, take the box out.'

Nick did as he was told. Bubba was referring to the box of condoms he had been showing off last week. 'There's only two left,' Nick said, peering inside.

'That's why,' Bubba said simply.

Michael snorted. 'You didn't have sex with her eight times before ice cream and the movies.'

206

'Four times before, three and a half times after,' Bubba said.

'I don't believe it,' Michael said. 'I bet you didn't even kiss her goodnight.'

'Maybe I didn't kiss her goodnight. I don't remember. She fell asleep in my arms.'

'That's BS,' Michael said. 'How could you get her in bed?'

'For the faithful romantic, no explanation is necessary. For the unbeliever, no explanation is possible.'

'You probably got her loaded.'

'I confess to offering her a couple of drinks.'

'I bet she was unconscious the whole time,' Michael said. He didn't know whether to believe him or not. In either case, he realised he was jealous.

'What was the half-time like?' Nick asked, curious.

Bubba smiled. 'And you said you were a gentleman.'

They ended up parking two blocks away. Climbing out of the car, Bubba donned a pair of sunglasses and a hat, even though the sun had set two hours earlier. He already had on a flowery Hawaiian shirt and a pair of brilliant red baggy swimming trunks. Nick offered to carry the case of Heineken Bubba had purchased – with the help of a phoney ID. Michael tucked his trunks in his towel, lagging behind his friends as they walked towards the huge, brightly lit house.

A number of people were gathered on the long steep front lawn. Michael thought he saw Dale Jensen, his main competitor for valedictorian honours, sucking on a joint. Neither of them let on he had seen the other.

Loud and crowded, the beautiful living room had changed from the last time he'd been there. Furniture had been cleared away from the centre of the floor, a thick clear plastic laid down. The dancers could have used a referee. You couldn't even hear yourself talking.

Nick deposited the beer in an ice chest in the kitchen, then he and Michael followed Bubba down the hall to a relatively quiet games room. The main attractions here were a pool table and three separate video games. Michael searched for Jessica, hoping to find her so he could avoid her.

Russ had planted himself in the corner in front of Demon Death. He had a controller, a full pitcher of beer and Polly to help him back to safety from the realm of the dead. She was all over him. Sara mustn't be around.

On the other side of the room, on a low couch behind a table covered with snack bowls, sat Bill Skater, Clair Hilrey and The Rock. The latter glanced up the instant Nick entered, leaned over, and whispered something to his quarterback. The team had lost the previous night: 17 to 7. Bill had thrown two interceptions and had spent the entire second half on the bench, when Tabb had scored its only touchdown. The Rock had played the whole game and had sacked the opposing quarterback four times. He was a strong SOB.

'Maria might be outside,' Michael said to Nick.

'She might be in this room,' Nick said. He had gained a measure of self-confidence in the last two weeks.

'She's not in this room,' Michael said. 'And there's no sense looking for trouble.'

'All right,' Nick said, turning to leave. 'But I can't keep avoiding him. You know that.'

'We'll see.'

Nick left. Apparently Bubba saw trouble, too. He didn't approach Clair right off the bat. He waited till Bill and The Rock were distracted, caught her eye, gesturing for her to meet him outside. Clair shook her head. She didn't mind hanging on to Bubba as long as no jocks were around. Yet Bubba persisted with his gestures, and finally she stood, excusing herself and silently passing within inches of Bubba as she left the room.

'There's a girl in love,' Michael observed.

'Even the best of them suffer from guilt now and then,' Bubba responded, not worried.

'Face it, she doesn't want to be seen with you when all her friends are around.'

Bubba didn't appreciate the remark. 'I didn't see Jessie running to welcome you with open arms at the door.' He went after Clair.

'Sorry,' Michael called after him. He was off to a great start. He noticed a ping-pong table set up in the garage off the games room. He often played against his mom at home; they were both good. He went and got in line for the next game.

He was a point away from being handed the bat when he saw Jessica enter the games room and sit down beside Bill on the couch. They seemed happy to see each other. Bill handed her his drink. She offered him a pretzel. Michael accepted the bat and crushed his opponent's initial serve into the table. They needed to get a fresh ball. He handed the bat to the guy behind him and got out of line.

I could walk home. It would only take a couple of hours.

He had once read a discussion about which was the worse pain: severe emotional or severe physical pain. The article had come to no conclusions. Now he could see why. One always brought the other. He actually felt as if he had been knifed through the heart. He felt the urge to shout, to run away, but he didn't have a shred of energy to move. Most of all, he felt angry at himself for caring. What did he have to care about? They hadn't gone together. He had nothing to feel sad about losing. What he had was exactly that – nothing. Looking at her didn't even bring him pleasure any more.

He would have left if Alice hadn't suddenly appeared at his side. He felt her before he saw her. She was hugging him. 'Mikey, you're very, very late,' she scolded.

He hugged her back. Touching her seemed to lessen his disappointment. 'How come I hardly ever see you at school?' he asked.

She stood back a step. She looked thinner than he would have liked, but colour had returned to her cheeks. Her clothes surprised him: plain blue jeans, an oversized green top – and she had a closet of dresses to choose from. She read his mind, as she often did.

'I wore this for you,' she said. 'Don't you remember?'

He smiled. 'When you came into the store at Christmas? Yeah, but you were ready to paint then.'

'I'm going to paint tonight,' she said, suddenly serious. 'When everyone's gone.' Then she smiled. 'I'm happy you're here. I have to talk to you.'

Bubba chose that moment to reappear, hat and dark glasses still in place. 'Hello, Crackers,' he said to Alice.

'Hi, Johnny,' she replied in the same flat tone. Michael

understood Alice's choice of greeting – John was Bubba's real name after all – but he had never heard the Crackers nickname before.

'Clair's changing,' Bubba told him. 'So are Nick and Maria. It's time for a little dip.'

Alice warmed at the suggestion. 'Yeah, Mike, let's go in the pool. Polly's been on at me all night about playing the hostess, and I'm getting sick of it. I'll dump a half gallon of bubble bath in the filter. It'll be great! You dive off the board, and you don't know what you're going to land on.'

'Isn't that dangerous?' Michael asked. He supposed he couldn't leave now.

'No, that's a great idea,' Bubba said. 'With the bubbles, we can all go skinny dipping.' He glanced at Alice. 'As long as that doesn't offend the kids?'

Alice didn't answer immediately, sizing him up. 'Sara's here. She's upstairs, in case you didn't know.'

'So?' Bubba said.

Alice slowly stepped around him, forcing Bubba to turn to follow her. 'She didn't expect to be elected president,' she said. 'She was really surprised. Everyone was, except me. I know you used your computer to change the vote count.'

It was Bubba's turn to size her up, his thoughts

effectively hidden behind his dark glasses. Michael had of course suspected Bubba had altered the outcome of the election. After studying how the votes were collected, however, and the structure of the program used to count them, he had been unable to figure out how it could have been done. He had, therefore, not confronted Bubba with it. In reality, Michael couldn't have cared less who was school president.

'I didn't,' Bubba said finally, his voice low and even. 'And I don't care whether you believe that or not. But I do insist you stop accusing me of having access to confidential files, especially when other people are around. I told you on that first day – talk like that could get Mike and me expelled.'

Alice laughed at his seriousness. 'You're such a wonderful liar! I love it! Don't worry, Johnny, I'm not turning you in. Not tonight at least. Come on, let's go swimming. Let me go change.'

As Alice left, Bubba looked at Michael and shook his head.

Polly was upset. She'd printed up sixty invitations and at least three times that number had barged through her front door. These people – they didn't care how much they ate, what they dropped on the floor. And they were so noisy! At Alice's insistence, she'd combined the speakers from their two bedroom stereos and arranged them in the corners of the living room. When the dial on the receiver was set at six, the house vibrated. Naturally, someone had jacked the setting up to ten! She already had a splitting headache. She almost hoped the police showed up when ten o'clock rolled around and neighbourhood noise restrictions went into effect. It was going to take something drastic to get this herd out of here. She wished she had never allowed herself to be talked into this blasted party. That Alice – she got her own way too much.

Polly had another reason to be angry at her sister. Despite her promise, Alice had invited Clark to the party.

'How do I kill these ugly critters here?' Russ asked, nodding at the TV screen, slurring his words. He'd asked for a little whisky in his beer. She didn't mind obliging him, though ordinarily she hated the smell of alcohol. She considered Russ a very special guy. He seemed to like her.

'You have to identify who they are first, what their powers might be. Most witches you can just shoot at and kill. But a disembodied spirit, you need a magic potion to get rid of them.'

'Huh,' Russ grunted, rubbing his red eyes. The poor

dear, it had been hot again yesterday afternoon when he'd run the cross-country race. She'd been one of the few present, shouting her support. She'd been glad when he won. Sara and Jessica hadn't bothered to stop by. 'What are these?' he asked.

'Witches,' she said. 'Just blow them away and go on.'

He fumbled with the button on the controller. 'They won't die,' he complained. They wouldn't die because he kept missing them by several inches. Frustrated, he dropped the controller on the floor and took a gulp of his beer. She had never seen anybody, teenager or adult, who had his thirst. He belched loudly. 'Where's Sara?'

She smiled pleasantly. 'She's not here. She's sick.'

'Sick?'

'She gets sick a lot. I never get sick. I'm one of the healthiest people I know. At the hospital, they're always having me come back to donate blood.'

Russ looked confused. 'I've got to talk to Sara.'

'Why? You can talk to me.'

He tried to stand, without much success. 'She's got my axe.'

Polly put him back in his chair. She had just spotted Alice heading for the living room, possibly for upstairs. That girl had better not be planning to go in the pool. Someone had to keep up with all these guests. Polly felt she had already done more than her fair share.

'Stay here,' she said, getting up. She still had the axe in the boot of her Mercedes. 'I'll try to find it for you.'

Russ scratched his head. 'Why did Sara give it to you?'

Leaving the games room, Polly noticed Jessica gossiping with Bill Skater. Clair Hilrey vanishes for a second and Jessica takes her place. The same thing had been going on all week at school. Polly thought Jessica a fool. She had a sharp guy like Michael Olson interested in her, and she pursued a lug like Bill. If she had a guy, Polly swore, any guy, who really respected her, she would treat him right. Jessica had a lot to learn.

Alice did indeed head upstairs. Polly followed her carefully. They'd placed a sign on the front door stating the top floor was off limits. A few people had ignored it, to use the second-floor bathrooms, which Polly supposed was better than their using the bushes.

Two short flights of stairs led to the upper floor. Polly paused on the landing. Alice was talking to that greasy guy from the gas station near the turn in the hall. *Kats* – another example of someone they had not invited. With the loud music, Polly couldn't hear what he was saying. But she didn't like how he was grinning at her sister. She wouldn't be surprised if Alice was encouraging him.

She changed her mind a moment later. Kats wouldn't

let Alice into her room. He'd stretched his hairy arm across her bedroom door. Alice looked around uneasily. Polly hurried up the remaining flight of stairs, strode down the hallway.

'Hi,' she said to Kats. 'How are you?'

He took his hand off the door frame, stepped back. 'Great! Good party you're having.'

She smiled. 'I'm glad you're enjoying yourself.' She took Alice by the arm. 'Excuse me, I have to speak with my sister.'

She led Alice around the corner and into the room at the end of the hall. It used to be their parents' bedroom years ago. Polly opened the door, turned on the light. A sudden flash dazzled her eyes. The light died. Old bulb, burned out. She stumbled forward, searching for the lamp on the nightstand in the corner. They were the only two pieces of furniture in the room. There wasn't even a rug.

'What was that all about?' she asked, turning on the lamp.

'Nothing,' Alice said, closing the door behind her. 'He wanted to talk, and I wanted to get into my room and change.'

The floor had recently been polished. The glare of the light from the lamp's naked bulb reflecting on the hard wood irritated Polly's eyes.

'You're not going in the pool.'

Alice put her hand on her hip, pouted. 'Yes, I am.'

'That isn't fair. I'm sick and tired of running all over the house making sure everybody's having a good time. I'd like a few minutes to relax.'

'Fine, relax. The party will carry on just fine without either of us.'

'Sure, just drop everything. In case you didn't know, we're out of paper cups downstairs.'

Although the room appeared empty, its closets were jammed. They kept Christmas decorations, party stuff, etcetera in the space where their parents had hung their clothes. Earlier, while preparing for the party, they had gone through the closets. There was still an aluminium ladder parked against the wall. Taking hold of the middle rungs, Alice spread it out beside one closet.

'I'll get the cups,' she said. 'Then I'm going in the water. I don't care what you say.'

'Who'll greet the guests? Not me.'

'Most of the guests are here. A lot of them are already leaving.'

Polly moved closer, stepping in front of the lamp, casting a shadow over her sister. 'Somebody is not here yet.'

Alice paused halfway up the ladder. 'He's not coming,' she said.

'He said he was when he called this afternoon. That's what he told me.' She took another step closer, put her hand out to support the ladder. It was old, unsteady. 'Why did you tell him about the party?'

'I didn't.'

'Then how did he find out about it?'

'I don't know.'

'I don't believe you.'

Alice closed her eyes briefly, leaning her head back, taking a deep breath. Her doctor had taught her that, just breathe and blow your troubles away. A bunch of hogwash. 'I told you, I'm not seeing him any more. I didn't tell him about the party. He must have heard about it from someone else. Jessica, or Sara maybe.'

'Neither of them has even met Clark.'

'He could have called when they were helping us get ready this morning. One of them could have answered the phone.'

'Did they say that?'

Alice shook her head, went up another step. 'Leave me alone.'

'You want me to let go of the ladder? If I do, you'll fall and break your neck. Anyway, why are you suddenly down on Clark? What did he do?'

Alice opened the closet, pulled out a mass of tangled Christmas tree lights. 'Nothing.'

'Did he say something about me?'

'No. What would he say about you?'

'Oh, excuse me, I guess you've forgotten I used to go out with him.'

Alice tried pushing the lights aside, trying to get to the brown box that held the paper cups. The Christmas lights kept tangling in her hands. 'I know who told him about the party,' she said softly.

'Who?'

'You.'

Polly let go of the ladder, chuckled. 'What?'

Alice glared at her. 'Admit it, you wanted him to come tonight. I've broken up with him, and you want to see if you can get him back. Well, he's not coming. I called him not three hours ago and told him he wasn't welcome.'

'Why, you little—'

'Listen to me, Polly! Stay away from him. He doesn't just have weird ideas, he does weird stuff. He's dangerous.'

Polly found herself trembling. How dare her sister, her *baby* sister, talk to her this way! Such filthy lies! Yet she didn't yell at her. The top of a ladder was no place to fight. There could be an accident, somebody might get hurt. She knew about that sort of thing. She tried to calm herself.

Besides, she was – *curious*. 'What sort of weird stuff?' she asked.

Shaking her head, Alice climbed down. 'I'm going. Goodbye.'

She opened the door. 'What about the cups?' Polly cried.

'I'll get them later,' Alice called over her shoulder, slamming the door behind her. Polly stood for a moment staring at the bright bulb, even though it hurt her eyes and made her headache worse. She hadn't invited Clark. Why would Alice say that? She was pretty sure she hadn't invited him. And she had a good memory for such things.

Polly resolved not to get the cups no matter who complained. Alice had said she would take care of it, and Alice had to learn to be responsible. But while the ladder was out, she figured she might as well change the overhead bulb. The lamp didn't go on when you threw the switch by the door. She didn't want someone looking for the bathroom stumbling and breaking a leg.

Polly found a package of 100-watt bulbs beside the Christmas lights. Holding the replacements in one hand, she scooted the ladder to the centre of the room with the other. Climbing the ladder, she reached around the shade and began to fiddle with the old bulb. She couldn't see it but she could feel it, dusty and delicate beneath her damp fingers.

All of a sudden, she realised exactly how wet her hands were.

Russ must have spilled some beer on me or something.

The light switch beside the door remained in the on position. The bulb couldn't have been completely dead. As she turned it counterclockwise, it flickered on. Liquid and light bulbs make poor companions. It exploded in her hand, and her fingers slipped directly into the charged socket.

The electric shock shot through the length of Polly's body. Her footing vanished beneath her. She had no chance to brace herself for the fall. She hit the floor on her right hip, hard, the impact sending a jolt through her spine and into her skull. Her headache blossomed from a minor irritation into a red wave of agony.

Then everything turned dark and cool, for how long she wasn't sure. When she opened her eyes next, the ceiling looked miles away. She sat up, shook herself. The fingers of her right hand were bleeding. She slowly got to her feet, using the wall for support. Glass from the shattered bulb lay scattered across the hard wooden floor.

Lord, I could have electrocuted myself.

She needed a bandage for her hand. She could fix the bulb another time. Clark might show up any moment. She did remember now; she had told him to come over late, after most of the people were gone. That didn't excuse Alice's insolence, though, not by any means. She would have to have a word with her about being respectful, for her own good.

Bill Skater didn't talk much. Jessica had always been attracted to the strong, silent type. Like Michael, she had discovered Bill to be an excellent listener. She did wish, however, that he would occasionally volunteer something. Hanging out with him, she often felt as if she were playing bounce with a flat ball.

The Rock, on the other hand, enjoyed talking, and surprisingly, had much of interest to say. He was telling her about the work he did with disadvantaged kids downtown. He had a loud, boisterous voice, and a childish enthusiasm she found appealing. In many ways he was like one of the kids he helped. She and Bill were drinking beer, but The Rock had ten minutes ago recoiled from her offer of one as if she had suggested a deadly shot of heroin. He quickly reassured her that he had nothing against her drinking, it just wasn't his style.

'We have it so easy in this part of town,' The Rock said. 'We have the ocean to swim in, the beach to run along. Everything's clean: the stores, the pavements. But in the ghettos, those kids have nothing but asphalt, plugged sewers and drugs. There're dealers everywhere. Crack's the big thing these days, that hard cocaine people smoke.' He shook his head in disgust. 'Just last week I was approached by a twelve-year-old kid trying to sell me the stuff.'

'How did you get involved in the Big Brother Programme?' Jessica asked. He had such obvious sympathy for black kids, she wondered how the feud between him and Nick had ever started. She didn't have the nerve to ask.

'I had to pick up a pal at the L.A. bus station. You know where that is, right in the heart of the city? There was this black kid – found out later he was only eight – bumming change at the entrance. He hit me up for a nickel. Imagine, just a nickel! I asked him what he wanted it for. He told me food. I took hold of his arm. It felt like a chicken bone.'

The Rock went on to describe how he took him for a sandwich and learned how the boy slept in a garbage dump. He discovered there were dozens of kids like him all over the city, that they had no parents, no one to help them. His conscience called. He became a Big Brother. To this day, he regularly saw that first boy – Emmanuel.

Then The Rock switched the topic to football, and almost immediately Jessica found her mind wandering, back to the previous Monday morning when Bill had approached her after Mr Bark's political science class. That morning she'd had to read a paper on why she thought the electoral college system should be abolished. Mr Bark had given her an A on the piece. She had spent three hours researching the paper in the library the previous day. Bill had wanted to compliment her on a job well done. Those were, in fact, his exact words. She had blushed.

'Thank you. But to tell you the truth, I didn't understand half of what I was saying.'

'I thought you were very clear,' he said. He had an unusually smooth complexion. The blue of his eyes reminded her of the Mediterranean skies of her vacation. 'What was your name?'

'Jessie.'

'That's right.' They talked for a few minutes about purely inconsequential matters: the weather, the state of the union. Finally the question came. 'What are you doing for lunch, Jessie?'

Life was good. Her legs felt weak. She told him she was free.

He took her for Chinese food in the mall. She had fun. Well, she had fun looking at him. They didn't exactly enjoy an instant rapport. Possibly because the team was doing badly, but he wouldn't even discuss football. She still didn't know what his interests were. Since Sara had told her how assertive he could be during student council meetings, she found his shyness confusing. Over lunch, and at other times in the week, he often seemed uncomfortable in her presence. She decided she would have to give it time. She had already made up her mind about one thing. She wanted to have sex with him.

A girl is always supposed to remember her first. Why shouldn't I start with the best?

Jessica was tired of day dreaming about making love. She had been doing that since she was in the seventh grade. It left her feeling unsatisfied, to say the least. It left her frustrated. She wanted the real thing, and she wasn't going to wait till she got married. It wasn't only because she was horny, she was just incredibly curious to see what it was like. When Bill finally asked her out on a real date, if he made a move, she had already decided she wasn't going to stop him. She couldn't wait to see the rest of that hard body. She was already investigating types of contraceptives.

Her decision surprised even her. A year earlier it would have been unimaginable. She had always considered herself fairly moral. For instance, her cheating on the chemistry quiz still bothered her. But her outlook had grown far more liberal in the last year, largely because of her European vacation. When she had first arrived on the beaches of southern France, and seen people nude sunbathing, it had been a shock. But by the end of the week – when her parents weren't around, of course – she had joined the crowd.

But there was still that big question – *when* Bill asked her out. When was that going to be? Clair had to be the reason for the delay. Jessica had never spoken to him when she was around. The one time she had broached the topic of his involvement with her, he had changed the subject.

The Rock wrapped up a story about some opposing lineman whose knee he had cracked in a dozen places and went off to change into his swimming trunks. Left alone with Bill, Jessica racked her brain for something to talk about. Bill continued to sip his beer, watching things go on about him. Suddenly Clair swept back into the room in an unfastened beach cover-up and red bikini. In a cheerleader uniform, Clair projected a certain sex appeal. In this reasonable excuse for total nudity, she looked positively nasty. All legs, chest – enough clear brown flesh to exhaust any red-blooded American boy's fantasy reserve. Bill started to stand up. Clair grabbed his hands and pulled him into her arms.

'Let's go big boy,' she said. 'Time to get wet.' She glanced up. 'Time to get down.'

'All right, I'll be there in a minute.'

Clair grinned and asked what on the surface appeared to be a redundant question. 'In the pool?'

'Yeah,' Bill said.

She patted his rump. 'OK, OK, the water first. Hurry.' And completely ignoring Jessica, she turned and left.

'Did you want to go swimming?' Bill asked uneasily, setting down his beer.

Why buy contraceptives when I might be able to borrow Clair's?

She had bought a new bathing suit for the party. To compete with Clair, however, she should have purchased breast implants. She smiled, although it hurt to do so. She wouldn't ask what the deal was, not yet. 'Another time, maybe,' she said.

228

Alone, she started to search for Michael. She'd seen him come in. She just wanted someone to talk to.

Summer had come to an end. Feeling the chill of the night-time air as he huddled his shoulders beneath the warm water and fluffy bubbles, Michael felt autumn inside. He always mourned the summer's passing and instantly began waiting for it to return. Somehow, this year, he could tell, it was going to be a long wait. He continued to think of Jessica and Bill together on the couch.

'Marco!' Bubba called, paddling through a bank of foam in the deep end, his eyes tightly clenched, playing the blindman in the oldest pool game ever invented.

'Polo!' three dozen people replied. Marco Polo in a pool as crowded as this was a joke. You just had to launch yourself in practically any direction and you were bound to tag somebody. Naturally, Bubba had been *it* for the last twenty minutes. Michael suspected he was slyly opening his eyes so he could stay *it* until he could accidentally rip the top off a girl of his own choosing.

'Marco!'

Maria and Nick swam to Michael's side. 'You two look like you're having fun,' he said.

'The water feels great after working all day,' Nick agreed.

'I think we should get out,' Maria said, glancing towards the diving board where several of the football players had gathered to taunt Bubba into coming their way.

'You might,' Michael said.

Nick shook his head. 'I feel just fine where I am. Anyway, what can they do to me in front of all these people?'

'They could drown you,' Maria said unhappily.

The boys on the team did not try to drown Nick. But they did pull a rather unpleasant stunt. Much to Bubba's obvious displeasure, he bumped into The Rock, and was no longer *it*. As the centre of attention, The Rock, with supposedly closed eyes, wasted no time in heading straight for Nick, who made the mistake of moving away from the side of the pool. Several guys on the team suddenly popped to the surface behind Nick. He saw them at the same time Michael did. It did neither of them any good. One grabbed Nick's right arm, the other his left. His head got pushed under and The Rock went diving.

They all reappeared a few seconds later, with Nick thrashing wildly and The Rock laughing heartily. The Rock had torn off Nick's trunks.

'Come get me, boy,' he taunted, moving into the shallow end where Nick would have to stay low – *real* low – if he didn't want to be the talk of the school on Monday. Yet Michael felt more afraid for The Rock than he did for his friend. The guys who had pinned Nick's arms seemed to have reassessed Nick's strength in the short time they'd had a hold of him. They backed off, gingerly rubbing their sides, as the other guys on the team watched from a respectful distance. For the moment Nick had The Rock to himself, and Michael could not have imagined such fury in Nick's face. It was out of a similar expression the many ugly rumours concerning his deadly rage must have sprung.

But Nick couldn't move, except on his knees. Bubba clearly recognised the problem, and Bubba loved to watch a good fight.

'Hey, Nick!' he called from the deep end, his hands out of sight beneath the water and bubbles. 'Take these!'

He didn't toss him a sword or a knife. Bubba threw Nick a pair of trunks – *his* own shorts. Nick caught them, put them on. The Rock backed into the side of the shallow end, stopped his taunting. Nowhere to go.

'Hey,' he said.

Nick launched himself at The Rock, who had decided a fraction of a second too late that the water was not a safe place to be. Nick caught The Rock by the right arm and the back of the neck just as The Rock put one foot on the deck. The Rock started a cry that ended in a strangled gargle. Nick had shoved him under. The festive atmosphere hushed into a tense silence. It was a struggle for Nick – The Rock's feet and hands kept thrashing to the surface but it was clear he could hold his prey's head under as long as he pleased.

'Stop!' Maria cried.

'No,' Nick said.

'You'll kill him!' she pleaded.

'Yeah!' Bubba cheered.

Nick smiled grimly, tightening his grip. 'Not yet.'

Maria dived towards Nick and pounded him on the back. 'Let him go now!'

Nick looked at her strangely for a moment. Then he held his hands up, as if he were displaying his innocence. The Rock broke the surface, his choking gasps material for pity. He lay bent over the steps, sobbing in recovery.

'We can't do this,' Maria said wearily. She could have been talking about more than The Rock's dunking.

'He started it,' Nick protested. Maria shook her head sadly. To her, it didn't matter.

Michael watched the next few minutes with a calm fascination. To a casual spectator, the hostilities appeared to be over. The usual chatter resumed across the pool. Yet Michael knew they had merely passed into the eye of the hurricane. Worried about Maria's feelings, Nick paid little heed to the movement of people around him. The Rock was making a swift recovery. He had moved from the steps and was now sitting on the side near the diving board. One by one, his teammates, including Bill Skater, swam to his dangling feet, conferring with him.

'Nick,' Michael said. 'Nick.'

His friend didn't hear, preoccupied as he was with convincing Maria that he hadn't intended to drown the fat slob. Perhaps it didn't matter, Michael thought. Help was on the way. Seconds before The Rock jumped Nick, Alice had been testing the pool's chlorine level. When they had a lot of people in the water, Alice had said, the level could drop rapidly. When The Rock had attacked Nick, Alice had dashed into the house, the pail of powdered chlorine in her hand. Now she reappeared with her sister holding the chlorine, just as The Rock entered the water with eleven backups – and began to swim towards Nick.

'Nick!' Michael shouted.

He said violence follows him, no matter where he goes. In the streets, the weight room, the store, the pool . . . Could he be right?

It didn't take long for a person, or a dozen for that matter, to swim the length of the pool. It took Polly about the same interval to stride from her back door to the steps of the pool. When Nick finally did look up, he found himself surrounded by friends and foes alike.

'Get out of the water, all of you,' Polly said.

'Sure,' The Rock said, a purple welt swelling beneath his left eye. 'After we take care of business.'

Nick flexed his shoulders, the water reaching to his waist, shooing a terrified Maria aside. 'Don't keep me waiting,' he said to The Rock.

'My man!' Bubba shouted, off in the corner with Clair. He would be pulling off the bottom of her red bikini next and offering it to Bill. Tabb's quarterback, another upstanding member of the lynch gang, waited expressionless by The Rock's side. Michael edged towards Nick. If he had to fight to save his pal, he decided it wouldn't be bad to get in a stiff kick to Bill's crotch.

After all, the guy stole my girl.

What a laugh. He would probably get his head smashed in, and yet, he was pleasantly surprised to discover he wasn't afraid.

'You better pray you were born with gills, boy,' The Rock said, glancing around to assure himself of his support. Nick did not move, but Michael could literally see the dark strength coiling in his muscles.

'No!' Maria cried.

'Get off my property!' Polly shouted at The Rock, jumping on to the first step, the water drenching the bottom of her black trousers. She stuck a hand into the pail of chlorine. 'Get!'

'Sod off,' The Rock said, raising his fist, intent on Nick.

Polly threw a handful of chlorine in his face. Unfortunately for The Rock, he was soaked. The white powder dissolved instantly. The Rock let out a scream, his hands flying to his eyes. Michael grimaced. Chlorine solution could eat out eyes in seconds.

'Put your head under the water!' Michael said. 'Get his head under!'

Bill tried to do just that. The Rock jabbed an elbow into Bill's jaw. *Don't you touch me.* Understandably, The Rock was not crazy about having someone submerge him again. He just kept screaming.

'My eyes! My eyes!'

Michael dived forward, grabbed The Rock's wrists. 'Go under water – now – and blink your eyes or go blind!' he yelled in his ear. The Rock nodded once, thrust his head beneath the surface. He came up a few seconds later.

'My eyes!'

'More,' Michael ordered, pushing him down. 'Stay under a whole minute. Flush them out.'

While he was submerged this time, Polly muttered something under her breath, dropped the pail on the ground, and strode back into the house. The others waited quietly. Alice entered the water to stand beside Michael. Finally The Rock reappeared.

'How are they?' Michael asked. 'Let me see.'

'They sting. They hurt.'

And they were a nasty red. 'But you can see,' Michael said. 'Go inside, into the bathroom, and take a shower. Let the cold water run straight into them for a few minutes, but not too hard. Keep your hands away from them. Then get dressed and have someone drive you to the hospital.' Michael patted him on the back. 'Go ahead, you're going to be all right.'

The Rock did not look at Nick as he left. Maybe it hurt too much. The boys on the team dispersed. It seemed to be over, for the time being.

The night deepened. The suds began to vanish. In groups of twos and threes, people got out of the water. Bubba finally gave up his carousing with Clair and consented to wear a towel on the walk to the house. And Nick and Maria were long gone when Michael began to slowly swim laps, on his back, staring at the black sky, wondering if Jessica was inside with Bill hearing about how the tall black dude had tried to kill The Rock for a second time.

Michael was alone with Alice and she was flying through space, like an acrobat, maybe an angel, in her white bathing suit and shining yellow hair, performing dive after dive.

'Watch this one!' she called, jumping on to the board again.

Michael rolled on to his side. Lithe but co-ordinated, Alice stepped forward, pounced the board's tip, soared upwards, gracefully spinning through two and a half somersaults. She disappeared head-first into the water with the faintest splash. Michael waited for her to resurface, ready to applaud her effort. *One . . . two . . . three . . .* Time passed so slowly when someone went under and didn't come up.

'Alice?' he said.

'Eeeh!' She laughed, popping up behind him, throwing her arms round his neck. 'Scared you?'

'Yeah, fish brain.' He grabbed her and threw her over his head as if she were made of air.

They got out a while later. From the positions of the stars, Michael knew it must be near midnight. The music continued inside but at a lower volume. No one seemed to be dancing. He could hear few people talking. Handing him a towel, Alice led him around the side of the house to the spot where she had been painting last week. They'd set up a couple of barbecues earlier that needed extinguishing, she explained.

'Do you think Polly damaged that boy's eyes?' she asked, slowly raking the smouldering coals with a black metal stick. She didn't have what most people would call striking features, but at that moment, the burning orange light warm on her young face, she was, to Michael, a child of beauty.

'No. Very little of the chlorine got in his eyes. He's a baby, cries a lot. Don't worry, he'll be fine.'

Alice smiled, not like an angel really, more like a mischievous devil. 'I told you I wanted to talk to you. Do you know what about?'

'What?'

'Jessie.'

'Oh?'

Alice stopped, watching him over the heat radiating from the flaked charcoal. The front of his body was burning, but goose flesh was forming on his back from a breeze that had begun to blow out of the east. He hugged his towel tighter. The tall silhouette of a two-armed cactus stood behind Alice in the garden like a prickly ghost.

'You knew she was the one I told you about,' she said.

'Not at first. Not until the football game.'

'Why didn't you tell me, after that?'

There was no accusation in her voice, simply curiosity. 'Why didn't you tell her when you found out we were going out?' he said.

Alice nodded, as if to say 'well answered'. 'Neither of us told her. What a coincidence. Or do you think the decision passed unspoken between us?' Before he could respond, she continued, 'Yeah, I think so. But I was still disappointed I didn't get to introduce you two, that you found each other without me.'

'Why?'

Alice returned to scattering the ashes. 'Jessie's always taken care of me. When my parents died, and Polly was in the hospital, she became like another sister to me. No, more like a new mom. I don't think I would have survived without her. And then, when I met you at Christmas, I felt like I had found – Does this sound corny?'

'Not at all, Alice.'

She smiled shyly. 'I love you, Michael. You know that. You've always been like the other half for me. Jessie and you – I had this dream for a long time. I was saving each of you for the other, for the right time. Then when our schools got put together, I knew that time had come. Do you understand what I mean? Maybe it was selfish, but I thought that you would come together through me, and then – then it would be beautiful.' Alice stopped. 'You love her, don't you?'

'I hardly know her.'

'But you still love her. I can see that. Don't worry, no one else can. I knew you'd love her.' She lowered her head, suddenly frowned. 'I hope everything will be all right.'

He chuckled. 'Everything's going to be fine. Why wouldn't it be?' He was glad she had not asked him to verify the truth of her statement. Her certainty, her insight, intrigued him, frightened him. She didn't even care how their date had gone. It was immaterial to her, or rather, it was simply material, and she was talking about something bordering on a spiritual bond. She stood on an edge where she could see in directions others couldn't. He'd known that from their first meeting, and it had drawn him to her. But how fine an edge? He worried for her.

'Because I wasn't there,' she said, vaguely confused. 'And in my dream, I was always there.'

'When Jessie and I met?'

'Yes.' She shook herself. 'I probably dream too much. That's what my doctor says.' She glanced up to the dimly lit second storey window above them. 'That used to be my parents' bedroom. Polly cleaned it out a

240

few years ago. Gave away all the furniture.'

'You must miss them a lot.'

She laughed suddenly. 'That's what I'm trying to tell you. I don't! When I'm awake, I have you two wonderful friends, and then, when I sleep, I walk in the forest with my mom and dad. I honestly do.' A spark flared between them, distracting her. She wrinkled her nose at the black and burning cinders. 'This is something Clark would paint. Looks like hell. But then, he's a weird guy.' She set aside her stick and slowly moved her hand inches above the centre of the barbecue.

'Careful, you'll burn yourself.'

'I'm wet, I can't get hurt.'

He had doubts about that. He wished she would stop. Who was this doctor she had mentioned? 'Tell me about your dreams?'

She nodded at his question. 'I bet you dream, too.'

'I do.'

'I knew it. I'll have to show mine. We can compare them. I'm going to finish my painting tonight.'

'Tonight? You should go to bed.'

She took her hand back. If she had burned it, she would never show it. He pushed aside his concern. She was sensitive – true, but also strong. 'I'm not tired,' she said. She glanced up at the window again. 'I'd better go in. This charcoal can burn itself out. I just remembered, I promised Polly I'd get out some paper cups.'

'But practically everyone's left.'

She stepped around the barbecue, took his hand in her warm one, and led him towards the back door. 'With Polly, it doesn't matter.' She laughed. 'Let's finish our talk later.'

All in all, Nick thought, it had been an eventful evening. He'd had a invigorating swim, been in a messy fight and had received the first kiss of his life from a girl only a few minutes after he believed he had lost her for ever. Sitting on the couch in the living room with Maria and Michael, listening to a Beatles album on the stereo, he was glad things had finally slowed down. He didn't wish to disturb his present feeling of contentment – it had cost him too much to achieve.

'It's lucky my parents think I'm asleep in bed at Jessie's house right now,' Maria said, nodding towards the polished brass clock on the wall as it struck one o'clock. 'At home, I have to be in bed by ten.'

'I haven't been in bed before ten since I was ten.' Michael yawned, leaning back into the soft deep cushions. He'd dressed, but his hair was still wet from his swim. 'I could go to sleep right here. Let's head out in a few minutes, Nick.'

'We can leave now if you'd like.'

'A few minutes. Where's Bubba?'

'I don't know.' For the moment the three of them had the living room to themselves. They had, in fact, only the foggiest idea who was left in the house. Nick had seen Clair and Bill not long ago, heading up the stairs, and Kats wandering around the kitchen searching for a knife. That was it.

Even with the music on, the house *felt* oddly still. Despite Nick's feeling of peace and contentment the sensation was not pleasant. Late at night on the streets, in the worst parts of town, it often felt quiet like this.

'I'm glad I won't have to keep lying to my parents,' Maria said. His reaction to The Rock's attack had terrified her as much as the attack itself. When they had got out of the pool, she wouldn't even talk to him. He'd feared that she thought he might one day go off the deep end and throw her around. But then, after she had changed into her clothes, her viewpoint shifted completely. The initial shock must have worn off. She told him how brave he had been. Then she had kissed him, briefly, but on the lips.

'What do you mean?' he asked.

'You're going to meet them,' she said.

'Your parents? I thought that was out of the question?'

She wouldn't explain. 'You're going to meet them,' she repeated, leaning closer towards him.

Sara and Jessica entered the living room from the direction of the games room. Michael sat up suddenly. None of them had seen Sara all night. Maybe she had only recently arrived.

'Why is the music so loud?' Sara demanded.

'Someone must have turned it up,' Jessica said. She sat in a chair at Michael's end of the couch. 'I was beginning to think you were going to stay in that pool all night,' she said.

Michael nodded. 'I might have overdone it. My eyes are sore from the chlorine.'

'They can't be as bad as that jock's in the garage,' Sara said, turning down the stereo volume. 'That Polly had a lot of nerve.'

'The Rock's here?' Michael asked, surprised. 'Didn't he go to the hospital?'

'He came back,' Jessica said.

Michael frowned. 'Why?'

Jessica shrugged, looking tired. 'Who knows?'

Wonderful, Nick thought.

Polly came into the room at that instant. Like Jessica, she seemed worn out, only more so. She wandered over to the record player. 'I'm turning this off,' she muttered. 'My head hurts.'

'Polly, where's Alice?' Michael asked.

Polly shook her head, trudged towards the back door. 'I don't know where no one is.' She pulled at the screen. 'I've got to check on the chlorine level.'

'Leave it until tomorrow,' Jessica said.

Polly paid no attention to her, going outside, shutting both the screen and the thick sliding glass door behind her. Nick watched as she walked over to the water and picked up the small, blue chemical test box and pail of white powder she had used to stop The Rock. He had meant to thank her for coming to his rescue. Perhaps he'd do it when she returned – and when he came back from the bathroom. He had been scrupulously avoiding anything alcoholic. He didn't want Maria knowing he had any bad habits. But he had been putting away the soft drinks. His bladder was full. He got up.

'Where's the bathroom?' he asked.

'There's one off the games room,' Sara said. 'But I think someone's in there right now throwing up.'

'Go upstairs,' Jessica said. 'Polly won't mind. There's one halfway down the hallway before you come to the turn. If that's being used, try one of the bathrooms in the bedrooms.'

And so Nick started a walk he would for the remainder of the school year replay again and again in his mind, searching for a clue, for a reason for the horror that came upon them all at the end of Alice's party.

The stairway lay near the front door, close to the kitchen. Putting his foot on the first step, he heard a low moan off to his right. He paused, stretching his head around the tall potted plant that stood between him and the sound. It was Bill Skater, bent over the kitchen sink, his shirt rumpled, his face pale, as if he were about to be sick. Nick wondered if he should go to him, but then he remembered Bill beside The Rock in the pool. He continued on up the stairs.

He probably drank too much.

In the first stretch of the hall there were four doors, three on the left, one in the middle on the right. Jessica had specified the bathroom was in the middle, but had not said on which side. He didn't want to barge in on someone sleeping. He decided to skip the first door on the left, but tried the second door, finding it locked. He thought he heard water running inside. Chances were this was the bathroom Jessica had referred to. Yet he couldn't be sure. The sound could be coming from the last door on the left, or even from the one room on the right. It disturbed him that he couldn't narrow it down more specifically. The harder he listened, the more the faint gurgling seemed to spring from all around him. Of course that often happened with a faint noise in a quiet place. He could not hear the others downstairs.

He tried the lone door on the right. It opened easily, silently; a whiff of night air brushed his bare arms and face. The door led to an elevated porch that overlooked the pool. A dark figure stood alone at the edge of the square space, staring up at the sky, his booted foot resting on the roof's wooden shingles, which went right to the floor of the porch. A blue glow from the lighted waters below danced over his rough leather jacket.

Kats.

Nick closed the door carefully, confident the quirky gas station attendant didn't know he had been there. He moved to the third door on the left.

It was also locked, and had faint stirring going on within. Nick did not intend to be nosy, but he stood long enough and close enough to the door to pick up on the sounds of breathing, of shifting bedsprings. He heard a cough, a sigh, enough, he decided, to keep him from knocking. He walked on, making a right at the turn in the hall.

This part of the hallway presented him with a choice of two doors, both on the left. The first was locked. He almost knocked. There were people inside; he could hear them. What stopped him was a sound of soft groaning. He or she or they – Nick couldn't be sure – seemed to be in pain. Nick thought of Bill downstairs. He wondered if there was a connection. Guilt pricked his conscience. What if someone was hurt, or being hurt?

Yet he walked on. He did not belong in a house this big, with its plush furniture and high-beamed ceilings. He was an outsider still, though for the moment things were going well, with his job and school, with Maria. He didn't want to mess up again. He didn't want to walk in on another fight.

Reasons. Excuses.

His guilt chased him into the final room at the end of the hall. Its door lay wide open, an invitation into a dark place. Nick reached inside without actually stepping through the doorway, found the light switch turned up. He flicked it down, then up again. The darkness remained. He glanced back the way he had come, uncertain what to do. The last light in the hall was around the corner. At the moment it was of little help.

Come on, after what you've been through, you can't be afraid of the dark.

Yet that was precisely the source of his hesitation. He did not trust the dark. It robbed him of his keenest sense, his first line of defence, and if The Rock really had returned to the party, as Sara suggested, maybe he was waiting inside this room with God knew how many of his buddies, waiting eagerly to pay Nick back for a near drowning and a pair of burned eyes.

At the last moment Nick almost turned and walked away. The reason he didn't was purely physical. Testing every upstairs door had consumed time. Now he either had to get to a place to pee immediately or he was going to have to run outside and find a bush. The Rock was only a possibility – his discomfort, a certainty. He stepped into the room.

It appeared empty, although he couldn't be sure. The illumination through the open windows – they faced east, away from the pool – couldn't have been more meagre. Yet the draught pouring in from the outside sent a chill through him. Polly and Alice must love the fresh air.

His eyes adjusted to the gloom. He noted the outline of another set of windows on the right wall, their shades down, and a second doorway off to the left, with a tiny room beyond. He felt his way forward. Inside the small room, his fingers found another light switch. Yet he chose to leave this one off. He had definitely reached a bathroom; he could see the outline of the sink and the toilet. If he put on the light he'd only startle his eyes, and then he'd have to exit into the dark room completely blind.

Nick moved inside, closed the door. He took care of business quickly, flushed the toilet and reopened the door. He was still in the bedroom, heading for the hall, when he suddenly paused in midstride.

Tommy?

That ominous silence he had noticed downstairs struck him again, only stronger this time. His head felt strangely full. He wondered for a moment if he hadn't accidentally drunk something alcoholic after all, even though he knew his uneasiness had nothing to do with booze.

My blood brother.

A seed of fear began to form deep in his mind. The feeling of *heaviness*, inside and out, was not entirely new to him. He had experienced it once before, two years earlier. But that had been in the middle of the night in a dark alleyway after a gang fight that had bought his best friend a switchblade through the heart. Later, he had come to understand he must have gone into shock lifting Tommy's head with its blank and staring eyes off the ground, watching the lifeless blood form a dark pool on the dirty asphalt beneath them.

He had not thought of Tommy since he had moved to this new neighbourhood. Why now? He did not know. He did not care. He just wanted to get out of the room, back to the others. The breeze coming in through the wide open windows was giving him the shakes.

Nick strode into and down the hallway. He didn't pause at any of the doors along the way.

He had reached the top of the stairs when the shot exploded in his ears.

No. Lord, please, no.

He froze, the bang resounding throughout the house. For several incomprehensible seconds, he did not move an inch. Then he bolted blindly down the stairs, colliding with Maria on the landing between the two flights, knocking her down. Picking her up, he noticed her eyes were as wide as saucers.

'What?' she gasped, trembling in his arms.

'A gunshot,' he said.

She nodded tensely, her eyes going past him, back the way he had come. 'Up there,' she whispered.

'Stay here,' he ordered, turning away from her. She grabbed his arm roughly.

'I'm coming, Nick.'

At the sound of the gunshot, Michael did not jump up or let out a shout. Instead, he closed his eyes for a couple of seconds. He did not think of who had died, who it might be, only that someone had died. He knew it to be true

251

with a certainty that went beyond reason. He felt *death* in the house. He felt sick.

When he did look up, Sara and Jessica were already on their feet, holding on to each other. A moment later the back sliding glass door flew open. Polly stood staring at the three of them for a second, her face as white and cold as fresh snow, then flashed by them towards the stairs. Yet Michael was the first to reach the top of the stairs. A gun that had fired once could fire twice. For a moment he tried to hold the girls back. He was wasting his time. They had to see, all of them, no matter how bad it was. They heard Nick's voice around the corner. In a tight fearful knot, they stumbled down the first hallway and turned right. Maria and Nick stood outside the last door on the left, peering in at the dark. Michael came up beside Nick, felt for the bedroom light switch.

'It doesn't work,' Nick said.

'Is anyone in there?' Sara asked them.

'There's a lamp in the corner of the room,' Jessica said. She stepped forward. 'I'll turn it on.'

Michael grabbed her arm, stopped her. 'No, all of you, stay here. I'll get it.'

The room was big. He could feel its size although he could not clearly see. He could feel a cold breeze in his face, the blood in his heart. It was cold, too, the blood,

252

and it felt as if it cracked – like ice – when his foot bumped into a soft heap on the floor. A body, a dead body. Michael could smell the blood.

Nick moved up behind him. Nick's eyes were sharper in the dark than Michael's. He noticed the body on the floor before walking into it. He knelt down beside it as Michael was stepping over it.

It. Not her. It. A nothing.

Michael knew who it was before he turned on the light. Why did he turn on the light? Why did he know who it was? The bulb drenched his eyes with harsh whiteness. He closed them again, for a moment, and counted to himself as he had while waiting for Alice to come up from her dive into the pool. He noticed that there was no carpet in the room. They had carpet in the garage, but not here. Nothing soft to land on like the water. He turned and faced the others.

Statues. Tragic sculptures. Four girls: Maria, Sara, Polly and Jessica – they all looked the same. Kats came up behind them. He looked different. Somehow uglier than usual. He was moving, that was it. All wired up and jittery. Michael did not want to move. He did not want to look down. But he did.

Alice.

Lying flat on her back. Gun in her mouth. Her lips

resting around the barrel. Nick took it out gently. Her lips closed, matching her closed eyes. She looked peaceful. Then a drop of blood appeared at the left corner of her mouth, trailed over the side of her face, plopping in her bright yellow hair. It was still wet, her hair. The drop of blood spread upward along the strand, trying, it seemed to Michael, to get back to her head, back inside.

There was something wrong.

Drop after drop began to trail out of the corner of her mouth. And each one splashed into her hair and spread upward, downward, wherever it found a path. Yet the hair at the back of her head was already soaked red. A thousand drops had already come and gone before they had entered the room. She lay in a pool of red. The reason was very simple.

She had a hole in the back of her head.

'She's dead,' Nick said, looking up at him. The gun in his hand and the quiet anguish in his voice hurt Michael almost as much as the sight of the blood. He stepped around Alice and stood close to the girls. Out of the corner of his eye, he saw Polly faint, Sara catch her. The others appeared, Bill, Bubba, Clair and The Rock – in that order. And he felt Jessica holding on to him, her face buried in his shoulder, the warmth of her tears seeping through his shirt.

'*I hope everything will be all right.*'

Michael didn't know these people. He didn't care about these people. Suddenly he saw and felt nothing that had to do with any of them. There were only the stars that had shone above him while he had swum on his back in the pool, the surprise touch of Alice's wet arms that had wrapped around his neck when he had begun to fear for her well-being.

'*I love you, Michael. You know that . . .*'

The yellow hair, the red blood, the repose of her sweet face – they all blurred into one ghostly form and began to move upwards towards the stars, faster and faster. He chased after her, as best he could, but her arms began to slip away. The spirit began to fade, to fail. The stars went out.

She had put on the veil of his dream. She was gone.

EPILOGUE

The funeral for fifteen-year-old Alice McCoy was held on the Thursday following her Saturday night party, at twelve o'clock in the afternoon. The McCoy family, though rich, was not large. And despite the many friends Alice had made during her short days on earth, few came to the funeral. People mourn easily the victim, the unfortunate, but seldom the suicide. A notice in the local paper had listed the cause of death as a self-inflicted gunshot wound to the head.

Standing beside the coffin above the open grave, a yellow rose in his hand, Michael looked around and counted, including the black-robed minister, only twenty-eight people.

There should be thousands.

He was in a tunnel. There was a dim glow up ahead, twilight behind, black enveloping walls all around. He had not slept since the party, nor had he been properly awake. Unfortunately, he wasn't in shock. He had been crying too much for that. But only when he was alone. That was how he wanted to be from now on, alone, always alone until the day he died.

He listened to the last words. Old written words – it didn't matter whether they were true or not, he thought, the lines about 'life everlasting' and 'the valley of the shadow of death'. They were still just words. It was foolhardy to believe they could bring any real comfort. They brought him none. It was ridiculous they even had funerals. He was glad when everyone began to leave.

He sat down beside the coffin, near the mound of brown dirt that would cover it. Clouds came and went overhead, and with them, the sun. He couldn't decide whether it was hot or cold. One minute he was sweating, the next, shivering. He still had his flower in his hand. He tried planting it in the dirt but it kept falling over. He couldn't imagine he was never going to see her again.

Time passed, a long time. Someone finally came up behind him. He assumed it was a grave digger, come to shoo him away. You have to go, Bud, we have to stick her in the ground now. But whoever it was said nothing, and finally Michael turned around.

'Hi, Nick,' he said. 'Were you at the funeral?' He honestly didn't know.

When Nick had come into the store that first day, he had trouble saying two words. Then he had gone out with a girl and stood off whole mobs. Now he seemed to be back where he had started. He bowed his head, mumbled his words.

'I'm sorry I was late. They just let me out of jail.'

'Lieutenant Keller let you out?'

'Yeah.'

'That jackass,' Michael muttered. 'He had no right holding you.'

'I wasn't alone.'

Michael nodded. The lieutenant had detained The Rock, Russ and Kats. Michael had spoken to Keller last night on the phone. Kats was the only one he was holding, he said, and that was only because they had discovered a number of unregistered firearms back at the hole Kats called his apartment. Keller did not feel Kats was guilty of murder. 'It was a suicide, Mike. None of those kids killed that girl. She put the gun in her mouth and pulled the trigger. Simple as that. Let it go.'

Ass.

'I want to talk to you about a few things,' Michael said. He hardly recognised the sound of his own voice. His

258

vocal chords felt as if they had been scratched with sandpaper. 'Could I see you down by the parking lot in a few minutes?'

'Sure.' Nick glanced nervously at the coffin, with its shiny azure-coloured paint and inlaid gold flowers. As far as boxes went, it was nice. But who wanted to be in a box. 'I didn't bring any flowers,' he said apologetically.

'It doesn't matter.'

Nick swallowed. 'I'll wait for you.'

When Nick left, Michael knelt by the coffin, touching it. A final goodbye, that's what he wanted to say. He thought about it a minute, but nothing came. And he knew why. She wasn't here, in this dead body. She had left that night. He had seen her leave.

Nevertheless, he suddenly wrapped his arms around the box as if he were hugging a flesh-and-blood person. He couldn't help himself. He cried as though she had just died in his arms.

Nick was sitting on the kerb, next to his bike, when Michael, calm and composed, finally descended from the rows of tombstones. Nick had bought the bike with his first – and – last pay-cheque from the store.

'I have some bad news for you,' Michael said. 'While you were in jail, you got fired. I told the bosses you had nothing to do with what happened. They didn't care.' He shrugged. 'If you'd like, I can quit in protest?'

'No, don't do that.' Nick did not seem surprised, nor did he seem to care. 'It's always been this way in the ghetto. Go in the slammer, lose it all. Everything.'

'Maria?'

Nick nodded.

'She doesn't think you did it, for God's sake?'

Nick winced, turning away. His voice came out small and hurt. 'I don't know. She won't talk to me.'

'Well, to hell with her then.' He went and sat beside Nick on the kerb. He had a bad taste in his mouth. He hadn't eaten that morning. He could taste only his bitterness.

'Did you want to ask me something?' Nick said hesitantly.

'Yeah, who killed Alice?'

That surprised him. 'I don't know.'

Michael sighed. 'I'm sorry. I know you don't know. And I'm sorry about Maria. And your job. But I'll speak to some people around town I have connections with. I'll find you another place to work.'

Nick nodded, hunched over. 'I'd appreciate that.' He paused. 'I'll tell you everything I know.'

'OK.'

Nick spoke as if he were repeating something he had

repeated endlessly at the police station. 'I got up to go to the bathroom. I saw Bill in the kitchen. He was by himself. He looked upset. I went upstairs. I passed the first door on the left. I didn't hear anybody inside. I tried the second door on the left, the bathroom. It was locked. I *thought* there was somebody inside. I heard water running. I tried the one door on the right, the door to the porch. Kats was standing out there, by himself.'

'Did he see you?'

'No.'

'Go on.'

'I tried the third door on the left. It was locked. It sounded like someone was sleeping inside. At the police station, Russ said it was him.'

'Yeah, he also said he slept right through the gun shot and all the commotion. I don't see how anybody could have done that.' He would talk to Russ himself, to all of them. 'Go on.'

'I went around the turn in the hall. There were two doors on the left. The first one was locked. But there were people inside. One of them sounded like they were crying.'

'Are you sure?'

'No. It sounded weird. I don't know what was going on in there.'

'But there was definitely more than one person in the room?'

'I'm sorry, Mike, I couldn't swear to it.'

'I understand.'

'I went to the last door. It lay wide open. The light wouldn't work. I went inside, anyway, went to the bathroom, and then came back out. That was it. I was on my way back down, at the top of the stairs, when I heard the gunshot.'

'You didn't see anyone in the room where Alice died, didn't hear anything?'

'No, but—'

'What?'

'There was something in that room.' He stopped for a moment, thinking, then he shook his head. 'I can't say.'

'Please, Nick. What did you see?'

'Nothing.'

'You must have seen something, heard something?'

'No, it – I was scared.'

'Scared? Of what?'

He shook his head again, perspiration appearing on his forehead. 'I don't know. Just something in that room scared me. It scared me bad.'

Nick had grown up in a dangerous environment. He could have developed instincts to recognise a threat, even if it was invisible. 'When you turned on the light in the bathroom, you didn't happen to notice anything behind you?'

'I didn't turn on the light. I could see enough without it.'

'That's odd.'

Nick was worried. 'The police thought so, too. They kept asking me about that. But you know, Mike, I'm telling you what I told them. I'm telling you the truth.'

'I believe you.' He thought of how often Bubba used that same line to call people a liar. Bubba had a way with words. The police hadn't arrested him. 'Could Alice have been in the room?'

'I didn't see her. The police think she could have been, waiting to, you know, waiting with the gun.'

'Or they think she could have entered the room from the bedroom next to it, right after you started back down? From the bedroom where you thought you heard someone crying?'

Nick nodded. 'They say that's probably what happened, that it was Alice I heard crying.'

A wave of disgust engulfed Michael. 'What did they say when you told them you thought you heard more than one person in that room next to the last bedroom? That you had heard wrong?'

Nick was watching him uneasily. 'Mike, they're not trying to hush anything up.'

'No! But they're not working overtime, either. They're looking for the simplest explanation. And they think they've found it. Alice put a gun in her mouth and pulled the trigger. Neat. Clean. Fill out the paperwork and close the file.'

Nick pressed his knees together, fidgeting. 'Who do you think killed her?'

'Someone! Another person. That's all. Or maybe a couple of people.' He buried his face in his hands, the tears too close. 'She was my friend, Nick. She was full of love, full of life. I know she didn't pull that trigger. I know it.'

Nick wisely didn't say anything, letting Michael be. Michael finally sat up. He could feel sorry for himself later. 'Lieutenant Keller told me last night where everyone said they were at the time of the shooting. Let me go over it again with you and see if it's any different from what you got out of him.' He held up his hand, counting off the points on his fingers. 'Bill said he was in the kitchen, having a glass of water. The Rock said he was in the upstairs bathroom, taking a shower. Kats said he was standing on the porch, looking at the stars. Bubba said he was out front with Clair, talking about the stars.' Michael clenched his fingers into a fist. 'The stars. Kats couldn't even tell you what one looked like, and Bubba and Clair . . .' He shook his head in disgust. 'Is that what Keller told you?'

'In the beginning, they separated us, got each person's story. They always do that. But this morning Keller told me exactly what you just said.'

'Did he tell you about the gun and the bullet?'

Nick nodded. 'The gun belonged to Kats. It was the same one he pulled on us in the store. Kats admitted it was his.'

'Right away? Before we identified it?'

'I don't think so.'

'What about prints? Keller told me yours, Alice's and Kats's were on the gun, but only Kats's were on the bullet shell.'

'Same thing he told me. Mike, I honestly don't think Keller's holding back on us.'

'I wonder. Did Kats have an excuse for how his gun got in Alice's hand?'

'He said he had no idea. He had it in his car, in the glove compartment. He didn't say why he brought it to the party. He's one of those strange dudes, you know, always has to have his piece handy.'

'If he was out on the second-storey porch, how come

265

he didn't get to the bedroom until after us?'

'I don't know. But he's in trouble. He didn't have a licence for the gun. Keller hasn't released him yet, and won't until someone bails him out.'

'That just breaks my heart.' Even if he hadn't pulled the trigger, if it hadn't been for Kats's weird hobby Alice would probably still be alive. Michael stood. 'Thanks for the information. Can I give you a ride anywhere? Your bike will fit in my boot, I think.'

Nick got up, too. 'No. Being cooped up these last few days – I feel like I need the exercise. What are you going to do now?'

'Go to Alice's house.'

Nick was concerned for him. 'Why?'

'To look around.'

Nick glanced in the direction of Alice's coffin, resting alone on the hill. 'She seemed like a real nice girl.'

Michael coughed painfully. 'I always thought so.' The McCoy residence, from the outside at least, had not changed: high roof, long driveway, steep front lawn – all that money and what difference did it make in the end?

The red sedan parked out front, however, was something new. Michael stopped his car beside it, got out warily. The front door opened before he could knock. The honourable Lieutenant Keller himself.

They'd met the night of the party. He was nothing to look at. Although a trim six feet two and less than forty years of age, he struck Michael as soft, someone on the physical road downhill. He didn't know how to dress. He favoured tartans but the squares on his sports jacket were much too big. He had a bald spot he tried to hide by parting his hair low and combing the thin brown strands over it; it only made his head look lopsided. And he had that greyish skin so often seen on the movie sleazeball. Michael disliked shaking his hand.

On the other hand, Michael realised, his appearance probably had nothing to do with the dislike. When Keller had arrived at the scene of the crime approximately half an hour after the shooting, he had failed to take charge. True, as Nick said, he did separate them and, along with his fellow officers, had taken down their accounts of the events. But Michael had watched him the whole time, and he never saw the sharp eye, the attention to detail he would expect from a good detective. Also, the lieutenant had appeared to decide right from the start what had happened. To Michael, that showed an unforgivable lack of professionalism.

Yet it would be unfair to discard his positive qualities. He had proven himself sensitive to the stress they were under. He had personally taken it upon himself to make sure Polly was immediately given over into the hands of a psychiatrist who specialised in the care of victims of emotional trauma. He was not a bad man.

He's just not Sherlock Holmes. Or his distant cousin.

They said hello and shook hands. He asked how the funeral had gone.

'Fine, I guess.' Michael shrugged. 'I haven't really been to a lot of funerals.' He nodded at the yellow ribbon in Keller's hands. 'What's that from?'

'The doorway to the bedroom. We'd placed it off limits until our investigation was complete.'

Michael found the remark ironic. Polly's aunt was staying with a cousin, and Polly was sedated in the hospital. Off limits to whom? His bitterness refused to stay down. 'So now you can go home early, I suppose?'

The lieutenant looked disappointed. 'Everyone keeps telling me what a sharp kid you are, Mike. They say you could be a genius. Think about it for a minute, the whole situation. Then tell me what you'd like me to do. Go ahead, do it.'

'I don't need a minute to know you shouldn't have told the papers it was a suicide. Why didn't you at least say she'd died from an accidental gunshot?'

Keller sighed. 'Mike, she had the gun stuck right in her mouth. How could that be an accident?'

Michael wished he would stop calling him by his name. He was going out of his way to be personal when Michael felt like screaming obscenities in his face.

'Right, you felt morally obligated to be a hundred per cent honest and to ruin Alice's reputation. But never mind that, your question's a good one. How could it be an accident?'

The lieutenant shook his head. 'We went over this last night. The facts have not changed since then.'

'I'd like to ask you about a few of those facts.'

Keller glanced at his watch. 'I have to be at the station in a few minutes. I really don't have the time.'

Michael chuckled without mirth. 'But you said it yourself, I could be a genius. I might spot something you missed. Or is that impossible, that you might have missed something?'

'Are you always this rude?'

'I must be in a bad mood.'

The lieutenant took a weary breath, looked past him over the lawn, northwest, in the direction of Jessica's house. Michael had seen Jessica at the funeral. She'd worn a black dress. It wasn't her colour. Although he remembered her saying hello, he was unsure if he had answered her. For reasons unclear to himself, he hadn't even wanted to stand near her.

'You're talking about a locked-room murder, you know that,' Keller said. 'The screens on the windows in that bedroom were screwed down. Our best man went over them with a magnifying glass. No one's removed them in years. There's an opening to the attic in the bedroom closet, but there's a stack of boxes pressed against it. Those boxes, by the way, couldn't have been moved and replaced in five minutes, never mind five seconds. When you get down to it, there was only one entrance into that room. The door.'

'And it was lying wide open. How can you call that a locked-room murder?'

Keller caught his eye. 'Do you think Nick did it?'

'No.'

'His prints were on the gun.'

'Because he took the gun out – away from Alice.'

'But if I was the murderer, I would have done the same thing. Touch the gun as quickly as possible so I'd have an excuse for having my prints all over it.'

'Nick didn't do it.'

'I don't think he did, either. But, from a purely technical point of view, he's the only one who could have.'

'That's not true. When the gun went off, he had the entire hallway behind him, all those rooms at his back that someone could have ducked into.'

'And how long did Nick take to get from the top of the stairway and back to the bedroom? Three seconds? Four seconds? He ran straight there, didn't he?'

Michael paused. He hadn't asked Nick that specific question. 'I would assume.'

'He did, he told me he did. And looking at him, I'd wager he can run pretty fast. Face it, Mike, there just wasn't time for anyone to enter the room with Alice, force a gun in her mouth, pull the trigger and then hide in one of the other rooms.'

Michael put his hand to his head. He couldn't think as clearly as he usually did. He needed sleep. 'You're overlooking something. You believe Alice entered the room immediately after Nick exited, right?'

'Yes. Or she could have already been in there when he used the bathroom.'

'But the first possibility, you feel that's the most probable?'

Keller nodded. 'Chances are she was the one Nick heard crying in the next-to-the-last bedroom.'

'Let's say she did enter the room right after he left. But let's also say she wasn't alone, that someone was with her, or that someone followed her. And let's imagine he, or she, killed her, but *didn't* leave the bedroom.'

Keller frowned. 'I don't know if I follow you?'

'The murderer didn't have to rush from the bedroom to hide in one of the other rooms. He could simply have stepped into the bathroom.'

'Did you see anyone step *out* of the bathroom?'

'No. But Alice was lying on the floor, and the – Well, in the shape I was in, Kats or The Rock or Clair or Bubba could have slipped into our group without my knowing it. To tell you the truth, I don't know where any of them came from.'

Keller thought for a minute. 'They came in through the door,' he said finally.

'Admit it, you never considered the possibility.'

The lieutenant started to protest, stopped. 'You are clever, Mike, like they said. All right, I didn't think of it. But I had a good reason. You had Maria, Jessica, Sara, Nick, Polly – part of the time – and yourself, and yet, not a single one of you said anything about someone coming out of the bathroom.'

'*We* may have had a good reason. Perhaps the murderer didn't come out of the bathroom until we left the room. That's what we did, you know. None of us could stand to stay in there.'

'And then, when you were all back downstairs, did this murderer calmly stroll out the front door in front of you all?'

'No. But he could have gone out on to the second-storey porch, off the roof, and into the backyard.'

'Are you ruling out those you've mentioned as possible suspects?' Keller asked.

'If the murderer joined our group without our seeing him, no. If he snuck off after we left, yes.'

'How did he get hold of Kats's gun?'

'He took it out of his car. Kats hasn't been able to lock that Mustang in years.'

Keller thought some more. This time he ended up nodding. 'There is merit in what you say. But it doesn't explain how he was able to get the gun into Alice's mouth and her fingers wrapped around the trigger?'

'That is a problem,' Michael admitted.

'And what about a motive? If you don't have that, you've got nothing. Who would want to kill Alice? Who was this outsider?'

'Did anybody tell you about Clark?'

'No. Who's Clark?'

'He was Alice's boyfriend.'

'Was he at the party?'

'I didn't see him.'

'Then why bring him up?'

'I told you, he was Alice's boyfriend. You asked for a possible motive. He was a weird guy.'

'What's his last name?'

'I don't know. I checked around and nobody knows. I even went to the hospital where Polly's being treated. I managed to get a note slipped in to her asking for his last name. She doesn't even know, and she used to go out with him.'

'I find that hard to believe.'

'He never told her.'

'Wait a second, Polly used to go out with Alice's boyfriend?'

'Yeah. I met him once.'

'And?'

'He had the strangest eyes.'

'Who cares about his eyes. Did he seem capable of murder?'

'Yes.'

'Do you know anything about him? Where he goes to school? Where he works?'

'No. All I know is that he's an artist, like Alice.'

Keller took out a tiny notepad, jotted down a couple of notes. 'How come I never heard about this guy earlier?'

'Clark is only a possibility. The others – they could have motives of their own.'

'Such as?'

Michael shook his head. 'Not right now. I need to think about it longer. But you could do me a favour. I want a look at the autopsy report.'

'What for? She was killed by the bullet that came out of the gun. It's cut and dried.'

'I'd still like to see it.'

'I appreciate your desire to clear your friend's name. But you are only that, a friend. You're not family. I can't turn over that report to you without permission from Alice's aunt.'

'If I get permission, will you give it to me?'

'What do you want it for? You're not going to discover something the coroner missed.'

'I like to be thorough. What was the name of the coroner?'

'I'd have to look it up.' He glanced at his watch again. 'I really have to go now. If you want to talk more, Mike, call me at the station in a few days. Try to get me Clark's full name.'

'I'll do my best.'

Keller went to close the front door. 'I don't have to tell you that what you've suggested is a long shot. From what Jessica Hart said, Alice sounded like a very unhappy girl.'

Michael found every muscle in his body suddenly

tense. When he tried to speak, he distinctly heard his jaw bone crack. 'What did she say?' he whispered.

'How Alice still hadn't got over her parents' death. In fact, it was Jessica who gave me the name and number of Alice's psychiatrist.' Keller consulted his notepad. 'Dr Kirby. I have a call into her, but she hasn't called me back.'

'She wasn't seeing a psychiatrist,' he said indignantly. 'I knew her as well as anybody and she never said a word about—'

'I probably dream too much. That's what my doctor says.'

He lowered his head. It changed nothing. Lots of people saw psychiatrists and didn't kill themselves. That goddamn Jessica, spreading such lies . . .

'Anything wrong?' Keller asked, peering at him.

'No.'

'What were you saying about her psychiatrist?'

'Nothing. I'd – forgotten.' He needed to change the subject, to get rid of this man. 'Could you please leave the front door unlocked? I promise to lock it when I leave.'

Keller trusted him. Giving Michael a fatherly pat on the shoulder, he got in his car and drove away.

Hope you have time to stop for doughnuts.

The instant he stepped inside the house, Michael felt

slightly nauseated. More than anything, he wanted to turn around and leave. He walked up the stairs slowly, listening to his heart thumping against his ribcage. It was the only sound he could hear. He realised he was holding his breath, and had to make a conscious effort to let the air out of his lungs.

The bedroom door where Alice died was closed. Turning the knob, he half wished it was locked. But it wasn't, and the first thing he saw as the door swung open was the yellow chalk outline the police had drawn on the floor around Alice's body. He hadn't stopped to think how short she had been. He walked into the room and closed the door at his back.

There was another outline on the floor, at the top of the yellow chalk, rounder, darker; blood always left an awful stain. For a morbid moment, he wondered if any had seeped through the floor on to the aunt's bedroom ceiling.

The rest of the house was furnished exquisitely. This room, except for the lamp and nightstand in the corner, the shades above the windows, was empty. No paintings, ornaments, not even a photograph, hung on the featureless white walls. Alice had told him Polly had simply cleaned it out one day. Why? The parents were dead. The parents had slept here. Alice had died here. Curious symmetry . . .

The police had drawn a small circle of chalk beneath the east-facing windows. A black dot pinpointed the centre. Michael knelt beside it. This was where the bullet had gone after it had exited the back of Alice's head.

He peered into the shallow hole. It appeared to go straight into the wall, parallel to the floor. He sat beside it and faced in the direction of the door. The hole was about level with his Adam's apple.

Was she sitting when she died?

The possibility filled him with disquiet. If a murderer had been holding her, it would have been easier for him to do so with her standing up. It would give the others another reason to think she had killed herself.

He noticed an aluminium ladder resting against the wall beside the bathroom. He figured the police had brought it in to assist in studying the room, until he vaguely recalled having seen it when they had discovered the body. Why had Alice or Polly brought a ladder into the room? To get down the paper cups?

He went through the room systematically, verifying Keller's points: heavy closet boxes blocked the attic entrance; dusty screen screws that didn't appear to have been touched in ages. Nothing he found proved or disproved either of the hypotheses he had presented Keller. But there were two things he noticed that struck him as unusual.

First there were the tangled Christmas tree lights hanging from the top shelf of the closet. The police had not pulled them out; he definitely recalled seeing them the night of the party. He wasn't quite sure why he considered it significant. The overhead light had been shorted out. Wires were often used to short out other wires. The connection seemed tenuous at best.

The second thing was not even properly in the bedroom. Peering out of the east-facing windows at the overhang of the roof, he noticed that a small portion of a nearby wooden roof shingle – at the very edge of the overhang – was broken off. Indeed, it looked as though someone had broken it off with the heel of a foot.

Did someone enter or exit the room over the roof?

It made no sense. With the screwed-down screens, any approach from the outside was impossible. And yet, when he searched both ways along the roof edge, he saw not a single other damaged shingle. Only this one directly outside the east windows.

He examined the bathroom, found the same immovable screens on the window.

He was leaving the bedroom when he noticed the fine glass shards in the centre of the wooden floor. A quick examination revealed them to be from a light bulb. He grabbed the ladder, spread it in the middle of the floor. Going up the steps, he reached up and unscrewed the overhead light shade. A minute later he was staring at a busted light bulb.

But what does it mean?

Probably nothing. That was what he was afraid of.

He went through the remainder of the rooms on the upper floor. When he was done, he sat down at the top of the stairs with a paper, ruler and pencil he had taken from one of the rooms and drew himself a diagram. He sketched the entire second floor, but only that portion of the bottom floor that seemed pertinent.

Who had been in the third bedroom appeared, on the surface, the crux of the whole matter. Yet in reality it could be of only minor importance. Alice and the murderer could both have already been in the fourth bedroom when Nick had entered. The guy could have had the gun in her mouth, and been whispering in her ear that if she so much as let out the tiniest sound . . .

Standing on the porch, Kats had had easy access to the roof of the house. Despite the window screens, it was something to think about.

The fourth bedroom had been extremely dark just before they had turned on the lamp. Michael didn't recall any light from the pool entering through the south-facing

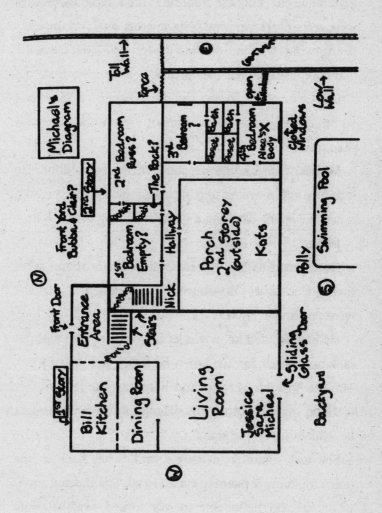

281

windows. Had the pool light been off or had the window shades been down? Would Polly have turned off the pool light while checking the chlorine? Those particular shades were certainly down now. Yet the other ones, on the east-facing windows, had definitely been up. Even now, he could almost feel that cold breeze.

Bill, who had been in the kitchen, had taken an inordinate amount of time to reach the scene of the crime.

Michael heard someone come in the front door. He stood up and moved a step back into the hallway, peering down the stairs, catching a glimpse of long brown hair.

Jessica.

He listened as she entered a downstairs room, went through a series of drawers. It sounded as if she were packing.

He had decided he would let her come and go without making himself known when he heard her start to cry. Mingled in with his grief and bitterness, he felt another emotion – guilt. Putting his diagram in his back pocket, he walked down the stairs.

She was standing in Alice's studio, her back to the door, touching a painting on an easel. She did not jump when he said hello. She merely turned, watched him through strands of hanging hair with those big brown eyes that had always worked such strange magic on him. They were red now, and puffy. She still had on her black dress.

'I saw your car out front,' she said.

'Why didn't you call for me?'

'I knew you didn't want to talk to me.'

He shrugged. 'I'm here. We're both here. Why shouldn't we talk?'

She closed her eyes, sucked in a breath, her hands trembling. His tone had not been kind. She turned away. 'I came to pick up some clothes for Polly,' she said. 'I'll be gone in a minute.'

'Take your time.'

Her back to him, her head fell to her chest. His guilt sharpened, yet so did his anger. 'Michael, I don't understand,' she pleaded.

The studio was the smallest room in the house. The numerous paintings and sketches were piled one on top of the other. Alice had had a dozen brushes and colour trays going at the same time. She hadn't been what anyone would have called neat.

Michael had seen much of the work before. She used to bring her pictures into the store as she finished them: forest animals building a shopping mall in the middle of redwoods; high schools populated with penguin students

– bright and silly situations that he had thought made up the best of her private universe.

As his eyes wandered over the room, however, he noticed a row of strikingly different works. A few were of alien worlds: a purple multi-tentacled creature feeding its hungry babies pieces of an American spacecraft; a hideous shivering skeleton trapped on an ice planet, trying to light a last match on the inside of its naked eye socket.

Before Clark. After Clark. I'll find that bastard.

Michael came further into the studio, feeling in no hurry to answer Jessica's question. There was no carpet in here, either; and this floor was also stained.

'*I* don't understand,' he said finally, leaning against the wall. 'Here Alice gets murdered and the first thing her best friend does is tell the cops she killed herself.'

Jessica stared at him, shocked, as if he'd slapped her across the face. Then her face collapsed in despair. A tear rolled over her cheek. Then another one. He held her gaze for a long moment, feeling his bitterness beginning to teeter as she began to tremble again. He turned away. This was bad. He had to stop. He wished he could stop. He just hurt so bad – it was as if pain had taken on a demonic character inside him and was demanding he make everyone suffer as he was suffering. But he didn't really hate Jessica.

I should have been there, in that room.

He hated himself.

It should have been me.

For being alive.

'I loved Alice,' Jessica said, struggling with each word. 'I loved her more than the world. And what I said to the police, I didn't say because I wanted to. It hurt me to say it, as much as it's hurting me now to stand here and have you accuse me of—'

She broke down then, completely, the sobs racking her body like shocks of electric current. He tried as hard as he could to go to her, to comfort her. Yet the insecure ego inside that he had deftly kept hidden all his adolescent years wouldn't let him. He was too afraid if he so much as touched her, he would break down, too. And that he could never do, not in front of her.

He stepped instead to the easel and pulled away the covering cloth.

Go forward, I will follow.

There was no desert, no bridge over a running river. Yet the lush forest and shimmering lake of Alice's final painting strongly reminded him of his dream. The colours were similar, and more important, the painting embodied the *feel* of his place.

He didn't quite know what to think. A lot of people,

he supposed, dreamed of a Garden of Eden. That Alice and he shared similar tastes in paradise probably meant nothing.

Nevertheless, the painting somehow evoked the peace he'd experienced in his dream. A faint ray of that peace pierced his heavy pain. He reached out and touched the canvas. Alice had placed the two of them together, walking hand in hand along the grassy path that circled the edge of the clear water. She'd had only to complete the details of his clothing and she would have been done.

Then he noticed something else, a photograph of himself propped up beside the easel. He picked it up, as Jessica began to quiet down.

'I took it the night of the game.' Jessica sniffed. 'After you helped me with my camera, when you were sitting at the end of the bleachers with Nick. When Alice saw it, she told me she had to have it.' Wiping at her eyes with her arm, Jessica gently plucked it from his fingers. She smiled suddenly. 'I sort of wanted it for myself, but Alice asked, and she was all excited and – what the heck, I thought.'

'Jessie.'

'No.' She set the picture on the easel at the base of the painting, picked up a small suitcase at her feet.

'Let's not talk, not now. I'll leave. I'll talk to you later. I'll see you at school.'

He nodded. 'Goodbye.'

She turned away. 'Goodbye.'

THE DANCE

---

part one

CHAPTER 1

'I can't wear glasses to school,' Jessica Hart said. 'I'll look like a clown.'

'But you can't see without them,' Dr Baron said.

'I don't care. There's nothing worth seeing at Tabb High, anyway. I won't wear them.'

The eye examination was over. Beside her best friend, Sara Cantrell, Jessica was seated on a hard wooden chair in front of Dr Baron's huge walnut desk. Jessica had been coming to Dr Baron since she was a child. A slightly built, kindly faced man with beautiful grey eyes and neatly combed grey hair, the ophthalmologist had changed little throughout the years. Unfortunately, neither had his diagnosis. He continued to say her eyesight was failing.

'Jessie,' Sara said. 'Even with your old glasses on, you almost ran over that kid on the bike on the way here.'

'What kid?' Jessica asked.

'I rest my case,' Sara muttered.

Dr Baron, as patient as when Jessica had been six and didn't want to peer through his examination equipment because she feared her lashes would stick to the eyepieces, folded his fine hands on top of his neatly polished desktop. 'You may be pleasantly surprised, Jessie, at the number of attractive frames this office has obtained since your last exam. Glasses have recently become something of a fad. Look at the number of models wearing them on magazine covers.'

Models on magazines aren't worried about being voted homecoming queen, Jessica thought. 'How about if I try the soft contacts again?' she asked. 'I know last time my eyes had a bad reaction to them, but maybe they'll be OK now.'

'Last time you started bawling whenever you had to put them in,' Sara said.

'That's not true,' Jessie said. 'I didn't give myself a chance to get used to them.'

'A few people,' Dr Baron said, 'less than one in a hundred, have hypersensitive eyes. The slightest bit of dust or smoke makes their eyes water. You are one of those people, Jessie. You have to wear glasses, and you have to wear them all the time.'

'What if I sit in the front row in every class?'

'You do that already,' Sara said.

'What if I only put them on when I'm in class, and take them off afterwards, at lunch and stuff?' Jessica asked.

Dr Baron shook his head. 'If you start that, you'll be taking them off and on between each class, and your eyes will have to keep readjusting, and that'll cause strain. No, you are nearsighted. You have to face it.' He smiled. 'Besides, you're an extremely attractive young lady. A nice pair of glasses is hardly going to affect how others see you.'

Sara chuckled. 'Yeah, four eyes.'

'Hardy, ha,' Jessica growled. Homecoming was only two weeks away, and she was beginning to have grave doubts about the 'attractive', never mind the 'extremely'. If not for the piercing headaches that had begun to hit her every day after school – and which she knew were the result of eyestrain – she wouldn't even have stopped in for an eye exam. She would simply have waited until after homecoming. But now she was stuck. Sara would hassle her constantly to put on her glasses.

'One thing I don't understand,' Jessica said. 'Why has my vision gone downhill so rapidly in the last few months? I mean, I don't have some disease that's making me blind, do I?'

'No, definitely not,' Dr Baron said. 'But sometimes a

stressful period can worsen an individual's sight at an accelerated rate.' He raised an inquiring eyebrow. 'Have you been under an unusual amount of pressure?'

The memory of Alice's death needed only the slightest nudge to flood down upon her in a smothering wave. Red lips round a black gun. Red blood dripping through beautiful yellow hair. Closed eyes, for ever closed. Jessica lowered her head, rubbed her temples, feeling her pulse. It was hard to imagine a time when she would be able to forget. Alice had been with her the last time she had visited Dr Baron's office. 'I suppose,' she answered softly.

The good doctor suggested she browse through the frames in the next room while he examined another patient. Jessica did so without enthusiasm, finally settling on a pair of brown frames that Sara thought went well with her brown hair and eyes. Before they left, Dr Baron reappeared, promising the glasses would be ready the following Monday. Only four days, and it used to take four weeks. Jessica thanked him for his time.

They had left Polly McCoy waiting in the car; Polly had wanted it that way. She was listless these days. Often, she would sit alone beneath a tree at school during lunch and stare at the clouds until the bell rang. She ate like a bird. She had lost twenty pounds in the last two months since she had lost her sister Alice. It was weird, she looked better than she had in years – as long as one didn't look too deeply in her faraway eyes and ponder what might be going on behind them. Jessica worried about her constantly. Yet Polly insisted she was fine.

'Do you need new glasses?' Polly asked, shaking herself to life in the backseat as Jessica climbed in behind the wheel and Sara opened the passenger door.

'She's blind as a bat,' Sara said.

'I can see just fine,' Jessica said, starting the car with the window up. It was the beginning of December, and after an unusually long, lingering summer, the sun had finally decided to cool it. Heavy grey clouds were gathering in the north above the mountains. The weatherman had said something about a storm in the desert. Flipping the heat on, Jessica put the car in reverse and glanced over her shoulder.

'Watch out for the kid on the bike,' Sara said.

'What kid?' Jessica demanded, hitting the brakes and putting the car in Park. Then she realised Sara was joking. 'I was going to put them on in a second,' she said, snatching her old glasses from her bag.

'I seriously doubt a single potential vote is going to see you on the way home,' Sara said.

'That's not why I hate wearing them,' Jessica said,

putting on the specs and wincing at how they seemed to make her nose stick out in the rearview mirror.

'I heard Clair Hilrey's a patient of Dr Baron, too,' Sara said.

'Really?' Jessica asked. The talk around campus had it that it was between Clair and her for homecoming queen. Jessica wondered. The results of the preliminary homecoming court vote wouldn't be announced until the next day, Friday. Wouldn't it be ironic if neither of them was even elected to the court?

It would be a disaster.

Sara nodded seriously. 'He's prescribed blue-tinted contacts for her to make her eyes sparkle like the early-morning sky.'

Jessica shoved her away. 'Shut up!'

Sara laughed, as did Polly, although Jessica doubted Polly felt like laughing.

They hit the road. Sara wanted to go to the bank to get money from the school account. She needed cash, she said, to pay for the band that was to play at the homecoming dance. A month earlier, acting as ASB – Associated Student Body – president, Sara had cleverly talked a local car dealer into donating a car to the school in exchange for free advertising in Tabb's paper and yearbook. The car had been the grand prize in a raffle put on to raise money for Tabb's extra-curricular activities. The raffle had been a big success, and Sara now had several grand to put into the homecoming celebrations.

Jessica, however, did not want to go to the bank. She was getting another headache, and besides, she had someone to see. With hardly a word, she dropped both girls off at Sara's house. Sara could always give Polly a ride home. She'd finally got her licence back. These days Sara was always quick to help Polly out.

Things have changed.

But life goes on – Jessica knew it had to go on for her. She had mourned Alice for two months. She had gone directly home after school each day. She had spent most of her time in her room, neither listening to music nor watching TV. She had spent the time crying, and now she was sick of crying. Alice was gone. It was the most terrible of terrible things. But Jessica Hart was alive. She had to worry about her looks again, whether Bill Skater found her desirable, whether she was going to pass her next chemistry exam. She had to live. But before she could properly start on all those things, she had to heal the rift between Michael Olson and her. It was time they talked.

She had obtained his address from the phone book. She preferred seeing him at his house rather than speaking to him at school. She hardly saw him on campus, anyway.

He came and he went, he said hello and he said goodbye. It was her hope that he would feel more sociable on his own turf.

With the help of a map, she located his place, parking a hundred yards up the street from the small white-stucco house. The late afternoon sun was ducking in and out of drifting clouds. She looked around: second-hand cars leaking oil on top of broken asphalt driveways; backyards with weeds instead of pools. This wasn't her kind of neighbourhood, and she realised the truth of the matter with a mild feeling of self-loathing. Nice things meant too much to her.

His garage was open, but she didn't see his car. She briefly wondered if he was at work, but remembered that he always took Thursdays off. She decided to wait. After pulling on a sweater, she reached for her SAT practice test book. The real test was to be a week from Saturday. With all her studying, she had only begun to score over a thousand. Compared to the average college-bound student, this was a respectable score, but next to the typical Stanford freshman – which she hoped to be this time next year – she was at the bottom of the pile. The maths sections were what was killing her. She could figure out most of the problems; she simply couldn't figure them out quickly enough.

They raise us with calculators in our hands and then take them away precisely when we need them most.

Jessica picked up a pencil and set the timer on her dashboard clock. She vowed to run through as many maths tests as it took for Michael to show up.

She dozed briefly in the middle of the third round, but a couple of hours later, when Michael Olson's beat-up Toyota pulled into his garage, she was still there. However, she did nothing but watch as he climbed out of his car and stretched in the orange evening light for a moment before disappearing inside. She remembered eight weeks earlier when he had cursed her for assuming Alice had committed suicide. And she remembered her inability to defend herself, to explain how it couldn't have been any other way.

Suddenly she was afraid to see him. Yet she did not leave. She simply sat there, staring at his house.

CHAPTER 2

'How much cash did you get?' Polly asked as Sara returned to the car from a quick stop inside the bank.

'Three grand,' Sara said, closing the door, setting down her bag, and reaching for the ignition. She never wore a seat belt. If she was going to be in a major accident, she was already convinced her car would explode in flames. She had that kind of luck. The last thing she wanted was to be tied in place. 'I have to pay the band, the caterer and that circus guy who's renting us the canopy.'

Homecoming would be a lot different this year, Sara thought, and a lot better. She again complimented herself on insisting at the start of the year that the dance be postponed until basketball season. The delay had given her time to raise the money necessary to put on a wild celebration that everyone could enjoy for a nominal fee, rather than a stuffy party that only a few could afford.

The plan was to have the dance at the school immediately after the first home game, outside, on the practice basketball courts. When she had initially proposed the idea to the ASB council, they had all told her she was mad. 'We come to this goddamn school every goddamn day,' the beautiful, bitchy vice-president Clair Hilrey had said. 'We can't stage an event as crucial as the crowning of the new queen between the peeling gym and the stinking weight room!'

Naturally, the negative reaction had only strengthened Sara's belief she was on to something. Yet the idea had its potential problems. What if it rained that night? And equally as bad, how could they create a party atmosphere when they would be surrounded by nothing but dark?

It was then Sara had thought of renting a giant tent. What a genius! With a tent the whole school could come; everybody, whether they had a date or not. And they could decorate it any way they wanted, and have a live band with the volume turned way up. Clair had loudly booed the idea, along with every other so-called hip person on the council. But the others in the room, those who figured they wouldn't be going to the dance, had nodded thoughtfully at the suggestion. That was enough for Sara. She hadn't even put it to a vote – she had simply gone about making preparations.

'You were able to get that money on your own signature?' Polly asked.

'No, it's a joint account,' Sara said. 'I needed the treasurer's signature, too. Bill Skater signed a cheque for me this afternoon.'

'Before you wrote in the amount?'

'What's your problem?' Sara snapped, before remembering she had promised herself she would be nice to Polly until Polly was fully recovered from Alice's suicide. Polly turned away at the change in tone, nervously tugging on a bit of her hair. Except for a streak of grey that had mysteriously sprung from beside her right ear, she looked – in Sarah's truly unbiased opinion – downright voluptuous. That was what happened when fat girls got skinny. Why did anyone pay for breast implants? Probably pigging out for a few months and then going on a fast would work just as well.

'I was only asking,' Polly said defensively. 'It's not safe carrying round that much cash. It's better to pay people with cheques. That way you get a receipt, too.'

'I realise that,' Sara said patiently. 'But take the band. None of them want to declare this money on their income tax. I can dangle the cash in their faces and tell them to make me an offer I can't refuse. And they'll make it.'

'Isn't that against the law?'

'I don't know. Who cares? Hey, has that engineer at your parents' company finished designing the float?' Another plus, in Sara's mind, of having the homecoming dance in a tent was that simply by pulling aside a flap, a special platform could be driven in for the crowning. The old custom of having the princesses cruise on to the track surrounding the football field with their papas had struck Sara as – well, old-fashioned. She had envisioned a castle float, with a central tower that the queen would ascend after the opening of the secret envelope. She had stolen the concept from a video on MTV.

'You mean Tony?' Polly said. 'Yeah, he called last week. He has it all worked out. He said he can use one of the trucks at the company to build it on.'

'Great.' That was one thing she wouldn't have to pay for.

'It's going to have to be towed to the tent,' Polly said. 'And Tony warned me that we'll need a good driver. It'll be hard to see, and the float won't be real stable.'

'I'll think of someone.'

'I don't want to do it,' Polly said quickly.

'OK.'

'I don't.'

'That's fine.'

Polly nodded, relaxing. 'All right.'

Sara gave her a hard look and sighed to herself. Who was she fooling? Polly was never going to get over Alice. None of them were. Sara hadn't even told Jessica this, but she could no longer stand to be alone. Occasionally she wondered if some sick impulse would suddenly strike her, like a demon whispering in her ear. And, like Alice, she would grab a knife, or maybe a razor blade, and cut open a vein, and bleed all that blood Alice had . . .

But, no, she was not suicidal and never had been. She was in no hurry to leave this world. Yet she would have given a great deal to see Alice again, even for a few minutes. Two long months, and still her grief was an open wound.

Before pulling away from the bank Sara noticed the clerk had forgotten to stamp the new balance in the ASB council's chequebook. A dash back inside remedied the situation.

On the way to Polly's house, they talked about Polly's guardian aunt. The poor old lady had had a mild heart attack immediately after hearing about Alice, and had only recently returned home. A nurse watched her during the day while Polly was in school, but Polly took care of her the rest of the time, cooking her food, rubbing her back, helping her to the bathroom. Sara admired Polly's charity but didn't understand – with the bucks Polly had

– why she didn't hire round-the-clock help. She'd get a lot more sleep that way.

After Sara dropped Polly off, she stopped by the market. Only this market wasn't just any market. It was six miles out of her way, below par in cleanliness and had an employee named Russ Desmond. She had asked around campus – discreetly, of course – where he worked. This would be her fourth visit to the store. The previous three times he had either been off or working in the back.

Naturally, she saw him practically every day at school, but being ASB president, she thought it beneath her dignity to go chasing after him there.

Starting in the vegetable section, her bag in her hand, she went up and down every aisle until she came to the meat section. She didn't see him. More disappointed than she cared to admit, she was heading for the exit when she spotted him wheeling a pallet into the frozen-food section. He had on a heavy purple sweater, orange gloves and a green wool cap that was fighting a losing battle with his bushy brown hair.

What a babe.

She didn't know why he looked so good to her. Most girls would have thought he had too many rough edges and was too sloppy to be handsome. Actually, she thought that herself; nevertheless, she always got a rush when she saw him. She liked the curve of his powerful shoulders, the insolence in his walk. Yet she didn't for a moment believe she was infatuated with him. She was too cool to be suffering from something so common.

She wanted him to notice her, to call her over. Acting like an ordinary, everyday shopper, she began to browse through the ice cream and Popsicles, drawing closer and closer to where he was working. She had approached within ten feet of him, and still he hadn't seen her. Feeling mildly disgusted, she finally spoke up.

'Hey, Russ, is that you?'

He glanced up. 'Sara? What are you doing here?'

She shrugged. 'Shopping. You work here?'

'Yeah.'

'I didn't know that. I come in here all the time.'

'Really? I've never seen you before.'

'I usually don't stay long. In and out – you know how it is.'

'Huh.' He returned to unloading his pallet, bags of frozen carrots. 'What are you looking for?'

'What?'

'What are you buying?'

'Oh – Spam.'

'Aisle thirteen, lower shelf on the right. You like Spam?'

'It's all right.'

'I can't stand it.'

Neither could she. 'I like the cans.' Brilliant. She cleared her throat. 'So, what's new?'

'Nothing. What's new with you?'

'Oh, just putting the homecoming dance together. You know I'm ASB president?'

'I remember you said that, yeah.'

'It's in a couple of weeks.' *Hint, hint, hint.* She didn't exactly have a date yet. Actually, no guy had even spoken to her in the last month. For all he cared. He finished with his carrots and went on to broccoli. She added, 'I'm going.'

'Huh.'

'Yeah, I have to. I open the envelope that announces the new queen.' She paused, swallowed. 'Are you going?'

'Nah. What for?'

'To have fun. We're going to have a cool band. They're called the Keys. I heard them a few days ago. They play great dance music. Do you like to dance?'

'Sometimes, yeah. When I'm drunk enough.'

She didn't know how to respond to that. Booze wasn't allowed at the dance. She stood there feeling totally helpless for the next minute, reading and rereading the label on a bag of frozen cauliflower – 'Ingredients Cauliflower' – while Russ finished with his vegetables. He

307

began to collect his empty boxes, stacking them on his pallet. 'I've got to go in the back,' he said.

'OK.'

He didn't invite her to accompany him, but she followed him anyway. Fortunately, there wasn't anybody else in the back, not beside the frozen-food freezer. Sara could hardly believe the cold rushing out of it or how Russ could work inside it. He began to restock his pallet, his breath white and foggy. He was a superb worker. He never stopped moving. He had excellent endurance. She remembered something she wanted to bring up.

'I hear you're going to be in the CIF finals,' she said. It was extremely difficult to even qualify for the CIF – California Interscholastic Federation – finals.

'It's no big deal,' he said, going further into the freezer, disappearing around several tall stacks of boxes. She took a tentative step inside, feeling goose flesh form instantly. She noted the huge axe strapped to the inside of the frost-coated door.

'Sure it is,' she called, hanging the strap of her bag around a dolly handle, cupping her fingers together. She couldn't even see him.

'Lots of people qualify,' he called.

'But I bet you win,' she called back.

'What?'

For some reason, shouting in the dark – particularly when you were repeating yourself – had always struck Sara as one of the most ridiculous things a human being could do. 'I said, you'll probably win!'

'That shows how much you know about cross-country,' he said, reappearing with his arms laden with boxes.

That sounded like an insult, and here she was trying to compliment him. 'I know something about it,' she said. She had been closely following his performances in the papers. He had won his last ten races, improving his time with each meet.

'Sure,' he said.

'I do.'

'What do you know?'

'That if you break fourteen minutes, you'll win.'

He snorted. 'Of course I'd win if I broke fourteen minutes. But the finals are down in Newport, on the hilliest course in the city. *Fifteen* minutes will be tough.' He dumped his boxes on the pallet, muttering under his breath, 'I'm not going to win.'

'Don't say that. If you say that, you won't win.'

'Who cares?'

'What do you mean, who cares? Don't you care?'

'Nope.'

She had begun to shiver. Another minute in there and

her hair would turn white. But at the same time she could feel her blood warming – or was it her temper? 'What are you saying?'

'That I don't care.' He pulled off his gloves, rubbed his hands together. 'It's just a goddamn race.'

'A goddamn race? It's the city championship! If you win, they'll give you a goddamn scholarship!'

He shook his head. 'I ain't going to college. I can't stand going to high school.'

'I don't believe it,' she said, disgusted. 'Here you have this tremendous natural talent that can open all kinds of doors for you and you're just going to throw it away? What the hell's the matter with you?'

He looked at her, frowned. 'Why are you always shouting at me?'

'Shouting at you? When have I shouted at you? I haven't even spoken to you in two whole months!'

'Yeah, but the last time you did, you were shouting at me.'

'Well, maybe you need someone to shout at you. Get you off your ass. The reason you don't care is because you drink too much. You're seventeen years old and you're already a drunk!'

'I'm eighteen.'

'You're still a drunk. I've seen you run. If you didn't

310

down a case of beer every evening, you'd probably be in the Olympics.'

He didn't like that. 'Who are you to tell me what I should do? You're as screwed up as anybody.'

'And what's that supposed to mean?'

He stood. 'You're insecure. Every time I talk to you – it doesn't matter for how long – you tell me you're the president of the school. All right, I heard you the first time. And who cares? I don't. I don't care if you're the Virgin Mary.'

Sara couldn't believe what she was hearing. Insecure? She was the most together teenager since Ann Landers and Dear Abby had gone to school. She was so confident that she had been nominated for school president when she wasn't even running – Well, that was only one example of how secure she was. There were dozens of others. 'Who are you calling a virgin?' she demanded.

He laughed. Why was he laughing? She'd give him something to laugh about. She stepped forward, shoved him in the chest. 'Shut up!' she shouted.

He laughed harder. 'That's it. That's your problem, Sara. You don't need a date for homecoming, you need a good roll in the hay.'

Sara clenched her fists, her fingernails digging into her

palms. She clenched them so tightly she knew she'd be able to see the marks the next day. If she hadn't done this, she probably would have ripped his face off. Only one other time in her life had she ever felt so humiliated: the last time she had spoken to Russ, at the end of their ill-fated date. She sucked in a breath, taking a step away from him rather than towards him. 'What makes you think I don't have a date?' she asked softly.

He stopped laughing, glanced at the floor, back up at her – still grinning. 'That's why you came in here, isn't it? I saw you looking for me.'

She smiled slowly, faintly. 'I was looking for you?'

'Yeah. I think you were.'

'I was looking for a can of Spam,' she said flatly.

He lost his grin. 'Sara, there's nothing wrong with—'

'Stop,' she said, taking another step back, her hand feeling for the edge of the freezer door. 'Just stand perfectly still and don't say another word.'

His eyes darted to her hand, panic twisting his face. 'Wait! The inside lock—'

She slammed the door in his face. On the way out, she picked up a can of Spam in aisle thirteen. She had decided to have it for dinner.

Yet she shook as she drove home. She wasn't worried Russ would freeze to death – if worse came to worst he could always chop his way out – she was worried he had been right about her.

Only much later did she realise she had left her purse in the store.

CHAPTER 3

The sound startled Michael Olson. Standing in the middle of his garage beside his homemade telescope, he paused to pinpoint its source, then laughed out loud at his foolishness. He had made the noise himself; he had been whistling. He used to whistle all the time, but this was probably the first time since the McCoys' party. He had forgotten what it sounded like to be happy.

Am I? I can't be.

The truth of the matter was that he felt fine, not overflowing with joy, but pretty good. And with that realisation came a flicker of guilt. He had promised himself at Alice's funeral that he would never let himself feel again, that he would never give pain such a clear shot at him. But that had been childish, he saw that now. He had actually seen that for a couple of weeks now, although he had not stopped to think about it.

314

He reached out and touched his twelve-inch reflector telescope, the hard aluminium casing, the well-oiled eyepiece knob. To a certain extent, the instrument was to thank for his comeback.

For two weeks after his blow-up with Jessica, he had stayed away from school. During that time, he had done nothing: he had not cried; he hadn't thought about who had killed Alice. Indeed, he had hardly thought about Alice at all, or rather, he had thought about nothing else, but without the comfort of allowing her sweet face to enter his mind. He had blocked every happy thought associated with her, picturing only her coffin, the gun, the weight of her dead body when he had accidentally kicked it in the dark bedroom. He had censored his thoughts out of shame – not just because he felt partially responsible for her death.

All his life people had told Michael what a great guy he was. And in his immense humility – what a laugh – he had always lowered his eyes and shaken his head, while at the same time thinking that he must, in fact, be quite extraordinary. He excelled in school. He worked hard. He helped his mother with the bills. He helped lots of people with their homework. He did all kinds of things for all kinds of people who weren't quite so great as himself.

That was the crux of the matter right there. He performed these good works, but he did so mainly to reinforce his image. This did not mean he was a completely evil person – only a human being. The day of the funeral had made that all too clear, although it had taken him a while to assimilate the full meaning of his behaviour. He had handled every sort of emotion since he was a child by bottling it up. But grief – crushing grief – had shattered Mr Cool Michael Olson. He hadn't been able to handle it at all. He had lashed out like a baby, attacking Jessica just when she was hurting the most. Yeah, he was human all right, and still in high school.

Exactly two weeks after the party, he'd had a sudden urge to drive out to the desert. The evening had been clear, the orange sand and rocks sharp and warm. When the sun had set and the stars came out, he lay on his back on top of a hill, miles from the nearest person, letting his thoughts wander the course of the Milky Way. Perhaps he had dozed. Maybe he had dreamed. He remembered lying there a long time, enjoying the first real rest he'd experienced since Alice's death. A calm, solid strength seemed to flow into him from the ground, and it was as if *something* else had touched him, something deep and powerful. He would have said it had come from above, from the stars, had it not touched so close to his heart. To this day, he couldn't say what had happened, except that for approximately two hours he had felt loved, completely loved.

By *whom* or *what* he didn't know.

Michael had never thought much about God. At a fairly early age, he had come to the conclusion that there might be one, but that it would be a sheer waste of time trying to prove it. He still held that opinion. But now he did feel there was *something* wonderful out there in the cosmos, or inside him – either place, it didn't matter. His feeling was more intuitive than logical. Then again, it could have been a desperate invention of his overly grieved heart, but he didn't care. It gave him comfort. It allowed him to remember Alice as she had been, without feeling pain.

When he had finally returned home that night, he dreamed of the girl he had dreamed about a couple of weeks before Alice had died. He had been on the same bridge, the same blue water flowing beneath him, the identical desert in front, the forest at his back behind the girl. Again, she had not allowed him to turn to see her, again saying something about a veil. But she had leaned close to his ear, to where he had felt the brush of her hair against his cheek. It had been the touch of her hair that had awakened him. He wished it hadn't. She had been on the verge of revealing something to him, he was sure, something different.

He had started on his telescope the next day, buying the grinding kit for the mirror from a downtown shop, purchasing other accessories as he went along: the aluminium tubing, the rack-and-pinion casing for the oculars, the eyepieces themselves – constructing the stand and clock drive from scratch. This was by no means his first experience at building a telescope. He had put together a six-inch reflector in eighth grade. But doubling the size of the aperture had squared the complexity of the undertaking. Yet working on it did give him much satisfaction.

He returned to school, and the telescope became central to his MGM (Mentally Gifted Minors) project. He designed it with an unusually short focal point, making it poor for high-resolution work – such as would be required for studying the moon and the planets – but giving it a wonderfully wide field of view, ideal for examining huge star groups. He explained to his project adviser that he was looking for comets. That was only a half-truth.

He was actually searching for a *new* comet.

It was a fact that the majority of comets were discovered by amateur astronomers working with fairly modest equipment. The odds against his making such a discovery, however, even after a dozen years of careful observation in the darkest desert nights, should have been a thousand to one. It was a strange universe out there.

Then just two weeks ago, searching from the top of the hill where he had begun his comeback, he charted a faint wisp of light close to the star Sirius that had – as far as he could tell – never been charted before.

He had followed the light for several days, and 'followed' was the word for it; the light was moving. It wasn't a nebula or a galaxy or globular cluster. It was definitely a comet. Perhaps it was *his* comet. He needed to complete a more detailed positional record before he could submit a formal application to a recognised observatory requesting verification of his discovery.

Unfortunately, the recent poor weather was frustrating his efforts. It had been cloudy in the desert the whole past week, and there was no way he could see the sky clearly in the city with all the background light. He was anxious to get on with the next step, but he was learning patience. It had been out there for billions of years – it would wait a few more days for him.

If it was a new comet, he would have the privilege of naming it. Probably that was why he had been whistling while cleaning his telescope. The weird thing was that when he had started building his new instrument, he had known he would find a comet.

He had also gone out for the basketball team. Their old coach had moved on to bigger things in the college ranks and their new coach was a bimbo, but Michael was having fun. Their first league game of the season would be a week from Friday. And the next game, the Friday after that, would be at home, right before the homecoming dance. It would be a good opportunity to show off his new jump shot.

Yet with all this new outlook on life, Michael had not given in to the common consensus that Alice McCoy had committed suicide. He could understand how others believed so, and he no longer blamed them for holding such a belief, but he was, if anything, more certain than ever that she had been murdered. Perhaps it was another intuitive conviction. Or maybe it was the product of dwelling too long on an idea that had come to haunt him:

Whoever had murdered once, could murder again.

Michael left his telescope in the garage and went into the kitchen. There was a call he had been meaning to make. Last night, while falling asleep, he suddenly remembered something very important about the way Alice had painted.

He dialled the police station, identified himself and asked for Lieutenant Keller. He had not spoken to the detective since the day of the funeral.

'Mike,' Keller said with a note of pleasure, but without surprise, when he came on the line. 'How have you been?'

'Very well, sir, thank you. How are you?'

'Good. What can I do for you?'

'First I'd like to ask if there have been any new developments on the McCoy case?'

Keller paused. 'I'm afraid not, Mike. As far as this department is concerned, Alice McCoy's death has officially been ruled a suicide.'

The news was not unexpected, but nevertheless disappointing. 'Does that mean you've completely closed the book on the matter? I think I might have another lead.'

'Did you obtain the full name of that boyfriend of Alice's you mentioned?'

'No, I haven't. No one seems to know anything about him. But I haven't given up trying. I think long enough has gone by that I can talk directly to Alice's sister, Polly, about the guy.'

'Sounds like a good idea.' Keller was being polite, that was all. Michael knew he still thought he was dealing with a distraught teenager. It bothered Michael, but not that much.

'What's your lead?'

'Do you have a CRT on your desk?' Michael asked.

'Yes.'

'Can you access the autopsy report on Alice McCoy?'

'Yes, but as I've already explained, I cannot divulge that information without written permission from the family.'

'I understand. But I'm not asking you to let me look at it right now, I'm just asking you to look at it.'

Keller chewed on that a moment. He seemed to sigh beneath his breath. 'Hold a minute and I'll punch up the record.' Michael listened as the detective tapped on a keyboard. It took Keller three or four minutes to get to the autopsy, an unusually long time. He was probably rereading it first. Finally he said, 'I'm looking at it.'

'Who performed it?'

'I told you, I can't—'

'How can the doctor's name be confidential?' Michael interrupted. 'The list of the city's coroners is public knowledge.' Poor logic, but his tone was persuasive. Keller admitted something significant.

'As a matter of fact the autopsy wasn't performed by a city coroner, but by a paid consultant.'

322

'Why?'

'Our own people were probably busy at the time. Look, if it will make you happy, the gentleman's name was Dr Gin Kawati.'

Michael jotted down the information. 'Do you know his phone number?'

'Mike—'

'All right, never mind. But let me ask you something else. You said that Alice's, Nick's and Kats's fingerprints were all on the gun. Is that correct?'

'Yes.'

'Does the report state which hand the fingerprints were from?'

'It does.'

'Which hand was Alice holding the gun in?'

'You were there. She had it in her right hand.'

'Were any fingerprints from her left hand on the gun?'

'Not that I can tell from this report. What's your point?'

'Alice McCoy was left-handed.'

Again Keller paused. 'Are you sure?'

'Yeah. I remembered last night how she used to paint. She always held the brush in her left hand. Interesting, don't you think?'

Keller sounded slightly off balance. 'Yes, yes, it is. But

it doesn't prove anything. She could just as well have held the gun in her right hand and put it in her mouth.'

'Are you right-handed, Lieutenant?'

'I am, yes.'

'If you were going to kill yourself, which hand would you hold your gun in?'

'What kind of question is that?'

'I know it sounds morbid,' Michael said quickly. 'But think about it for a moment. Even if a girl is about to commit suicide, she would still handle the gun carefully. She would be worried about getting off a clean shot, of doing it right the first time. She would be nervous. She wouldn't hold the thing in her weak hand.'

'Now you're getting into the psychology of someone suffering from depression. For all either of us knows, she could have intentionally done everything backwards.'

'She wasn't depressed!' Michael snapped, before catching himself. 'When you go home tonight, think about it for a while. That's all I ask.'

'All right, Mike, I'll do that. Anything else?'

'Yeah. Could I swing by and pick up that permission form you keep saying I need?'

'I have to go in a few minutes, but I can leave it at the front desk for you.'

'I'd appreciate that. One last thing. Was Alice's right hand dusted for prints?'

'I can't tell from this report. But during the party, she could have shaken hands with any number of people. Such prints would have been meaningless.'

'I wonder,' Michael said.

They said their goodbyes, both sides promising to be in touch. It was four o'clock; the sun set early this time of year. Michael dialled a number that gave up-to-the-minute weather reports. The word was that it would be raining again in the desert. He decided to finish cleaning his telescope and put it away.

The garage was somewhat stuffy. He pushed open the door, deeply breathing the crisp evening air. It was then he noticed the car parked up the street.

Michael had never seen Jessica leave school in her car, but he remembered the silver-blue Celica in her driveway the evening of their date. This car appeared to be the identical make, and someone was sitting in the front seat. Because of the lighting, however, he couldn't tell who it was, whether it was a male or a female even. Well, he had just the thing to solve the mystery. He positioned his telescope in the driveway behind a bush. With a little manoeuvring, he was able to see the person between the branches without being seen. A moment of focusing presented him with a clear view of every detail on Jessica Hart's face.

She was working on something and had a pencil in her mouth. He watched for a minute while she scratched her head, wrinkled her forehead, glanced at her watch and grimaced. No matter what the expression, to him she was beautiful.

Since he had returned to school, he had gone to great pains to avoid her, more than he had during the week following their one date. He'd asked and received another locker. He'd avoided the courtyard during both break and lunch. He'd obtained a list of her classes from the computer at school and mapped out in his head where she should be at any particular moment, planning his own routes accordingly.

'I loved Alice. I loved her more than the world. And what I said to the police, I didn't say because I wanted to. It hurt me to say it, as much as it's hurting me to stand here and have you accuse me ...'

Naturally, despite his precautions, he had occasionally bumped into her, anyway. But they'd exchanged few words. Hello. How are you? Take care. Goodbye. But he'd seen enough of her to know his longing for her had not died with Alice, as he had thought it would. It had only grown stronger.

She was parked in front of Julie Pickering's house. He hadn't realised they were friends. She was probably waiting for Julie to come home. From what he could see, he guessed she might be finishing up some homework before knocking on Julie's door. She could disappear any second.

He didn't give himself a chance to think about it, to chicken out. He started up the street. He had decided that first night in the desert that he owed her an apology.

Halfway to her car, he saw her notice him. He waved.

'Hi. Jessie?'

She rolled down her window, peeped her head outside, her long brown hair covering her shoulder. 'Yeah, it's me,' she said, her smile strained. 'Hi, Michael. I guess you're wondering what I'm doing here?'

He nodded towards the Pickerings' residence. 'You know Julie, don't you?'

Jessica glanced at Julie's house. 'Ah, yeah, Julie. Yeah, I know her.'

'Are you two going to study together?' He remembered Julie, like Jessica, was taking chemistry.

'Yeah, that's it. I mean, I didn't know you and Julie lived on the same block?'

He gestured vaguely back the way he had come. 'I live over there.'

'Oh.'

He put his hands in his pockets, looked at the ground. That was the neat thing about the ground. It was always there to look at when you were talking to a pretty girl. He didn't know how to begin.

'I haven't seen you around school much,' she said finally.

'I've been around.'

'Do you have a new locker?'

'Yeah, they gave me one. Somebody transferred to another school.' He shrugged. 'It was available.'

'I bet you have a lot more room now?'

'You never crowded me.'

'Sure I did. With my bag and my make-up and stuff. I don't know how you put up with me.'

'I was the one who ruined your sweater.'

'You didn't ruin it.'

'Yeah I did.'

'No.' She reached out, brushed his arm. 'Look at me, Michael.' He did so, seeing her large brown eyes first, as he usually did when he looked at her. She chuckled. 'Don't you see? I have it on.'

He smiled. 'That's right. How did you get the stain out?'

She touched her chest. 'I don't remember. It doesn't matter. It's gone.'

'It looks great on you.'

'Thank you.' She paused, her face suddenly serious. 'Did you ask for a new locker?'

He couldn't lie to her. 'Yeah.'

The word seemed to startle her. She recovered quickly, however, nodding. 'That's OK.'

'Jessie—'

'No, I understand. It's fine, really, no offence taken. It's just that I sort of, you know – I used to like talking to you between classes.' She smiled briefly. 'That was fun.'

'I'm sorry,' he said.

'It's all right.'

'No, I'm sorry about what I said to you.' He lowered his voice, his eyes. 'When we were in Alice's studio. I shouldn't have said – what I did.'

She sank back into her seat, taking a breath, putting her hands on the steering wheel, pushing them off again. Obviously, it was a topic she would have preferred to avoid. 'You were upset,' she said quietly.

'I was an asshole.'

She started to shake her head, stopped. She could have been talking about the stain again. 'I don't remember what you said. It doesn't matter, anyway. It's past.'

'Do you forgive me?'

'I don't have to forgive you for loving her.' She caught

329

his eye. 'That's all I heard in that room, Michael – that you loved her. All right?'

She did forgive him, and she was asking him to drop it. 'All right,' he said, feeling much better. He should have come to her weeks ago. She picked up her papers and books from the passenger seat, glad to change the subject.

'You can see I'm still studying for the SAT,' she said. 'I have to take it, not this Saturday, but next.'

'That's when I'm taking it. At Sanders High?'

She brightened. 'Yeah. Maybe we'll be in the same room.'

'Maybe.'

She nodded to her test book. 'I'm not so hot on these trial tests. How do you score on them?'

He had not given a thought to the SAT. 'I haven't taken any.'

'Really? You're just going to walk in there and do it? That's amazing.' She glanced at her scratch papers, frowned. 'I wish I could do that.'

'You'll do fine. Don't worry about it.'

'I'm not worried.' She laughed. 'I'm terrified.'

He smiled. 'If worse comes to worst, I can always slip you my answers – if you'd want them?'

She looked up at him. 'Don't tempt me.'

'Of course you'd have to pay me in advance.'

'Oh! I do have to pay you. I mean, I still owe you a movie.' She paused. 'Would you like to go to the movies with me?'

He felt much much better. 'When?'

'How about tomorrow?'

Tomorrow was Friday, and he *had* to work because he was already taking Saturday off to play in the final practice game of the season. He couldn't do that to his bosses – disappear two days in a row during the busiest part of the week. They'd already given him a break by not firing him when he had stayed at home for days on end after the funeral.

On the other hand, this last pre-season game was against a marshmallow of a school. And Coach Sellers was still trying to make up his mind about a couple of guards. If he did call in sick, the team would still win, and the two guys would get more playing time, and have more of an opportunity to prove themselves. By working Saturday, he could rationalise taking Friday off.

'Tomorrow would be great,' he said.

They worked out the details. He would pick her up at six at her house and they would take it from there. She squeezed his hand just before she drove away. He decided she had changed her mind about studying with Julie.

331

He didn't know what was the matter with him. He could never sit around and enjoy a happy moment. His brief conversation with Lieutenant Keller suddenly came back to plague him. He hadn't had enough information to challenge the detective. He needed more. He needed to study that autopsy report.

He got into his car, drove to the police station. There he picked up the permission form. The sooner he got it back to them, the sooner he might clear Alice's name. He headed for the McCoy residence.

Polly answered the door. There were shadows beneath her eyes, and the rest of her features looked drawn and tired. She had lost a great deal of weight, particularly in her face. He had never realised how pretty she was, or how much she resembled her sister.

'Hi, Mike,' she said. She had on dark wine-coloured trousers, a white blouse, a red scarf around her neck. 'How are you?'

'I'm all right. How about you?'

'Fine. Would you like to come in?'

'Yeah, thanks.' He stepped inside, bracing himself involuntarily. Even twenty years from now he doubted that he would feel comfortable in this mansion. The plush carpet, the high white ceilings – he remembered it all too well. There was, however, a slightly stale odour in the air he did not recall. Polly led him towards a sofa in the living room where he'd been sitting with Nick and Maria when the gun had gone off.

'I was in the neighbourhood, and thought I'd stop by and see how things are,' he said as they sat down.

'That was nice of you.'

He glanced about. 'It's amazing how neat you're able to keep this place.'

'Polly.' A thin voice sounded from the direction of the hallway. Polly immediately leaped to her feet, but stopped at the start of the hall.

'It's a friend from school, Aunty. Do you need anything?'

'No, dear, talk to your friend first.'

'First? *Do* you need anything?'

'Go ahead and talk to your friend,' said the old woman.

Polly shook her head, mildly irritated, and returned to her place beside Michael on the couch. 'She'll probably call out again in a minute,' she said.

'How is she? Someone told me she'd had a heart attack?'

She nodded. 'Yeah. The doctors say it was mild, but she's so old. She hasn't really got her strength back. She has to stay in the downstairs bedroom. The climb upstairs is too much for her.'

'Do you have a nurse?'

'I can take care of her. If she'd tell me what she wants. She doesn't know half the time.' Polly shook her head again and then looked at him, smiling, pain beneath the smile. He almost decided right then and there not to bring up the reason for his visit. 'I'm glad you stopped by,' she said. 'It gets kind of boring sitting home every night.'

'You should try to get out.'

Polly glanced towards the front hall, or was it up, towards the bedroom where they had found Alice. That was one room he'd like to look at again. 'Not yet,' she said.

He cleared his throat. 'Polly, I have a confession to make. I did have another reason for stopping by. I have a few questions I want to ask you.'

'Would you like something to eat?'

'No thanks. What I wanted—'

'How about something to drink?'

He smiled. 'Sure. Juice would be nice.'

She jumped up. 'What flavour? We have pineapple-coconut?'

'That would be fine.'

She was back in a minute with a huge ice-filled glass, a

slice of orange stuck on the rim. She hadn't bothered about one for herself. She sat on the couch a little closer this time, her expression now more alert than hurt. 'Is it good?' she asked.

He took a sip. 'Great.' He set it in his lap, stirred the ice with the straw she had provided. 'I wanted to ask about Alice,' he said carefully.

'We can talk about her,' she said quickly. 'Jessie and Sara – they think I'll break down if I hear her name. But I won't. She was my sister, after all, why shouldn't I talk about her?'

'That's a good attitude.' Man, this was hard. Despite what she said, he felt as if he were treading on thin ice on a hot day. 'What I wanted to say – Do you think Alice killed herself?'

'Didn't she?'

'Do *you* think she did?'

Polly turned her head away, stared off into space for a moment. 'What?'

Michael set down his drink on the coffee table. 'Do you think she was the suicidal type?'

She frowned. 'Do you mean before she killed herself? She only killed herself the one time. At least that was the only time she tried, that I know of.'

'Do you think there might have been other times?'

'She never told me about any other time. She didn't tell me about this time, before she did it, I mean. But she didn't always tell me everything. We were close, but she had her secrets, which I think is all right.'

'Polly.'

'What? Did I put too much ice in your juice?'

'No. What I'm trying to say is I don't think she killed herself.'

'No?'

'No. I think she was murdered.'

Polly was impressed, to a certain extent. 'Really?'

'Yes.'

'Who murdered her?'

'I don't know. That's why I'm here. I'm trying to find out.'

Polly was suddenly confused. 'You don't think I did it, do you?'

'No.'

She relaxed. 'I didn't. I thought she did it. That's what that doctor at the hospital told me. The man with the electricity.'

'The man with the what?'

Polly shook her head. 'Never mind. I see what you're saying. You think someone killed her on purpose, and not accidentally.'

'Yeah.'

'And you don't know who it is?'

'Right.' He sat up, folded his hands. 'Polly, just before Alice died, you went outside to check the chlorine in the pool. Do you remember if you turned the pool light off?'

She nodded. 'Sure I remember. I have a good memory. I turned it off.'

'After you put the chlorine in the water?'

'Yes.'

'How long before you heard the shot did you turn off the light?'

'Not long.'

'A minute?'

'Yeah.'

That would explain why the room had been so dark. 'When you were outside at the pool, did you see anybody?'

'No.'

'Did you hear anything? Like up on the roof?'

'No.'

'Are you sure?'

'No. Yes.'

'What did you do when you heard the shot?'

'Wh— I came inside. You saw me. Don't you remember?'

'I remember.' She had been about to say something else. 'Tell me about Clark?'

Polly spoke defensively. 'I don't know his last name.'

'I understand. But can you tell me anything about him? How did you meet him?'

'On a hike in the mountains. I sprained my ankle and he came and drew my picture.'

'Where in the mountains?'

'I don't know what the place is called. We took that road that leads up and away from the racetrack.'

'The Santa Anita Racetrack?'

'Yeah, we went up there.'

'You and Alice?'

'Yeah.'

'What school did Clark go to?'

'I don't know if he went to school.'

'But wasn't he our age?'

'I don't know. He never talked about school. Alice told me you met him?'

'I did, yeah, at the first football game. Tell me, what did he talk about?'

'Weird stuff. He was a weird guy. But he – he was interesting, too.'

'Why did Alice go out with him?'

'He was an artist. He was showing her all kinds of new

338

techniques, opening her up.'

'Were they romantically involved?'

Polly's face darkened. 'What do you mean?'

He had to keep in mind Polly had gone out with Clark before Alice. 'Were they boyfriend and girlfriend?'

'You mean, did they sleep together? Of course they didn't. Do you think I would let my little sister have sex with someone like that? I was the one who told Alice not to invite him to the party. If she was here, she would tell you that.'

Michael stopped, feeling a chill at the base of his spine. 'Did Clark come to the party?'

'What?'

'Was Clark at the party?'

'I told you, I told Alice not to invite him.'

'But did he come? Without being invited?'

'He wouldn't have come without an invitation. He was weird, but he wasn't weird like that.'

'But—'

'Polly,' the aunt called.

Groaning, Polly got up. 'Coming,' she said, disappearing down the hall off the central foyer. She reappeared a moment later. 'I'm sorry, Mike. I can't talk any more. I have to take care of her. I'm really sorry.'

He stood up, pulling the permission form from his

back pocket. 'That's OK, I shouldn't have barged in on you like this, anyway. Maybe we can talk about this some other time?'

'Sure.'

'Hey, could I ask a big favour? You see this paper? It's a legal document that gives me permission to review the report that was done on your sister.'

'What report?'

He hated to use the word. 'The autopsy report.'

She accepted the sheet, glanced at it. 'You want me to sign it?'

'No, I want your aunt to sign it. She was Alice's legal guardian.'

'But why?'

'I feel there may be something in the report that the police overlooked.'

Polly folded the form. 'I'll ask her to look at it.'

'I'd really appreciate it. Another thing. Could you please keep this visit between us private? Don't talk to Jessie or Sara about it? They think – I don't know, that I should just drop the whole thing.'

Polly nodded sympathetically. 'They're like that a lot of the time.'

She showed him to the door. As he was stepping outside, she put her hand on his arm, looked up at him.

Again, the pain behind her eyes was all too clear, and he wondered if he'd added to it with his questions. She seemed to read his mind, as Alice used to do.

'I don't mind talking to you about how she died,' she said. 'She always told me what a great person you were. She told me I could trust you.'

Michael smiled uncomfortably. 'That was nice of her.'

She continued to hold on to him. 'Don't go after Clark, Mike. Alice told me about him, too. The night she died — She said he was no good.'

'Are you saying he might hurt me?'

'I don't know. I don't want you to get hurt.'

'Was he at the party, Polly?'

Now she let go of him, raising her hand to her head, trembling ever so slightly. 'I don't remember,' she said softly. 'There were so many people there. Too many uninvited people.'

He patted her on the shoulder, thanked her again for her help. Climbing into his car, he felt vaguely disoriented. If she hadn't loved Alice so much, and if he hadn't seen her go out to the pool immediately before the shooting, he would have added Polly to his list of suspects.

'That's what the doctor at the hospital told me. The man with the electricity.'

CHAPTER 4

It was later. Michael was gone, her aunt was sleeping, and the sun had gone down. Polly sat alone in the dark, the TV on, the sound off. She preferred it that way, watching people she didn't have to listen to. Sometimes at school she felt as if she would go mad, all those people talking all the time. Even her best friends, Jessica and Sara, they never shut up. And whenever she had something to say, they were too busy to listen.

Polly reached for another carrot. She had read that eating a lot of carrots improved your ability to see in the dark. Since she spent most nights awake answering her aunt's calls, it was important to her. Besides, carrots helped you lose weight. That's what Alice used to say. And look how skinny Alice had been. Thin as a stick.

She wasn't sure what she was watching, some stupid sitcom. Practically everything on TV these days was stupid. She didn't know if many people realised it, but the networks were even beginning to rerun the news.

Polly sat up suddenly. What was that sound? She had heard a banging noise. It seemed to be coming from out the back. She hoped it was a cat. She was terrified of burglars. She didn't have a hand-gun in the house, only her dad's old shotgun, which she couldn't even find. Getting up, she peeped through the curtains covering the sliding-glass door.

There was nobody there, at least nobody she could see. But with the approaching storm, it was unusually dark outside. She stood still for a moment, listening to the wind, the rustling of the trees. The noise was probably nothing but a branch knocking against the outside wall. There was probably no need to call the police.

Oh!

A bolt of white light split the sky, causing her to jump. Instinctively, she started to count, as she had been taught as a child. The crack of thunder hit between two and three. The rain followed almost immediately, pelting the pool water like sand particles blasting a windshield. Like sometimes happened in the desert when a car went off the road.

Polly bowed her head, leaning it on the glass door. All of a sudden she missed her parents, missed them really badly. *Their* car had gone off the road, right into a ditch, where it had exploded. She had been small at the time, but she remembered exactly how it had happened. There had been an argument about something, and then the car was burning and the doctor was telling her everything was all right. She didn't understand why doctors always lied.

'*The wires won't hurt. You won't even feel them.*'

But she felt everything. Liars.

Polly walked upstairs, headed down the hall, and turned right, entering the last room on the left, her parents' bedroom and the room where Alice had died. The chalk outline the police had drawn had been washed away long before she had returned to the house after her sister's death, but she could still distinguish a trace of it on the hard wooden floor – even in the dark. Sometimes, when she felt sad as she did now, she found it soothing to come into this room and rest on the spot where they had found Alice. Stretching out on the floor, she lay with her eyes open, staring at the ceiling.

Lightning flashed, thunder rolled. The gaps between the two seemed to lengthen. But the rain kept falling, and the storm was not going away. She noticed that the time between her breaths was also growing. She counted ten seconds between inhaling and exhaling, then fifteen.

She wondered if her heart was slowing down. Lying there, she often felt as if she understood what it had been like for Alice when they had found her on the floor. It hadn't been so bad. The dead might bleed, but they never cried.

Polly realised she was crying. It was all because she was alive. They had all gone and left her alone. A wave of despair pressed down on her, but she fought it, fighting to sit up. They hadn't cared about her. They hadn't asked what she wanted with her life. Her dad had decided to drive off the road. Her mom had gone ahead and burned. And Alice had taken that stupid gun and –

No!

Polly leaped to her feet. That banging sound again. Only now it was coming from outside the window. She crept to the shades, lifted it and peered down, seeing nothing at first but the garden, the rainy night. Then there was another flash of lightning. And there he was! Someone in her backyard!

'Hey, you! What are you doing there?'

The sound of her voice didn't cause him to run away, nor did it startle him. He cupped a hand over his eyes, looking up, his long scraggly hair hanging over his shoulders. She took a step away from the window, her heart hammering. She should have kept her mouth shut, she thought, and called the police. But then he spoke.

'Is that you, Polly?'

Relief rushed through her, followed by a fear of a different sort. 'Clark? What are you doing down there?'

'Trying to get in. It's wet out here. I rang the front doorbell a dozen times. Why didn't you answer?'

'The front doorbell doesn't work.' It had broken the night of the party.

'I knocked, too.'

'I'm sorry, I thought – I don't know. Just a sec. Go around to the back patio. I'll let you in.'

He had on the black leather jacket and pants he wore on his motorcycle. For the most part, the rain had left him untouched. Except for his tangled red hair. Soaked, it seemed much darker.

'I was beginning to believe you'd left this big box to the ghosts,' he said as she slid open the sliding-glass door that led out on to the roof-covered patio. 'How are you, babe? Been a long time.'

'Yeah, months. I can't believe you're here. Why didn't you call before coming?'

He wiped at his pale face with his long bony fingers. He had always been skinny. Now he was close to emaciated. 'I wanted to see you, I didn't want to talk to you.' He grinned. 'You look exotic, Polly, real tender.'

She beamed, relaxing a notch. She didn't know why she had felt she had to warn Michael away from Clark. Why, here he was right in front of her and everything was cool. 'Thanks, you look nice, too. Do you want to come in?'

'Nah,' he said, nodding to his mud-caked boots. 'Better not. Don't want to spoil the scene. I like to keep pretty things pretty.' He turned towards the side of the house where she had first seen him, and the grin seemed to melt from his face as if he were a clay sculpture in the rain. His entire manner changed.

'Why didn't you tell me?' he said.

She bit her lip. 'I thought you knew.'

He looked at her, his green eyes darkening. 'I didn't know until I read about the funeral in the papers.'

'Did you go?'

'You know I didn't.'

'I didn't know. They had me in the hospital.'

He was angry. 'But I called. I left messages.'

'My voicemail was acting up. I didn't get them.'

He shook his head, stepping away from the door, turning his back to her, reaching his palm out from beneath the shelter of the patio. The rain continued to pour down. 'Who killed her?' he asked.

'The police say it was a suicide.'

He thought about that a moment, then his mood changed again, and he chuckled. 'The police. What else do they say?'

'Nothing.'

'Did they ask about me?'

She hesitated. 'They didn't.'

He whirled. 'Did someone else?'

She had never been able to lie to him. He had some kind of power over her she didn't understand. 'A boy at school.'

'What's his name?'

'Michael.'

'What's his last name?'

'I'm not sure.' She added weakly, 'He wanted to know your last name.'

He moved to her, briefly touched her chin with his wet fingers, and it was almost as if an electrical current ran through his nails; she couldn't help quivering. 'Remember when we met?' he asked. 'On that sacred ground? The Indians buried there believed if you knew a person's secret name, you could make him do anything you wished. Anything at all.'

'Is that why you never told me your full name?'

He grinned again. 'Do you believe that nonsense?'

'No.'

He held her eyes a moment. 'I remember this Michael. I met him at the football game. Do you know if he saw me at the party?'

Lightning cracked again, thunder roared, the smell of ozone filling the air. Polly put a hand to her head, rubbed her temple. She didn't feel pain, only a slight pressure and immense surprise. 'You were at the party?' she said.

'Yeah, I came at the end like you told me to. Don't you remember?'

'Yeah,' she said quickly. 'I had just forgotten for a moment, that's all.' She really did remember, not everything maybe, but a lot. The three of them had been in the room together. They had got into an argument about the paper cups, or why Clark hadn't come earlier, something like that. Then she and Clark had left Alice alone in the room and gone downstairs. He had left on his motorcycle and she had gone out the back to check on the chlorine in the pool. Then Alice had gone for the gun . . .

The loneliness Polly had experienced in the bedroom suddenly crashed down on her, and she burst out crying. Clark's wet arms went around her, and she leaned into them.

'All I did was fight with Alice and make her think I hated her when I loved her more than I loved anything,' she said. 'And now she's gone, and Aunty's here, but she can hardly breathe. Help me, Clark, you've got to help me. I can't live like this. I feel I have to die.'

He didn't say anything for the longest time, just held her as he used to hold her before he had started to see Alice. When he finally did release her, she felt a little better, though slightly nauseated. He brushed the hair from her eyes, accidentally scratching her forehead with one of his nails.

'You'll be all right, kid,' he said. 'You don't have to die. You didn't do nothing wrong. Nothing at all.'

'But I—'

'Shh. Enough tears. Mourn too much and you disturb the sleep of the dead. Tell me, does Michael say Alice was murdered?'

She dabbed her eyes. 'He's suspicious.'

'Hmm. What else?'

'He gave me a paper he wants Aunty to sign.'

'Show it to me.'

He barely glanced at the form when she handed it over, folding it and sticking it in his coat pocket. 'I'll look at it later,' he said.

'If you want, I can read it to you now. I've been eating lots of carrots. I can see in the dark.'

He brushed aside her comment, sticking his head in

the doorway, sniffing the air. 'It stinks in this place. That old lady's still here?'

'Yeah. She's sick. She had a heart attack. I take care of her.'

'Why? Old people – when their number's up, they die. It doesn't matter what you do.'

'Don't say that!'

'That's reality, babe. Sometimes they choke to death on their tongues. It's a hassle watching her all the time, isn't it?'

'I don't mind. I take good care of her.'

He grinned and started to speak again just as someone knocked at the front door. 'Who's that?' he snapped.

'I don't know. I'll go see.'

'No, wait, I'll go. My bike's parked at the end of your driveway beneath that ugly tree, but it's probably getting wet.' He grabbed her by the arm, pulled her towards him. She thought for a moment he was going to kiss her, but then he let her go, gesturing for her to follow him away from the patio. 'Come here.'

'Out in the rain? I'll get wet.'

'Who cares?' She walked over and stood beside him in the downpour. The person at the front door knocked again. She hardly noticed. The water felt delicious atop her head, the drops sliding down inside her blouse and over her breasts. Clark took her into his arms again, leaned close to her ear. 'I like you this way,' he whispered. 'Cold, like me.' He kissed her neck lightly, and she could imagine how the rain must have drenched deep into his flesh while he had raced through the night on his motorcycle; his lips sent a chill into her blood, a warmth up her spine. 'Do you love me, Polly?'

'I-I'm glad you're here.'

'Do you want me to come again?'

'I do.'

'Then I will.' He kissed her again on the neck, took a step back. 'I have a secret to tell. Can you keep a secret?'

'Sure.'

'First you must promise not to talk about me to anybody.' He scratched her shoulder lightly, pinching the material. 'You must cross your heart and hope to die.'

She sketched a cross over her chest. 'I promise. What is it?'

'Michael knows something. But what he knows, he knows it backwards. Alice didn't kill herself.'

'How do you know?'

'Your sister was too cute to wash her hair with her own blood.'

'Who did kill her?'

He stared at her with his bright green eyes. The person

352

at the front door knocked a third time. 'You don't know?'

'No.'

'Would you lie to me?'

She began to feel a bit sick again. 'I honestly don't know.'

His face softened with a sympathy she had never seen in him before. 'Maybe I can't remember, either. But I paint what I see. Listen closely and ponder deeply. It wasn't you who killed her, and it wasn't me who pulled the trigger.'

She smiled at the absurdity of the idea. 'Well, of course we didn't.'

He turned to leave, spat on the grass. 'Stay alive, babe, and stay cold. It's the only way for the likes of us.'

He disappeared around the west side of the house, in the direction of the gate. He was such an interesting guy, she thought. She hurried to answer the door.

It was Russ. All he had on was a green T-shirt and blue jeans. Someone had punched him in the eye. The swelling reached to his nose. It was absolutely cool he had come over to see her messed up the way he was. 'I need a place to stay,' he said.

She had always known he liked her. Suddenly she was quite happy, and not the least bit lonely. All these nice boys wanting to talk to her and kiss her. It should rain more often.

But Clark might not like Russ kissing her. She could see his motorcycle at the end of the long driveway. Her eyes darted towards the side of the house. He probably hadn't even got past the gate yet. She reached out, taking Russ by the arm, pulling him inside. 'You poor dear,' she said. 'Let me make you dinner and you can tell me all about it.'

She cooked him a steak and fries. There wasn't any beer in the house, but he seemed to enjoy the expensive bottle of French wine she fetched from her aunt's closet. He finished it off before getting to dessert. When she asked who had belted him, he just shrugged, which was OK with her. She wasn't the nosy type, not like a lot of people she knew.

They watched TV. He liked the old *Star Trek* reruns – with the sound on. They talked a little, but then he started to yawn. She led him upstairs to her own bedroom. He was such a gentleman, he didn't expect her to put out right away. He just said goodnight and closed the door. She crashed on the couch downstairs.

Her aunt kept her up half the night. She didn't mind. It was nice having a man in the house.

CHAPTER 5

'How could you be so careless?' Jessica asked.

'I took it into the store because I was trying to be careful,' Sara said.

'Leaving a purse stuffed with three grand sitting in a supermarket freezer isn't my idea of being careful,' Jessica said.

'I didn't just leave it. I set it down and then he chased me out of the place.'

First period would begin in minutes. Jessica and Sara were in the parking lot, sitting in Jessica's car. Sara had let Jessica drive all the way to school before admitting she'd lost the majority of the ASB council's money.

'Russ chased you out of the freezer?' Jessica snorted. 'More likely you locked him in the freezer. What did you find when you went back last night?'

'Well . . .'

'Did you find your bag?'

'Yes.'

'With all the money gone?'

'Yes.'

Jessica studied her old friend, suspicious. 'What else?'

'The freezer door was gone, too.'

'What happened to it?'

'The store manager says Russ chopped it down.'

'*What?* You did lock him in! What the hell got into . . . Never mind. I don't want to know. Was Russ there when you went back?'

'No. His boss fired him for ruining the door.'

'Did you explain that it was your fault?'

'No. I was trying to get my money back. I didn't want the boss mad at me.'

'Man, you are dumb. You are the dumbest president I have ever seen.'

'I was hoping you would cheer me up.'

'You don't deserve it.' They sat in silence for a moment. 'He must have taken it,' Jessica said finally. Sara only shook her head. 'But you tried to turn him into a Popsicle. Why wouldn't he have taken it in revenge?'

'Russ wouldn't do that.'

'Have you spoken to him?'

'I called his house.'

'And?'

'He isn't living there any more.'

'Great. Fabulous. What are you saying?'

'His old man kicked him out. I don't know where he is.' Sara scratched her head. 'After Russ got fired, half a dozen people ran in and out of that freezer for a couple of hours. They were moving all the frozen goods to another store so they wouldn't spoil. One of them must have found the bag, and stolen the money.'

'Half a dozen employees shouldn't be that hard to check out.'

'Oh, yeah.'

Jessica drummed her fingers impatiently on the dashboard. 'You've screwed up everything. You won't be able to afford the band. You won't be able to pay for the food. Homecoming will have to be postponed again. It'll probably be called off.'

'And your crown might start to rust.'

'That's not what I'm talking about.'

'The hell it isn't! I'm in trouble, Jessie. And all you care about is winning some horse-faced beauty pageant!'

'That's not true!'

'It's all you think about!'

'So! What do you want me to do?'

'Give me some moral support! Quit telling me how

dumb I am!'

'You are dumb! You go in to buy a can of Spam and find a date and you end up spending three grand and almost killing a guy!'

Sara gave her a weird look and sat back in the car seat. 'You've made your point,' she muttered.

Jessica took a deep breath. 'I still think Russ must have taken it. I would have taken it.'

Sara sighed. 'No. I know him. He's not that kind of person. The money's gone, and it's gone for good.'

'How much is left in the account?'

'About two thousand. But half of that will be eaten up by cheques I've already written.' She shook her head. 'There isn't going to be enough.'

'How about hitting up Polly?'

'I tried that already. I talked to her this morning. She says she needs her aunt's signature to get hold of that much cash.' Sara shrugged. 'I believe her.'

'Could you find another car to raffle?'

'There isn't time.' Sara gave a miserable smile. 'I'm open to suggestions?'

Jessica thought a moment. 'I don't have any.'

The varsity tree was at both the physical and social centre of Tabb High. A huge thick-branched oak, it stood halfway between the administration building and the library, near the snack bar. At lunch, without fail, at least half the jocks would gather under it to enjoy the good looks of half the girls on the pep squads. For the most part, except for the week before the party when she had been vigorously pursuing Bill Skater, Jessica avoided the area. Crowds, even friendly ones, often tired her. But today was different. The results of the balloting to determine who would be on Tabb High's homecoming court would be announced from a platform set up beneath the tree.

'Where's Sara?' Maria Gonzales asked. 'Isn't she going to read the names?'

'No, I hear Mr Bark, my political science teacher, is playing MC,' Jessica said. 'Sara's got a lot on her mind.'

Maria was sympathetic. 'It must be hard for her to keep track of everything.'

'Tell me about it.'

'Are you nervous?' Maria asked.

'I feel like I'm waiting to be shot.'

Maria nodded to the crowd. 'You're the prettiest one here. Anyone can see that.'

'Anyone but me.' Dr Baron had been right about the letters and the numbers on the board making more sense when she had her glasses on, but all morning she couldn't help feeling people were staring at her and thinking she looked like an encyclopedia. At the moment, however, she had her glasses in her hand, and for that reason, she wasn't sure if she was hallucinating when she saw the long-legged blonde sitting all alone on one of the benches that loosely surrounded the varsity tree. Jessica pointed to the girl. 'Who is that?' she asked.

Maria frowned. 'Clair Hilrey.'

'What's she doing?'

'Nothing.'

Glancing around, Jessica quickly slipped on her glasses. The cheerleader was indeed by herself, and if that wasn't extraordinary enough, she looked downright depressed. 'I wonder what's the matter with her.'

'She's probably worried she won't be on the court.'

'Clair's got the self-confidence of a tidal wave. No, that's not it. Something's wrong.' Jessica took off her glasses and hid them away. 'Which reminds me. During chemistry this morning, you were looking pretty worried.'

'I'm fine.'

'Come on, Maria. Haven't we been friends long enough? You're not happy. What is it?'

Her tiny Hispanic friend shyly shook her head. 'I'm happy.'

'Are you still thinking about Nick?'

'No.'

After Alice's party, when the police were running in and out of the McCoy residence and questioning them all, Maria's parents had suddenly appeared. When Jessica had called her mom to explain what had happened, she forgot to tell her not to call the Gonzaleses. That had been a mistake. Mr and Mrs Gonzales didn't even know their daughter was at a party – and at two in the morning. And then Maria's parents arrived precisely when Bubba was telling a detective about the fight in the pool between The Rock and Nick. Of course Maria had played a vital role in that fight, which Bubba mentioned right in front of her parents. It took them no time at all to figure out that Maria had been dating Nick. And it didn't help that the police chose Nick – along with Russ and Kats – to detain for further questioning. Jessica didn't hear exactly what they said to Maria, but from a quick glance at their faces as they were leaving, Jessica knew it couldn't have been anything gentle.

Parental law was still in effect in Maria's family: for absolutely no reason was she to go near Nick Grutler.

'Liar,' Jessica said. She knew Maria was still thinking about Nick.

Maria started to protest again, but stopped herself. 'I wish I could choose what to think about,' she said sadly.

361

'It'll work out. It usually does.'

Maria had her doubts. 'I can't even talk to him about it.'

'Sure you can. Your parents won't know. Explain the situation to him.'

'How can I say that because he's black, my mom and dad assume he murdered Alice?' She shook her head. 'It's better if he thinks I don't like him any more. It's simpler this way.'

Mr Bark climbed on to the platform. The crowd quietened. Jessica hoped he wouldn't give a speech. A minute more of this waiting and she would scream.

He gave a speech – fifteen minutes – about how wonderful it was to be a teenager and to be alive in such exciting times. Bless him, he even worked in the need for nuclear disarmament. Jessica ground her teeth. Finally he pulled out the envelope.

'And now, the new homecoming court,' he said, excited, opening the list. 'Princess number one is . . .'

Jessica – Jessica – Jessica – me – me – me.

Mr Bark paused, perplexed. 'There seems to be some mistake. There are supposed to be five girls on the court . . .' He stepped away from the microphone, spoke quietly to Bubba for a moment. Bubba kept nodding his head no matter what the teacher seemed to ask. Finally Mr Bark returned to the mike. 'The vote has resulted in an unusual situation,' he said. 'There was a six-way tie for fifth place. It has, therefore, been decided that there will be only four girls on the court this year. They are: Clair Hilrey, Cindy Fosmeyer, Maria Gonzales and Jessica Hart.'

Maria dropped her books and pressed her fingers to her mouth. Jessica let out a totally involuntary scream. Then they hugged each other and laughed with tears in their eyes. It felt good, Jessica thought. It felt better than just about anything had ever felt in her whole life. She couldn't stop shaking.

'I can't believe it,' Maria kept saying. 'I can't believe it.'

'We don't have to believe it.' Jessica laughed. 'We're living it!'

People they knew and didn't know gathered around to offer their congratulations. Cindy Fosmeyer was one of them. She had huge breasts and a big nose. Jessica gave her a kiss. Everything seemed to be happening so fast. Pats on the back, smiles, hugs, kisses. But none of them were from Polly or Sara, and Jessica had started to look for them when Bill Skater came up and shook her hand.

'I knew you'd get on the court,' he said.

'If you knew, why didn't you tell me!' She giggled, giving him a quick hug, which took him by surprise.

'Well, Jessie, you didn't ask.'

She felt brave. She felt like a tease. 'So I didn't. So why don't you ask me something?'

Such boyish blue eyes. He gave her a sexy look – with his face, it was the only kind he could give – but his voice was hesitant. 'Do you want to go out tonight?'

The icing on the cake. Maybe she'd get a scoop of ice cream later. 'Absolutely!'

She was a princess. She had a prince. She gave him her number, another hug, and went to find her friends.

She accidentally bumped into Clair instead, in Sara's locker hall, far from the hustle and bustle. Clair was alone. She in fact *looked* lonely. But they shook hands and she offered Jessica her congratulations.

'Four little princesses,' Clair said. 'Sounds like a bad fairy tale, doesn't it?'

'It's amazing about that tie,' Jessica said.

'I wasn't surprised. Is Maria a friend of yours?'

'Yeah.'

'Give her my regards.'

'I will.' Jessica smiled. 'Aren't you excited?'

Clair turned to dial the combination on her locker. 'Ask me in a couple of weeks, when they call out my name during the dance.'

So that's how it was. 'Maybe you'll be asking me.'

Clair paused, giving her the eye. And now she

smiled, slow and sure. 'You may as well know, honey, I can't lose.'

CHAPTER 6

Unknown to Jessica, Sara had watched the announcement of the homecoming court. But she had shied away from congratulating her best friend for a couple of reasons. First, as she had told Jessica in the car that morning, she thought Jessica had become overly preoccupied with the whole queen business. Second, with the loss of the money and Russ's getting fired, she was in a rotten mood and was afraid she'd say something nasty just when Jessica was enjoying her high moment. The fact that these two reasons were contradictory didn't make any difference to Sara. In reality, she was happy for both Jessica and Maria, and not the least bit jealous. She wouldn't have wanted to be a princess for anything. Being ASB president was enough of a pain in the ass.

She needed money and she needed to get Russ's job back for him. She didn't know which troubled her most.

She was still smarting from his comments. She liked to think she didn't care about being popular. She had always thought of herself as subtle. But Russ honestly believed – and it didn't matter whether he was right or wrong (although he was most definitely wrong) – she was using her position of authority to seduce him, then maybe there was something in her approach. It was a possibility.

He was not at school today. All right, she'd worry about him the next day. Big bucks and fat Bubba were what mattered now. She followed Bubba as he left the varsity tree after the announcement, watched him disappear into the computer-science room. It was general knowledge that Bubba dealt in the stock market, and after checking around campus, she found out that he did extremely well. He was, in fact, a genius when it came to turning a few dollars into a few thousand. Knocking on the computer-room door and turning the knob, she hoped he didn't charge for advice.

He was already at a terminal, typing a million words a minute on the keyboard. He blanked the screen the instant she entered, but appeared happy to see her. He offered her a chair.

'What do you think of our new batch of princesses?' he asked.

'I was surprised Maria Gonzales and Cindy Fosmeyer

367

were selected,' she said. 'Maria's probably the quietest girl in the school, and Cindy – she's not exactly the princess type.'

'You mean she's a dog?'

'Yeah.'

Bubba nodded. 'But she does have big breasts, and those babies go a long way with half the votes in the school.' He glanced at his blank screen. 'She's always been one of my favourites.' He seemed to think that was funny, smiling to himself. 'What can I do for you, Ms President?'

'I have a small problem. I've been told you might be able to help me with it.'

He leaned back in his seat, apparently satisfied that it was his reputation that had brought her to him. 'Is it a financial or a sexual problem?' he asked.

'You have a lot of nerve.'

'I also have a big bank account, and a huge . . . Well, let's just say I am willing and able to help in either department.'

'It's a financial problem.'

'A pity.'

'I need three grand, and I need it by next week.'

'Why?'

'There'll be no homecoming unless I get it.'

'Why?'

'What do you mean, why? I need it to pay for everything.'

'Have you already spent the money from the car raffle?'

'No, not exactly.'

'What happened to the money? Did you lose it?'

'I . . . yeah, I did.'

'How did you lose it?'

'What difference does it make? I lost it!'

'If you lost it on a guy, then I would have to say you have both a sexual and a financial problem. I like to know what I'm dealing with before I invest my time.' He picked up a pen. 'Are you going out with Russ Desmond?'

'What business is it of yours? No, I am not going out with him. Look, can you help me or not? Because if you can't, I haven't eaten lunch yet.'

'Where would you like to go for lunch?'

'What?'

'I'll buy you lunch. Where would you like to eat?'

She stood. 'Nowhere. Thanks for your time.'

She was at the door when Bubba stopped her with the line, 'I can get you the money, maybe.'

'How?'

'Come back here and sit down.' She did as she was

told. He put aside his pen, leaned towards her, studying her face. 'You're cute, Sara.'

'How?' she repeated.

He shrugged. 'Does it matter? You should be asking what it's going to cost you.'

'What is it going to cost me?'

'Sex.'

She chuckled in disbelief. 'What?'

'Sex.'

'Are you crazy? Are you saying you'll pay me three grand for my body?'

He sat back, shook his head. 'No offence meant, but I would have to be crazy to spend that much money to sleep with you, or any girl for that matter. No, I said I can get you the money. I didn't say I would *give* it to you.'

'Where are you going to get it? From your own account?'

'No, most of my money is tied up.' He thought a moment. 'How much do you have left?'

'A grand.'

He considered again. 'Can you get to that money this afternoon?'

'Not without Bill Skater's countersignature on a cheque.'

'Do you have a copy of something Bill has signed?'

'Yeah.'

'Then you can fake his signature.'

'No, I'm not that desperate. I see what you're driving at. You want me to turn over the thousand to you.'

'You *are* that desperate or you wouldn't be here. And, yes, I'll need what you have.'

'No way. What are you going to do with it?'

'Invest it.'

'Can you invest money and get that big a profit that quickly?'

'In the commodities market, you can lay out a hundred dollars today and have five hundred tomorrow.'

'But I've heard investing in commodities is the same as rolling dice.'

'Not if you know what you're doing. But I only mentioned commodities as an example. I haven't decided exactly what I will do with the grand. I'll have to think about it.'

She shook her head. 'This sounds pretty thin to me. I told you, I need this money within a few days. If you're not willing to get it out of your personal investments, then I can't take you seriously.'

He was amused. 'I notice you haven't said anything about my demand for sexual favours?'

'What am I supposed to say? You were kidding, weren't you?'

'No.'

She realised she was blushing, and that he could tell she was blushing. 'But you need to triple whatever I give you in less than a week,' she persisted. 'Nobody in the world can guarantee they can do that.'

'Nobody in the world can guarantee anything. But I do believe – in fact, I'm almost certain – I can do great things with your money. Now as far as your deadline is concerned . . .' He picked up his pen again, reached for a piece of paper. 'Who do you owe?'

'Mainly the caterer and the band.'

'I need their names and phone numbers. I'll arrange it so we can pay them later.'

'They won't go for that.'

'They will after they talk to me. Give me the information.'

'Wait! Let me get this straight. I'm going to give you a thousand dollars, and in return you're going to take responsibility for all the homecoming bills?'

'What is this responsibility crap? I'll do the best I can. That's all a man can do.'

She swallowed. 'And when you pay everything off, I have to sleep with you?'

'Yes.'

'How many times?'

'Once.'

'Is that all?'

'When it's over, you'll wish there were a hundred times yet to come.'

'But you've been through half the girls on campus. God only knows what diseases you have.'

'My vast experience has only made me all the more careful. Trust me, Sara, I'll take exquisite care of you.' He paused. 'Have we got a deal?'

She grimaced. 'Has anyone ever told you what a sleazeball you are?'

Bubba threw back his head and laughed.

CHAPTER 7

If anyone else had chased after him so long to do something he didn't want to do, Nick Grutler thought, he probably would have punched him in the nose by now. But he respected Michael, and he learned it paid to listen to him. Michael was trying to persuade him to go out for the basketball team.

They were near the end of a one-on-one game, playing on an outside court near the girls' baseball field. The storm the night before had left an occasional puddle for them to dodge, but the water was slowing neither of them down. School had ended about an hour earlier, and the varsity team's official after-school practice had been cancelled. The new coach had wanted the gymnasium floor waxed, and Tabb High's most recent crop of janitors had never done it before – and probably shouldn't be allowed to do it again; at the rate they were going, the floor wouldn't be ready for the homecoming game.

Michael had asked Nick to hang around to help him with his jump shot. Naturally they had ended up trying to show each other up. It was no contest. Nick was ahead forty-four to thirty in a fifty-point game. Michael had trouble stopping Nick because Nick was able to palm the ball with equal ease with either hand, hit three-quarters of his shots anywhere within a twenty-foot radius of the basket, and – according to Michael, though Nick thought he was exaggerating – fly.

'But if this new coach you guys have is such a jerk,' Nick said, tossing the ball to Michael to take out of bounds, 'why should I put myself out for him?'

'You won't be doing it for him,' Michael said, wiping the sweat from his forehead. Nick admired Michael's gutsy determination, especially on defence, even though he knew if he really wanted, he could score on him every time. 'You'll be playing for yourself.'

'On a team sport? Sure you don't want to take a break?'

'I'm all right,' Michael said, dribbling slowly in bounds. 'I mean you don't know how talented you are. I bet you could average thirty points and twenty rebounds a game if the rest of us didn't get in your way.' He paused, panting, his free hand propped on his hip. 'Are you ready?'

'I'm ready.'

Michael nodded, continuing to dribble at the top of the key. 'You get that kind of stats over the first half of the season and you'll have every college recruiter in the area coming to watch you play. Have you ever thought about that, going to college?'

'I never thought of graduating from high school till I met you,' Nick said, not exaggerating. It had been Michael who had got him into academics at Tabb. Michael had done it by forcing him to read one book, from cover to cover, each week. It had been quite a chore for Nick because initially he'd had to go over each page three or four times with a dictionary. But he had learned that Michael's belief that the key to success in school was a strong vocabulary was absolutely true. He had found that even in maths he could figure out how to work the problems now that he could follow the examples. He had also learned he enjoyed reading – he especially liked war stories – and that he wasn't dumb. Indeed, Michael had told him not more than an hour earlier that only someone with a high IQ could quadruple his vocabulary in the space of two months.

Nick was going to look up the exact definition of IQ as soon as he got home.

'Would you like to go to college?' Michael asked.

'I don't know what I'd do there.'

'You would go to classes as you do here. Only you'd be able to major in any subject you wanted.' Michael stopped suddenly, let fly with a fifteen-foot jump shot. Nick sprang up effortlessly, purposely swatting it back in Michael's direction. 'Nice block,' Michael muttered, catching the ball.

'Do people major in history?' Nick asked.

'Sure. You enjoy reading about the past, don't you?'

'It's interesting to see how people used to do stuff.' Michael appeared undecided what to do next. 'Why don't we take a break?' Nick suggested.

'Only if you're tired?'

Nick yawned, nodded. A week after Alice McCoy's funeral, Michael had called him with a job lead at a vitamin-packing factory. Nick had immediately ridden to the place on his bike. He had been hired on the spot. Only later had he come to understand they'd taken him on as a favour to Michael. Apparently, Michael had once helped the owner's son – Nick didn't know all the details. He was just thankful to have cash coming in so his dad wouldn't throw him out. But the hours were long and there was a lot of heavy lifting. He usually worked swing – three to twelve. He couldn't imagine taking on the extra burden of daily basketball practice. He told Michael as much as they walked to the sidelines and collected their sweats.

'You shouldn't be working full-time,' Michael said. 'You're only in high school. Does your dad take all your money?'

'Just about.'

'That's not fair.'

'If you ever met my dad, and he wanted your pay-cheque, believe me, you'd give it to him. Anyway, *you* work full-time.'

'That's different. My mom needs the dough. And that's beside the point. You've got to take the long-term perspective on this. Imagine – you go out for the team, blow everybody's mind, get offered a college scholarship, earn a degree, land a job where you don't have to kill yourself every day for the rest of your life, and you can see how it would be worth it to sacrifice a few hours of sleep for the next few months.'

Nick wiped his brow with his sweatshirt, slipped it over his head. 'Forget about psyching me up for a minute and tell me this: am I really that good?'

'You're better than that.'

Nick shook his head. 'I can't believe this.' In response, Michael snapped the ball towards his face. 'Hey!' he shouted, catching it an inch shy of the tip of his nose. 'Watch it.'

Michael nodded. 'There isn't another kid in the school who could have caught that ball. The best somebody else might have done was knock it away. You've got reflexes. You've got hands. And you've got a four-foot vertical jump. Trust me, you're *that* good.'

Nick lowered his head, dribbled the ball beside his worn-out sneakers; he'd had only one pair of shoes in the past three years. 'The Rock and a couple of his football buddies are on the team,' he said. 'What kind of welcome are they going to give me?'

'Oh, they'll try to make you feel like dirt. Especially when you start bouncing the ball off the top of their heads every time you slam-dunk. But I can't believe you'd let *them* stop you?'

'It's not just them. It's – something else.'

'What?'

'Somebody's out to get me, Mike.'

'Who?'

Nick grabbed hold of the ball, squeezed it tight, feeling the strength in his hands, and the anger, deeper inside, that seemed to give fuel to his strength. Except for brief moments it was as if he had been angry all his life . . . or alone and unwanted. It was often hard for him to tell the feelings apart. 'There's this guy who goes to school here – his name's Randy. I don't know his last name.'

'What's he look like?'

'He's ugly. He's got dark hair, bushy red sideburns and a beer gut. He looks older. You know who I'm talking about?'

'I've seen him. What's he doing to you?'

'He's trying to sell me drugs. I know that doesn't sound like a big deal, but he keeps on at me, even after I've told him half a dozen times I'm not interested. I think he's trying to set me up.'

'That serious?'

'Yeah. This afternoon, when I went to my locker, I found a bag sitting on top of my books, and a note that said "On the House". The bag had a couple of grams of coke in it.'

'What did you do with it?' Michael asked.

'I gave it to Bubba.'

'What did you do that for?'

'He was with me when I found it. He wanted it.'

'But Bubba doesn't do drugs.'

'Maybe he wanted to sell it, I don't know.'

Michael considered a bit. 'The fact that he looks older could be important. It might be possible to use the computer to check on— Hey, what is it?'

She was coming out of the girls' shower room, her long black hair tied in a ponytail as it had been the day they first met. Although small and far away, for a second, she was all he could see. 'It's Maria,' Nick said.

Michael was not impressed. He thought Maria was a phoney for dumping Nick simply because the police had detained him at the station after Alice McCoy's death. Michael didn't know about her overriding fear of calling attention to herself, of being found out for what she was – an illegal alien. But maybe the knowledge wouldn't have made any difference to Michael. Often it seemed a poor excuse to Nick, too. Yet there wasn't an hour that went by when Nick didn't think of her.

'She must be feeling like hot stuff being elected to the homecoming court and all,' Michael said.

'Not Maria.'

Michael glanced at him, then at Maria. 'I shouldn't have said that.'

Nick rolled the ball in his hands. He would pop it next; he knew he could make it explode. 'It's driving me nuts.'

'What do you want to do?'

'Talk to her. But she doesn't want to talk to me.'

'Have you asked her why?'

'I've tried.'

'Try again. Try now.'

'No. No I can't.'

'You have a perfect excuse to approach her. You want to congratulate her on making the court. Here, give me the ball. I'll wait for you.'

'Mike . . .'

'Go before she's gone.'

He went; he only needed a shove. She saw him coming and turned to wait. He took that as a positive sign.

It wasn't.

'Hi,' he said. 'How are you?'

She appeared so calm, he thought she must surely be able to see how he was trembling inside. Yet a closer look showed her calmness to be no deeper than the welcome in her expression. She had waited for him out of politeness, not because she wanted to.

'Good,' she said. 'And you?'

'Oh, I'm all sweaty.' He nodded towards Michael, and the courts. 'We're playing some basketball.'

She nodded, solemn as the day they'd met, only more distant now, not nearly so comfortable. 'I saw you. Say hello to Mike for me.'

'I will.' That sounded like a goodbye. 'I hear you're a school princess. That must be exciting?'

Her mood brightened, a bit. 'I still don't believe it.

I didn't think anyone knew who I was.'

'It didn't surprise me. I voted for you.'

'You did, really?'

'Of course.'

'Who else did you vote for?' She sounded genuinely curious.

'Jessica and Sara and that girl Bubba sees – Clair.'

'That's only four people. You could vote for five.'

'They were the only ones I wrote down.'

She seemed happy, in that moment, standing there listening to his praise, probably replaying in her mind the afternoon's announcement. But it didn't last. She looked at the ground. 'I've got to go.'

The word just burst out of him. 'Why?'

'Because, Nick, because—' She clasped her books to her chest, her head still down. 'I have to.'

'I see.' Then he said something that had been on his mind since the cops had led him to the jail cell with Kats and Russ the night Alice McCoy had taken a bullet through the head. 'Is it because I was running down the stairs after the gunshot?'

She jumped slightly. 'No.'

'You think I killed her.'

She turned away. 'No!'

'You're the only one who knew I was coming down

those stairs.' He stopped, and now a cold note entered his tone. 'Or are you, Maria?'

Her back to him, she nodded slowly. 'I'm the only one. But that doesn't matter. None of that matters.' She glanced over her shoulder, her eyes dark, lonely. 'I have to go.'

He shrugged. 'Go.'

When he returned to the court, Michael asked him how it had gone. Nick repeated everything that had been said, except the bit about his running down the stairs. It wasn't that he didn't trust Michael, he simply felt guilty for having lied to him after the funeral when they had originally discussed the matter. Back then, after having spent a few days in the slammer, he'd been afraid to say anything even remotely incriminating.

He needed respect, not just from Michael, but from everyone in school. Then maybe Maria would see him as something other than a threat. As they walked towards the showers, he said, 'I think I will go out for the team.'

CHAPTER 8

Although he had been badly beaten on the court, Michael felt better for the exercise. The thought of his date that evening with Jessica wasn't slowing him down, either. He'd had trouble falling asleep the night before thinking about it.

After saying goodbye to Nick, Michael headed for the computer-science room. He'd been meaning to have a talk with Bubba. He decided now would be a good time.

Michael had not purposely avoided his old friend after Alice's death the way he had avoided Jessica, yet since then, he had spoken to Bubba very few times. He suspected Bubba may have been keeping his distance. Whatever the reason, it was time to clear the air between them.

On the way to Bubba, he thought of the form he'd given Polly. She hadn't been at school that day. He decided to give her a quick call. She didn't answer till the seventh or eighth ring.

'You barely caught me, Mike. I'm on my way out.'

'I won't keep you then. I was wondering if I could swing by this afternoon and pick up that form I left last night?'

'What form?'

'The permission form I wanted your aunt to sign. Did she have a chance to read it over?'

Polly hesitated. 'I don't know. I don't think so.'

'Is there a problem? If you'd like, I could explain what it's for to your aunt.'

'No, you don't have to do that.'

'Do you have any idea when I could pick it up?'

'I'll see. I'll get back to you, all right?'

'Sure. I'll talk to you later.'

Hanging up, he knew he'd wait a long time before Polly McCoy contacted him.

He was not surprised to find Bubba seated in front of a computer. Hardly lifting his eyes from the screen, Bubba waved him into a chair. Michael sat patiently for a few minutes before finally asking, 'Should I come back later?'

'No.'

'What are you doing?'

Bubba continued to study the screen, zipping through rows and rows of figures. 'Did you know Tabb High is paying to receive the latest Wall Street numbers over our modem?'

'No.'

'Neither does the administration.' Bubba pointed to the screen. 'Look at Ford. Yesterday it was ninety-five and three quarters. Now it's down to ninety-two and a half.'

'Did you buy an option on it?'

'No. I've been shying away from options altogether. Too risky with the way Wall Street has been dancing since the bond market choked.' He tapped a couple of other numbers, then put his finger to his lips, thoughtful. 'But when the market's like this, it's also the best time to make a quick killing.'

'Are you in some kind of hurry?'

'Greed always is.' He flipped off the screen, relaxed into his personal swivel chair, giving Michael his full attention.

'What's up?'

'The usual – nothing. How about you?'

'What can I say? The world revolves around me.' He paused, giving Michael a penetrating look. Bubba was no dummy. 'You want to talk about something, Mike?'

'Am I that obvious?'

'No, I'm that perceptive. Besides, we've known each other a long time. What's on your mind?'

He reminds me we're old friends. He knows I don't trust him.

Michael did not suspect Bubba of murdering Alice McCoy. He realised, however, that Bubba did not have to be a murderer to be a liar. Nick had heard groans coming from the locked bedroom next to the room where they had found Alice. Cries of distress, Nick had thought, perhaps mistaking what had actually been cries of ecstasy.

'All right, I did want to talk to you about something.'

'Shoot.'

'Were you having sex with Clair in the bedroom next to the one where Alice died?'

Bubba chuckled. 'Wow, now that's a fine question.'

Michael smiled. 'Were you?'

'What did I tell the police?'

'That you were outside in the front with Clair, stargazing.'

'Then the answer must be no.'

Michael leaned forward. 'Come on, Bubba, it had to be you. It couldn't have been anybody else.'

'How does this tie in with what happened to Alice?'

'If I knew for a fact you were in there with Clair,

it would allow me to cross that room out of the whole equation.'

'Are you still talking to the police?'

'The police think it was a suicide,' Michael said. 'I keep in contact with the detective that was in charge of the case. Why?'

'Just wondering.'

'I'm not going to go to them with this information if that's what you're worried about.'

'I wasn't in the bedroom. I would tell you if I was. Why don't you believe me?'

Michael knew from experience what a phenomenal liar Bubba was. Yet he didn't understand why Bubba would lie to him now. Surely he couldn't be trying to protect Clair's reputation, not after bragging about how many condoms he had gone through with her. On the other hand, the question remained – who could it have been?

Could Bubba have been in the room with Clair and Alice? Michael sat back in his seat. 'I hope Clair enjoyed the astronomy lesson. Did you show her the Little Dipper?'

Bubba grinned. 'Hey, that sounds like a personal insult. But I'll forgive you this time. How's the telescope? Discovered any comets?'

No one could change a subject as smoothly as Bubba. Michael decided he would wait and broach the topic later. 'I'm still looking,' he said. 'It's a big sky.' He had made a vow to himself not to discuss his find with anyone until it was definite. He nodded to the computer screen. 'I need a favour.'

'What?'

'Use those codes you swiped from Miss Fenway and call up the files on that Randy guy who's been hassling Nick to buy drugs.'

'On Randy Meisser?'

'Is that his name?'

'Yeah. I already have. He's a narc.'

'Are you sure?'

'I can't be absolutely sure, but he came out of nowhere. He has no transcripts. He has no home address. I think he was planted here by the police. They're doing that these days.'

'Why do you think he went after Nick?'

'Because he's black.'

'What did you do with the cocaine you got out of Nick's locker?'

'Spiked a Pepsi with it and gave it to Randy.'

Michael laughed. 'Did he drink it?'

'Yeah. He was bouncing off the walls in creative writing. The teacher had to send him down to the office.' Bubba yawned. 'I'll spread the word about him. He won't last.'

Michael thought of Polly and the permission form. 'I'd like you to do me another favour. I want a look at the report on Alice's autopsy. I'm having trouble going through official channels. I was wondering if you could tap into the police files and—'

'Forget it,' Bubba interrupted.

'Why?'

'The police department deals with highly sensitive information. It's not like the school district. They have experts protect those files. I won't be able to touch them.'

Michael had suspected that would be the case. 'The coroner who did the autopsy isn't a full-time employee of the county, but a consultant. His name is Dr Gin Kawati. I checked around at lunch. He has an office downtown.' Michael pulled a slip of paper from his pocket, gave it to Bubba. 'That's his business address. You can see he belongs to the ARC Medic Group. They're fairly large. They must be computerised.'

Bubba fingered the slip. 'Even if I'm able to break into the Group's files, who's to say the good doctor will have a copy of a report he did for the city in with his private records?'

'There's no way of telling without looking. Can you do it?'

'It all depends on how their system's set up. It may be that I'd have to go down there at night and use one of their terminals.'

'You mean break into the office?'

'Yeah. Or I might be able to do it from here.' Bubba set the paper aside. 'I'll look into it.'

'I really appreciate it.' Michael shifted uncomfortably. 'I suppose you think I'm nuts for keeping up the investigation?'

Bubba turned away, snapping his screen back on. 'I understand how much she meant to you, Mike. You don't have to explain anything to me.'

'Thanks.'

The door burst open. It was Clair Hilrey. Michael got to his feet, went to congratulate her on her nomination to the homecoming court. The words caught in his throat. Her usually bright blue eyes were bloodshot, and she hadn't been out drinking and celebrating. She had been crying. She smiled politely when she saw him, though, wiping a hand across her cheek. 'Hi, Mike. Am I interrupting something?'

Bubba had stood up, too, and knocked over his chair doing so. Bubba jumped for a girl about as often as he went to Sunday Mass. Michael took the hint. 'I was just leaving,' he said.

'He was just leaving,' Bubba repeated, catching Clair's eye. She lowered her head. Michael hurried towards the door.

'I'll leave you two alone,' he said.

Obviously he wasn't the only one with a lot on his mind.

CHAPTER 9

Polly hadn't lied to Michael. She really had been on her way out when he called. She had to go to the market for groceries, and to the family clinic for contraceptives. If Russ's sexual appetite matched his appetite at the kitchen table, she figured she had better be prepared. All day he had done nothing but watch TV and eat. Her aunt didn't know he was in the house, and since she never left her bedroom, Polly saw no reason for her ever to know. Polly had told Russ to keep his voice down when they talked.

But after speaking to Michael, Polly couldn't find her keys. They weren't where she always left them, on the counter beside the microwave. She was searching in the drawers when Tony Foulton, the architectural engineer at her construction company, called. He had some concerns about the float he was building for the dance.

'As I told you last week, Polly, this is a little out of my line. I think Sara would have been better off hiring a company that specialises in floats.'

'I told her the exact same thing. But she says the school can't afford it. How's it coming along?'

'The platform itself is no problem; it's the fact we're building it on top of a pickup truck that bothers me. How far did you say it has to be driven?'

'Only a hundred yards. We can have it towed to the school.'

Tony considered. 'Would it be possible to rent a real float carrier?'

'How much would it cost?'

'They're scarce this time of year with all the holiday parades, but I could check around town. Less than a thousand dollars.'

'A thousand dollars is a lot of money.'

'I don't think it would be that much.'

'But haven't you already begun construction?'

'We're about half done with it, yes. But it wouldn't take long to pull it down.'

Polly knew what her carpenters charged per hour. This was turning out to be expensive. Sara had a lot of nerve putting her people through all this. 'But why? It's not going to cave in if someone stands on it, is it?'

'No, it won't do that. But as I said before, it lacks stability.' He paused. 'As an engineer, I would feel better if we didn't use the truck.'

'Are you going to be in tomorrow, Tony?'

'Yes. I usually work till noon on Saturday.'

'I'll come by about ten and look at it. Oh, how's Philip?'

Philip Bart was a foreman who'd been with the company since her father had founded it fifteen years earlier. Recently McCoy Construction had won a big contract in the mountains near Big Bear Lake for a two-hundred-room hotel. Prior to laying the foundation, a hard vein of granite had to be removed from the soil using dynamite. Somehow, in the middle of one of the blasts, Philip had been struck on the head by a flying rock. He'd gone into a coma and the initial prognosis had been poor. Fortunately, in the last couple of days, he had regained consciousness.

'Much better,' Tony said, his voice warming. 'He's sitting up in bed and eating solid food. He told me to thank you for the cheque you sent his family.'

'It was the least I could do. I'm glad he's going to be all right. Give him my best. But Tony, next time, have everyone stand back a little further, OK?'

He laughed. 'I'll see you tomorrow, Polly.'

Russ came into the kitchen as she set down the phone. He had not shaved. He looked very masculine. When he had arrived the night before in the rain, he had a suitcase outside in his truck. Now he had on running shorts, shoes and socks and nothing else. 'Where are you going?' she asked.

'I have to run,' he said, sitting down and checking his laces.

'Why? I thought cross-country was over?'

'I run year round.'

'Where are you going to go?'

'Wherever my feet take me.'

'You won't tell me?'

He glanced up. 'I don't know where I'm going, Polly.'

'But it might rain on you. It rained yesterday.'

He stood, stretching towards the ceiling, then reaching for his toes, his powerful back muscles swelling around his shoulder blades. 'The rain and I are old friends.' Straightening, he headed for the door. 'I'll catch you later.'

'Wait! I have to talk to you about something.'

He stopped, his hand on the knob. 'What?'

'Jessica called a few minutes ago. She told me how Sara locked you in the freezer. I never knew she hated you that much. God, it must have been awful for you. I knew last night something was wrong when I saw how red and sore your hands were.'

'Yeah, well, it was probably my fault.' He nodded. 'See ya.'

She watched him go. He sure was cool, maybe too cool. He let people walk all over him. She used to have that problem. She hadn't told Jessica where Russ slept last night. She respected his privacy, and hadn't wanted to brag.

Polly never did find her keys, and had to fetch a spare set from her bedroom. Backing out of the garage into the driveway, she rolled down the window, feeling a chill in the air. It had been her practice last winter to always keep an extra sweater in the boot. Stopping the Mercedes, she jumped out to check and see if it was still there.

She found the sweater, but that was all she found. It wasn't until she was back in her car and heading down the road that she realised the axe she had taken from Russ the first week of school – and which she had been meaning to give back to him ever since – was no longer in her boot. She had no idea what could have happened to it.

She screwed up by going to the market first. She bought all kinds of frozen goods and milk and stuff and then realised it would have to sit in the car while she was in the family clinic. It was really a question of priorities, she thought, after deciding not to go home before visiting the clinic: the welfare of her body over the welfare of a few lousy frozen carrots. Obviously, if she was going to have sex like a mature woman, she was going to have to act like one and take the precautions necessary to keep from becoming pregnant.

Walking up the steps to the clinic, Polly congratulated herself for coming here instead of making an appointment with her personal physician. Dr Kline had known her since she was a child. He was old and conservative and would have asked her lots of nosey questions. Besides, it was more fun this way. She might run into someone she knew.

Polly did precisely that. But first she had a hard time making the nurse – Polly assumed she was a nurse, she was dressed in white – understand what she wanted. They weren't speaking the same language. Sure, she had read about condoms and diaphragms in women's magazines, but all the articles had been written with the assumption you knew what those things were. Polly wasn't even sure which ones the boys wore. She finally told the nurse she wanted a birth-control method that wasn't too gross. The nurse smiled and told her to have a seat. The doctor would see her in a few minutes.

The waiting room was crowded – thirty people at least, and only three of them were guys. The few minutes had become more than a half-hour and Polly was beginning to feel restless when Clair Hilrey suddenly appeared through the inside swinging green door. A nurse was holding on to her elbow; she was having trouble walking. The nurse guided her into a chair directly across from Polly, who had never seen Clair with a hair out of place, much less ready to keel over. Before leaving, the nurse asked if she'd be all right. Clair nodded weakly.

Polly sat and watched Clair for several minutes, all the time wondering what her problem could be. The girl was perspiring heavily, her eyes rolling from side to side. At one point, she even bent over and pressed her head between her knees. Polly was relieved when Clair didn't throw up.

'Are you all right?' Polly asked finally.

Clair took a deep breath, rested her chin in her hand, didn't look up. 'Yeah,' she mumbled. 'I'm waiting for someone.'

'But you look sick. Are you sick?'

'No, not now.'

'That's good. I didn't go to school today, but Jessica

told me the two of you were elected to the homecoming court. That's great.'

Clair sat up. 'Huh?'

Polly smiled. 'Jessica said—'

'Jessica Hart?'

'Yeah, she's my best friend. Don't you remember me? I'm Polly McCoy.'

Clair put a hand to her head, dizzy. 'Yeah, Polly, yeah. Of course, I remember you.' She glanced towards the exit door. 'How are you?'

'Great. Just stopped by to buy some contraceptives. You know Russ Desmond? He's staying at my house. What kind of contraceptives do you use, Clair?'

'I don't.'

'You don't?'

'I mean, I don't need any.' She got up, staggering slightly. Bubba had appeared in the hallway. 'I've got to go, Polly. Take care of yourself.'

Bubba took Clair by the arm and helped her across the floor. Clair said something to him about his being late, but they were out of the door before Polly could hear his response. Polly didn't know why Jessica didn't like Clair. She seemed a nice enough girl.

CHAPTER 10

Michael stopped at the petrol station where Kats worked on the way home from school. Because of his one-on-one game with Nick and his talk with Bubba, he was late leaving campus. The sun had already begun to set, and he was anxious to shower and get dressed for his date with Jessica. But he had set the investigative ball in motion and felt he had to stop to have a little chat with Kats – just for a minute. If he'd been asked to pick Alice's murderer, it would have been Kats. He parked at the full-service isle – something he never did – and got out. Kats appeared from beneath a jacked-up Camaro inside the garage. He had on an oil-stained army-surplus jacket that could have used a rinsing in a tub of gasoline, and a cigarette dangled between his lips. He must have just been in a fight. Michael noticed he was missing a front tooth and he had been ugly to begin with.

'Hey, Mikey, how come's I never see you any more? Where you been hanging out?'

'I've been around. What are you up to these days?'

Kats wiped at his greasy black moustache. 'Working and going to night school. You know, I'll probably get my diploma when you guys do.'

'I didn't know that.'

Kats giggled. He might have been high on something. 'Yeah, I might be at your graduation! Imagine that!' He lowered his voice. 'You wouldn't let me come last year.'

'Not me.'

'Huh?'

'Nothing.' They were the only ones at the station. Michael nodded to his car. 'Could you fill it up with unleaded please?'

Kats paused, eyeing him. 'Since when are you too important to pump your own gas, Mikey?'

'Since I started paying for full serve.'

Kats glanced at the pump, grinned. 'Hey, you're right. You're parked where all the big shots park. Sorry, I didn't see that.' He threw away his cigarette and started to unscrew the petrol cap. 'You mustn't be counting your nickels and dimes any more. Things going good? They're going good with me. The day I get hold of that diploma, I'm out of this joint.'

'Are you still planning on joining the army?' Michael asked, leaning against the car. He'd opted for full serve, feeling it would give him a psychological advantage while questioning Kats. For the moment, he was the boss.

'You kidding me? Those pussy-foot children?' Kats unhooked the pump. 'I'm going to be a marine, or I ain't going to be nothing.'

'Have they accepted you already?'

Kats nodded. 'Get your schoolin' done and you're in. That's what they told me.'

'Was that before or after you got arrested the night Alice McCoy died?'

He had purposely phrased the question to shock Kats. Yet Kats was either too smart to fall for the bait or else too stupid to recognise it. He stuck the nozzle into the tank, set the grip on the handle to automatic feed. 'I don't remember,' he said, whipping a rag from his back pocket. 'Want your oil checked?'

Michael could have backed off at that point and asked Kats a couple of civil questions about the night of the party. But he decided to push him further. He would get more out of an upset Kats, he decided. The guy had one of those mouths that split wider the greater the pressure inside.

'Yeah, you remember,' he said. 'It was before Alice

died. But the way things are now, I bet the marines wouldn't let you hold an empty rifle in basic training.' He knew this wasn't true. The marines were looking for a few good men, but weren't above taking a few good killers. Kats didn't know that. He started to warm to the discussion.

'I didn't do nothing,' he said, throwing open the hood. He sounded both hurt and angry. 'I didn't kill that girl. I wouldn't do that, Mikey. You know me. We go way back. When did I ever kill a girl?'

Michael followed him to the front of the car. 'It was your gun in her hand. It was your bullets. Your finger prints were on both. Explain that to me, why don't you?'

'I had it in my car. I don't know how she got hold of it. I told the police that. They had no right to go to my place and take all my pieces.'

'A girl dies, and you're worried about your gun collection?'

'I didn't kill her!'

'Who did?'

'I don't know!'

'What were you doing on the roof porch when the gun went off?'

Kats's pride had been offended. He began to sulk. 'I wasn't doing nothing.'

'But you were on the second floor. Why did you take so long to get to the bedroom after the gun went off?'

'Why should I talk to you? I thought you were my friend. You're worse than the police.' He let the hood slam, turned to walk away. 'Get your own petrol and get the hell out of here.'

Michael grabbed Kats's arm, realising he might have made a mistake with his hard-nosed tactics. Here he thought he was proceeding logically when deep inside he probably just wanted to find someone to blame. Michael realised he hadn't changed from the day of the funeral, not really. Kats shook loose, jumped back a step. 'Lay off!' he snapped.

Michael raised his palms. 'All right, you don't know anything. Neither do I. But you can still answer the question.'

Kats fumed, debating whether to talk to him. Finally he said, 'I didn't go straight to the room. I went into the backyard first.'

'What? You jumped off the roof?'

'No, I didn't jump off the roof. I'm not that dumb.'

'But why didn't we run into you going up the stairs?'

Kats shook his head impatiently. 'I was out on the porch. I thought I saw someone in the backyard.'

'Polly was the only one in the backyard.'

'I didn't know that. I went to the edge of the roof to see who was there. That's when I saw Polly. She was running into the house.'

'Yeah, after the shot,' Michael said.

'That's what I'm talking about, after the shot. I saw her run through the back door. I figured someone must be after her. I kept looking for whoever fired the gun, but didn't see them.'

'Go on.'

'Then I went downstairs, and out into the backyard.'

'What did you see?'

'I told you, I didn't see nothing.'

'Then what are you talking about?'

'You asked me why it took me so long to get to the room and I've told you. I told the police the same thing and they kept me in jail for a week.' Kats was disgusted. 'I don't know what's wrong with all you people.'

Kats must have still been searching the backyard from his vantage point on the second-storey porch when they passed his door in the hall. But the main inconsistency in his explanation was so obvious Michael almost missed it. 'Wait a second,' he said. 'We were downstairs, and we could tell where the shot came from. How come you couldn't?'

'Quit hassling me, would ya?'

'But you're supposed to be an expert when it comes to guns. Christ, you've practically slept with them since you were twelve. How could you make such a mistake?'

Kats paused, and he seemed honestly confused. 'I don't know.'

Could someone have shot Alice from outside?

It made no sense. The bullet couldn't have passed through the screens on the windows. Certainly, it couldn't have penetrated the walls without tearing out the plaster. And she'd had the gun in her hand. No, Kats was either lying or else he needed his hearing checked. There hadn't been anyone in the backyard except Polly. And even if there had been, even if, say, Clark had been somewhere in the bushes, he couldn't have got to Alice. The only way he could have put that bullet in her head was if he had been in that room with her. Now that was a possibility.

He paid Kats for the petrol and left.

When Michael got home, his mom told him Jessica had called. She wanted him to call her the moment he came in. His heart sank. Something must have come up. Maybe she'd changed her mind. He hadn't realised how much he had been looking forward to being alone with her.

'Don't be so glum,' his mother said when she saw his

face. 'It might be that she wants you to pick her up half an hour later.'

'Did she say anything else?' he asked.

'Nothing about why she wanted you to call. But I talked to her a few minutes. She seems like a nice girl.' His mother smiled. 'She sounds like she likes you.'

He blushed. She knew how to embarrass him when it came to a girl – she just had to bring them up. She had been a hippie in the sixties and was still extremely liberal. He had to be the only guy at Tabb High whose own mother thought her son was a prude. 'What gave you that idea?' he asked, very interested to know.

'The way she says your name,' she said. 'I notice she always calls you Michael, not Mike. Also, she went on about how smart you are. Of course, I told her you got all your brains from me.'

'Take credit where credit's due.' There was no mistaking they were related. They both had the same black hair, the same dark eyebrows and eyes. Neither of them had ever had to worry about their weight, and nature had given them exceptionally clear skin, although Michael occasionally wished – especially during the summer when he burned lobster red on the beach – they weren't so fair.

Their mannerisms, however, were quite different. His

mom talked enthusiastically, using her hands a lot, while he normally kept his fingers clasped in most discussions and seldom raised his voice. She was a strong lady, although in the last couple of years or so, Michael had begun to feel her secretarial job – what with the traffic she had to fight commuting and the crap she had to put up with from her boss – had begun to take its toll. She always seemed tired, no matter how much she slept.

Yet today she positively glowed. She had on a light green dress and had curled her hair. Plus there was blood in her cheeks that gave her face a youthful sheen. 'What is it?' she asked in response to his stare.

'Have you been exercising? You look – alive.'

She laughed. 'I'll take that as a compliment. But the only exercise I did today was to carry in the groceries.' She nodded at her dress. 'Do you like it? Daniel gave it to me. I'll be at his place this weekend. I'm leaving in a few minutes.' She added mischievously, 'You won't need to spring for a motel on your hot date.'

He headed for his room and the phone. 'I'd be happy to go to a movie with her.'

'Mike?'

He paused, saw the sudden seriousness in her face. 'What is it?'

'I'd like to talk to you about something.'

'Can it wait a minute?'

She hesitated. 'Sure. Call Jessie. I'll be here.'

He had memorised Jessica's number when she had given it to him the second week of school. Before dialling, he sat on the edge of his bed and took a couple of deep breaths. Then he dived in. She answered quickly. He knew the date was off the instant he heard her voice.

'Hi, can you hold a sec?' she asked.

'Yeah.' He listened to his heart pound while she went to another phone. It didn't sound like it was going to break, yet it ached, and suddenly it hit him again, how much he missed Alice. Those hugs she used to give him when she would sneak up on him . . . He closed his eyes, sat back in the bed, mad at himself. He was reacting like a child. Jessica came back on the line.

'I tried to get you earlier. I talked to your mom.'

'Yeah, she told me.'

'She's such a cool lady. I hope I didn't give her the impression I'm stupid. I'm not very good at talking to people on the phone that I've never met. I start rambling.'

'She liked you.'

'Really? That's good.' She took a breath. 'I suppose you're wondering why I called? Tonight, Michael, it's not good. Something's come up. I have to cancel on you.'

'That's OK.' Hey, the sun just blew up. That's OK. I

411

can carry on as a collection of cooked carbon molecules. No problem.

But, Jessie, I need to see you. I need you.

'I'm free tomorrow,' she said. 'Would that be all right?'

He couldn't call his bosses and expect them to rearrange his schedule again. 'No, I can't. I have to work.'

'Can't you get off?'

'I wish I could.'

'Oh, no.' She sounded distressed. He began to feel a tiny bit better. 'If I had known . . . Dammit. I'm sorry.'

'Don't worry about it. Things come up. I understand.' Since she wasn't volunteering what this *thing* was, he thought it prudent not to ask. 'I heard the announcement at the varsity tree this afternoon. I was happy to hear your name called.'

'Oh, you were there? I was looking for you.'

When he had seen her talking to Bill Skater, he had decided he would save his congratulations for another time. 'I want to wish you luck with the next vote. I think you'd make a wonderful queen.'

'Thanks. How about next Friday?'

'We have our first league game then. I'll be playing.'

'Then how about next Saturday? We could go out after the SAT test. We could compare answers! Come on, Michael, I'll need someone like you about then to help put my brains back together.'

He had to work next Saturday evening as well. Yet that was a week away. He might be able to swing something with the boss's son. 'That should be fine, but I'll have to double-check at the store.'

'I'm *carving* you into my appointment book for next Saturday,' she said. 'If you don't show, I'm coming to your store to get you.' She giggled. 'How come you're always so understanding?'

'Don't be fooled, I have my days.' The words were no sooner past his lips than he realised she was one of the few people who knew precisely what he meant. He hadn't intended to bring up the scene in Alice's studio, not again. He said quickly, 'I'll let you go, Jessie. See you at school.'

She paused. 'Take care of yourself, Michael.'

Her last remarks had soothed his feelings somewhat. But now he had absolutely nothing to do. He glanced out of the window, at the clouds. They were heading west, towards the ocean. He dialled the weather service. They assured him there would be patches of visibility throughout the night in the desert. Good news. He hadn't seen the comet in weeks. If he could find it tonight, he would be able to construct a yardstick with which to plot its course.

Preparing to spend the night in the desert, he forgot all about his mom's asking to speak to him, not until she came into his bedroom. 'What are you doing?' she asked.

'Cleaning my Barlow lens.' He held the unusually long ocular up to the light, lens paper in his hand, searching for dust particles. 'Use this with any eyepiece and you double its power.'

'Are you going to the desert tonight? Is the date off?'

When he'd started his comet hunt, she used to wait up for him, worrying. So he'd taken her with him once, and hanging out with him beneath the stars on the wide empty dark sands, she'd come to realise he was safer outside the city than in his own bedroom.

'We're going out next Saturday.' He shrugged. 'It's cool.'

'You're not upset?'

'I'm fine. What did you want to talk about?'

Her eyes never left his, not even to blink. 'I'm pregnant.'

He set down his lens. He heard himself speak. 'And?'

'Daniel doesn't know. I'm going to tell him this weekend.'

'And?'

'I don't know what he'll say.' She glanced above his desk at a painting of a kindly mother polar bear feeding a bottle to a cute baby penguin. Clark hadn't completely spoiled Alice's artistic fun. It had been one of the last things she had done. His mother wasn't the type who cried easily, but as she looked at the painting he saw that her eyes were moist. 'And this time, it doesn't matter what he says.'

Michael smiled. 'I always wanted a sister.'

She laughed. 'They're still making brothers, too, you know?'

'It will be a girl.' He *knew* it would be.

'Who was that?' Bill Skater asked. Jessica whirled around. She had not heard him coming up the stairs.

'No one,' she said. 'A friend.' She felt sick with guilt. When Bill had asked her out at lunch, she, in all the excitement, completely forgot about her date with Michael. And then later she had figured she could simply see Michael on Saturday night, no harm done. Naturally, being Ms Free Time, she had conveniently overlooked the fact that he had other responsibilities. She shuddered to imagine what he must think of her. If she'd had any integrity at all, she would've called Bill and cancelled the instant she remembered her original commitment.

But you didn't because you're as phoney as that phoney crown you're hoping to wear in two weeks.

'I thought I heard you say somebody's name,' Bill said, stepping into her bedroom. He had on a turtle neck sweater the identical shade of blue as his eyes. And he had brought his body with him. What a stroke of good luck. She could practically *feel* it beneath his clothes, waiting for her. She honestly believed she was going to lose her vaunted virginity tonight.

That's why I forgot my date with Michael.

'Huh?' she asked.

'Were you talking to Michael Olson?'

'Do you know him?'

He nodded. 'He's a decent guy. Did you invite him along?'

'What? No.' That was a weird question. She picked up her bag, knowing her glasses were not inside. She would have to listen hard during the movie and try to figure out what was going on that way. She smiled, offering him her arm. 'I'm ready. Let's go.'

CHAPTER 11

Aunty's dying, Polly thought. Sitting on the bed beside her, holding her dry, shrivelled hand, watching her sunken chest wheeze wearily up and down, Polly wondered when it would be. Next week? Tonight? Now? She hoped it wasn't now. She didn't want to be there when it happened. She had seen enough family die.

'I'll go now and let you sleep,' Polly said, moving to leave. Her aunt squeezed her hand, stopping her.

'Are you unhappy, Polly?' her aunt whispered, barely moving her lips. Since the heart attack, it was as if the nerves beneath her already lined face had gone permanently to sleep. Nowadays her expression never changed; it was always old, always waiting for the end, impatient for it even. Only her eyes, the same blue as Alice's, held any life. Whenever Polly entered the room, she felt those eyes on her. Polly, could you

417

do this? Polly, I need that.

'I'm all right,' Polly said. 'Don't I look all right?'

'No.' Her aunt shifted her head on the pillow so that they were face-to-face. Polly felt a momentary wave of nausea and had to lower her eyes. Aunty had lost so much weight, for an instant Polly imagined she was speaking to a skull. Yet, in a way, no matter whom she talked to lately, she felt that way. All that lay between youthful beauty and clean white bone was a thin layer of flesh, she thought, a thread of life. They were all going to die someday, someday soon.

'What's wrong, Polly?' Aunty asked.

'Nothing.'

'Are you lonely?'

'Why would I be lonely? I have you to talk to. I talk to you all the time.' She glanced at the clock. Twelve forty-five. Russ had been asleep in her bed upstairs since midnight. He had only stayed up for *Star Trek*. She was beginning to hate that show. She had told him she had been to the family clinic and he had just grunted. He hadn't asked her why she had gone.

Her aunt tried to smile, her stiff cheeks practically cracking. 'You've been very good to me, Polly. You're good to everyone. I remember how you used to watch over Alice.' Aunty's eyes rolled towards the ceiling, going slightly out of focus. 'Her first day at kindergarten, she didn't want anyone but you to walk to school with her. I remember driving the car slowly behind you. You were holding hands, wearing bright-coloured dresses. Yours was yellow, and Alice had on—' She paused, trying to picture it. No matter how the conversation started, Aunty always went off on something that had happened years ago. 'It was green. I bought them both in Beverly Hills, at a shop on Wilshire. Of course, you wouldn't remember.'

'I remember,' Polly said. 'Why wouldn't I remember?'

Aunty coughed, raspy and dry. 'You were hardly seven years old.'

'So? I remember when I was two years old. And, anyway, Alice's dress wasn't green. It was red.' She was suddenly angry, restless. If she didn't get out of the room now, she felt, she would never be able to get out. She would be trapped there for ever and ever, feeding Aunty, helping Aunty to the bathroom, wiping the spit from Aunty's pillowcase.

'You must miss her terribly. It must be so hard for you.'

Polly leaned over and kissed the old lady, smelling her stale sticky breath. 'I have you. I don't need anyone else.' She brushed a hair from the woman's forehead, and it stuck to her fingers like a strand of steel wool. 'Now get some sleep.'

Polly had just sat down on the living room couch when she heard the sound of the motorcycle roaring up the street. She hurried to the front door.

Clark had parked his bike beneath the tree at the end of the driveway. He waved as he walked up the long front lawn, his leather gloves in his hand, his red hair hanging over the shoulders of his black jacket. Polly glanced back inside the house, up the stairs. Russ sometimes snored. Loud.

She smiled. 'Hi, Clark. What a pleasant surprise.'

He nodded, stepping past her, putting his gloves in his back pocket. But the instant she closed the door, he whirled around, grabbing her, pressing his mouth hard against hers. She could taste his breath, feel it, clean and cold as the night air. She leaned into him, a warm thrill going through the length of her body. Then his finger dug into her lower back, caressing her roughly. She pushed him away, and his face darkened. For a moment she thought he would explode.

'What's the problem, Polly?'

She let go of him, stepped towards the living room. 'You surprised me. I didn't know you were stopping by.'

'I told you yesterday I'd come back.'

'Oh, yeah.' She gestured for him to have a seat on the sofa. 'Can I get you something?'

He remained standing in the area between the kitchen and living room, near the stairs. 'I want you.'

She laughed nervously. 'What do you want with me?'

He came towards her. 'Let's go up to your bedroom.'

'No, I can't.'

He took hold of her arms. He was thin as a rail, but strong. 'Why not? A few months ago you used to take off your clothes to tease me. You were dying for it.' He squeezed tighter, moistening his lips with his tongue. 'Tonight, Polly, I think you'll die if you don't get it.'

'But that was modelling.' She tried to shake loose and couldn't. 'You're hurting me!'

He grinned, releasing her. 'I'm very sorry.' He turned and walked into the living room. There were red marks on her wrists, and she massaged them gently, following him. She hated it when he was like this, but couldn't really say she wanted him to leave. Aunty had been right; since Russ had gone to bed, she had been feeling terribly lonely. Clark went and stood by the sliding-glass door, staring out the back.

'What are you looking at?' she asked, coming up beside him.

'The dark. The past. Can you see it?'

'I don't understand.'

'Alice's party. All the beautiful people in the pool.'

She wished he wouldn't keep bringing up that night. She had thought about what he had said yesterday, as well as what Michael had said, and had decided they were both wrong. The evidence couldn't lie. Alice must have killed herself. 'They weren't all beautiful,' she said.

'Jessie, Maria, Clair – those three were here that night, and now they're princesses.'

'Maria isn't that good-looking.'

'But she's Jessie's friend.'

'How did you know that?'

'You told me.'

'No I didn't.'

He looked at her, along with his faint reflection – *two Clarks* – in the glass door. 'Then how did I know?'

'I don't know.'

'You can't remember?' he asked.

'I didn't say that.'

He nodded, his eyes going back to the night. 'Jessie meets Maria, and now she hardly talks to you any more. Sara becomes president and she only calls you when she wants money. Isn't that true?'

'No. Jessie's my best friend. She called me tonight.'

'Why? To brag to you? She's not your friend. None of

them are.' He raised his palm, touched the glass, almost touching his reflection. The line between them seemed so thin. 'Think about it, Polly. If Jessie and Sara had not talked you into the party, your sister would be alive today.'

It was a horrible thought, one she refused to consider for even an instant. But before she could tell him so, Russ bumped the wall with his elbow or leg or something in the upstairs bedroom. Clark turned at the sound. 'What was that?' he asked.

'My aunt.'

He paused, sniffed the air. 'Her. She doesn't smell very pretty.' He stepped towards the hall. 'Where is she?'

'She's in bed, asleep.' Polly went after him. 'Please don't disturb her. She's not well.'

He ignored her, going to her aunt's bedroom door, peering inside. She tried frantic gestures, tugging on his arm, but he refused to budge. He smiled big and wide. Watching her aunt unconscious and fighting for breath seemed to give him great pleasure. 'What would you want if you were that old?' he asked.

'Shh,' she whispered. 'Nothing. I'd want to die.'

'Why?'

'I wouldn't want to be sick like that.'

'And ugly?'

'Yeah. Come on, shut the door.'

'She's no different from you. Inside, she thinks the same way you would if you were inside her.' He nodded towards her aunt. 'She wants you to do it.'

'Do what?'

'Take a pillow, put it over her ugly face, and hold it there.'

'Are you mad? That would be murder.'

'It would be a kindness.'

'Stop it. She's all I have.' Polly began to shake, her eyes watering. She could never do anything to hurt Aunty. She would sooner hurt herself. 'I'm closing the door.'

He let her. He began to put on his gloves, heading for the front door. She followed on his heels, confused. He always had that effect on her. 'I'm going now,' he said.

'But you just got here. I thought you wanted . . . don't you want to see me?'

He grabbed a handful of her hair, tugged on it gently, then let it go. 'I've seen you.'

'I meant—'

'See you naked? That would be nice. Maybe next time.'

'But what's wrong with tonight?'

'You pushed me away.' He opened the door, looked at her a last time, his expression hard. 'Push me away again,

Polly, and I won't forget it. Not as long as you or your aunt lives.'

He strode down the front lawn, jumped on his bike, and drove away. Frustrated, Polly went upstairs, took off all her clothes and climbed into bed beside Russ. His snoring kept her up most of the night.

Looking at Bill, Jessica would never have thought he went in for foreign films. Yet he had taken her to a French movie, complete with subtitles, and she'd had a terrible time discussing it with him afterwards over ice cream and pie. The screen had been a colourful blur, the music loud and deceptive. She'd thought it was a war movie, but the way Bill talked, apparently they'd seen a love story. He probably thought she couldn't read.

All that, however, was behind them. They were at his place, sitting together on the couch, his parents asleep upstairs, the lights down low, the last pause in their conversation stretching to the point where she was thinking, *If he doesn't take me into his arms soon, I'll scream.*

He brushed her shoulder. A start. She felt the warmth of his touch all the way down in her toes. She honestly did. She was one big nerve. 'You have a thread,' he said, capturing the offensive little thing between his fingers, flipping it on to the floor and returning his hand to his lap.

'This sweater draws them like a magnet,' she said, smiling. She had been smiling all night. Her cheeks were beginning to get tired.

'Magnets only pick up metal, not material.'

She laughed. 'Very funny.'

He frowned. 'No, it's true.'

She stopped laughing. 'Yeah, you're right. My chemistry teacher talked about that in class.' Either she didn't appreciate his sense of humour, or else – *it doesn't matter, he's still a babe*, she told herself – he didn't know he had one.

'I never took chemistry,' he said.

'You didn't miss much. I have to study all the time. I got a C-minus on my last test.' Actually, she had received a B-minus. For maybe the first time in her life, she wasn't worried about coming off as smart.

'You should get Michael Olson to help you. Did you know he wrote the textbook you use?'

The rumour – which Michael had already told her was false – was that he had written the lab manual. 'Really? That's amazing.'

'He's an amazing guy,' Bill said. 'When we were in seventh grade and took all those IQ tests, I remember they had to bring out a psychologist to retest him. He kept getting a perfect score.'

'I didn't know you knew him that well?' She'd never seen Michael and Bill talking at school.

'We go way back.' He looked at her, instead of at the wall he had been admiring for a while now. 'How do you know him?'

'We – ah – share a locker.'

'But Michael's in my locker hall.'

'Yeah. He moved.' Her guilt over standing Michael up had hardly begun to abate and talking about him was not helping. She wished Bill would start kissing her and get on with the evening.

He's probably shy. I'll have to make the first move.

She touched the arm of his blue sweater, letting her fingers slide over his biceps. 'Do you work out now that football season is over?' she asked.

'No.'

'You feel like you do. I mean, you feel strong.'

He shifted his legs, recrossing them the other way. Then he scratched the arm she was supposedly stimulating. She took her hand away. It had worked in a movie she had seen. 'The season only ended a couple of weeks ago,' he said.

'Oh.' Somehow, despite a shaky start, Bill had managed

427

to remain the starting quarterback throughout the season. Tabb High had finished next to last in the league. 'Are you going out for any other sport this year?' she asked.

'Track.'

'That's neat. What are you going to do?'

'I haven't decided yet.'

She twisted her body around so that she didn't have to turn her head to look at him, tucking her right leg beneath her left, her right knee pressing against the side of his hamstring. 'I had a wonderful time tonight,' she said.

'It's late. You must be tired. Would you like a cup of coffee, some tea?'

'No, thanks.' She let her right arm rest on the top of the sofa, near the back of his neck. If she put her fingers through his hair, she thought, and he didn't respond, she would feel like a complete fool. 'You have beautiful hair,' she said.

'How about a Coke.'

'I'm not thirsty, Bill.' She contemplated asking him to massage a tight spot in her shoulders, but decided that would be as subtle as asking him to undo his zip. 'That's a beautiful zip you're wearing,' she said.

He glanced down. 'My zip?'

I didn't say that! I can't believe I said that!

'I mean, your belt, it's nice.'

'It's too long for me.'

'I thought the longer the better.' Talk about Freudian slips. This was getting ridiculous. She leaned towards him, letting her hair hang over his left arm, smiled again. 'I'm really glad you asked me out tonight. I've been hoping you would.'

'I've been meaning to for a while. I've always thought you were a nice girl.'

She giggled. 'Oh, I'm not that nice.'

'You're not?'

'I'm not exactly the person people think I am,' she said, serious now, touching his arm near his wrist, drawing tiny circles with her finger. 'Just as I don't think you're the person people think you are.'

He sat up straight. 'What do you mean?'

'That you're not just some super-great athlete. That you are a real person.' As opposed to an *unreal* person? she had to ask herself. 'I think the two of us have had to grow up faster than most people our age. I'm not saying that's a bad thing.' She tapped his left hand. 'It can be a good thing.'

Her little speech was not leading him in the direction she planned. He began to grow distinctly uncomfortable. 'What are you saying, we've had to grow up faster? Are you talking about what happened at the party?'

The question startled her. 'No.'

'I don't know what you heard about that night, but none of it's true.'

'Wait. None of what's true?'

He stood suddenly, reaching a hand into his pocket. 'I don't want to talk about it. I've had a nice time tonight, Jessie, and I don't want to spoil it.' He pulled out his keys. 'It's time both of us got to bed. Let me give you a ride home.'

She didn't even have to fix her bra as she got up. She decided there must be something wrong with his parents' couch.

Bill dropped her off in front of her house. He didn't walk her to the door, nor did he give her a goodnight kiss. When he was gone, she stared at the sky, feeling lonely and confused, and saw a bright red star. For no reason, she wondered what its name was. Had he been beside her, Michael would have been able to tell her.

To the inexperienced eye, the wisp of light in the centre of the field of view of Michael's telescope would not have looked significant. Because it was so far from the sun, the comet's frozen nucleus had no tail to set it apart from the star field. It was its position – its changing position relative to the unchanging stars – that had initially caught Michael's attention. In time, it was possible it would develop a halo of gas to further distinguish it in the heavens, but he had no illusions about it sweeping past the sun and lighting up the earth's skies. Very few comets came in that close.

He now had an accurate reading on its position and course. The comet was definitely not listed in any astronomical tables he had access to. If no one else had discovered it in the last few months, it would be *his* comet.

Orion – Olson.

He was really going to have to think of a name for it.

And for my sister.

Michael recapped the telescope and took a stroll around the desert hilltop to warm his hands and feet. Although he could see little of his surroundings in the deep of the night, he sensed the serenity here, the silence. Yet perhaps he had brought a measure of contentment with him. He couldn't stop thinking about the baby. He had been surprised when his mother told him she was already three months along. Her due date was the end of June, a couple of weeks after graduation.

Michael had walked down to the base of the hill and was hiking back up to get ready to go home when a brilliant shooting star crossed the eastern sky. He was not superstitious, but he automatically made a wish. It was not for the health and happiness of his unborn sister, which would have been the case had he thought about it for a moment. Instead, he found, even in this peaceful place and time, a portion of his mind was still on that night two months ago.

He had wished for the name of Alice's murderer.

A few minutes later he was unscrewing the balancing weight on the telescope's equatorial mount when he noticed how bright Mars was. He had been so preoccupied with comet hunting, he had forgotten it was coming into opposition. Changing his ocular for one of higher power, he focused on the planet. No matter how many times he studied Mars, the richness of its red colour always amazed him. No wonder the ancients had thought of it as the god of war.

Of blood.

The one time he had met Clark came back to Michael then, hard and clear. The guy's hair had been a dirty red, his eyes a bright green. He had spoken few words and what he said had not made much sense. Nevertheless, as Michael remembered, his heart began to pound.

'Where are you from?'

'Why?'

'I was wondering, that's all. Do you go to school around here?'

'No.'

'Where do you go?'

'The other side of town . . . Our team's as lousy as yours. But in our stadium, you can always lean your head back and look at the trees in the sky.'

Trees in the sky. What could it mean? Michael didn't know, not yet.

CHAPTER 12

Holden High's gymnasium was older than Tabb's – pre-World War II. It desperately needed an overhaul. The lights flickered, the bleachers had begun to splinter and the court had so many dead spots it actually seemed allergic to bouncing balls. Crouched in the corner beside the water fountain – exactly one week after her Friday night date with Bill – her Nikon camera in hand, trying to get a picture of Nick as he leaped to rebound a missed shot, Jessica wondered if a major earthquake might not be the ideal solution for the building's many problems.

'The lighting in here makes everybody look a pasty yellow,' she complained to Sara. 'Even Nick.'

'What difference does it make?' Sara asked. 'They're all going to be completely out of focus. Where're your glasses?'

Nick passed the ball to The Rock, who walked with it.

Holden High took the ball out of bounds, going the other way. Jessica set down her camera, glanced at the scoreboard. Tabb 30, Holden 36. One minute and twenty seconds until half-time.

'I can't wear them now,' Jessica hissed. 'Half the school's here.'

'They're watching the game, not you.'

Jessica eyed the cheerleaders, bouncing and twirling in front of the stands. All except Clair, who was standing by the microphone leading the cheers. 'A lot of them are watching Clair,' she grumbled.

'And here I thought you were sacrificing your night out to take pictures for the school annual,' Sara said. 'You're only worried about getting equal time.'

'Well, it's not fair. She gets to wear that miniskirt and flash her goods in front of everyone all night. The election's less than a week away – Wow!' Nick made another spectacular defensive rebound, tossing the ball to one of Tabb's guards. Jessica positioned her camera to catch the breakaway lay-up. She got her shot. Unfortunately, the guard missed his. Holden rebounded and went back on the offensive.

'That guy's missed everything he's put up tonight,' Jessica said. 'I don't understand why the coach doesn't put Michael back in.' During the first quarter, when

435

Michael had played, she'd used up a whole roll of film on him. It was her intention to plaster him throughout the yearbook.

'That's Coach Sellers,' Sara said. 'He was the coach at Mesa, remember? I hear he used to coach boxing in a prison until the inmates beat the hell out of him one day.'

In the final minute, Holden scored twice more, leaving Tabb ten down. Jessica waved to Michael as the team headed for the locker room. His head down, obviously disgusted, he didn't wave back.

'He's going to hear about it if he hasn't already,' Sara said as they walked towards the steps that led to the stands. The air was hot and humid. People poured off the bleachers, heading for the entrance and the refreshment stand.

'He didn't wave 'cause he didn't see me,' Jessica said.

'But Bubba will tell him.'

'And how will Bubba know I was out with Bill?'

Sara shook her head. 'Bubba knows everything.'

'Has he taken care of your bills?'

Anger entered Sara's voice. 'He's put them off. We'll have food and music, but when homecoming's all over, we're still going to have to pay for it. I swear to God, I think he's already lost the money I gave him.'

'You've got to give him a chance.'

'Believe me, sister, I'm giving him more of a chance than you can imagine.'

'What?'

'Never mind. When's the SAT tomorrow?'

Jessica groaned, feeling the butterflies growing. 'It starts at nine.'

'That's how it was for us.'

Sara had taken the test two months before. She had not told Jessica her score. She was waiting, she said, to hear Jessica's score first. But Jessica had the impression Sara had done fairly well.

'Is Bill here?' Sara asked.

'I haven't seen him.' Bill had avoided her all week at school. She wouldn't have felt so bad if it had been because he was feeling guilt for having taken advantage of her. She worried that she had come on too strong.

'Is Russ?' she asked.

'No. And don't ask me where he is, I don't know.'

Jessica snickered. 'Doesn't Bubba know?'

Sara stopped in midstep. 'I'll go ask him.'

While Sara went searching for Tabb's sole omniscient resident, Jessica rejoined Polly and Maria in the stands. The three of them had come together. But one of the reasons Jessica had gone picture hunting – and Sara, damn her, *had* hit on another of the reasons – was because Polly had insisted they sit in the middle of the second row, which was precisely three feet away from where Clair Hilrey and her amazing band of cheerleaders sat between cheers. Jessica liked to keep an eye on the competition but she wasn't crazy about smelling the brand of shampoo Clair used.

At the moment, however, Clair wasn't around. Jessica plopped down between Maria and Polly. 'Enjoying the game?' she asked.

Polly nodded serenely. 'I love it. It's not like football. You can always see where the ball is.'

Jessica turned to Maria, who was fanning herself with her notebook. Maria had brought her homework to the game. Jessica thought that was why Maria was getting an A in chemistry while she was only getting a B. On the other hand, Maria had not known Nick was playing, and it looked now as though she hadn't been reviewing the methyl ethyl ethers section tonight.

'What do you think of Nick?' Jessica asked.

Maria appeared awed and sad – a strange combination. 'He's very good. They should let him shoot the ball more.'

'Michael passed it to him practically every trip down the floor.' Jessica glanced in the direction the team had exited. An idea struck her. 'Maria, you once told me what a Laker fan your father is?'

'He is, yes.'

'Next week's game is at home. Bring him.'

'My father would never come to a high school game.'

'But you may be crowned queen that night! Both your parents have to come.'

Maria was worried. 'It wouldn't make any difference.'

'Sure it would. When they see what a tremendous athlete he is, they'll forget his colour. Look, just think about it, OK?'

Maria nodded, already thoughtful. 'I will.'

Maria excused herself a few minutes later. She needed some fresh air, she said. The place was awfully stuffy. Jessica amused herself by listening in on the cheerleaders' gossip. Too bad they knew she was listening; they didn't say anything juicy. Clair hadn't returned yet.

Then Polly started to talk.

'I'm glad Clair's feeling better,' she said casually.

Jessica paused. She had been unpacking her telephoto lens to use in the second half. 'What was wrong with Clair?'

'I don't know, but last Friday she looked pretty sick.'

Polly had not been at school last Friday, Jessica thought. 'Where did you see her?' she asked carefully.

Polly sipped her Coke, yawned. These days, she lived on sugar and raw carrots. 'At the family clinic.'

Jessica set down the lens. The cheerleaders, the girls on either side of them – in fact, everyone around them – stopped talking. They were all listening. Jessica knew they were listening and she also knew that if she continued to question Polly she would probably hear things that could hurt Clair, things that could damage Clair's chance of being elected homecoming queen.

Jessica started to speak, but stopped. If Clair had a personal problem, she told herself, it was nobody's business but Clair's. At the same time, Jessica couldn't help remembering how gloomy Clair had appeared last Friday. She'd had something *big* on her mind. And then – what a coincidence – she'd been at the clinic, looking sick.

She had an abortion.

The thought hit Jessica with sharp certainty. She had not a shred of doubt she was right; she had no reason – not even for the sake of curiosity – to question Polly further. She had no excuse for what she did next – except for another idea that struck her with every bit of force as the first.

I am cute. Clair is beautiful. I don't stand a chance against her. I never did.

440

Jessica closed her eyes. 'What were the two of you doing at the family clinic?' she asked in a normal tone of voice.

'I was getting birth control.'

She opened her eyes. '*You?* For what?'

Polly appeared insulted. 'I need it.' She added. 'Russ is staying at my house, you know.'

Sara had gone to ask Bubba where Russ was, Jessica remembered. She silently prayed Bubba didn't know everything. 'I see.' She had to push herself to continue, although she could practically hear a tiny red devil dancing gleefully on top of her left shoulder. 'But what was Clair doing there? You said she looked sick?'

'Yeah,' Polly said. 'I was waiting to get my contraceptive – so I won't get pregnant when I have sex with Russ Desmond – when Clair came out of the doctor's office. A nurse was holding her up. She looked totally stoned.'

No one leaned visibly closer, but if they had stopped talking a moment ago, now they stopped breathing. 'Like she had just had an operation?' Jessica asked.

'Yeah!' Polly exclaimed, the light finally dawning. 'Hey, do you think Clair got—'

'Wait,' Jessica interrupted. 'Let's not talk about this now. We'll talk about it later.'

What a hypocrite.

That was fine with Polly. Jessica listened as the shell of silence around them began to dissolve, being replaced by a circle of whispers that began to expand outward, growing in strength, in volume, and – so it seemed in Jessica's imagination – in detail. Then she saw Clair coming back, smiling, happy, pretty, ignorant.

The whispers would soon be a wave, a smothering wave.

The poor girl.

Jessica got up in a hurry, shaking, close to being sick. Grabbing her camera equipment, she dashed down the stairs, past Clair, pushing through the crowd until she was out in the cold night, away from the gym and the noise. Along a dark wing of the school, she ran into Sara, alone, leaning against a wall. Sara glanced up wearily, saw who it was, then let her head drop back against the brick.

'The world sucks,' Sara said.

'It's true,' Jessica said, leaning beside her.

'Bubba says Russ is staying at Polly's house.'

'Good old Bubba.'

Sara sniffed. 'What's your problem?'

Jessica wiped away a bitter tear. Her victory now would be meaningless. 'I'm going to be homecoming queen.'

Then she realised Clair's unborn child must have belonged to Bill, and she felt ten times worse.

Michael had just figured out the fundamental problem he had with Coach Sellers. The man was totally incompetent. Yet he wasn't a bad person. He had just asked for their input, something Iron Fist Adams would never have done. Sitting on the concrete floor of Holden High's uniform cage with his teammates, half-time almost over, Michael raised his hand and requested permission to speak. The coach nodded.

'I think we need to make serious adjustments if we're going to win this game,' Michael said. 'As you've already mentioned, we have to block out more to stop their offensive rebounds. But that's only a symptom of our main problem.'

'Oh?' Sellers said. Although only in his mid-forties, he was not a healthy man. He had a terrible case of liver spots on top of his balding scalp, and for some reason, which must have been connected to the slight egg shape of his head, his thick black-rimmed glasses were for ever falling off his nose. He also had a tendency to shake whenever they had the ball – a quality that did not inspire confidence. 'And what is our main problem?'

'We are not playing like a team,' Michael said. 'On

offence, whoever has the ball only passes off when he can't put up a shot of his own.'

'Aren't you exaggerating a bit, Olson?' Sellers asked.

'No. Everybody's trying to show off.' Michael pointed at The Rock, who was still red and panting from the first half. The Rock couldn't hit from two foot out, nor could he jump, but with his strength and bulk, he was able to manoeuvre into excellent rebounding position. 'The Rock's a perfect example. In the second quarter, Rock, Nick was open half a dozen times on the baseline when you had the ball, and you tried to drive through the key.'

'I made a few baskets,' The Rock protested.

Sellers consulted the stat sheet, nodded. 'He's scored seven points so far. That's three more than you, Olson.'

'But I didn't play the whole second quarter,' Michael said, glancing at Nick, who sat silently in the corner, away from the rest of them, his head down. Nick had already pulled down a dozen rebounds but had taken only three shots, making all three.

'Are you saying if I let you play more, we'd be a better team?' Sellers asked.

'To tell you the truth,' Michael said, 'I don't know *why* you took me out so early. But that's beside the point. We're too selfish. We have plenty of plays we can run.

Why don't we run them? Why don't we help each other out on defence? We're down by ten points.'

'I don't think a ten-point deficit is any reason to despair,' Sellers said.

'Yeah,' The Rock agreed. 'Don't give up the ship, Mike. We'll come back. I'm just getting warmed up.'

'That's the spirit,' Coach Sellers said, smiling. Apparently that was the end of the discussion. He had them all stand and place their palms on top of one another and shout out some mindless chant. Then they filed out to return to the court. Except for Michael. Coach Sellers asked him to remain behind.

'You're a good kid, Mike,' Sellers said when they were alone. The uniform cage stank of sweat. The coach removed his glasses and began to clean them with a handkerchief. 'I understand that you're trying to help us.'

'I am,' Michael said.

The curtness of the reply took the coach somewhat aback. 'You may be trying, but I don't believe you are succeeding.'

'Sir?'

Sellers replaced his glasses on his nose. 'Let's be frank with each other. You think I'm a lousy coach, don't you?'

The question caught Michael by surprise. 'No, I think

you're inexperienced.' He added, 'That's not quite the same thing.'

An uncharacteristic sternness entered Sellers's voice. 'But if you don't feel I'm capable of coaching this team how can you be on it?'

Michael considered a moment. He had mistaken Sellers for a kindly klutz. And here the bastard was threatening to drop him! 'I'm the best guard you've got,' he said flatly.

Sellers looked down, chuckled. 'We like ourselves, don't we?'

Michael's pride flared. 'Yes, sir, I do like the way I play. I put the team first. All right, I scored four points in the first quarter. Look how many assists I got. Six. Except for Nick, I'm the only one on this team who knows the meaning of the word *pass*, or even the word *dribble*.'

'If you are so team-oriented, where were you last week when we had our final practice game?'

'I came to your office and told you I would not be at the game. You said that was fine.'

'But you didn't say why you couldn't come?'

'I had personal business to attend to.'

'What?'

'It was a private matter.'

Sellers shook his head. 'I'm afraid that's not good

enough. You're a gutsy kid, Mike, I'll grant you that. But you're not a team person. You don't fit in. You're a loner. Basketball's not the most important thing to you right now.'

The words struck home with Michael; there was a measure of truth in them. He'd always played basketball for fun, not out of passion. And now the games, along with practice, had become a drag. There really was no reason for him to stick around.

Nick will survive without me.

Still, Sellers had no right to can him. When he was angry, Michael knew how to be nasty. 'I played in every game last year on a team that took the league title and went to the CIF semi-finals. How did your team do last year, *coach*?'

Mesa High had finished last. Sellers tried to glare at him, but lost his glasses instead. Fumbling for them on the floor, he stuttered, 'If you think you're going to play in the second half, Olson, you have another thing coming.'

Michael laughed. 'Thanks, but I won't be in uniform in the second half.'

The coach stalked out. Michael changed into his street clothes. He was tying his shoes when Bubba appeared.

'Are you injured?' Bubba asked.

'No. I'm no longer on the team.'

Bubba didn't care to know the details. 'Sellers is a fool.' He sat beside him on the bench. 'What kind of mood are you in?'

'I'm mad.'

'Seriously?'

'No. What's up?'

'I've got some good news, and I've got some bad news.'

'Give me the good news first so I can enjoy it.'

'I went down to your coroner's office today. I told them my dad was a doctor who was thinking of computerising his office. The chick there believed me. She demonstrated their system. She even left me alone for a minute to get me a cup of coffee. I took notes.'

'You can get into Dr Kawati's files?'

'Yes. I can hack in from school. But it'll take a while. I'll probably have to dump the entire medic group's files on to one of our hard discs.'

Michael was pleased. He'd asked Polly about the permission form again and had got nowhere. 'Can we do it tomorrow?'

'Next week will be better for me.'

Michael knew not to push Bubba. 'All right. Thanks for checking it out. What's the bad news?'

'You won't like it. Girls – they're all sluts.'

He groaned inside. 'Jessie?'

Bubba nodded, disgusted. 'She went out with Bill last Friday. That's why she cancelled on you.'

Michael tried to keep up a strong front. He didn't know if he succeeded. The situation was familiar, as was the pain. Yet neither was exactly as it had been before. When he was alone with the thought of Jessica, she seemed endlessly charming, always brand-new and different, and perhaps for that reason, he was always unprepared for the heartache she could bring. She could come at him from so many different angles.

Or else stay away.

Bubba excused himself to return to the gym. He'd heard about a rumour that needed tracking down. He didn't say what the rumour was.

Michael had not come on the team bus, but had driven to Holden High in his own car. That was one break, and breaks were in pretty short supply right then.

He was heading for the parking lot when he saw Jessica standing alone in the shadows of a classroom wing. He didn't want to talk to her. He didn't trust what he might say. Yet he did not feel angry with her. If anything, he wanted her more.

Then she saw him. 'Michael?'

Trapped. 'Hi. Jessie?'

She walked towards him slowly, looking small and frail beneath all her exotic photo equipment. He sure could have used one of those cameras to record his comet on film. But he'd already sent in the finder's application to an observatory.

'How come you're not playing?' she asked.

'Oh, the coach and I – we had a difference of opinion.'

'You didn't quit the team, did you?'

'Not exactly.'

She sounded upset. 'But you won't be playing? That's terrible.'

'There are worse things.' He glanced around. They were alone. The crowd in the gym sounded miles away. 'What are you doing out here all by yourself? You know this isn't the greatest neighbourhood in the world.'

Her gaze shifted towards the gym. He couldn't be sure in the poor light, but it seemed she had been crying. He hoped to God it hadn't been over Bill Skater. 'I'll be all right.' Then she looked at him, her eyes big and dark. 'I'm really sorry about last Friday.'

'It's no problem.'

'I had no right to do that to you. It was totally inconsiderate of me.' Her voice was shaky. 'Can we still go out tomorrow?'

450

He smiled. Maybe Bill had left a sour taste in her mouth. 'You bet, right after the test.' He had to work later that night.

A gust of wind swept by and Jessica pulled her jacket tighter. She gestured north, towards the dark shadow on the horizon. 'If it's not too late, and it's a nice day, maybe we could go up to the mountains. What do you think? Michael?'

Holden High was approximately five miles south of the mountains. On a clear day, particularly during the winter when there was snow, the peaks were undoubtedly beautiful. Yet there were other campuses, possibly two or three in Southern California, that must be situated within a mile or two of the mountains. At those schools, the mountains would dominate the scene. And the forest trees . . .

Would seem to stand in the sky.

CHAPTER 13

Dashing down the hall of Sanders High School to the SAT examination room with Michael, Jessica spotted a drinking fountain and stopped to pull a prescription bottle out of her purse. Removing a tiny yellow pill and tossing it in her mouth, she leaned over and gulped down a mouthful of water, feeling the pill slide home.

'Should I be seeing this?' Michael asked, perplexed. She laughed nervously.

'It's just a No-Doz. They're mostly caffeine. My dad always keeps a few in this old bottle for when he has to fly to Europe on business.'

Michael looked at her closely. 'Didn't you sleep?'

'I counted sheep, thousands of noisy sheep.' She took hold of his arm. She was glad they would be together in the same room. She seemed to draw strength from him.

She needed it. She hadn't slept a minute all night. 'Come on, we'll be late.'

'Are you sure we're going the right way?' he asked.

'I'm positive.'

When they reached the examination room, everybody was seated, and the proctor had already begun to explain the test rules. The woman hurried to meet them at the door. Michael presented the letters they had been sent a couple of weeks earlier. The proctor glanced at them, shook her head.

'You're L-Sixteen,' she said. 'Go down this hall and take the first left. About a hundred feet and you'll see the door on your left. Hurry, they'll be starting.'

Outside, jogging to the room and feeling properly chastised, Jessica said, 'I hope they don't ask for the definition of *positive* on the verbal sections.'

Michael smiled encouragingly. 'You'll be fine.'

This proctor wasn't explaining the rules. She had already finished with those, and was about to start the timer when they stumbled through the door. Jessica had only herself to blame for their tardiness. The night before she had made Michael promise he would wait for her in front of Sanders High. Naturally, on her way to Sanders, she had got lost. No matter, Michael was true to his word, and was sitting on the front steps when she finally pulled into the school lot. Everyone else had gone off to their respective examination rooms. She couldn't get over how cool he was about the whole thing.

This lady – a prune face if Jessica had ever seen one – was all business. After scolding them for being late, she asked for their letters and identification. Satisfied everything was in order, she led them to a table at the rear, handing them each a test booklet and a computer answer sheet.

'Print your name, address and booklet number on the side of the answer sheet,' the woman said. 'Use only your pencils and scratch paper.' She nodded to Jessica. 'You're going to have to find another place for that bag, miss, besides my tabletop.'

Jessica put it on the floor. Michael sat to her right. There was no one between them, but with the wide spacing, she would have needed a giraffe's neck to cheat off him.

I haven't seen the first question and I'm already thinking about failing.

The proctor walked back to the front. 'I didn't know she brought the goddamn tables from home,' Jessica whispered to Michael. The lady whirled around.

'There's to be absolutely no talking. I thought I made that clear.'

'Sorry,' Jessica said. Michael laughed softly.

The lady pressed the button on top of the timer. Jessica took off her watch and laid it on the table beside her computer sheet. Six half-hour tests. Just like at home. No sweat. She flipped open the booklet.

Christ.

Her practice books had stated that the first third of each section would be easy, the middle third would be challenging and the final third would be outright hard. She couldn't believe it when she got stuck on question number one.

1. WORDS: WRITER
    (A) honour:thieves
    (B) mortar:bricklayer
    (C) chalk:teacher
    (D) batter:baker
    (E) laws:policeman

She was supposed to select the lettered pair that expressed a relationship closest to that expressed in the original pair. She quickly eliminated *A*, but then she had to think, which was never easy even when she was wide-awake and relaxed. Words were used by writers. Mortar was used by bricklayers. Teachers used chalk, bakers used batter, policemen used – No, policemen didn't exactly use laws. She eliminated *E*. Now what? Mortar and batter were crucial to bricklayers and bakers. But a teacher could teach without chalk. There went *C*.

Jessica swung back and forth between *B* and *D* before finally deciding on the latter. But she had no sooner blacked out *D* when she erased it in favour of *B*. Then she remembered a point in the practice books. If you were undecided over two choices, the authors had said, take your first hunch. She erased *B* and darkened *D* again.

She glanced at her watch. She had to answer forty-five questions in thirty minutes. That gave her less than a minute a question, and she had already used up two minutes! She was behind!

I'm not going to make it. Stanford will never accept me.

Paradoxically, her panic brought her a mild sense of relief. She had been worried about freaking, and now that she had done it, she figured she didn't have to worry about it any more. She plunged forward. The next question was easy, as was the third. Then the fourth had to start off with the word *parsimonious*. She skipped it altogether. Not even Michael could know what that word meant. Their proctor had probably made it up and typed it in out of spite.

In time, Jessica began to settle into a groove. She forgot

about the rest of the room, even blocking out the fact that Michael was sitting close. But she could not say this tunnel vision was the result of a high state of concentration. On the contrary, she had settled *too* much. She couldn't stop yawning. Finishing the analogies and starting on the antonyms, she found she was fighting to stay awake. She couldn't wait for the break to take another caffeine pill.

It was good to be out in the fresh air again. The stress had been so thick inside, Michael thought, it had been as bad as a noxious gas. He understood why many kids, like Jessica, took the test seriously. Most name colleges, after all, demanded high SAT scores. But for him, it had been a piece of cake. He wouldn't be surprised if he had a perfect score so far.

'The team got snuffed last night after you left,' Bubba said.

'Serves the coach right after what he did.' Jessica said.

'How did Nick do?' Michael asked.

The three of them were standing near Sanders High's closed snack bar. Bubba was taking the exam in another room. They had only a minute to talk. They still had two thirty-minute sections to complete.

'When our guys gave him the ball, he put it in the

basket,' Bubba said. 'But that didn't happen much until it was too late.'

'Nick will make his mark,' Michael said confidently. 'I'm surprised to see you here, Bubba. You say you're not going to college. Why are you taking the test?'

'For fun.'

Jessica groaned, taking out her bottle of yellow pills and popping a couple with the help of a nearby drinking fountain. 'I can think of a lot of other things I'd rather be doing this morning,' she said.

'What are those, morning-after pills?' Bubba asked.

'Bubba,' Michael said. Jessica didn't appear insulted.

'They're No-Doz,' she said.

'Since when does No-Doz require a prescription?' Bubba asked.

'This is just a bottle my dad puts them in,' Jessica said.

'Let me see it,' Bubba said. Jessica handed it over. Bubba studied the label. 'Valium,' he muttered. He opened the bottle, held a pill to the light. 'You've got the wrong bottle, sister. These *are* Valium.'

Jessica snapped the bottle back. 'That's impossible. I asked mom which bottle to take and she said the one on top of the—' Jessica stopped to stifle a yawn. Then a look of pure panic crossed her face and she spilled the whole bottle of pills into her palm. 'Oh, no,' she whispered.

Bubba chuckled. 'How many of these babies did you take altogether?'

'Three altogether.' She swallowed, turning to Michael, her eyes wide with fright. 'What am I going to do?'

The hand bell signalling the end of the break rang. 'You only took the last two a minute ago,' Michael said. 'Run to the bathroom. Make yourself throw up.'

'Better hurry,' Bubba said, enjoying himself. 'They dissolve like sugar in water.'

Michael took hold of Jessica's elbow. 'There's a rest room around the corner. Go on, do it.'

'I can't! I can never make myself throw up.'

'You just haven't had a good enough reason,' Bubba said.

'Shut up,' Michael said. 'It's easy, Jessie. Stick your finger down your throat. You won't be able to help but gag.'

The bell rang again. Jessica began to tremble. 'I don't have time,' she said anxiously. 'We have to get back. I might mess up my blouse.'

'And I hear Stanford doesn't stand for messy blouses,' Bubba said sympathetically, shaking his head.

'What is the normal dosage for those pills?' Michael asked.

'One,' Jessica said miserably, close to tears. 'I can't

throw up, Michael. Even when I have the stomach flu, I can't.'

'You've got to try,' Michael said. 'You're tired to begin with. If you don't get the drug out of your system, you'll fall asleep before you can finish the test. Go on, there's time. I'll wait for you.'

Nodding weakly, she headed for the bathroom. Michael turned on Bubba. 'Why are you hassling her at a time like this?' he demanded.

'She stood you up last week to go out with Bill and you're worried about her test score?' Bubba snorted. 'Let me tell you something, Mike – and I say this as a friend – forget about Jessica Hart. She's not who you think she is. She doesn't care who she hurts.'

'What's that supposed to mean?'

'Never mind. I've got to finish the test. If she passes out, be sure to give her a goodnight kiss for me.'

Michael didn't understand Bubba's hostility. Jessica's going out with Bill didn't explain it. In Bubba's personal philosophy, all was fair in love. Also, Bubba hurt people left and right, and always rationalised his actions by saying the people in question must have bad karma.

Michael decided to wait outside the test room. He wanted to keep an eye on the proctor should she restart the examination before Jessica returned.

He received a surprise when the lady came into the hallway to speak to him. 'Are you the Michael Olson who won the work-study position at Jet Propulsion Laboratory last summer?' she asked.

'Yes, that's me.'

She smiled, offered her hand. 'I'm Mrs Sullivan. My son is an engineer at JPL – Gary Sullivan. He spoke very highly of you.'

Michael shook her hand. 'Gary, yeah, I remember him. He was a good guy. No matter how busy he was, he always took time to answer my questions. Say hello to him for me.'

Mothers always loved him. Too bad he didn't have the same luck with their daughters. The lady promised to give Gary his regards.

Jessica reappeared a few seconds before they started on the next section. She didn't speak, just looked at him, her eyes half closed, and shook her head. He should have checked those blasted pills before she had swallowed them. From the beginning, he had wondered if they were really No-Doz.

They went inside and sat down and started.

If $2X - 3 = 2$, what is the value of $X - .5$?
(A) 2 (B) 2.5 (C) 3 (D) 4.5 (E) 5.5

On this section, they were allowed slightly more than a minute per question. Michael found he could solve most of them in ten seconds. A was obviously the answer to the first problem. He didn't even need his scratch paper. When he got to the end of the section, however, and glanced over at Jessica, he saw she had blanketed both sides of both her scratch papers with numbers and equations. He also noticed she had filled in only half the bubbles on her answer sheet. Her beautiful brown hair hung across her face as she bent over the test booklet. But every few seconds her head would jerk up.

She's hanging on by a thread.

The proctor called time. Jessica reached down and pulled a handkerchief from her bag, wiping her eyes.

'Jessie,' he whispered. 'Hang in there.'

'I can't think,' she moaned.

'No talking,' the lady ordered.

They began again. Reading comprehension. Michael had to force himself to concentrate. The miniature essays from which they were supposed to gather the information necessary to answer the subsequent questions were distinctly uninteresting. Also, he was peeping over at Jessica every few seconds, worried she might suddenly lose consciousness and slump to the floor.

She's not going to get into Stanford with these test scores.

It was a pity she had waited until now to take the SAT. She would not have a chance to retake it in time to make the UC application deadlines. He really felt for her.

And what are you going to do about it?

Much to his surprise, Michael realised a portion of his mind was methodically analysing the best way to slip her his answers. Of course he'd have to make a list of them on a piece of his scratch paper. The real question was how to get the paper into her hands without the proctor seeing. He did have a point in his favour. The lady obviously thought he was a fine, upstanding young man. Nevertheless, a diversion of sorts was called for, and the simpler the better.

It came to him a moment later. He immediately started to put it into effect. He faked a sneeze.

During the next fifteen minutes, while he polished off reading comprehension, Michael faked a dozen more sneezes. Then, after pencilling in the final bubble, and without pausing a moment to recheck his work, he began to copy the answers. Yet he jotted down only those that dealt with the final two sections. This was his way, he knew, of rationalising that he wasn't really helping her cheat.

What if you get caught? What if she doesn't even want your precious help?

463

He had an answer to that. At least he would have tried.

Carefully folding his list of answers into a tiny square, he closed his test booklet, collected his other papers and stood. There were nine minutes left. The proctor had her eyes on him. She was smiling at how clever he was to be the first one done. He began to walk towards the front.

He was half a step past Jessica when he sneezed violently, dropping everything except his tiny square. 'Excuse me,' he apologised to the room as a whole as he turned and bent down. Jessica hardly seemed to notice his presence. Both her hands were situated on top of the table. He took his tiny square of scratch paper and crammed it between her tennis shoe and sock. Then he glanced up, and – it took her a moment – she glanced down. Their eyes made contact. Knocking on dreamland's door, she still had wit enough left to recognise his offer. She nodded slightly, almost imperceptibly.

When he handed in his stuff, the proctor proudly observed how he hadn't needed any of his scratch paper. Thankfully, she didn't observe that he was a page short.

'It was nice to have it handy, though,' he said. 'Just in case.'

He waited for Jessica in the hallway. She came out with the group, ten minutes later, and immediately pulled him off to the side. Her big brown eyes were drowsy – he imagined that's how they would look if he were to wake up beside her after a night's sleep – and she was obviously wobbly on her feet, but she practically glowed.

'I would kiss you if I wasn't afraid my breath would put you to sleep,' she said. 'Thanks, Michael. You're my guardian angel.'

'Did you have time to put down my answers?' His big chance for a kiss and he had to ask a practical question. She nodded.

'I had to erase a lot of mine, but I had time.' She yawned. 'How do you think you did? Or we did?'

He laughed. 'Pretty good.'

She laughed with him.

He didn't want her driving. She said they could still go to the mountains as they had planned, as long as she could crash in his car on the way up. Even though he protested that he should take her home, she insisted an hour's nap was all she needed to get back on her feet.

On the way to the parking lot, she excused herself to use the bathroom. Michael had to go himself. He ran into Bubba combing his hair in the rest-room mirror.

'Did she conk out or what?' Bubba asked.

'She did just fine – thanks for your concern.'

Bubba chuckled. 'Hey, what's a few Valium before a little test? I made it once with a six-and-a-half-foot Las

Vegas showgirl after chugging down an entire bottle of Dom Perignon. Talk about a handicap in a precarious situation. She could have broken my back and paralysed me.' He straightened his light orange sports coat. 'So what did you think of the SAT?'

'A pushover.'

'Really? I had to think on a couple of parts. I probably got the hardest test in the batch.'

'I believe you,' Michael said. Bubba was pleased to hear his favourite line turned on him. 'I'm serious. I think the difficulty rating varies considerably between the tests.'

Michael stopped – stopped dead. 'What are you talking about? There's only one test.'

'No. Didn't you hear what they said at the start? They use four different tests so you can't cheat off your neighbour.'

I'm in a bathroom. This is a good place to be sick.

Michael dashed for the door, leaving Bubba talking to himself in the mirror. He had one hope. They had come in late. Perhaps the proctor had not taken the time to select two different exams.

The lady was sorting the booklets when he entered the room. 'Forget something, Mike?' she asked pleasantly, glancing up.

He had to catch his breath. 'No, it's not that. I was just

466

wondering – My girlfriend and I, we're going to talk about the test on the drive home, and it would be nice to know if we were talking about the *same* test. If you know what I mean?'

He smiled his good-boy smile that mothers everywhere found irresistible. 'I don't want to change any of my answers.'

She laughed gaily at the mere suggestion of a scholar like him doing such a despicable thing. 'I can check for you, of course. But I'm sure I wouldn't have given you the same series. What's your girlfriend's name?'

'Jessica Hart.'

She flipped through the computer answer sheets, found his first and set it aside, and then picked up Jessica's, placing the two together. 'No, you were code A,' she said. 'Jessica was a C.' She smiled. 'Don't worry, you'll know your scores soon enough.'

'How long?'

'Oh, with the District's new computer system, you could receive the results in the mail in about a month.'

'Is there any way of finding out sooner?'

'You could call the test office. They might know the score as early as this coming Friday.'

He thanked her for her time. Outside, he wandered around the campus like someone who had swallowed a whole bottle of Valium, the thought *I should have known* echoing in his brain like a stuck record.

When Jessica finally caught up with him, he was standing in the campus courtyard holding on to a thin leafless tree that felt like a huge number-two marking pencil in his hand. She looked so happy that he debated whether or not to give her the next few days to enjoy it. Unfortunately, he was too devastated to psych himself up for a good lie.

'Where did you go, silly?' she asked. 'I've been searching all over for you.' She grinned. 'What's wrong?'

'We have a problem.'

She put her hand to her mouth. 'No.'

He nodded sadly. 'A big problem. Our tests, Jessie, they weren't the same.'

'No, that's impossible. What does that mean?'

He spared her nothing. 'It means you got a zero on the last two sections.' He coughed dryly. 'I'm sorry.'

She stared at him for the longest imaginable moment. Then her face crumbled and her eyes clouded over. She began to cry.

This was another date they were never going to go on.

TO BE CONTINUED . . .

Final Friends

VOLUME TWO

High school horror at its best.

They just wanted to finish high school, but high school might finish them …

The sinister death at Jessica's party has everyone on edge. What if it is wasn't suicide? Will the death toll rise at the homecoming dance? Michael Olson needs to find out who the killer is, before another victim is claimed at graduation. But will he be too late?

Final Friends
VOLUME TWO
The million-selling author
CHRISTOPHER PIKE

The Last Vampire

THE LAST VAMPIRE
BLACK BLOOD

Alisa Perne is the last vampire.
Beautiful and brilliant, for five
thousand years she has hunted
alone, living among humans,
living off humans. But somebody
knows her secret – and they
want her dead …